LONG WAY FROM HOME

Books by Frederick Busch

FICTION

Long Way from Home (1993)

Closing Arguments (1991)

Harry and Catherine (1990)

War Babies (1989)

Absent Friends (1989)

Sometimes I Live in the Country (1986)

Too Late American Boyhood Blues (1984)

Invisible Mending (1984)

Take This Man (1981)

Rounds (1979)

Hardwater Country (1979)

The Mutual Friend (1978)

Domestic Particulars (1976)

Manual Labor (1974)

Breathing Trouble (1973)

I Wanted a Year Without Fall (1971)

NONFICTION

When People Publish (1986)

Hawkes (1973)

LONG
WAY
FROM
HOME

❖

Frederick
Busch

Ticknor & Fields

NEW YORK

1993

For information about permission to reproduce selections
from this book, write to Permissions, Ticknor & Fields,
215 Park Avenue South, New York, New York 10003.

Library of Congress Cataloging-in-Publication Data
Busch, Frederick, date.
Long way from home / Frederick Busch.
p.   cm.
ISBN 0-395-63415-6
I. Title.
PS3552.U814L6   1993   92-40727
813'.54 — dc20   CIP

Printed in the United States of America

Book design by Robert Overholtzer

BP 10 9 8 7 6 5 4 3 2 1

Excerpts from fairy tales on pages 195–198 are reprinted
with permission of Macmillan Publishing Company
from *The Golden Bird and Other Fairy Tales* by the Brothers
Grimm, translated and introduced by Randall Jarrell.
Copyright © 1960, 1962, 1963 Macmillan Publishing Company.

For Paula Fox

AUTHOR'S NOTE

This began as a twenty-page short story called "Privacy." It would have remained one except for the insistence of Richard Bausch that it become a novel. He deserves none of the blame and all of my gratitude.

I have made free with the names of places in New York, Pennsylvania and New Mexico. Burroughs is an important name, but not of a town you can go to except in the imagination.

Sometimes I feel like a motherless child,
Sometimes I feel like a motherless child,
Sometimes I feel like a motherless child,
Long way from home;
Long way from home.

ELIZABETH BEAN MASTRACOLA: Head Mother, as one of the always-embattled guidance people called her; The Bitch to several generations of high school boys whom she drove with all but spurs, whip and electric prod through to their implausible graduation; also named Sweetie by the fifteen-year-old mothers whom she counseled, calling them that as they dropped out of school to raise their babies proudly for a while in rural-slum mobile home or sweat- and tinderbox apartment three blocks and all of their lives from school. One child, in filthy weightlifter's shirt, sweat-stiffened denims and high-top sneakers from which the soles flapped when he walked stiff-legged past her office to sneak out for a smoke, called her Fuckface when she asked him where he was going. She had reached for his hair, pulled him into her office and seized what she could of each lean and unloved side of his jaw in her big hands. She had put her nose down to press it against his nose and had stared into his eyes. "I want you here at three o'clock to talk to me about manners," she'd said. "Come here at three and talk nicely," she'd said. "I'll tell you a story about your life." The boy had called her Ma'am before he went home that afternoon. Her husband usually called her Lizzie Bean. Her daughter Sarah hadn't called her for a very long time.

"Dr. Bean," her secretary said over the chest-high counter of the general office. Lizzie stood before the glassed-in trophy case. She wasn't certain how she had come to stand and stare through plastic disguised as metal commemorating the triumphs of lanky athletes who were gone by now to fat and the sadness that comes with remembering what your body did on its own, in spite of the *you* still trapped in its flesh gone frailer.

"Here I am, Karen." She heard her voice drift idly. She could hear herself not concentrating. She sounded to herself the way she had when she gardened or cooked or tried to write a letter, and Sarah was small and calling shrilly for her attention. It was the sound of a grownup in hiding.

"I *know* you're there, Dr. Bean. That's why I called out to you. Would it be possible for you to like *drop in?*" As Karen scolded, Lizzie heard the pounding of the school again, as if she had turned the sound down with a dial and now were turning it up: the hooves of boys who slapped through the corridors, the purposeful screams of girls who were jostled by boys at whom they'd aimed themselves, the hive sound of hundreds of voices urgently fitting into the four-minute passage between periods everything they had said before class and would need to reiterate afterward.

In the cool, dark interior office, its hallway door closed and only the desk lamp on, Lizzie seated herself as Karen pointed with a long, bony finger at the paper she had centered for Lizzie's attention. Karen said something and Lizzie nodded and Karen spoke again. "Hello?"

Lizzie said, "Excuse me?"

"Where *are* you? What's wrong?"

"It feels like something's happened to Sarah," Lizzie said.

Karen said, "When doesn't it?"

Gloria Dodge was a county nurse who rolled from farm to mobile home to semi-leanto over the rutted, unpaved roads in her tan

4

station wagon — "Dust-colored car for a dust-colored world," she very often said. Gloria was a small woman, maybe half an inch taller than five feet. She wore heavy work shoes that made her little feet look smaller somehow. She never wore a uniform, but always carried a bulky black doctor's bag that she thought engendered confidence in her patients — her "customers," she liked to call them, laughing a tidy laugh that was more like a bark. Gloria took temperatures and left off sample packages of antibiotics, though she'd been warned not to. She diagnosed pneumonia in old people and called out the local volunteer fire company's ambulance and saw to their hospitalization. They often wept as she converted their slow, quiet desperation into clamor, into an irrevocable public event.

She could tell you how to soak dandelion roots in vodka, then after six weeks strain the liquid through a cheesecloth and drip it into antique colored bottles with stoppers. Keep them by you and take a few drops with your tea, she'd advise: clean your blood up like an Electrolux. Waiting in a dooryard for a frightened woman to bring her baby to the door, Gloria could show the older children, muddy at the porch and staring, how to make a whistle of timothy leaves you folded and held to your lips just right. When robins dove and fluttered near the deep maroon berries hanging from pokeweed, she would tell the children that the birds had got drunk eating them. "Fact of life," she said. "Even though your mother could boil up the shoots and serve them for dinner tonight. That's an actual fact."

In farmhouses smelling of mildewed sills and damp earth basement, in shanties where the people smelled more powerfully than their animals, Gloria searched out interesting newspapers. She sought anything from small towns in other states, shoppers' tabloids filled with advertising from elsewhere. "I'd be pleased to take this off your hands if you don't need it for reading or the stove," she said. In her station wagon, eating wet sandwiches — cucumber and cottage cheese, pickled herring fillets — she read

5

the little ads in the Personal columns and copied into her small looseleaf notebook the rates for ads and the address of the paper.

ARE YOU MY MOTHER? was what she looked for.

AM I YOUR MOTHER? was what she sent off.

You could make a paste from beechnuts and press out the oil for cooking. You could grind the dried paste fine and use it instead of flour. You could roast the nuts and grind them instead of buying coffee. You could drink the coffee and sit with your face squinting into the morning sun and look at one of the newspapers from someplace like Boise, Idaho, or Metuchen, New Jersey. ARE YOU MY MOTHER? you might find one time. You really might. It happens like that. It's a fact.

So there came Barrett, from Doylestown, Pennsylvania, steaming over Route 81 at night to bear his son to his in-laws and tell them that their daughter was gone. He was a husband. He was a father. He had come a pretty long way with his child, and he had just howled and wrenched at the steering wheel of his motionless car. "Will you help me?" he had asked his son, or anything in the darkness beyond the windshield. "Will you *please* try and fucking *help* me?"

Barrett was a father. He was a husband. He had driven since just before dusk into the orange-red sun that seemed so sore, so enormous, that its light lay on everything and the world, as he drove, looked unnaturally bright. Now the sun was down, and the coming darkness felt like comfort. He knew enough about what was happening to tell himself to take the comfort he could as it came. He knew that he was a father and a husband and that on reaching the home of his in-laws, bringing his little boy to abandon, he would continue pursuing his wife. And he knew, or he told himself he knew, that she would not willingly be caught. He was a husband, and his wife had left. He knew this. He was

6

a father who would leave his child behind. He knew that too.

Off 81, at a place that had "Bend" in its name, he had pulled over to buy coffee and sandwiches at an all-night diner. He locked Stephen in the car and talked to the woman behind the counter without studying her face or the signs behind the coffee urns. He bought hamburgers and fries and a soda and coffee and, as he left, wondered what he might have been able to buy for his son if he had taken the time to focus on the words behind the woman with the high, pink growth on her forefinger. As she served him, he'd become enchanted by it and had looked at nothing else. At least he had noticed that, he thought. At least he was still attentive to distortions of the flesh.

When he had come back to the car, Stephen had stared out at him. He saw his son watching his face. He was the boy's captor, he thought. So, "Hey *ho!*" he had cried with too much glee as he unlocked the door. Stephen, now, was looking at the key, Barrett saw. The guard had come with the key.

And when he had seen to ketchup packets and napkins, to straws, to the even distribution from a cardboard box of clammy french fries, he had sighed as loudly, and almost as long, as he had wanted to. And he'd heard himself say it again: "She'll be back. She's coming back."

Stephen said, "You'll get her back."

"Yes, sir," he said. "I will."

Stephen said, "I'll be fine with Grandma." And then: "Her closet smells like flowers."

"Herbs," Barrett said. "She likes the smell of herbs."

Stephen asked, "What do you call it again? That thing like a ball that smells so sweet?"

But Barrett was holding on to the steering wheel, then, with both hands. He couldn't stop. He pulled it and pushed back against it and turned it hard, as if he were in motion and couldn't slow down and had to hold on. He heard his voice grinding its

7

way from between his teeth. He heard it say, "Will you help? Will you *please* try to fucking *help* me?"

At night he stopped the car outside the large house in Burroughs, New York, where Sarah's parents lived. He'd always wondered how they kept the grass down between the bricks of their walk, how they mowed the wide lawns and painted the white clapboard. Her father was always humped under unfinished chores when they visited. He had not thought *used to visit*, he caught himself thinking.

Stephen, pale in the weak light from the porch fixture, his neck rigid, his eyes grown huge, pointed and told him, "You can always tell Grandma's house by the door. It's the same color as the, you know, shudders."

"Shutters," Barrett told him. He touched the back of his son's head and gently squeezed. His fingers were as long as the diameter of his boy's neck, he thought. He could almost make his fingers meet around the little throat. He'd been entrusted with this round, thin skull and small neck, and this was what he did. He whispered, "You won't get lost, Sluggo. You'll be all right."

"Sure will," Stephen said, leaning his head back hard against his father's hand.

"I'll come back soon. I'll bring Mommy with me."

"You'll get her," Stephen whispered back, as if they had to keep this truth a secret.

"You'll be fine."

She had actually started her run, Sarah thought, back on a February morning that felt like years before, not months. She had walked from the shower, left it running and, in her bathrobe but still untoweled, her hair slimy with shampoo, wet and cold and confused, she had gone into Stephen's room to watch him sleep.

His mouth was closed as if he disapproved. But of what? She

looked at his eyes pulsing with dream beneath the pale, soft-looking lids with their dark and widely separated lashes. Those were not Barrett's closed eyes, and surely not the eyes of either of her parents. Maybe they were hers. Maybe, through the dark chemistry of the history sealed away from her, she had passed another person's lashes and temple bones and socket bones and pallor and — who could tell? — nightmares along to Stephen. Maybe she was like those women who, themselves untouched, hauled terrible ailments to men. Maybe she was a carrier.

Stephen's eyes opened and she flinched. But he smiled, as if she often stood before him, wet and probably goggle-eyed. Then Sarah felt herself relax away from Barrett and the work she didn't like that well, and from the feeling — like a low-grade stomach-ache, like a faint throb in the shoulder joint or wrist — that something was lost.

"Stephen," she whispered. He sat up. He crossed his legs and put his palms on his knees. He sat like a child who waited for a story to be told. "There's a little emergency feeling in the air," she said. "No!" she told his furrowing face. "Not a terrific one at *all*. No. But it's telling me I can't go to work. And you can't go to school."

"No school?" He was grinning now.

"*Utterly* no school," she whispered. "I am convinced by omens and portents that we have to play hooky."

"What's a portent?"

"Kind of a message that nobody sends. You just get it. Get it? Listen: a picnic. There's —"

Stephen pointed out the window. "Mommy. It *snowed*."

"A last gasp. A piffle. Onion snow, it's called."

"Why?"

"We have to get out in it and see if it's because it tastes like onions." Stephen grimaced, a burlesqued distaste, she knew, that was meant to match his antic mother's mood. "Don't tell Daddy,"

9

she said, putting a finger to his dry, cool lips. "He'd make us be good."

"We're being bad?"

She fell onto his bed and hugged him to her and rolled back and forth, squeezing him. "Would I do something bad? Would I make you do something bad?"

Barrett, behind them, at Stephen's door, said, "You left the shower on."

Stephen stiffened. Sarah rubbed his shoulder and said to Barrett, "Did not."

"Sarah, you did," he said as he tried to button down the collar of his starched oxford shirt.

"Did not," Sarah said. Stephen giggled. Barrett threw his light blue shirt up into the air and walked away down the hall. She heard the water shut off. She heard Stephen's quick breaths. "He isn't angry," Sarah said, "he just thinks I'm a bubblehead." She prodded her hair, lacquered with drying shampoo, and she said, "I guess I am." She got off the bed, retrieved the shirt, said, "You get washed and brush your teeth and get dressed, little man. You better do it fast, and it better not be for school. Picnic duds, all right?" She put her finger to her lips. Stephen nodded, and he did the same.

Sarah buttoned the collars of the shirt as she walked down the hall and into their bedroom, saying, before she saw Barrett, "Here you go. It's easy when you use your thumbs." She saw him, then, sitting on the edge of their bed, looking down. She said, "What?"

"You're making me nuts. You're making me worry. You're scaring hell out of me, Sarah. Are you all right?" He turned, looking at her wet bathrobe and unrinsed hair with large, liquid, angry eyes.

She shook her head. "I'm sorry," she said. "No."

"Can you tell me what it is?"

"I don't know," she said.

"Is it your parents?"

"Why them, for godsakes?"

"Because you don't call them. We haven't gone there for months. You haven't asked them to come down here."

"No," she said. "No. I'm on leave from childhood is all. I don't want any complications."

He was standing now. She looked at the mole near his collar-bone, at the sparse, harsh hair of his chest. She looked at his narrow face. She thought he was going to cry.

"Sarah," he said, "they don't give sabbaticals from being some-body's kid."

"Then you have to take them," she said.

He shook his head. He asked, "*What* complications?"

She remembered later, driving away from him and Stephen, how reasonable she wanted to be. She said to him now, very reasonably, "You know how my friend Emma had a face-lift? That little chin-tuck thing? You remember how we had this time when you and I thought every other person we knew was having an affair? And that nurse on Long Island who went through the hospital unplugging the life supports of the old people? You remember the one about the boy with the automatic rifle in the hamburger joint? You ever hear the one about the kid, he gets left off in a garbage thing outside a restaurant, he's two days old and it's snowing? The car-bomb deal in London near Harrod's when everybody's shopping for Christmas? The father who ran his children over by mistake, backing down the split-level drive-way in Avalon?" She wiped her lips and tried to take a breath. She remembered thinking that now she'd done it. Now she'd made him cry. Now she'd made them cry. "Because it isn't such a *bad* marriage. It isn't such a *bad* childhood. It's a — that movie? Where he — what's it called? The *Wonderful Life* movie? It isn't so terrible, really. How could anyone think it's so terrible? And

11

Stephen's so *sweet* and everything. I mean, we *love* each other, after all, don't we?" She remembered asking Barrett, "What can we *expect* from each other?"

His face was crooked-looking, the features somehow disorganized. He stared past her, so she turned. Stephen was a step or two inside the doorway of their room. He wore a pair of corduroys and a flannel shirt he often wore to school. Everyone looked and no one spoke, and then Stephen shrugged at her, raising his eyebrows as, possibly, she often did when she shrugged at him, she thought. She looked at his eyes, the color of hers, and she wondered if he understood anything he saw. She remembered wondering just what he saw. If he did understand, she'd thought, maybe he could explain it to her.

"Another time," she said, as Barrett sniffed behind her and Stephen watched his father try not to weep. "Another time."

Now it was another time, she thought, and she wondered as she fled whether it was only bad luck or bad timing that prevented Barrett from making a way to be alone with her, and calm, and saying, "Sarah. Love. What's the complaint?" and her from telling, with affection and reasonableness, what it was.

She wondered what she might have thought to tell him.

When he'd courted Lizzie Bean — his word: *courted* — Willis Mastracola had told her, had said it aloud with a serious face, that he was one of the South Carolina Mastracolas.

"Do you still have slaves?" Lizzie had asked.

He knew that he would remember his declaration and her response all his life. It is my shame before you that's as strong as my need, he often thought of telling her but never did. With the wind right and his mood derisive, he could still hear himself — with his actual hat in his clumsy hands as the usual cold spring rain of the Chenango Valley soaked him and ran into her eyes while they stood outside his car, before their date had a chance to go wherever it might take them — saying, "I was only trying to tell you that I'm not just a dago on the run from big-city newspapering. I'm an old-line dago on the run. And *I'm* the only slave left. If you'd rather go back inside, I'd be pleased to come to the door and try this all over again."

He was fifty-six years old and he was trying to remember when he'd not defined a good portion of himself in terms of Elizabeth Bean. One year and four months older than she, and he more and more considered her significantly his junior, he thought: a sign of the times — of *time*, which he'd begun to wear like a shirt one size too small. He had the feeling that if he mentioned to Lizzie that the pain in his back ran down through his leg every morning, that when he set the date for each week's issue he felt cornered, she would strike him. She was as tall as he was, and probably stronger. She made a point of towering over bad boys in school. He might be shrinking with age. She would maybe lean over and look down into his shifty eyes and tell him to grow up. And he'd be tempted to tell her that he *was*, and that was the problem.

He poured them cups of the morning's reheated coffee, thick and sour, and he said, "It's the leaving her *kid*, you know, that has me so angry. No: crazy. Because you know what he's going to do is —"

"Wait," she said, moving a week's worth of unsorted mail and receipts, the detritus of two busy people. "Before you tell me what has you crazy and me crazy and anybody else crazy, can we agree on something?"

"I'll agree right now."

"I mean it. Let's remember it has to be *Sarah* who's crazy. Who's whatever she is bad enough to leave her little boy behind. She *loves* him."

"I hope he finds it a comfort someday to recall that."

"Will, she isn't doing it to *you*."

"Oh, no? You think Barrett isn't coming here to drop Stephen off for good?"

"He wouldn't leave his son."

"His wife just did."

Lizzie leaned over the cup and sniffed it. "Yuck," she said. "And you think we're going to have to raise him?"

"Who else should? We're his grandparents, for chrissakes."

"We're young enough to do it, almost."

"No sweat," Will said. "He's six, right? When he's ten, I'll be sixty. When he graduates from high school, I'll be most of the way to seventy. When he graduates from college, I'll be — never mind."

"We'd better look into College Board tutoring," she said.

"It isn't funny, Lizzie."

She looked down at her coffee again, and he thought she was going to weep. She said, low, "When you're those ages, I'll be too. And don't make any stupid jokes about me as a younger woman, please."

"I should have included you. I do. I just don't always say it right."

"Please say it right," she said, "so I don't think you're planning your life entirely without me."

"You know, I never believed it when I turned fifty."

She sighed. "You didn't believe it when you turned forty."

"But I believed it about Sarah when Barrett called. Didn't you?"

She nodded. Her long face was pale. In the dimly lighted kitchen she looked young enough, to him, to be her daughter. They were going to watch their diet and work out together and he was going to conquer cigarettes and they would never retire and never slow down. They were going to travel, beginning this summer. And he was going to learn from her the secret of ac-

14

cepting his life. But now they were about to become the parents of their grandchild while Sarah, who had never quite broken their hearts and never quite given them ease, had yanked herself out of Stephen's life and Barrett's, and like a suicide had done as much damage to the world as to herself.

"I don't believe this," Lizzie said. Her eyes were wet.

"Sarah and Barrett and Stephen and — whatever?"

"No," she said. "I believe that. I believe it. It's that I'm *crying*. I didn't think my magical bitch daughter would make me cry again. At my —"

"You were going to say 'age.' "

"Forget age," she said.

He leaned across and ran the edge of his hand along the tears. When his hand was at her chin, he cupped it and leaned in to kiss her. Her lips were very soft, her breath full of coffee and fright. "I'll try," he said.

"Because we're required to be a good deal younger for a while," she said. "But — *bitch!*"

"Maybe she fell in love with somebody else," he said.

"I'm assuming that. I'm hoping that."

"Well, I just had a thought about that," he said.

"What?"

"Fuck love."

That was why they were trying to suppress giggles, were clearing their throats and blinking their eyes that bulged with laughter and tears, when they stood at the front door which Will pushed open, crying, "*Here* you are!"

Daddy carried in his suitcase and his book bag and coat. Grandma stood in the hall and watched everything. Stephen watched her eyes. They looked wet from crying. But Stephen thought she looked angry, not sad. In the kitchen, Grandpa

15

talked to Daddy. Daddy said something about "daughter." Then, Stephen heard, he said, "Your daughter."

"She'll be back," Stephen told Grandma.

Grandma looked at him. Stephen took a step toward the kitchen, then he stopped. He looked over at Grandma. She was watching him.

Daddy looked at him and Grandma. He looked skinny when Grandpa came over and stood next to him. Grandpa looked happy. His eyes inside his glasses looked big, and so did the rest of him. He had ears that stuck out and a big head and long arms with wide hands that had hair all the way up the fingers. He looked like he could hold Daddy and rock him the way Daddy got down on his knees and started rocking Stephen. He saw Grandma come closer. She looked at him and Daddy, and Stephen thought she was going to cry.

"We're a family and a half, folks, aren't we?" Daddy said to Grandma. She put her hands over her eyes. Daddy made a sound in his throat and Stephen thought *he* was going to cry. Stephen looked at the hallway table that had piles of newspapers and magazines and books and a bird's nest on it.

"Where'd you get the nest, Grandma?"

"Birds," she said, and she started to laugh. Her hands came away from her face. "You know, darling. *Birds.*" Grandma started to laugh, and then Grandpa did. His voice was deeper than Daddy's. Grandma stopped. She said, "Oh, Barrett, I'm sorry. It's just craziness, you know? Forgive us." She covered her mouth with her hand.

"I'll be back with her," Daddy said. He took out his wallet.

"Don't," Grandma said.

"No," Barrett said, "it's, you know, mad money. For Sluggo here. So he can buy stuff when he wants. Wouldn't that make him feel good, Lizzie? Or, anyway, better?"

"Better than what?" Grandma said.

Stephen said, "You'll be back pretty soon." They looked at him, and he thought maybe he said it too loud.

Lizzie stood at the doorway and watched Will tucking Stephen in. He stared at his grandfather as if to learn something he might use for tomorrow's waking.

"I'll only be sleeping over a little while, Grandpa," Stephen said. "Hi, Grandma."

"Hi, sweetie."

Will said, "You can stay here as long as you want to, little guy. We like it that you're here. It's like Christmastime or something."

"Thank you," Stephen said, "but I won't be here terribly long."

"You're a courtly fellow," Will said. "You're how old?"

"Six, going on seven," Stephen said. "You sent me a birthday card, remember?"

"That's right. And was there maybe something inside it?"

"A dollar," Stephen said. "Thank you."

"Oh, you're welcome. You're pretty courtly for six going on seven. Are you scared about your mother and father?"

"He'll bring her back," Stephen said.

"Yes," Will said. Lizzie heard it in his voice: a man not sounding desperate, a man not wanting a cigarette. Will said to Stephen, "Did you know this was your mother's room?"

"This was Mommy's room?"

"This was your mommy's room."

"This was her bed?"

"Her very bed."

"Did you tuck her into it?"

"Not after a while," Will said. "She got to want her privacy after a while. But at first, I did. You know about privacy?"

Stephen shrugged. Lizzie felt certain that he knew the word. She thought she knew from whom.

17

Will said, "She's anyway consistent, isn't she? Good night, Stephen. Don't worry."

"Nope."

"I'll leave the door open so you can come get us if you want us."

His eyes looked as large as Barrett's to Lizzie. Barrett had wept when Will shook his hand. Will had embraced him and patted his back very clumsily. Now he surrounded Stephen with his arms and head and hands.

Lizzie said, "You come and get us anytime you want."

"Yes, ma'am," Stephen said.

"I might leave a night-light on tonight," Lizzie said.

Stephen and Willis nodded.

She said, "We love you, sweetie. We love you and Mommy and Daddy. We'll take care of you."

She saw Willis close his eyes and step back from the bed.

"It's really all right, Grandpa," Stephen said.

Lizzie said, "You heard him, Grandpa. It's fine."

In the woods past the field behind Grandma and Grandpa's house there was a river that could sweep them away, Grandma said. He was to play in the yard, or in the woods behind the yard, but not at the river. Stephen stood touching the tree at the edge of the river, looking at the thick rope that hung from a heavy branch. It had a knot at the end, and Stephen knew that children would swing back and forth, in wider and wider circles, until they were above the middle of the river. They would let go into the air and sail out and then drop in, making a foaming splash. Their mouths would be wide and their eyes would be closed and they would make long, loud noises.

Stephen was throwing rocks into the muddy river when he saw Grandpa, in his dark blue bathrobe, looking for him. "Privacy," Stephen said.

Grandpa called his name. Stephen didn't answer. He threw a thick piece of fallen branch into the river. It spun in the air, then spun in the water, and Stephen was deciding between sharks and piranha tearing the flesh from the terrified ox when Grandpa called his name again.

Grandpa came up, wearing high green rubber boots with his pajamas tucked into them. He looked at Stephen, but didn't say anything. Then he smiled. He took a cigarette from his bathrobe pocket and lit it with a silver lighter that clicked open and shut.

"I didn't go too close to the edge," Stephen said, watching the blue cigarette smoke fall apart.

"Can you swim?" Grandpa asked.

"Not good."

"Can you float?"

"Dead man's float."

"Well, if you fall in, then you float really hard, you hear?"

"I'll hold on to a log until I get downstream."

"That's a good idea," Grandpa said. "Where *is* downstream, anyway?"

Stephen shrugged. Grandpa said, "I'll ask Grandma. She knows these things. So, how'd you sleep?"

Stephen shrugged. His mother was always saying *"Answer"* when he did that. But he didn't know the answer.

Grandpa said, "Good. I thought I heard the water running this morning, early. That you?"

"Washing up," Stephen said.

"Good man," Grandpa said. He clicked his lighter open and shut and Stephen looked at it. "I got this in the navy," he said. "My faithful Zippo. Here." He offered it to Stephen, who held it, then clicked it open and shut. Grandpa asked, "Can you read what it says?"

"Cuda?"

"That was my boat. The *Barracuda*. A submarine — you know what they are? I was a machinist's mate on her. I used to work in the engine room on the *Barracuda* off of the Philippines. I was a boy."

"You used to have torpedoes?"

"We did, that's right. Of course, we weren't at war with anybody, officially. But, yeah, we had some fish, we fired some dummies for drill." Grandpa grunted and slid his back down along the tree until he was sitting. Stephen sat next to him. Grandpa rested his arms on his knees and leaned against the tree and smoked his cigarette. It smelled good to Stephen, even though it could kill him for smelling it. He breathed it in. Grandpa clicked the lighter. "We actually sank a ship, one time," Grandpa said. "A Swedish freighter. She was burning already, no one could salvage her. They sent us out to clear the shipping lanes."

"Did it blow up?"

Grandpa said, "Well, I didn't see it hit, of course. I was below. I heard she just turned over on her side. A lot of greasy black smoke, then lots of steam, then she rolled under."

"Were there sharks?"

Grandpa squinted and looked at Stephen. "I expect so," he said.

"And piranha?"

"No. I think I can state that we didn't encounter piranha. You find those only in Brazil, I think, and in movies."

"When you were a boy, did you ever wet your bed, Grandpa?"

Grandpa sat very still, just holding the lighter. Then he pushed his cigarette into the ground and rolled it until it was out. He put it in his bathrobe pocket, took out another cigarette and lit it. "I remember getting up very early and washing so nobody would know. I got a little embarrassed at first."

"What'd you do with the sheets?"

"I took them off the bed and carried them downstairs to the pantry off the kitchen where the washing machine is. I stuck them into the machine — tell you what: why don't I show you before we eat breakfast? It's easier to explain that way. Can I borrow your sheets?"

"Sure," Stephen said. "And then it stopped?"

"I don't know one grownup man who wets his bed," Grandpa said. "It goes away by itself. Every man does it, though, when he's a boy. Then it stops. You hate it because you can't help it and you think you should. But then it stops. I remember what my father told me about it."

"What?"

"He said it wasn't my fault."

Stephen said, "Do you think girls do it too?"

"I believe they do," Grandpa said, "but boys get it worse, I think. I don't know why that is."

"We can ask Grandma," Stephen said. Then he said, "Does my mommy know about the ship that rolled over?"

"I can't imagine I ever had the occasion to tell her. I'd say no, she doesn't. Why?"

"Maybe I can tell her sometime," Stephen said.

When he drove away, Barrett knew that he should have stayed the night with his in-laws instead of racing off, with his skin tingling, as if exhaustion were a rash. He knew that it was less the panic to pursue Sarah that sent him off than it was his fear of staying with Stephen, whose eyes had grown so large and whose pale face looked stiff and somehow sore. But he was frightened of what he must say, might say, couldn't say to his son, and he found it easier to continue his pursuit. There were so many directions and so few choices he might make correctly. He had thought of Santa Fe, and pottery, and the pueblos and the pots. He thought of a small old woman with a starched white apron over her clothes. "Blue Corn," Sarah had told him, and he'd nodded, he remembered, embarrassed before the old woman and his wife. The woman had told them where she took the clay from and how, with horse manure, she created the gleaming black pots that Sarah held with reverence. "The San Ildefonso do their pots this way," Sarah had told him, as if Blue Corn weren't standing there in her living room before the glass showcase in which her bowls were displayed. "It's a great tradition," Sarah had said. "They make their choices within the tradition. It's about limits." He'd understood none of it until now, he thought. He had picked a tradition, and he would travel in it.

He tore along the two-lane that would take him to the highway west. He drove too quickly and with loose loops of the wheel. He didn't much think about what might be coming in the opposite lane, in darkness and at high speed to explode upon him with its bright lights. "You have to take *care*," he told himself, but didn't drive any differently.

But Sarah hadn't chosen according to any tradition *he* had heard of. Sarah had run away. Maybe that was the great tradition she was working in. People were always leaving each other, not loving each other, or loving some stranger, or not loving anyone. Maybe that was the tradition. Maybe she was nuts. Well, she was. She always had been. But maybe she was in real trouble now. He, surely, was. And he was going to find her. She would travel toward the Indians and the clay pottery and the city they'd had fun in when they were new to each other and marriage and before Stephen was born.

He heard Sarah say, in a future time, when she'd come back, and Stephen was happy and all right and maybe they had another child, and Barrett was away at work and Sarah was meeting a friend for lunch, "Barrett knew exactly where I went." He heard her voice, rueful and rough with derision of her wild, younger self. He would have brought her home, and he would be away at work, knowing that she wouldn't leave again. "It was like coming to, you know? After you faint?" he heard her say. "All of a sudden, there he was. He knew exactly where to find me. Out of the whole country — *continent* — he picked the right hotel in Santa Fe, New Mexico." She would sound a little mastered, a little proud of him and even them, a little ashamed. He would have been working to make her feeling of shame diminish.

This is what pioneer men would have done, Barrett thought, or cowboys, even. He drove south before driving west, and he thought of men in greasy chaps, of scrawny and haunted men in leather caps who couldn't stand company. He thought of John Wayne in *The Searchers*, carrying Natalie Wood back from the Indians when he had thought, at first, to kill her. Barrett thought of riding, of a man on a horse, and then of a man on a woman. Then he thought of the woman on the man, of Sarah, her breasts dipping toward Barrett as she bit her lips and rode him toward her satisfaction, and the thrill he always insisted upon: seeing her achieve it, her features going soft, her eyes fluttering under the lids, her breath sighing out as she came down upon him, covering his eyes and mouth with her flesh. She sometimes said, lying over him, "You looked again."

He smelled her and heard her and saw a man with no face beneath her, in some salmon-and-beige-colored motel room on an east-west highway. He saw them, collapsed in nakedness upon each other as his car, smelling of hot bearings and filthy oil, toiled past them on a turnoff to, say, Michigan City, Indiana, as he dipped away, forever, in the wrong direction.

He should fly to Santa Fe. But that was so risky. It was such a one-shot effort. Miss, and he was standing alone in a gallery hung with ugly turquoise paintings of skulls and teepees, or in a group of tourists who paced the line of Indian vendors outside the Palace of the Governors, offering earrings and genuine Native American sterling silver golf tees. This way, driving like this into nothing but his headlights, slithering off the verge of Route

12 and heading for Route 81, then 80, he would at least cover the miles of westward-running road. He might even see her. It could happen. Coincidence must be part of the larger plan. And mustn't there be some larger design in this? And mightn't he, truly, see her on the side of the road, maybe beside a broken-down rental car or — what? — the van or sports car or fucking rusted pickup truck belonging to whoever it was she might have chosen to run with?

Let her be alone, he prayed. Let her flee me by herself.

Grandma said she and Stephen could stay home, but Grandpa had to go to work. Stephen and Grandma went out so she could clean up a patch of garden near the woods. He was supposed to help her, but when they got to the garden, Grandma told him to sit down while she talked.

"Why don't you sit on that piece of log, sweetie? It's Grandpa's splitting block. He splits kindling there, except every time he does it his back gets sore. It's the splitting block I never let him use." Grandma sat down on the chopping block and Stephen sat down on the ground. The sun was shining, but the ground felt cold.

"Sweetie, don't bite your lip, all right? It'll swell up and keep on hurting. You'll be all right, Stephen. Listen. Your father and your mother —"

"He has to go after her. She isn't thinking straight."

"That's what your daddy said? She isn't —"

"— thinking straight," Stephen said. "But she'll get better. It's going to be a hell of a long drive. It'll take him days and days. And then finding her in the right place. He thinks it's a hotel someplace. And then driving back with her. He'll be tired as hell."

"Tired as hell?"

"That's what Daddy figured."

"Well, I'm sure he's right. Your daddy knows his way around."

Stephen said, "It just happens to a woman, sometimes."

"Does it," Grandma said. "Look. Stephen. What if they can't get back? What if your daddy can't make it back here?"

"Well, why would that be?"

"I don't *know*, sweetie."

"He loves me."

"Yes, he does. And he loves Mommy."

"And she loves him," Stephen said.

"That's love for you."

Stephen said, "You know, I could stay at a hotel if I'm a nuisance or anything. I have money Daddy gave me."

Grandma took her hands off her jeans and held them wide. She held them out toward him. Stephen didn't know if he was supposed to go get hugged or if she might flap her hands and shoo him away. Her face was squinty, and she shook her head. Then she put her arms down and said, "Well, we'd just as soon you stayed with us if you can stand it, dear."

Grandma got down onto her knees and picked up a wooden-handled trowel. She moved around until he was looking at her bottom, and, over her shoulder, she said, "Stephen, will you come over here and take the little fork and scratch this earth soft? We'll dig in a little early. We'll try."

Stephen got down beside her, but he didn't pull the fork through the lumpy, cold soil. He was on his hands and knees, the way you are when you crawl, but he just stayed there. He watched the backs of Grandma's hands move. Things were moving under her skin, inside, while she turned the earth and picked up stones.

He knew he would have to ask it sooner or later. He knew that was why she was so upset. "Am I going to have to stay here, Grandma?"

"Oh, no," she said. "We can do this, and then I thought we could do a little baking. I haven't had time to bake for months. We could make a cake if you like. Or we could go to the store and buy a cake and find a movie to watch tonight. We could buy some popcorn. It's like a holiday for me with you here, Stephen, so today we get to play. What would *you* like to do?"

He said, "Am I going to *stay* here, I mean."

She sat up from digging. She nodded her head. Her hair was dark brown with little bits of red and gold and gray. The sun moved in it, and Stephen thought with surprise that his grandmother, with her long face and long nose and wide mouth, was pretty. "I know what you mean," she said.

"For a very long time?"

She said, "I honestly don't know." She looked at him. "I don't."

"No?"

"I don't, darling. I'll take care of you if it happens. If — Grandpa and I will take care of you. But nobody knows."

"Does Daddy know?"

Grandma's eyes got big and she shook her head. She looked past him and he turned his head. He saw the woods, the sunlight on the trees, the bugs in the light, and then the part of the woods that looked dark. When he turned back, Grandma was scratching with her trowel at the ground.

Barrett awakened and knew it all at once — his location on the highway in Pennsylvania, the reason for his being there and the size of what was behind him and what was ahead. He peed behind brush at the edge of the road, possibly visible to passing cars and not caring. He considered turning around to show them his scorn, but he knew that, finally, he couldn't. He wasn't a violent man. He smiled to think of his penis as a violence committed on strangers who passed him at seventy miles an hour.

Back in the car and starting up, he smelled again the mingled odors of fried food, his sour body and — he sniffed, as dogs do in the wind — the hair and skin of his child. He turned the motor off and leaned away from the wheel. He was close enough to the turnoff to the Northeast Extension to be at his own house in a couple of hours. That was the progress he had made. He had driven all night, put hundreds of miles on his engine and tires and his sore muscles, had terrorized his child and abandoned him to his in-laws, who were now beleaguered and confused, and this was where he had got: close to home.

Yet he was to locate, among all these miles of road and sign-board and gasoline-wilted leafage that mostly screened his nation from him, a woman who had fled her life with him and their child as if she were one of those television teenage murderers on a cross-country spree. She's too little to find, he thought. She can hide behind something thin. She's a guerrilla fighter, and she's sheltering under bushes and the mossy sides of trees. He couldn't remember whether moss grew on the north or not. It ought to be the eastern part, he thought, where it catches the sun. Except it would catch the sun as it went down westward as well. He wanted to cry for the not knowing which. And then he thought of Sarah, her back against a birch tree, which was the only tree he knew, in a camouflage suit, her face blackened with cork so she looked like a lady football player. He saw Sarah in khakis and black headcloth, Sarah in muddy motorcycle boots and tight, faded jeans and a soiled T-shirt: Sarah in a T-shirt in the woods, east or west, without a brassiere, her nipples broad against the shirt, her breasts wide and flattened.

With an erection that outraged him — "It isn't *fair*," he said, as if his arousal had been brought on by her wish, according to her plan — he started the car again and pulled out onto a road that was only loosely clotted with traffic.

"First," he instructed himself, ignoring his groin, "you find someplace where you can eat and rinse out a shirt."

He nodded in response. His obedience made him smile. That

27

was how he would do it, he thought, slipping on his sunglasses. He would work in small sequences: food here, a stop for gas and a restroom there, a stop for more coffee later on, and then a long accumulation of miles. He would do it in steps. He would achieve small chores. He would let his quieter mind, the part that mightn't be as terrified as his conscious brain and his disobedient body, work on finding Sarah. He would drive, meanwhile, so that he would be in motion when he thought of nowhere else. He would settle on Santa Fe, he knew. In his pinched, nightmare thinking, it had been Santa Fe again and again. He would try to find an alternative, but he knew his uncunning: he would think of noplace else. He would land in Santa Fe, he thought. And, setting himself in motion, he drew contentment from the knowledge that he would be well westward by the time he believed he was right.

He wouldn't call the police, who would trace the credit card if they ever believed him that she was a Missing Person. That would be easy, and that would be official. Structured as Barrett liked to think he was, organized and as much of a maverick as the president of a local Rotary, he would not be logical and call the cops. Because he'd be too embarrassed, she thought. He would have to admit that the little lady, instead of shopping Victoria's Secret in the Bucks County malls for ruby silk bedclothes, had taken her bank cards and a canvas plumber's bag filled with jeans, underwear and socks, some shirts, a cotton sweater and a long skirt that hung out quickly, and had driven away in the family's 1989 cherry-red Blazer with its underpowered engine — Barrett complained whenever they climbed the long, slow hill up the Black Horse Pike — and its litter of blueprints, drawings, contractors' brochures, catalogues and the plastic box wrapped in bright silver duct tape and labeled, in Barrett's wobbly hand, EMERGENCY.

So Barrett would be too dishonest with himself, she thought, to call out the police. He would wait at home because it was sensible to wait at home. He would take care of Stephen. Here was where she always had trouble. She could manage the part about being a thief of her own property. She could juggle the stuff about Barrett's being stunned, then crazy with fear, then so bewildered that his stomach would ache and his head feel tight as a bell somebody was beating on — for that he would take too much acetaminophen and cure his head but ruin his stomach. She wouldn't say *sorrow* and she worked at not thinking it, hearing herself as a grade school girl crying *Yahdeeyahdeeyahdee*, as she had done to drown out feuding girlfriends on the playground during lunch break. Whenever she thought that word she didn't wish to entertain, she would think in her loudest voice of those drowning-out sounds that were always followed by a mocking *I ca-an't hear you*. Nevertheless, there was a scuffed wooden yo-yo, an old one her father had found in their garage, that Stephen had tried to use, trailing it flat and unspinning instead of Walking the Dog. It lay near the spare tire and liquor carton containing the tire iron, jack and other tools she didn't wish to use. It was a scratched and faded bright red, like a well-washed, very old and often used nightshirt.

"He got your note," she said, leaving the motel outside of Mechanicsburg, Pennsylvania. "He's got your note." She was well into traffic and doing 65 before she leaned forward to adjust the radio and noticed that she'd forgotten to clip her seat belt. She pulled it down and over and locked it with her right hand, steering with her left and feeling suddenly vulnerable. She said, "He will *have* it." She did not add that lots of kids never had a note like that, much less six years of tenderness. "You say 'Plus three squares a day,' " she said, "and I'm pitching your skinny ass out of the car."

It simply had to happen, and everyone would have to understand. She hadn't gone looking for it. She wasn't — "Am god-

29

damned well not," she called, in a voice that sounded to her uncomfortably like that of Elizabeth Bean Mastracola, but she *wasn't* — one of those adopted kids who mooned around orphanages or haunted the overworked women at Catholic Charities or the nightmare lawyers who were said to sell infants flown north from Arkansas. Nor did she put whimpery ads about mother-and-daughter bonding, for Christ's sake, in the Personal columns of big-city papers or the more high-minded magazines. This one had come looking for her, and when something arrives in that fashion, you are required to respond.

She had borrowed a batch of magazines from Sonny Fischer because she'd wanted something new and trivial to read. Because Sonny had a crush on Barrett and liked to prove herself remarkable to him every few weeks, she had given Sarah copies of some glossy magazines for intelligent women over forty who wanted to look like twenty-year-olds while admitting to thirty, along with back issues of *The New Republic* and *The Village Voice*. For *New Republic*, she'd decided, you were better off as a reader if you wanted the separation of church and state in America but adored Israel and were enchanted by renouncing idealism in world affairs. For the *Voice*, you had to see the depraved vie everywhere with totalitarian forces. But she'd remembered the famous sexy Personals and, turning to them, reading past the boys who wanted to be whipped by bigger boys and the middle-aged men who searched for teenage boys to advise and discipline, she had moved on to the back cover. There were notices from people dumbstruck by someone they saw while riding three stops on the subway two weeks before — *Call Me*, the ads pleaded, *Call Me* — and Sarah envisioned New York City, its citizens passing each other on trains and buses, pulsing to the heartbeat of fugitive love. It was the New Chastity, she thought, looking over the descriptions of cheap HIV testing. You fell in love with your eyes and then forever lived apart with broken hearts, and don't think I didn't catch that *fugitive*, she thought, but *I ca-an't hear you.*

AM I YOUR MOTHER? it said. Then underneath: *You were born on November 29, 1963, in St. Elizabeth's Hospital, Schuylkill Street, Wyandotte, Pa. Long arms and legs, long fingers, blue eyes and black hair. Shouldn't we know each other? The future belongs to the past. VV Box 942Y.*

Sarah continued to work at that: the future belongs to the past. She'd felt deceitful asking, but had anyway asked, and Barrett, supervising Stephen's shower and dripping water from his ears and nose because he had, as usual, stuck his face through the shower curtain — at precisely the moment in their conversation when he always stuck his head through the shower curtain to bark like a sea lion, but *I ca-an't hear you* — and, as Stephen toweled himself, had said, "It sounds like it's one of those really wise things you're supposed to know. You know? And I *don't* know. Not being a really wise person. Montaigne? Gertrude Stein? Richard Nixon? You think it's true?"

"I think I do," she'd answered.

"Do you know what it means?" Barrett had asked, mopping himself with a dishtowel and making a face at the chicken broth she'd earlier cleaned up with the towel.

"No. Sort of. Probably not."

"Then it's bound to be true," Barrett said.

"Because we don't know what in hell we're talking about so we think whoever said it has to be smarter than us?"

"Well, we *are* intellectuals," he said. "Where'd you find it?"

"In an ad someplace."

"For brassieres."

"Something cantilevered, yes. I don't remember what."

"Cantilevered support, you got either buttresses for medieval cathedrals or brassieres for ladies' jugs."

"God, you're a pig, Barrett."

"I am easily excited by architecture is all," he'd said as Stephen emerged with a towel around his waist and his lean chest bare, so white, she remembered thinking, that she looked for the blue of veins beneath it, and reached with a finger to feel the rounding of his ribs.

I ca-an't —

She pumped her brakes and was able to drop down to 62 and make her face go innocent as she cruised past the radar trap. She insisted of herself that she think about business, Barrett designing houses and suburban office buildings, Sarah doing what her teachers called interior design and what she knew was interior decorating. Together they had made money until the Reagan-Bush time bomb went off and there was no money from expanding businesses because businesses were going bust. There was no money from new homes because developers were leaving the commonwealth, leaving the country, leaving their brains, in one case, in a spray of mush against the gazebo walls.

Leaving letters, she thought. People were also leaving letters, like hers to Stephen, for example. He would find it in the pocket of his *I Ate Alligator* shirt from the seafood house where none of them had dared to order alligator steak but where Barrett had bought the shirt because, seeing it on their waitress, Stephen had said, "Cool."

Barrett had said "Cool" too, but had been tasteful enough not to mention the waitress's chest, which, Sarah knew, was what he'd meant.

And Stephen would find his mommy's note. He wouldn't feel alone and abandoned, and anyway Barrett was a good enough father. Stephen trusted him. Barrett complained, often, that he failed as a father because he got angry. Sarah, so far, had been unable to make clear that some kinds of anger were reassuring. And who in hell was he going to be angry with around here? Where was this line of thought going? He'd be merciful to *her?*

That's right.

That's right.

And last night, she remembered, alone in a motel for the fourth or fifth time since they'd been married, she'd lain on the bed in a T-shirt and a pair of Barrett's boxer shorts, and she'd remembered a time she often thought of but was somehow embarrassed to mention. She thought it was interesting that she couldn't mention it to him. It was a night in summer when she'd worn his boxer shorts to bed because of the heat, and he'd walked his fingers over her thigh to the fly of the shorts and had walked them in.

"I like these on you," he'd said, and they'd made love while she wore them. And she, excited by his excitement, by their sweating on each other in the humid dark, had reached for him soon again and, kissing his penis, had brought him back, and they'd made love again, this time with the boxer shorts off.

She had felt peaceful — "Mm, gluey," she said as he grazed on her, kissing and licking the sweat in her navel and then nuzzling between her legs — but she hadn't been peaceful, she remembered, thinking in the motel how, in their bed at home, she had opened her legs for him and, when his tongue began to take her too quickly, when she'd wanted to feel everything but at the slightest, friendly distance, she'd said, "You know what I would love to do now?"

"What?" he'd said, like a child who looked over the next unopened present set before him.

"I would love to stop."

"Sarah," he'd said, "Jesus. Why *stop?*"

"And go to sleep a teensy little bit horny, maybe. So we can see what we feel like. You know what I mean? So we can see if it's just fucking or —"

"Fucking isn't *just* fucking, Sarah. Jesus."

"It doesn't have to be," she'd said.

33

"This sounds like some kind of a back-seat-of-the-car teenage cocktease, Sarah. You know? This is some kind of a nightmare or something. Jesus."

And she had put her hand on his stomach, which jumped and felt hot, and Barrett had gone still, waiting for her hand to slip down. She'd said, "I'm going to sleep, Barrett. All right?"

"Jesus," he'd said, "no."

She remembered sitting up and pulling the pillow onto her, covering the front of her with the pillow and saying, over it, "*No?*" He tore the pillow from her and stuffed his hand up her legs while, with the other, he pushed her shoulders back. She'd been moist and had resented how she'd let her legs slide apart and how he had put a finger, then another finger, up inside her. She'd resented and enjoyed it, had hated her pleasure as she rode his hand and as another finger pried and pushed between her buttocks and then had entered her so that he held her and, with his strong hand, worked on her like some kind of master crafts-man.

"Bastard," she'd said, to the rhythm of his hand and of her body on it. "Bastard. What're you doing, bastard, you *ow!* bas-tard, you bastard."

In the motel, not watching television, lying alone in his boxer shorts on the wide bed, she had touched herself, then stopped. "You're such a jerkoff," she said aloud — and without thinking, except to reflect that it might have been easier to *be* there with them and speculate on driving away than to be here in a nameless place, she found herself seizing the telephone and decoding the secret to making a long-distance call to Stephen and Barrett for only twice the usual cost. She whisper-sang telephone company commercials to herself as the phone rang. She play-acted scenes from melodramas in which people said, "Thank God it's *you*. Just tell me you're all right, the rest will take care of itself." It didn't ring. It never sounded like a bell. It burred. It clicked. It was like the monitor on the IV drip in the hospital when you almost lose your kid but have him. This is the patient calling, hello. Hello? She hung up. She tried to snort a kind of laugh. Then she tried to cry. All she could do was read the first section of the Harrisburg papers and fall into dreamless, unforgivably uninterrupted sleep.

And on the road next morning, thinking of a pause for coffee and a bathroom, she thought of her parents. They would be pestering Barrett to bring Stephen over, to let them come to him, and Barrett would insist on being private and aloof in his pain. He would think she was leaving him, leaving them. When Stephen found her note, he'd know differently, of course. She was still puzzled by her inability to write to the man she had lived with and worked with for seven years, counting their living together in Chinatown in Philadelphia. There was too much to say, she thought, too few choices of words for all of it. With Stephen, it was easier. She and Stephen were alike — oh yeah: a couple of orphans. But *I ca-an't hear you.*

She'd slowed without realizing it and was passed by a truck that pawed her with its airstream. The Blazer rocked and she tailgated the truck and then swung out, without signaling, and passed him at 75, slid over in front of him without a signal, and kept her foot down for two or three miles. One reason, she realized, as she dropped down to 60 and watched the truck come into her mirror again, one anger that drove her out into the passing lane again was her sudden understanding that Barrett would *not* stay home and chew his thoughts and cheer their child. He would go to her parents. He was the boy whose mother and father had died in a car when he was less than what you'd call mature. It was Barrett who chased after parents — after anyone older who bought him a shot of milk, she had told him during an argument. She was, you could say, betrayed. So she was justified. She speeded up, and she felt herself smile.

*   *   *

35

The office, he often thought, was the best of the job. In a small two-story brick building at the end of the little east-west shopping street, it was as much museum and hideout as newspaper office. If you liked living a century ago, Willis knew he said too often, this was your kind of place. The old press was in the front room, which stank marvelously of ink and metal type. At the counter was the phone extension that Stovall Stratton, his typesetter, refused to answer. Upstairs, Willis hid, opened his mail, wrote checks, received some, edited the reports of his correspondents flung out as far as Smyrna, New York, and Georgetown, cropped and taped the borders onto photographs, made up the ads, and cringed — he knew he said this too often also — lest something actually *happen*. The next-to-last big news had occurred when the cold-cream-factory workers learned through Willis's front page that their factory was closing in a month. Most recently, a local boy had been run over by a British armored personnel carrier during Operation Desert Storm. Willis had published the letter from the boy's commanding officer and, next to it, his editorial entitled "Your Sorry Letter," which he'd addressed to the President of the United States. He had lost some ads and subscriptions as well as the plate glass window with its gold lettering: THE PRESS. In future, he'd warned his correspondents, nothing more violent than bad weather and impolite divorces would be acceptable in their weekly columns.

Now he'd been flushed from his office and required at the Village Hall, a squat and undistinguished low building near the railroad tracks. It was his favorite part of town, because the old feed mill and the Agway reminded him of what Burroughs must have felt like when it was a market hub for big farms, a tannery and a lumber mill, which still collapsed on itself to the west of the railroad tracks.

The rest of the council were there — Ben Pierson, Dick Pearson, Sidney Sherwood and Mariah Kasselbaum. They were known as selectmen until Mariah Kasselbaum ran for office and won. She demanded they be called the Village Council, and, despite remarks at the final meeting of the Village Selectmen about burning brassieres in front of the Dale Carnegie library where the Civil War monument clock — the Union Soldier with his vast mustache stood on top of it — told a wronger time than the clock in the steeple of the Methodist church, Mariah Kasselbaum had won. They were the Village Council of Burroughs, New York, 60 miles south and west of Syracuse, 50 miles north of Binghamton, 265 miles north of New York City and approximately — this was according to Lizzie's secretary, Karen Kelly — one million miles from civilization.

Ben Pierson took notes for the official minutes. Mariah Kasselbaum often asked that the minutes be read aloud, and she liked to make motions to amend them. Ben Pierson said he was certain that she enjoyed rubbing in what she'd said on her first day among them: "I will not consider being the girl who takes notes. One of you boys will have to be the girl. And I would just as soon not hear anybody clear his throat and start off with 'Gentlemen —' "

So they listened to Ben summarize the matter that convened them: the refusal of the son of their local hippie lawyer to salute the flag before sporting events. He was fat, gawky, unathletic, strong and full of errant confidence. He was fifteen, an immature eleventh grader, and he was entitled to be on the basketball and baseball teams despite his lack of skill. The coaches never played him. He seemed not to care. He practiced hard, though mouthily, and arrived on time for games. That was when the trouble began. In the gym, before basketball games, he refused to place his hand over his heart and pledge allegiance to the flag. At baseball games, when the coach played his tape recording of "The Star-Spangled Banner," the boy, Loren Macy, Jr., liked to sneer during this moment of high public patriotism, and adjust his clothing or rub his face — the gestures, Willis figured, were meant to draw attention to his unsaluting hand, his unsinging mouth. Parents of other players wanted him thrown off the team. Lizzie demanded that she be permitted to deal with him. But the parents had sent angry letters to Willis, and he'd printed them. And in their letters they had insisted on the council's involvement, since the village's reputation — at the United Nations? Willis had asked one of them — was endangered. The American Legion would be calling, another said. Willis asked why not the Ku Klux Klan, and he saw from one or two faces that the idea had already, like manure in springtime, been in the air.

Loren Macy, Jr., was the son of Loren Macy, a lawyer from New York who had come up with his wife and son to build his own house and work part-time while — well, no one knew what. They assumed, in the village, that he smoked marijuana and maybe did worse. They didn't like his thick dark beard, his rumpled suits, his big smile, his tired and maybe desperate eyes with the dark brown semicircles of exhausted flesh beneath them. They didn't like it that he and his family had survived a bad winter despite burst pipes and his need to twice hire a bulldozer at a hundred dollars an hour to scrape down to ice the winding drive up his steep hill to the house hidden in the woods of his land. "The man drives roofing nails like a girl and he don't know shit about wall," Sidney Sherwood had said. "He left the headers off where he cut his windows in. The windows *will* blow out someday. I hope to see it happen."

After the minutes were read, and after Mariah Kasselbaum had suggested that the location "being that" be replaced, in the interests of literacy, by "since," and after the motion had carried, the Village Council ate their sandwich lunch and drank their iced tea in the little room with its yellow walls and green linoleum, the Franklin stove and the red telephone that connected them to the volunteer fire department at the back of the building. As they ate, they discussed the Loren Macy, Jr., matter.

Mariah Kasselbaum, an organizer for the Democratic Party and therefore the resident leftist, said, around her sandwich, "It's the boy's right not to pledge and not to sing. Freedom of speech means you have a right to *not* speak. There is no law that says you have to parrot along."

"In view of the dead bodies this village gave to three or four wars, I would think every citizen would want to kick the little hippie prick's ass. Some people had their way, he'd be lucky to get off with a thumping or two." So said Dick Pearson, hardware mogul and veteran of World War II.

Mariah snorted.

Dick said to Ben Pierson, "Can she just *do* that?"

Will said, "The boy's father knows what he can do. When he commutes to Vestal, he works there in a storefront law office. He argues cases in court. He's supposed to know the law a little. We could end up spending the village budget on court costs — you know how expensive lawyers are. They charge by the hour, don't forget. And anyway, it'd be either really rough on the kid, or give him just what he wants. I figure that we, as the grownups, maybe ought to drop it."

Mariah said, "Your wife wants that?"

"Now, don't go holding the man's wife against him," Dick Pearson said.

Ben Pierson said, "I think she's got whatever jurisdiction there is, Dick. And it doesn't insult somebody if you say out loud he's married to Elizabeth."

"Thank you, Ben," Will said. To Mariah Kasselbaum he said, "You're on the school board. What's the word over there?"

"Same rush to mob rule. Same indignation. The boy's skin hasn't cleared up yet, and he's Public Enemy Number One. I believe that he'll be used, come school-budget time, as an excuse for voting down books for the library and enough money for one pennywhistle production of *The Sound of Music*."

"What kind of *mob-rule* crack would that be?" Dick Pearson

asked. He stuck a finger behind his upper teeth and pried away a wad of gummy bread, which he inspected, then replaced in his mouth and swallowed, staring thoughtfully at Mariah Kasselbaum.

Will was thinking of Stephen and Barrett, of Stephen's wide eyes and his pallor, of the soiled sheets he had washed for the boy while running on about an upcoming visit to the baseball Hall of Fame in Cooperstown. He recalled how Sarah had shouted on the phone at Lizzie, and how Lizzie's voice had wobbled when they talked about it afterward, and how Sarah hadn't called anymore, how he and Lizzie made the calls and how stiff and difficult the calls had been — how desperately they'd chattered to fill the emptiness between them and their child, how sad and then angry they'd grown. Lizzie had been a guidance counselor and now, as principal of a large central school, she seemed to Will to qualify as a major expert on people younger than they. And who, he had asked her, is *not* younger than they? And Lizzie, curling her lip at his comment, had said, "I haven't got an idea worth saying out loud, Will. Maybe it's what happens to adopted kids sometimes. They get angry."

"Because they've been ditched?"

Lizzie shrugged.

"But we didn't ditch her, Liz. We did the opposite. She isn't lost, godammit. She is *found*."

"Will? Jesus, Will, how about it?" Dick Pearson was bent close to the dull maple top of the meeting table, as if looking underneath a stone to see whether Will was there and might reply.

"Sorry," Will said.

"You all right?"

"Yes, Dick, thank you, I'm fine. I'm just puzzled."

"That's why Miz Kasselbaum is moving to table. We all seem confused."

"Second," Will said.

Dick said, "Sidney already did that."

Will said, "All right, Dick. What shall I do?"

"Vote yes."

"Yes."

"I knew you could do it," Dick said.

Stephen was swinging out over the water when she found him. He had both sneakered feet pressing against the rope, just above the big knot, so that his feet were sole to sole and his knees poked out sharply. His body was bowed, with his rump out in the air, and he seemed terrified. Yet he was swinging in circles that grew wider and wider as he pumped at the rope. Lizzie tried to find his expression but could see only the familiar features — slightly rounded nose that was a little flatter on his face than you'd expect; the blue eyes that seemed so old in a boy because the color was not of a brilliant sky but faded, as if cloudy; the small, determined mouth — and yet his face didn't seem familiar to her at all. Either he was a new person in this new world his parents had made for him or he was going to be an unpredictable boy, hard to grasp, harder to hold. Like his mother, Lizzie thought.

She didn't call out to Stephen about his disobedience in being at the river, and about his actual risk in being on that rope in widening circles that threatened to flatten out beneath the branch to which the rope was tied and pulp him against the side of the maple or hurl him into the river, which wasn't shallow or slow. She watched him as she had watched Sarah since she was six days old and had been, suddenly, theirs. So we wished, Lizzie thought: so we as a matter of fact *prayed*. All he's doing, she told herself — and her thoughts sounded to her like something you'd say in surprise — he's simply taking the shortest path, and therefore the riskiest, into his mother's life.

She stepped back into the woods and sat on a broad gray stone that was going green with lichen. It was cold, as everything there was cold in April — rocks unwarmed by sun, the ground you tried to drive seeds through, the kitchen in early morning because Willis had decided to hell with winter and turned off the furnace they'd need, in fact, through the first week of May at least. And she thought of Willis, rumbling his cough until she came downstairs to the coffee he'd made after sneaking his first cigarette in the yard. He was a problem. He said age was the problem. Well, here was what you'd call perspective, she thought. You want a problem, try the old mom-and-pop routine with your vanished daughter's six-year-old. *Vanished*, she decided, was a word she might not use again.

Lizzie realized that she'd been rummaging through dead leaves and sparse grasses with her right hand. She allowed her hand to continue the search, and it found what her flesh had known would be there: Will's cigarette filters, rubbed emberless against the rock and then buried. You think you don't leave a trace, she thought, and then you're found.

She listened for Stephen, for the smack of his flesh against the tree, the splash in the ice-cold river. She leaned forward and groaned as she stood. She thought: I sound like you, godammit, Willis. She walked toward the river out of the shade of the woods and called, "Stephen! For goodness' sakes. I didn't know *where* you'd gone. Can you swing back over here, sweetie?"

He let his arcs diminish, then worked, first with his feet, then pumping with his hands and feet, to aim himself at Lizzie. As he came over the cold water, he seemed to sweep its chill at her. His face was red with his efforts, and his nose ran. He looked like a child coming in after playing in the snow. He landed with a casual fall to the ground at her feet, stood up, kicked his right foot as if he'd twisted it, then stood before her. He looked up with scrupulous attention, and after that pause he said, "Are you mad?"

She shook her head. She hadn't been asked that, in that tone of voice, by a child so young, in over twenty years — by a child of *hers*, she'd heard herself think. "No," she said, forcing herself to keep her distance as he drew lines with his sneakers into the slippery dark brown clay on the bank. "No, I was a little worried. I didn't think you'd come down here without telling me."

"I couldn't tell you. I wasn't supposed to come."

"That's right, isn't it? And you wouldn't have considered *not* coming, I suppose."

"Sorry, Grandma."

"No, that's all right. You aren't that sorry anyway, are you? You really like going out there."

He smiled an impersonal, elusive smile and nodded. "It gets out pretty high," he said.

"Do you feel brave when you do it?"

"And scared."

"But it doesn't take you all that far, does it?"

He shrugged.

"Not far enough," she said.

He said, "I guess."

"Your mother used to swing on that rope. She used to come out here when she wasn't supposed to and swing and swing whenever she got mad at Grandpa and me. She *flew!* We used to — one of us would come out after her and hide in the woods and watch. To make sure she was safe. You see, the river's fast enough, it could carry you downstream a good distance if you fell in, if you were small. It's deep enough to drown in, Stephen. You should wear the life preserver hanging in the pantry."

"I didn't see it."

"I put it back there today. We haven't used it for a while. It's orange and it has white straps and it's a pain to put on, but I really wish you'd wear it."

"What did Mommy say?"

43

"About what?"

"You and Grandpa sneaking up on her like that."

"I don't believe she ever spotted us. Interesting question, Stephen."

"Thanks."

"Will you be more careful?"

"Sure."

"Really."

"Sure," he said. "Did Mommy or Daddy call up today?"

"No. Nobody called. I'm sorry."

"He'll find us," Stephen said.

"Who, darling? Find —"

"Daddy. He'll find her."

On an unpaved country road that was really little more than a lane, in her tan car thick with the brown-black dust of coal country, Gloria sat with her window open, her cream cheese and tomato sandwich beside her, a newspaper opened to the Personals. She was reading of Special Orders Taken at a bait shop, of Rubber Stamps Made to Order and of Fresh Silk Flowers available for all occasions. She was parked beside a pond that was, already, with spring barely begun, rimed near the banks with a sudsy yellow scum and going green overall. Soon the mayflies would come, she thought, floating to the surface, shedding their skin and flying up. In a day or less they'd become shiny spinners and live the few hours' length of their lives. She looked at her large-faced men's watch, then back at the ads, then over at the pond. Their mouths, she thought, wouldn't function. She sighed. So many other creatures' mouths are the sites for fakery. Why not the ridiculous mayflies? They'd mate in the air, on the run, like the rest of us. She thought of a boy she knew years before, Chester Terrell. He'd explained about mayflies to her and they'd watched them in the air — "Fucking in flight," he'd cackled. They would swarm over the water, mating. The females, laying their eggs near the water, would die. She said, "It's like that, ladies. Mid-flight mating, then you're dead." She thought of Chester's dirty laugh. Country boys could lecture on the sex of any creature, large or small, except for human females. You could leave a flashlight on the banks of a pond at night, and the mayflies would heap themselves onto it, ten inches deep, a foot sometimes. Of course, then you had yourself a foot's worth of mayflies to contend with.

She reached out and broke off a twig of waxy-limbed sweet gale, a kind of myrtle, she thought. She rubbed her fingers but the scent was thin, not rich.

"Oh, well," she said to the remains of her sandwich, to the Personals and the business ads, and to her recollections of Chester Terrell, who, when she was a teenage girl, had pinned her arms above her head and forced her torso still with his. Someone apparently had told him that tonguing a girl's neck got her hot, and he had laved her like a mother cat on the job. She remembered the feel of his hard chest on her breasts. She wondered if she was the first girl he had felt that way. He humped up and down and mewed a little, and she said, she remembered, beaming ahead in her filthy tan car, "Chester, don't you go licking me like that. I'll have a grass stain on my jeans and spit all over my neck and I don't want to have to change my clothes and take a bath on account of *you*." Two years later, he had her writhing in the back of a Buick Roadmaster he'd salvaged with junkyard parts.

"Mayflies," she said, pulling out in what she figured was the direction of the farm she sought. The ridge along which she drove was made of dense low brush. What looked like stubble in the distance, she found as she drew near, were softwood forests some company had cut, either for paper or for log-cabin homes like hers. Most people here weren't buying them or anything

else. Here, they would sell out if they could and live in apartments in town, or in mobile homes. This was the part of Pennsylvania that was better off dead, the statehouse calculated. This
was the ridge above the played-out coal mines where aspen and
some birch too young to harvest and the rows of ancient, half-
rotten maples lined side roads that once had led to prosperous
farms. One of the roads was called O'Neill Road, and she turned
onto it, passing what would be — what could have been, if there
were some nutrients left in the coal-dust soil — fine blackberries
for late-summer picking.

You look for life and what do you find?

AM I YOUR MOTHER?

It was a terrible place. The roof, shingled with shakes, had to
leak, she thought. Some of the shakes stood straight up, and
others lay buckled out of line. The posts of the porch were
telephone company poles, painted white one time so that the
dark brown creosote showed through. The porch was a slab of
crumbling cement. A number of cats fled as she knocked on the
warped storm door.

The woman who answered was tall and very thin and very
dirty. Her right sleeve was rolled up, probably to ease the friction
of her greasy green men's flannel shirt on the three-inch-wide
blister that was red and brown and moist with pus in the center.

"Mrs. Bruchak? Mrs. Benjamin Bruchak? I'm the county
nurse? Gloria Dodge. I'm here to see about your husband's —"

Mrs. Bruchak shook her head. The fine brown hair cropped
at ear length was stiff and dirty and didn't shake, but moved
with the motion of her head as if it were a helmet. "He went,"
she said.

"Went. I thought he was sick."

"He was sick, but he had to go. They offered him a run."

"He's a trucker?"

"Bus," she said. "Chartered bus to Atlantic City. A church or a club or a class trip. I don't know. I hope they don't smoke."

"Your husband's chest."

"All the time. It hurts him to cough. It hurts him when I make him breathe steam and the phlegm comes up. He can't talk no more, barely."

"So why'd he go, Mrs. Bruchak?"

"For money to live, Mrs. Nurse."

"No offense, no offense. I understand."

"Not as much as I do."

"No. And your arm? You want me to dress that? You keep it up, you'll need it debreeded. That could be staph, honey."

"If he has the cough, I have the burn. It's fair."

Mrs. Bruchak, she figured, was hardly thirty. She looked more like fifty. What had seemed to be repose, as she stood with her head cocked and a shoulder pressed against the molding of the door, was really exhaustion, Gloria thought.

"I could make it feel a little better. You could be more helpful to him when he comes home."

"No." She stood straight now. "We decided. No county nurse, no welfare, no food stamps, no nothing but us. Only us."

"You and the staphylococci, Mrs. Bruchak. Let me at least dress it."

"Thank you. No."

"You have any children, Mrs. Bruchak?"

Her cheeks went red high up on the bone. "No."

"That's a blessing, I'd say. Take care. Good luck." Gloria backed away from the door.

"Why do you say 'blessing'?" Mrs. Bruchak asked hoarsely.

"Your husband is almost dead. He dies the week after next. He'll hemorrhage, I'm afraid. On Thursday. No, I'm sorry, it's a red-colored day in my mind, so then it's Wednesday. Wednesday, of course. Wednesday a week. It's a fact."

Gloria turned, walked back to her car and got in. She heard

47

a loud, long cry from Mrs. Bruchak. She started the car and pulled out into the dark dust. She thought she heard Mrs. Bruchak's voice more than half a mile away. It was what happened when you acquired knowledge, when you skimmed the wind for information. People howled like that. Gloria was hurrying. She was soon to have a guest, she thought. She would file her reports at the hospital and then go home to bake.

Gingerbread, she thought. That was what mothers made.

I N HIS ROOM, in his mother's room, Stephen was getting dressed in his main going-to-restaurants shirt because Grandma and Grandpa were taking him someplace for pizza. Under the *A* of *Alligator* he felt a rough bump when he put the shirt on. He was standing in front of his mother's mirror in a wooden frame. It hung on a wire from a hook on the wall behind her bureau. He had looked inside the bureau for her clothes, but he found only sheets and blankets and towels. He had looked in the closet for her old toys, but he found only boxes of books about girls. There weren't any secrets in the room, and there was nothing to look at except the lamp on her desk. It was black metal, and it had springs and things you tightened to make the light steady. On the metal shade his mother had pasted little colored pictures from magazines. There were men with a lot of hair and there were women with big eyes. Two of them had brown skin. A little red sign with black letters said *I Hate Disco*.

Stephen stood in front of his mother's mirror and pulled at the paper folded into his pocket. It was little and yellow with green lines. It was from his mother. She printed dumb, he always told her. When he remembered that, he looked away from the paper and there he was, in front of him, watching. "You look like you ate snakes," Stephen said to him. That was what his mother had said when he came home sick from school once.

The note was in her funny printing.

Darling Stevie,

Mommy *always* loves you! I got this feeling, it was kind of an emergency feeling. You and I have talked about how we feel when we get them, remember? I had to rush off on a crazy errand. It's not dangerous. I'm coming home in a little while, I think. Meanwhile, I love you and I think about you *all* the time. I *miss* you! Will try to call you. Take care of Daddy. He will take good care of you. What a crazy lady, huh? Love and love and love, baby.

Mommy

In the overheated restaurant in town, Grandpa kept using napkins to wipe his face. Grandma watched him, and she watched Stephen. She was always looking hard at something. You could tell she was thinking about things. When she had seen Stephen's T-shirt, she had gone upstairs and changed into a black T-shirt that said *Harley*. Then Grandpa started in hugging and smooching her, and she smiled her pretty smile at him, but she was thinking. You could tell.

Grandma said, "Do you like anchovies, sweetie?"

"I don't know, Grandma."

"They're little salty fish."

"Gross!"

"No anchovies," Grandma said.

Grandpa said, "Good. I hate 'em."

"We don't need the salt, anyway," she said.

"You look pretty salty to me," Grandpa said.

Grandma said to Stephen, "So, how are tricks, chum?"

"Tricks? Oh, how am I?"

"How are you?"

"I'm great. You're worried about Mommy."

"Aren't you?"

"She had this, well, you could call it a emergency feeling. You get those once in a while."

"Did she *tell* you that?"

"Nope."

Grandma said, "She did tell you that, right?"

Stephen shook his head and sucked up soda through his straw until it made loud noises.

"Emergency feeling," Grandpa said.

Grandma kept looking at Stephen. Stephen watched her in the mirror alongside their table. When she looked into the mirror and found him, he looked at the table where her big hands were slowly making a fork turn around and around. He heard Grandma say, "You can tell."

Grandpa said, "What, Lizzie?"

She said, "Stephen knows." Her voice was low and almost mean.

"Hey," Grandpa said.

Stephen saw the fork stop and stay straight up and down. "And what am I being so serious about?" Grandma said. "It's not as if somebody's forcing us to swallow live *anchovies*."

Stephen knew he should say a kid thing. He said, "Yuck."

"Yuck," Grandma said.

Grandpa said, "And yuck again." His hand went to his shirt pocket, and Stephen thought maybe he got a letter too.

Grandma saw him. She said, "No smoking."

He said, "I'm sorry, but what makes you think I want to smoke?"

"You're caressing your cigarettes through your shirt."

"Auto-eroticism," Grandpa said.

"What's *that*?" Stephen asked them.

"Oh," Grandpa said, "just wait and see."

"Enough," Grandma said. "Stephen, what does alligator taste like?"

"We didn't eat it. Daddy just bought the shirt."

"So how did the shirt taste?" Grandpa asked. His grandfather was being funny, Stephen thought, but his face looked sad. Then he saw that his grandmother's did too.

Stephen said, "It tasted kind of green," and looked at the three of them in the restaurant mirror to see whether he had made anyone smile.

Barrett told himself that west was west, even if you did drop somewhat south onto five different minor roads to reach Zion Hill after seventy minutes of curves, Caution signs and places called Morgan's Furnace and Hayden's Choice. Sheila Mason lived in Zion Hill, not far from the West Virginia border, in countryside that looked blighted, harsh, maybe recently bombed from the air. Sheila and Sarah had roomed together in college for two years, and they told each other secrets even now, he knew. They never talked on the telephone, but wrote long, infrequent letters, calling each other Mason and Mastracola, as if Sarah had never married him, as if Sheila hadn't married the man who had moved, after eighteen months of marriage, to New Castle, Pennsylvania, with his secretary from the bank. For a while, Sheila had signed her letters Fuckless and Fucked Up and Blind Fucking Fool. Sarah had never let him see the body of any letter, and then, after showing him a signature that said only Sheila, she had shown him no more.

He'd met her at her wedding to the banker, and he remembered her flat nose. "Nose job," Sarah had greeted her, tweaking and then embracing her before the rehearsal. They had stayed at a hotel that smelled tarry and medicinal, like Mercurochrome, and while he had been full of lust — "*Amore*," he remembered crooning, in what he thought was the spirit of weddings but in what Sarah told him was the spirit of hostelries — she had been tearfully annoyed by his attentions. He remembered wanting to ask if, as he had heard about friends at all-female colleges, Sarah and Sheila had been lovers once. He was amused, now, by how he'd qualified their loving: once. He had been unable, at first, to imagine Sarah in bed with a woman, and then he'd been very able, and then he'd been unable to find any language that forestalled some permanent damage. So he'd said nothing. As he drove past bright yellow earth-moving machinery that seemed to be engaged in digging vast holes, and with nothing in sight to be buried, he thought of how often he had said nothing because no language lay at hand. "At brain," he said. That was the trouble with so many people who lived by their eyes, he thought. They lived in silence, or anyway lived like immigrants learning the difficult local patois, meanwhile making do with the natives' simpler terms for common foodstuffs, for obvious essentials, for the usual civic codes.

According to the telephone directory for a number of smaller municipalities outside Altoona and north of Hagerstown, a Sheila Mason lived on a Mercersburg Street, which looked about as long as all of Zion Hill's business district. There were five or six good houses, and two he slowed at. One was a huge Victorian with enough of a touch of Italy at the pediments of the porch posts to interest him. Another had a tower with a helm roof where a sloping turret must once have been: a factory owner, a boss of a mill or the richest farmer in this meager countryside, he'd have bet.

He stopped at a house made of gray squared stone to which a clapboard wing had been added at right angles. An arched porch joined the sections downstairs, while a terrace next to french doors sat on top of the porch. Merchant Banker Arriviste, he thought, the worst of the twenties. And here he was, the worst of the nineties, Fin-de-Siècle Gutted, at his fled wife's former roommate's door — and it was, indeed, hers, because Sheila answered, looked behind him, then inspected him with a wrinkled brow, with eyes that squinted as if in ocean light, with lips compressed as if against a queasiness. "Where is she?" Sheila asked in the voice he remembered from her wedding, low and very harsh.

"I thought maybe you might know," Barrett said in the casual tone he'd rehearsed while he drove. "Sarah isn't home."

"And I am."

"Well, in fact, silly as it sounds, I was almost passing through. Give or take a couple of hours. I think I know where to look, but —"

"But you don't. She running away from you?"

Barrett found that he couldn't answer her. His throat felt swollen, sealed. He was embarrassed by the dampness of his eyes, by the power of his memory of Stephen's face, as his father went away from him, to stop the breath in his chest. He finally shrugged, with perhaps a sort of smile, then shook his head. He cleared his throat and said, "It's very clear she's running away. She's gone. She didn't tell us why."

"No," Sheila said, "she wouldn't."

So an hour later he sat in a sunroom off the porch, eating an omelette with peppers, onions and sliced potatoes and drinking a bloody mary to keep Sheila company. She wore baggy dungarees and floppy cloth bedroom slippers. Her football sweatshirt was stained.

She asked, "Are you staring at my tits or memorizing how to spell 'Steelers'?"

"Excuse me."

"I hate it when people stare at my chest."

"I wasn't, Sheila."

"This is how I was born. Even when I was skinny, I felt fat because of them."

"They're — it's — Jesus, Sheila. You're not, you know, pe-culiar-looking. You're a normal woman who — Jesus."

"You're trying to say I embarrassed you."

"At least."

"Apologies."

"What — offered, accepted, unnecessary, demanded? We're supposed to be friends, Sheila."

"No," she said, "you married somebody who's my friend. You're the friend's friend. Worse: you're the friend's husband. No, it's worse. You're the husband who the friend ran away from."

"How do you know *she* ran away from *me?*"

"What," Sheila said, putting her cigarette out, "she ran away from her kid? What kind of mother runs away from her kid?"

"The kind of mother," he said, standing, "who you talk about later on, after the damage is all done, ended up doing it. A person."

Sheila lit another cigarette and surprised him by nodding. "Another fucked-up person like the rest of us. Sit down, Barrett. Don't pout around and stalk off with your skinny little legs all tight at the knees."

He sat. It was either sit in distress in this cold, unsunny sun-room in a cold, unlighted house or drive against a bright white sky in what had become a slow and constant panic. He asked, "What was that about my legs?"

"Sarah said one time how you didn't like to go to the beach because you thought your legs were skinny."

He looked hard when she moved to the kitchen to raise the level of the vodka in their drinks. Her breasts looked broad and prominent even under the shapeless sweatshirt, and he remem-bered Sarah talking about how often Sheila was dated in college by boys for whom her fascination was simple and lascivious. She used to say to them, according to Sarah, when they came to the apartment, "Let's be up front about a couple of things."

57

Barrett said, "No, I haven't got great legs. I didn't know you two talked about things like that."

"We wrote each other everything," Sheila said, returning with their drinks and sipping at hers as she walked. He touched the base of his glass but didn't drink.

"Everything," Barrett said.

Sheila, lighting a cigarette, raised her brows, as if she teased him.

Barrett said, "Did she ever —"

"What? I don't mind if you ask."

"Complain?"

"Sure."

"About me?"

Sheila pushed her long hair behind her neck and readjusted two clips made of silver and decorated with long strips of onyx. She nodded.

"Could you tell me?"

He was looking at the glistening lipstick on her white filter in the ashtray. She'd put on makeup since he'd come, he realized. Her oval face was a little thicker under the chin, and the generosity of that flesh made him uncomfortably aware of the rest of her body.

"It wasn't anything people leave people about," she said. "You were apparently congenitally unable, despite holding several degrees, to turn a clothing washer on."

"Jesus."

"It comes with the chromosomes," Sheila said. "You don't have to look so *earnest*, Barrett. You look like a little boy when you make that face." She stood and walked around the table and leaned into him where he sat, cradling his head against her. Her belly was hard, not soft as he'd expected, and he felt her breasts on the top of his head. The sweatshirt smelled stale, but the smell excited him. She stepped back, as if she'd been waiting for him to relax beneath her hands. "My," she said.

58

"I'm going. I have to get on the road. I have —"

"It's okay. You have to go."

"I do."

"You should go, then."

"I really have to."

"Look," she said, "call me up when you think of it. Maybe I'll remember something. Call me up even if I don't. Of course, you wouldn't know that, would you? What I was remembering. Well, take a *guess*, then, and give me a call." She put one foot behind her for balance. "Don't worry about your drink," she said. "I'll stick it in the fridge for if company comes by."

"I'll stay in touch."

"I want to know how Sarah is."

"I'll call you."

"And how you are, Barrett. And your boy, little Stephen, and the rest of you."

"That's all there is," he said, walking to the door with Sheila's hand on his arm. "Just the three of us."

"And me," she said. "I'll be here, and you can call me."

"Yes. I will."

"You know, when you cried, when you were standing at the door when you first came, you looked the way I bet your boy looks. Sarah sent me infant pictures, but not anything else. That was something she didn't want to share with me. What he was like as a boy. Maybe you'll send me a picture. Bring it by. Bring Stephen. You know," she whispered harshly, as if unsealing a secret, "there are limits to friendship."

Barrett stopped on the porch, turned, put his hands on Sheila's shoulder and kissed her on the temple. He smelled the vodka in her skin. He heard her breathe out. She leaned against him and he patted her shoulder so that she would lean away. She did, and then he said, "I've been scared of hearing that for the last two days. That's the worst news you can give me."

"It isn't news," she said.

59

When he was driving north to Route 80 the next morning — an hour before dawn, really; he had wakened to the pain of a deep toothache except that it pulsed in his forehead; he had wakened to a sore body and the panicked certainty of having forgotten something crucial — he thought that it was Sheila's sad announcement, the mourning certainty with which she told him everything was always lost. It was that, he decided, driving west again to find his wife.

Barrett had stopped on her porch and had turned, and then he'd walked back. He was afraid to look at Sheila, so he closed his eyes. Standing before her, maybe like a rutting college kid, he feared, his chest just touching hers, his lips at the level of the middle of her nose, and smelling time grown long and difficult as he leaned forward to be met by her mouth, he said on her lips, "I'd like to stay, please."

Sheila put her hands inside the waistband of his battered twill trousers and pulled him closer, kissed him harder, chewing his lower lip until he cried, "Ow!"

" 'Ow' is right," she said. "This whole fuckin' thing is 'ow.' "

On her unmade bed, in her dark room, among bedclothes that smelled, like her sweatshirt, of a laboring organism, of not caring terribly much, of having noplace to go, they made love. Her stomach was warm and he found it so welcoming, so abundant, that he kneeled to chew at it and then to kiss her generous navel in gratitude. He nuzzled her ribs, he kissed between her breasts and the heavy flesh of the breasts themselves, and he tongued her nipples and finally — he heard her sigh in either pleasure or acknowledgment of the usual — he sucked on her, sucked *at* her, as if he tried to draw her into himself.

Her pubic hair was as harsh as her voice, he thought. It rasped on his groin and the friction excited nerves not only there. He was certain that he felt her on the soles of his feet. They labored at each other, grunting as if pummeled each time their bodies rose and fell. Each time they struck on one another they winced or groaned.

"I feel you," Sheila said. "I *feel* it. You're —"

He heard himself call something wordless. He felt her tremendous presence, the assurance inside his body and on its surface of her being there with him, of how heavily and sweatily she gave. He gave what he could.

Sheila straightened, she arched her body, and she lifted him. She embraced him and — *buttress*, he couldn't help thinking — held rigidly above the bed as he, flown by her, pumped and pumped and slowly shook his head.

She subsided and then embraced him harder, squeezing with her legs, rising again, shuddering. He drove on instead of slumping on her, worked as if it were his turn now to keep them aloft. He wondered later, in the car, at dawn, driving west, whether when she shuddered again and drove her head forward and up, slamming hard against his nose, she wasn't nodding *yes* in contradiction of the way he had shaken his head against her. Yes about what? he wondered as he drove Route 80. But in her bedroom he drove into Sheila, holding with forearms and knees and belly and breast to feel as much of her as he could.

It was she who fell asleep, as if she'd been waiting for a way. Barrett lay beside her, then rubbed her broad back. It felt rubbery now, and the resistance of her flesh moved him from the bed to the bathroom of foggy black and white tile, of uncleaned toilet, of damp towels balled on shelves. He found aspirin and swallowed four, washing them down with water from a black plastic drinking cup that was scummy with toothpaste at the rim. He took a very hot shower and he washed his hair twice with her strawberry-scented shampoo. Naked, he lay beside Sheila again, curled beneath the comforter, his face partly buried in the pillow now grown cool.

"You fucked your wife's old roommate," she whispered.

He whispered back, "You fucked your roommate's old man."

Sheila reached a hand back and cupped his balls. "Too bad she isn't here for both of us to fuck." She snickered and squeezed and, when he was about to react by moving hard against her hand, she took it away, grazing his belly with the backs of her fingers. Instead of imploring or demanding, he cupped himself, then lay his hand on her hip and slept until his own snoring woke him and he rose to dress in the dark.

Standing on her side of the bed, he pulled the comforter back and kissed her nipple. She murmured, and he kissed her goodbye on the mouth. Sheila whispered, "You can come back sometime, you know. Whatever happens, the world won't do you a favor and end. It doesn't."

"I've been bad with you," he said. "I had fun when I shouldn't have, and I'm afraid I cried on you."

"I squeezed you dry, buster. I got most of you. Come back sometime with the rest. I'm going to sleep. You gave me a great night's sleep. Bye-bye." She exhaled a smell that was oily and like a root cellar at once. She lifted her mouth to be kissed again, and then she fell back to her pillow and into her sleep, and Barrett went down to his car.

When he turned on his headlights, the headache beat harder. As he navigated out of town and toward the highway, it occurred to him more powerfully than it had since she'd left that Sarah might be fraying herself on someone else's skin. He shook his head as if to lose or deny his thought. The pain made him hold his head very still. His thought remained, and it grew to a vision. He saw her in bed with a man he'd never met, he saw her wincing in pleasure. He thought of her in bed with Sheila, and he said, as Sheila had, "There are limits to friendship."

Karen sat behind the girl's mother and took notes while Lizzie sat tall behind her desk. The girl seemed to imitate Lizzie as she sat in the straight-backed chair before the principal's desk. Her feet were planted side by side, her knees were together, her jean skirt was smoothed and on the lap lay her clasped hands. A cold sore swelled her lower lip, and her face was pasty, her eyes swollen-looking.

Her mother wore her raincoat despite the excessive heat of the building. She looked like her daughter, but more exhausted. Her hair was dyed a pathetic bright maroon and her eyes were heavily made up. She said, "That kind of talk'll ruin her life, it'll ruin mine. To say nothing of her father's professional life."

Lizzie nodded. They spoke low, even though both doors to her office were closed against the corridor roar. "I understand the awful difficulties this makes for you, Mrs. Berg. I find it almost impossible, myself, to talk about them with you, and I lost a lot of sleep last night trying to decide, frankly, if this is the right way to handle it. I've tried other ways in the past —"

"There's that much talk about this sort of thing?"

"Mrs. Berg, there's that much of this sort of *thing*. Look, the signs are unmistakable. Madeleine has lost weight, she's started to fail one course and she's received warnings in two others. She's late to school. She reacts inappropriately — Maddie," she said, "that doesn't mean you're rude. It means you cry at surprising times, you get angry when you didn't used to." She returned to the mother. "There are ways professionals have of discerning these problems. Three of us have spoken with Maddie."

"*That's* what that was about?" the girl said.

"We try to keep an eye on you, sweetie. On everyone."

Madeleine's lips twisted, and Lizzie didn't know whether she might snarl or wail. She said, "Didn't you ever hear of freedom?"

"Yes."

"Well, why can't I *have* any?"

"Believe it or not," Lizzie said, "this is about your freedom to grow up happy. It's your right. We're trying to find it for you."

"What about my freedom for you to leave me alone?"

63

"Sometimes that one's hard to get hold of. Freedom's messy stuff, I think. But listen, Maddie. It's pretty evident from what we've heard that your father is abusing you. That has to stop. You want it to stop. You know you want it to. Does he cry about needing you?"

Mrs. Berg stood up. "We're not listening to this. This is libel."

"It's slander, I think, that you're thinking of. But it isn't either one, Mrs. Berg. It's the truth, and you hate it. I hate it too. The man is raping his daughter, Mrs. Berg. You're helping him. You're in the bind too. But you turn your back on it. You tell yourself, or you don't even say it, I bet. You *feel* it, yes? You believe that he'll stay if you shut up, and leave if you don't. So you're — oh, God help us. You're pimping her, Mrs. Berg."

Madeleine's mother put her hands on the desk. She leaned forward and stopped herself with her straightened forearms from falling across the desk. Her face, before Lizzie's, was furrowed, her eyes squinted in rage. She spat into Lizzie's face and stood up. "Pimp, Mrs. High and Mighty Educator? Pimp?"

Lizzie wiped at her face with her sleeve. "We'll call the county, Mrs. Berg. I was hoping to help. Now you'll get your help from the police and the social welfare."

"You won't call the police," Mrs. Berg said. "Madeleine, let's go."

Lizzie said, "Karen?"

"She'll call the police," Karen said. "When your foot's out the door, I'll be picking up the phone for her. By the time you get to your car, she'll be spilling your private can of worms."

Madeleine said, "Can I talk to my mother?"

Lizzie nodded. Karen stood. Mrs. Berg said, "No."

"We'll go outside," Lizzie said. "Use this office."

"No," Mrs. Berg said. Madeleine was crying into her hands, beginning to rock as she wept. Her mother sat down. She was crying too, but not into her hands. She looked at her daughter and cried, watching her daughter cry.

In the hall, Karen blew her nose into a tiny silk handkerchief that matched her man-tailored shirt and slacks. "Don't you hate this shit?" she said.

Lizzie nodded until she could talk. "Yup," she said. "What's next?" Then she said, "Oh, good. There's Will. Thank goodness. Karen, make sure I see Mrs. Berg and Maddie before they leave, all right? I don't want them going unless I talk to them."

"Check."

"And set it up with Social Services, all right?"

"Check again."

Will walked through the mob scene of the hall with a startled expression. Lizzie greeted him by calling, "You'd think you never went to school, the way you look."

"The girls are twenty-six years old. The boys keep saying 'motherfucker' and 'excellent.' Nobody has any books."

"It's morning in America."

"How did Stephen do?"

"Oh," she said. "It was terribly hard for him. Actually, Will, it was terribly hard for me. Yes, Kent," she said to a boy with a large, soft behind squeezed into leather pants, "very alluring."

"It's my S & M look, Dr. Mastracola," he said. "Hi, Mr. Mastracola. I'm stepping up the sophistication level in the building."

Will looked at Lizzie. She waved Kent along. "He's another one I'm going to have to really deal with one of these days. Nothing I can do will help him, I'll mess him up worse, and I'm over my head. Otherwise, I'll handle it competently. Remember curriculums? I used to worry about them before I went into the psychiatry business. He looked so *vulnerable*, Will. With his little green book bag and his head so straight. His eyes weren't any bigger than the headlights on my car. He said, 'As long as I'm staying a while, I better be going to school, I guess.' He didn't want me to feel bad, you see. God. Will. What must he feel like."

She watched him blink his eyes and nod. She did too. He

said, "You're so goddamned wonderful, you know? Is your office free? Could I get you in there and ravish you or anything?"

"We're all so wonderful. And all these kids are getting so completely worked over. It's like watching a prizefight, and one of the boxers is bleeding on the one who's hitting him, and on the towels and the ring ropes and the floor, and he won't fall down and they let the other one keep hitting him."

Willis began to cough, and he turned from her and coughed more, gagging. "Sorry," he said, looking at her again. "It's all right. It's allergies. You know what early spring does to me."

"It's cigarettes, Will."

"I'm cutting down. Anyway, the subject isn't coughing."

"I'd like you around with me for Stephen. For whatever we find out about Sarah. So it is."

"I'm fine, Lizzie."

"I'd like you around for *me*."

Karen called. She pointed at the principal's office.

"I have to get back anyway," Will said. "I just got worried about the little fellow. I needed to see you."

"I was thinking I could use a little of you, too. And you had the graciousness to appear. Here I come," Lizzie called to Karen. "Here I go," she said to Will. "Tonight."

"Tonight what, Dr. Mastracola?" he asked.

"If you need to ask, you're too young."

"If you need to tell me, I'm too old."

"And don't start *that*, or forget it."

"Forget what, Dr. Mastracola?"

"Oh," she said, "the usual. Vitamins followed by artificial respiration. Here I come," she called to Karen, moving down the hall, waving behind her back to Will and letting her ass ever so slightly, just for two paces, sway.

Then it was Mrs. Berg and her daughter and Lizzie. It was time to apologize for the remark about pimping, and to talk about how their lives had officially been taken hold of by more than a high school principal. She told Maddie about the Social Services interview that was being scheduled, and about doctors who would see her if she or her mother wished, and about the psychologists. Maddie was past crying now. She watched Lizzie and she nodded. It was her mother who couldn't stop and, holding a box of tissues that Lizzie knew Karen had given her, she tore off a handful and blew her nose noisily while Lizzie talked.

Maddie said, "What about the police? Do they have to call the police?"

"What he did was a crime," Lizzie said.

Maddie said, "He's pretty screwed up, Dr. Mastracola."

"Now you are, too, Maddie. He was good enough to share so much with you."

Maddie looked at her mother, but her mother looked ahead, at Lizzie, and blew her nose.

So that was a sixteen-year-old girl. That was family life. She thought of Sarah, she thought of Lizzie Bean Mastracola as a Mrs. Berg with henna running down her neck, the neck like a ladder under chicken skin, the tears running down from her cheeks and nose to sagging breasts and the same helpless look, the same expression of docile uninvolvement in her own corruption. She sat up straighter at her desk and examined her hands. She turned them over to look at the creases, the fingertips abraded from grabbing papers and books and children. She pushed her hair where it tumbled onto her forehead. It was a dark chestnut brown with only a little gray, and all the colors were her own. It was cut stupidly because she grew impatient at the hairdresser's and bored with the magazines they showed her, and contemptuous of their advice: *She* wears it like that, and you'd look great that way. She'd ask, *Who's she?* And they would look at her as if she'd farted or, before them, shed a leg. And they would rush the cut and send her home as she'd come in. Here I am, she thought: the usual. And there her daughter was — no, that was the trouble. Nobody knew where her daughter was. She wondered if Stephen knew. Or Sarah herself. All that mother-daughter bonding everyone wrote about and read about in the eighties, she thought: I used to be so jealous of those fantasy relationships in the magazines. My Mother, My Best Friend. How I Found the Daughter in Me, by Dolly Parton. Madonna's Mother: Abandoned by My Kid.

Karen appeared in the doorway. Behind her were a pale, panting teacher and two bloodied ninth graders. She said, "We got a fight, a damage to school property, a refusal to give the teacher their names, insubordination, indecent conduct and the necessity for a shop teacher and a basketball coach to intervene. The men are outside if you want them, Pardee wants to go lie down until you need her, and these two boys here want to discuss out-of-school suspension with you."

Lizzie said, "Bring in the students and Joanna Pardee. Give her smelling salts if you have to. The others can leave."

"Smelling salts," Karen said. "We don't —"

"Figure of speech!"

"Oh. Well, then."

"I'm sorry, Karen. I'm sorry. I'm a little thwarted, here."

Lizzie opened her hands and lay them on the desk. She studied the lines as you might query a map for a road. She searched them until she heard Karen's footsteps cross the office floor. She looked down and in, as if she might find the car and its passenger, until she heard Karen usher in the combatants and their teacher, who was young enough — that's right — to be Lizzie's daughter.

On the verge of 76, before turning south for New Geneva, Sarah sat in the car and did what she hadn't wanted to do for the past hundred miles. She held on her lap the flat plastic box that he had wrapped in silvery duct tape on which he'd printed EMER-GENCY. He was always so neat, she thought. When as little more than kids they had lived in a slum above a restaurant with which they shared rats, water, plumbing, and the smells of old vege-tables, he had swept the floors daily, had always promptly washed the dishes that she might leave for a week if allowed, had swabbed the grim bathroom and fastened pegboard to the flaking kitchen wall so they could hang their two pots and frying pan and plastic-handled spatula.

He left her notes in his spiky handwriting, everything neatly vertical, in fine lines. He organized his time and helped to or-ganize hers. It was he who had taught Stephen how to make his bed. It was he, of course, who kept the financial records, paid the bills and balanced the books. And he was the one who said each car had to have an emergency kit. And here it was. And here was the emergency. She put the kit on the passenger seat and pulled out, driving slowly, so that dozens of cars had to pass her. A sign said that local services were off the next exit ramp, and she drove there, to a cluster: truck and trailer rental, ham-burger joint, a gas station and convenience store. She found the public phone outside the convenience store and she filled the car with gas, decided again to ignore the oil until next time and, after paying, went to the telephone and dialed her number.

He might be home alone, she thought. He might be there in the afternoon, with nothing to do, and he might pick up the phone. Maybe if it was one of the sitters who answered, if she kept her tone light and stayed fast on her feet, if she sounded as though nothing much were wrong, the sitter might pass the phone to Stephen if she asked and then she could tell him hello. Hello, I deserted you. Hello, you might have noticed that I'm not there. Hello.

No one answered, and she returned to the car, found Route

76 and dipped west and south on it, looking for 119 to 166 and New Geneva. But she found herself slowing down, drifting to the right, then pulling off past the breakdown lane onto the sparse grass that gasoline and a bitter spring had left. There were beer cans, plastic cups and a large puddle of cigarette butts where someone had cleaned out a car. "You wanna keep them cars clean," Barrett always said on finding such a mess. "Might track all that shit into your *truck*, you ain't careful." He had always annoyed her with his imitations of people he never had lived with. He'd grown up smart and sassy and sure of his importance in suburban Philadelphia, shady Devon Street in Mount Airy. She wondered if he'd ever ridden in a truck. Sure. Probably when the contractors drove him around a site. Man of the people, she tried to say with disdain. But she was holding the emergency kit, she found.

Unwrapping the tape, she couldn't force the smile away. He had wrapped several yards around it, just as when he sealed parcels he used too much strapping tape, just as when he sealed a business envelope he licked the flap so thoroughly that the paper wrinkled with moisture. Barrett was a man who had to be sure — who tried, she thought, to be sure. What a present she had given him.

The box was the hard plastic container from a cordless drill and bits she had bought him for a birthday. Inside were a safety razor, a tube of antiseptic cream, two broad sterile compresses, a roll of tape, several Band-Aids held together with a rubber band, a sewing needle and thread, a box of safety matches, a pair of tweezers, a thin rubber tube — maybe a tourniquet, she thought, trying to remember how you'd use one — and a felt-tip marking pen, a small pad of yellow paper — for messages in bottles, to be floated out to sea when stranded? — small plastic bottle of suntan lotion, burn spray, aspirin, digestive tablets and a copy of *Goodnight, Moon*. She imagined the three of them in a broken-down car, lost or unnoticed, sick or afraid, and she imagined Barrett in the back seat, Stephen as an infant on his lap, going loose and losing his sense of catastrophe because Barrett, in a low voice, read to him about the little old lady whispering, "Hush."

Sarah carefully replaced everything in the kit. There was nothing here she could use, she decided. Clearly, she had picked the wrong kind of emergency. Or he hadn't considered a wide enough variety when he'd set up the kit. Maybe, she thought, you can evaluate a marriage according to its emergencies. What makes you shriek and run in circles and tear at your flesh? Does your spouse rend his skin likewise? Often. Sometimes. Occasionally. Never. Use a number 2 pencil and fill in the entire space provided. Do not guess. Credit is deducted for guesses. Answer only what you know. All right, she thought. All right. She reopened the kit, took the aspirin out and forced open the little tin. All right. She swallowed some dry. We are not entirely emergency-unsuited, she thought. She closed the kit and wrapped the sticky silver tape around it a good deal less neatly than she'd found it, thinking, So maybe *that's* a little all right.

She got out of the car and walked across tarry pebbles and yellow-green grass to the saplings that seemed to her to be shaking in the winds of the wakes of passing trucks. The sky was as white as it was blue, and though she couldn't see the sun, she squinted and felt forced to look down, at cigarette butts and half of a gray-green carton of eggs and an oozing flashlight battery. Her throat tightened. She thought she might strangle there, dying on her knees in garbage, kneeling at the edge of the blighted woods. She spat, she tasted herself and retched and spat, and although she lost whatever it was she had drunk and eaten over the last day and night, it felt to her that the aspirin remained in her throat, acid and bitter and large as stones. She pictured Stephen on Barrett's lap. She heard Barrett read "Hush," and she saw Stephen's eyes, wide and liquid, flutter under their lashes, then close.

Asarabacca: it loves our limestone countryside, and while you might want to dig the roots for her visit especially, it's too early in the season. You lose a certain pungency, too, when you use the roots of wild ginger recently harvested. Try this, instead, when it's late spring or full summer, and you've a chance to find the dark red, nearly brown, really, flower. Find the little flower and you'll find the two big heart-shaped leaves. Hairy things they are, sometimes half a foot wide and a silvery green from the hairs. Dig the roots, and instead of drying them, boil them up the way you'd boil a dinner of greens. Remove from the water and add to a basic sugar syrup. Let them sit. Later on, roll them in table sugar. Take them for your stomach's sake. Take for your sore throat. But for gingerbread men, use them dried and ground, adding somewhat more than you would your ordinary, store-bought ginger. Make it, say, three teaspoons instead of the usual two. Blend your quarter cup of butter and your half cup sugar until they're creamy. Beat in half a cup of dark molasses. Sift into your three and a half cups flour the baking soda, cloves, half teaspoon cinnamon, the wild ginger and a touch of salt. Now, work it. You'll need water so it's pliable. I use a paring knife like a pen and I cut out boys and girls. They may call them ginger-bread men, but I make boys and girls. The oven should have been at 350, and you lay them on a greased sheet and bake them eight minutes. Push down on their heads and bellies. If their bodies push back, then they're done.

Gloria sat on the stool in front of her clean counter, regarding her ingredients, feeling the heat of the stove pulse up. From the window behind the counter she could see the edge of her pond and the spruce limbs as they stirred in rising wind. The house smelled cold and lonely. It smelled like someplace nobody had lived in for years. Yet she had lived here since having it built nine years before, when she had moved from the little village in which she had spent her girlhood and young womanhood and the heart of her middle age. She had moved away and returned and had stayed there until the chalet-style house went up. She lived with buttonbush and swamp rose, with ash and black willow, with droneflies and water mites and a wild white cat that came to the far side of the pond about as often as the great blue heron that came down to stand near the pickerelweed in terrible stillness. The cat and the heron, never there together, arrived to be alarmed, she thought. They didn't hunt or flee. They seemed condemned to appear there. They waited, she thought, until released. What released them? she wondered. She wondered what it was that summoned them back.

AM I YOUR MOTHER?

She thought of her child, of maybe-her-child, of her dark hair and pale skin and long limbs. She remembered them. She was convinced that she remembered them, for she had embraced the baby, had begged to suckle her, and she had been refused. The doctor was so handsome and haggard, he looked always to be walking against an awful event, like a hurricane that kept blowing into him. And he had asked the nurse to move her baby away. "She shouldn't have seen her in the first place. You both know that. It's wrong. And it isn't seemly." What had begun as a kind of crush on the man who plumbed your body had become something like hate because of that "isn't seemly." But the baby, to whom she hadn't been permitted the giving of a name, disappeared. "As you instructed," she remembered being reminded by the doctor. She would not remember his name. "As you instructed," he had said, in too kindly a tone to be chastising her, she knew. But she was chastised nevertheless. "As you instructed."

73

She had been thinking of something to tell the child, the woman who was the child, when she came. She had refined it on the long drives over rutted roads, on the two-lane blacktops so repetitive she sometimes had to read the map as she drove in order to remind herself where she was *today*. She had thought to tell her why. She had pondered why for years, of course, and there were practical and sensible, logical, explanations. *Because*, she could say, and then she could tell her. But a couple of weeks before, as she drove away from the four-apartment home, the high green square Victorian house on the corner of — how could it ever be anything else? — Main and Broad in a town once famous for its asbestos, where she had insisted on treating as well as she could the cigarette burns on the belly of the undersized six-month-old boy who was sentenced to the rest of his life, she had thought of something important she ought to say to her. She should say, "People always think they want to ask you *why*. Not whether because of it your blood pressure spikes high enough to strike you down in the tuna fish aisle of the supermarket. Not whether you bear a man's body printed on your skin like a burn. They think they want to know *why*. I was going to talk to you about that. But then I thought, one day, after I saw something unbearable, I thought how we're all pretending not to hear the real question we want to ask. What we all want to know, you see, really is *why not*."

She cut the gingerbread figures into round-bellied boys and girls. She put cinnamon candy drops on the faces of the girls for eyes and mouths and noses. The boys were blank. "Company's coming," Gloria said. "Into the oven with you."

Stephen walked down the curving sidewalk at the front of the elementary school, past the lines of children, past the buses they waited to board, past teachers too, and down the hill to the street.

There were a couple of cars there, and one of them had a smiling mother who looked a little bit like his. She leaned along the seat to push the door open for her little girl and she said, "Oof!" when she did it, and when she grinned she looked like a kid. She said, "What'll it be, kiddo? Whole-bran muffin or a pack of Twinkies? Boy, do I wonder about that!"

When they drove away, after the mother fixed the girl's seat belt, Stephen said, "What'll it be, kiddo?"

He knew where to turn because he had made himself memorize the houses and stores on the way. He went left past the street of big houses until he got to the white one with the black door, where he went left again. Then there was the street with gas stations and the video store and the place where they cut your hair, where they had a room full of aluminum foil and sun lamps. Then there was the Great American, the drugstore and the pizza place, then the post office and the Superette. That was where the bus stopped. You could buy a ticket inside, he guessed, or maybe you asked the driver. You could ride the bus out. He was thinking about that. He was scared, but he was thinking about it anyway. He figured you could ride the bus to Utica — that was where Grandpa said the bus went. They had a bus station there, and you could get a bus to Santa Fe.

He wondered, if he went there, if he got from the station in Santa Fe and found his parents, whether his father's face would go hard and tighten up. His mother called it Walnut Face. It would be terrible to ride all the way there and have that happen. A man in boots and dungarees with straps nodded his head at Stephen and said, "Son." Stephen smiled as pleasantly as he could. He got to the Superette and stood near the telephone on the outside wall. That was where the bus had stopped when Grandpa drove them past. Now there were kids on bikes buying sodas from the machine. One of them was pretty big and pretty fat. He had blond hair cut really short and he looked mean.

"The fuck you lookin' at?" he said to Stephen.

He smiled his most pleasant smile, but he knew it wouldn't do any good. He was holding his green book bag and looking dumb and too small, and he knew he was going to get pounded.

The big kid kicked the soda machine and slammed the side, but nothing happened. He waited with his hands open at the slot, but nothing came out. The kid looked funny with his hands that way and his knees bent.

He turned around and said to Stephen, "You fuckin' think I'm funny?"

Stephen smiled his pleasantest smile and shook his head.

"So don't laugh."

Stephen nodded. There was nothing to laugh at. There was traffic going by, and people coming out with groceries and going to their cars in the parking lot on the side of the Superette, and this big kid with crummy sneakers and jeans that looked like they had mud smeared all over them and a white T-shirt that said *Buffalo Bills*. He and his dirty-looking friends with their pale faces, red mouths and mean eyes were going to jump all over him. He knew it. And he couldn't stop laughing. It was a horrible giggle kind of noise that he hated when kids did it in school. But they did it on purpose — "Heh heh" — to show you they got the joke or knew how to cheat or they were tough. This was because he was so frightened he thought he was going to wet his pants. He closed his eyes because he could see himself on the bus to Santa Fe, crying and bleeding and with a big pee stain on his pants. He saw his father's face tightening up. He didn't want to see any of that, or the boy with the buzz cut who was coming over, so he closed his eyes and waited to get pounded and he laughed the weird laugh he couldn't get rid of. It was like having a terrible cough with your eyes closed, except they were going to pound you in the middle of it.

He heard somebody say, "Hi, fellas." Then he heard a shuffling noise and the rattle of their bikes, and then the man — it was Grandpa — said, "Bye, fellas."

There was a hand on his head, and Stephen opened his eyes. Grandpa was standing next to him in his white shirt and necktie, and he was lighting a cigarette. After he blew the smoke out, he said, "You all right?"

Stephen nodded. "Yes, sir."

"You took a walk, I take it. Or did somebody drive you here?"

"I wouldn't go in a car with a stranger, Grandpa."

"That's good, Stephen. Would you go in a car with your grandfather?"

Stephen smiled, but this time because it was all right. They went to Grandpa's car and he drove them in a direction Stephen didn't know. After a long way, past farms mostly, they came to a bunch of drive-in stores, and Grandpa bought them malteds. Then he drove them along the highway to a little road that went to a lake that was so big he couldn't see the other side. When Grandpa turned the motor off and rolled down their windows, Stephen couldn't hear anything except the wind, and ducks and geese on the water.

"I sometimes come out here to have a smoke and think a little," Grandpa said.

Stephen worked on the strawberry malted.

"That doesn't take long," Grandpa said. "Compared, say, to a bus ride to someplace. Where?"

"I wasn't sure," Stephen said. "I didn't know how to do it."

"You go to the lady behind the counter where they sell the doughnuts," Grandpa said. "You tell her where you want to go, and she sells you the ticket. Of course, your choices are limited. You can go to Norwich or Sidney or Binghamton, going south, or Sherburne, Earlville, Hamilton, Oriskany Falls or Clinton going north. Or Utica, of course. Now, *that's* where you could get a ticket to someplace farther away than sixty miles, in Utica.

Matter of fact, the bus stops right at the train station. You can get a train to Canada, or New York City, or someplace along the Hudson — Poughkeepsie, say."

"Is that near Santa Fe?"

"No, you'd have a good distance to go from there to New Mexico. Where Santa Fe is."

Stephen nodded. Grandpa lit a cigarette. "You remembering all this?" Grandpa said, blowing the smoke out. Stephen liked the smell because it was Grandpa's smell. "You going to run away?"

Stephen swallowed a mouthful so cold his throat ached. "I wasn't running away from you and Grandma. I wasn't running away at all."

"You were studying on it."

"Thinking about it?"

"That's what it means," Grandpa said.

Stephen said, "I was studying on it. Do you think my mother will come home?"

"Wow," Grandpa said. "Wow." He clicked the top of his lighter. "Stephen, if you were waiting at home, I would get there if I could."

"Why couldn't you? The emergency feeling?"

"I don't know what that is," Grandpa said. "Let's walk around the reservoir, would you like to? There's a path that goes partway around. We could look at the ducks." He held his hand out and Stephen took hold of it. It was wide and hard, and it pulled him across the seat and out Grandpa's door. Stephen left his soda, but he kept his hand in Grandpa's, and they walked. It was soft and full of leaves and mud on the path, and people had left all kinds of things there, but there were more ducks than he'd ever seen before, brown ones, black, the shiny green ones. When he asked Grandpa what they were called, Grandpa said, "I know mallards and wood ducks to guess at, and that's about it. I like to look at them, and I never wanted to bother to know their names. I'm an ignorant man, Stephen. I just look at 'em."

After a squishy part, where they got into mud up to their ankles, the path got hard and it went up. They followed it, bending to get under branches with thorns, and they came out onto a hill. They could look down at the reservoir and see all the ducks and the white geese. Everything was moving around and making noises. They sat and watched. Grandpa lit a cigarette and Stephen sat in front of him, leaning back against Grandpa's legs and smelling the smoke.

"So, what's the emergency feeling?" Grandpa asked him.

"Where you just have to go and *do* something?"

"Panic?"

"I don't know," Stephen said.

"Who gets the emergency feeling, Stephen?"

"I don't know."

"Do you?"

"Sometimes."

"After school? When you went down to the buses?"

"Kind of."

"Mommy gets it, of course."

Stephen sat still.

"It's all right," Grandpa said, "I won't tell anyone."

"You'll tell Grandma."

"I have to tell her everything."

"Sure," Stephen said, "but then it won't be secret."

"And you're supposed to keep it secret." Stephen shrugged. "It's between you and her. It's what you got from her. What you can keep now." Stephen shrugged again. "Makes sense to me. Your mother told you something or — did she call you? Probably not. Probably a note." Grandpa breathed more smoke out. "Well, listen, amigo. You better just keep it between you and her, all right?"

Stephen felt his shoulders go loose. They had been so still, his neck had begun to hurt. He leaned back again, and put his head on Grandpa's legs.

Grandpa said, "Stephen, will you do me a favor?"

"Okay."

"Will you not take a bus trip without checking with me? I got worried when you weren't outside school. I got so worried, I left the printing of this week's edition to Mr. Stovall Stratton. He can run a Linotype, but he will not read for style. Wasn't trained to, he'd tell you — just accuracy. The chances are excellent we'll be accurately illiterate this week. But that's all right. We'll survive. We're the paper of record for more people than anyone on any city daily could imagine. What I'm really trying to say, Stephen, is I was really worried about you. And if you think those guys outside the Superette were meatheads, wait until you see the guys outside the *big* bus stations."

"Are they tough, Grandpa?"

"Like stringy meat."

"Tougher than you?"

"Yeah, they're that."

"Okay."

"Good man," Grandpa said. "I'd worry about you, Stephen. You know?"

"I'm worrying too, Grandpa."

"I do know that," Grandpa said.

He was all right going through Johnstown on 70/76, then staying with 70 as it dropped southwest. He had planned that, and he went through Indianapolis and on, aiming himself at St. Louis, stopping at gas stations and eating whatever was ready and wrapped. He suddenly almost fell into the wheel, as if he'd been slammed in the head from behind. He pulled over and shut the engine off, cracked the windows open, locked the doors and, sitting on the margin of the highway, unable for an instant to distinguish it from any of the other highways he had been on, reached for the book of maps. He couldn't remember what state he was in, so he opened the wide book at the front and traced his fingers over the red lines indicating cross-country highways. He forced himself to say the names of places he had passed, or names he'd read on signs. He said, in a hoarse voice he thought sounded different from his own, "Mattoon. Vandalia. Right, then Festus happened. And Lebanon. Fucking Indiana," he said. "I'm in Indiana."

Although he had showered at Sheila Mason's house, after going berserk and being loved halfway to death for a while — he slumped into cheap pride, as he afterward thought of it, and her dark, unhappy enchantments. "But," he said, and then forgot to speak. He did think it: *But* you smell like her skin and her sheets and the sweat between her wonderful breasts. And he was in a car on the side of the road, Route 70 on its way to being 44 and going to, Jesus, *Tulsa*. Well, he'd probably never get to St. Louis, much less Tulsa, and all that cowboy shit after it along the way.

Missouri, he thought. He heard the word and knew that he was asleep, that if a runaway tractor-trailer swerved off the road and crushed the car flat and him into jelly, then burned the jelly black, he would not wake up. There were the sounds of cars and trucks, and then there was the sense of being in a vast tunnel through which engines and voices made their drifting, slurred sounds. Then it was he and Sarah. But this isn't a dream, he dreamed himself thinking. This is true.

He was with another woman, in the lobby of a hotel or in an airport. He was worried that he wore no shirt, that he'd left his luggage in the room with Sarah, that he and this tall, broad woman with a thick waist around which he kept his arm were going to have to live separately forever. She said nothing, only

81

leaned over from time to time and kissed his neck, up under the ear, with a lingering and passionate kiss that was almost a bite. The soles of his feet ached. The sadness of their imminent parting was enormous. He heard himself tell her, I have never had a feeling like this. She reached, with a black-gloved hand, and lovingly touched his naked chest above his heart. Like this? she asked. Oh, he answered. Oh. And he woke, expecting to be cold because he'd left his shirt in the room with Sarah, but he was sweating.

And he fell asleep again, but he wasn't far enough under to dream. He drifted on his thoughts, like a swimmer on the surface of the sea. He remembered this. They were hurrying to dress for a dinner outside Perkasie, a matter of business, of contacts, of the awful glad-handing at which neither of them was very good, but which they agreed they would work at. The babysitter was downstairs. Stephen, about three, was going through a time of worrying about their absence, especially Sarah's, and he came wet-eyed and red-faced and clearly alarmed into their bedroom. Barrett watched Sarah's face go white, as if she'd been injured. He saw her mouth move peculiarly, as if the bottom lip fought the top for definition of her face. Her nostrils flared, her mouth worked against the background of her pallor, and her eyes were hard. She looked like a policeman trying not to swat a drunk or vagrant with his club, and about to lose the struggle not to. He remembered how he had walked in front of her and scooped up his hot-faced kid and held him, waltzed a phony, carefree waltz with Stephen's legs against his chest and waist, as he squeezed and patted and sang unmusical tunes in the hallway of their house. The sitter came to Stephen's rescue, or Barrett's, and Barrett went back to his bedroom as if to the scene of a car wreck.

He actually looked around the room as he entered, searching for debris. There was only Sarah, in a black dress with long sleeves and a high, simple neckline. She was fastening beads around her neck, amber that he'd bought her two or three years before.

"That looks great," he said.

"Thank you."

"Is that early frost I hear in your voice? Are you pissed at something?"

"I'm not used to having my child rescued out from under me, that's all."

"Oh, now, it wasn't out from under, Sarah. Come on. I picked the little guy up and defused it."

"Defused precisely goddamned what?"

"I don't know. I don't know. You seemed very angry, I guess."

"Is that what you guess? Gee, what a guess. So I'm a child-beater because I'd like a few goddamned minutes to myself to get dressed? I'm so *terribly* sorry."

"Sarah, this is blowing up out of noplace. Honey. I just thought you needed some time, so I went and got him. It really isn't anything immense, you know? Don't fight. Don't make a fight out of this one."

" 'This *one*,' I could have sworn I heard. Do I make a lot of things into fights in your recollection? In your experience with the defendant? Am I blowing up these storms all over the place, Barrett, and filling our lives with gusts of paranoia or something intrusive like that?"

She pulled the amber necklace off and threw it at the wall behind the bed. He couldn't help himself. He jumped and stuck his arm up and rolled on the bed, holding the necklace aloft as a center fielder might after chasing down a long potential triple into the left-center gap.

She held her hand out. Her eyes were as hard as they'd ever appeared to him before. But they were softening. Color began to infuse her skin. Her lips, though, bit against each other and

83

fought. He stepped toward her from the bed and let the necklace drop gently into her palm.

"Thank you," she said. "Thank you for them the first time, and thank you for them tonight. You look very nice. You didn't wrinkle your shirt up. I'm afraid I made us late."

"Yeah," he said. "You're welcome and all right and all. But how do you *feel*, Sarah?"

In the car he answered for her, waking to his memories: "Sometimes I feel like a motherless child." He said it as he had heard Leontyne Price sing it, but in his mouth the words were unresonant. He tasted his breath, and he was tasting his age.

In fact, Sarah had looked away from him, had picked up her purse and told him, "I'm going to kiss Stephen good night. You want to stand guard?"

He was awake now. He was going to find a gas station, brush his teeth, wash up and buy lots of coffee and things with sugar in them. Then he was going to drive through St. Louis and down the southwest corner of Missouri, passing — he touched the map — places he had never heard of, like Lebanon, like Carthage. Both his parents were dead, and for the first time in years he wished he could call them. He thought he ought to call Willis and Lizzie. He ought to talk to Stephen. His stomach ached as he thought of the loneliness and fright he might hear in Stephen's voice.

Would hear in Stephen's voice.

Hi, babe, it's Daddy.

Did you see Mommy? Did you find her yet? Are you coming home?

Barrett rolled the window down and sucked in the chemical air. Not *when* are you coming home, you son of a bitch? Not even when you make it up for him? Just: *are* you. He remembered when they were younger and drove a station wagon with a padded playpen in the back, and Stephen clung to the rails and whooped as they rode. His greatest fear in those days was an accident in which he and Sarah were killed, and Stephen in his booted pajamas with the hatch in back was thrown from the car. In those days he would see the little boy crawl, and then haul himself erect enough to sit. He always, in his darkest times, saw little Stephen, his face contorted in terror unbearable to watch, crying by the side of the road, unrescued.

But he still fastened his seat belt. He still turned his lights on and put the car in gear and got himself back on the road going south and west.

It was the same catching-up time they had sneaked when Sarah was Stephen's age. It had been a different house in a different place, and Lizzie had been head of guidance for a superintendent who was fired for comforting troubled high school girls, and Willis had been trying to work for the papers in Syracuse, and their bodies had lain less gratefully at the end of a day, perhaps. But it was still Lizzie Bean and Willis Mastracola, looking up in the dark bedroom and whispering as lightly as if each or both of them were part of the air of the house and not just the shape alongside. They had done this since adopting Sarah when she was six days old — stolen time from what they said they most desired, the breathing baby more fragile than anything they had known. They rose at dawn to whisper over coffee about the day to come, before they sat in Sarah's room to watch her nurse from the formula bottle. They whispered at night while they listened for a cry from down the hall. They never discussed their reason or their custom. They stole the time, and they used it.

And now, so many years later, they were doing it again. Their whispered sibilants hissed in the darkness. Willis's rumbling voice and his occasional suppression of a cough, the harsh, comfortable smell of tobacco and of his skin, were a kind of background music, Lizzie thought. It was like talking over the ring of silver on china, or drinking whiskey in a hotel lounge in a small city where a pianist played unexceptionally. She breathed in so sharply that Willis whispered, "What?"

"I was thinking," Lizzie said. "I've been doing this for twenty-nine years."

"What?"

"Smelling you."

"Am I offensive?"

"You smell wonderful. But you've also been smoking cigarettes for as long as I've known you."

"Worrisome," Willis said.

"Scary as hell."

"As soon as this all stops, I'll stop too."

"No," she said, "you stop now. It'll bring us luck. Please."

"Luck?" She reached out until she touched her bedside table and she knocked on it. "You're knocking on wood?"

"I'd sacrifice a virgin if I thought it would help."

"You'd have to import one," Willis said.

"You stop first," she said. "Consider this begging, will you?"

"What do I get for stopping?" She felt his hand on her stomach. She lay her hand on top of his.

"I get more of you," she said. "Please." He seized gently on the flesh of her belly and he squeezed. She said, "All right?" He patted her as if to say yes, and she knew that nothing was assured. "Say you promise," she said. "Say you're stopping."

He moved his hand. "Stopping the cigarettes, not this."

"Yes," she said.

"I'll try," he said.

"Because everything else seems to be going to hell. I don't want to do it alone. I don't want you to —"

"Is the word *die?*"

"I want you to be well. We have a *life*, Willis."

"Yes," he said, "we're the oldest parents of a six-year-old between New York and Alaska."

"Barrett is not going to leave his child. For that matter, neither is Sarah. She of all people ought to know something about being left behind, don't you think?"

Willis's hand lay on her hip bone — there is still a verifiable bone, thank God, Lizzie thought; it isn't all lard yet. He touched her idly. That kind of lazy stroke was, she thought, the great gift. It felt better, in the soul, than the best sweaty, wild and bedbreaking screw. You weren't as relieved or wrung out by it, and you didn't get delusions of immortality or even well-being. But you were saved by hands like that, you were found and given comfort by hands like that. By *those* hands, she thought, reaching to touch one of his fingers on her, then leaving it alone.

He said, "You think it's something about being adopted? Some kind of a mental — I don't know — a time bomb? Something goes off in the spring before their thirtieth birthday and they run amok? I don't mean to make it a joke. You know that. I don't feel that way. But, Lizzie, I have to tell you: I stopped thinking about it. Didn't you?"

"A lot of the time."

"Yeah. It would be you to worry some of the time about something that's so goddamned beautiful — she and we get together, out of all the people in the world, and we love her and she loves us. Fuck. I always *assumed* she loved us, you know? But who really knows, I guess. I'm such a simpleton. I just thought it was all okay and she was glad and we were glad and we'd all live happily ever after. And you had the brains to worry about it. I was, I probably was just ducking out on it. You knew there was something wrong?"

"Oh, no," Lizzie whispered, turning onto her side, leaning her head on her hand and propping herself on an elbow. She looked down in the dark and realized that she'd been talking with her eyes closed. "God. No. I was just frightened. It's my Irish: you always *know* you're guilty of something and you'll any minute be punished. I'm a worrier. That's what I do for a living."

"And I'm a carefree guinea."

"Of the South Carolina carefree guineas," she said.

"You remember that, huh? Still?"

"Only because it drives you nuts." He touched her forearm. "You know," she said, "you have the peculiar ability to create unusual erogenous zones."

"If you are asking me to commit perversions," he said in a pompous, priggish voice, "you will have to provide both directions and lubrication."

"So I don't know," she said. "It could be. It could also be their marriage blowing up. Did you think things were going okay?"

"I never knew how to tell. In my experience, no one knows if the marriage is going okay. All of a sudden it blows a head gasket and they know." He said, "Do you hear me? Perversions, blowing, *head* gaskets. I'm mildly deranged. I'm a sick man."

"You're only a mildly cunning man. But what about Sarah? I am so frightened about her. And Stephen. No: I'm also *angry* about her. That poor little boy. I'm so sleepy, Willis."

"And Barrett. Crazy Barrett. He goes from yuppie architect to road tripper. I don't know if he's equipped for that."

"I can't stay awake one minute longer," she suddenly said. She felt as if she were falling into the bottom of the mattress. "What a day."

"But this has been such wonderful sex. Just let me catch my breath before I whisper good night."

Lizzie rolled her head on the pillow on which she'd collapsed. She kissed his ear. "I know I'm being perverse," she mumbled. "But you *were* on the hunt for perversions. I'm gone. Love you. Night."

Willis mumbled, or she heard what he said as a mumble, but

she was dreaming about a tall, hairy man who shouted at her and whose words — she could see them leave his mouth as if in a comic strip bubble — burst apart with the sound of shattering glass.

It was the Motel Dreadful, she decided, and it was her punishment for cowardice heaped on cowardice: she had fled her baby — *I ca-an't hear you* — to follow the directions she'd received from the woman who was probably her birth mother. She had therefore, possibly, fled her mother, who was too much woman for any girl but maybe a terrific friend to have sometimes, and possibly a person you could fruitfully imitate, the way junior high school girls will emulate the snooty one with first breasts and best wardrobe. Her father was the person you sought for comfort and a quiet resistance to plans you made that you knew were stupid but needed help avoiding. Barrett was another story, but that was why she had married him. She had wanted another story. And Stephen.

But she had stopped here. She thought of Road Runner, skidding to his cartoon halt on the edge of a high, pink, sandy cliff, like the ones they had seen in New Mexico. Here she was, *meep-meep*, in her cloud of cartoon dust. She could have been at the woman's house by now, this was hardly what you'd call the fall of dark. But she had nevertheless checked into the Motel Dreadful and was in the brown room, breathing brown air, smelling mildew and cat shit on the wind, maybe on the window screen for all she knew, and here was her fried imitation chicken and her six-pack of warm Rolling Rock — four-pack by now — and there was the telephone, probably sticky with the drooling of someone whose call had been shortened by contagious hemorrhage.

April had gotten harsher in these Pennsylvania hills. It was a different place from soft Bucks County, with its nouvelle cuisine and high tax base, its shops that specialized in fire screens and andirons, in reproduction Victorian brassware, in DKNY clothing, in challenging toys for gifted and talented kids. Here, people seemed pasty and afflicted with skin eruptions. Their clothing looked stiff with either dirt or artificial fibers. Houses were for sale where no one ever, except with their eyes closed, would buy. The restaurant chains were absent, two gas stations had been closed on the local roads. Color seemed leached from the brush and trees, from the paint on the houses as well as from the people who sat outside them on half-built or partly ruined porches. Even the blacktop of the road seemed bleached.

This is where I could have grown up, she had thought, driving away from the highway because she was there, where she'd been instructed to go, and driving aimlessly because she was frightened of getting closer. Maybe I'd have been you, she thought, looking at a round woman with great, flabby arms who was lighting a cigarette and seemed to be staring over a fence where there wasn't one. Four cars and a truck were parked on her front lawn, and her children played among them. Sarah would have bet her Lay-Zee Eight Diner chicken with coleslaw and french fries and roll that only one of the vehicles worked. Maybe you'd have been me. Maybe you are. AM I YOUR MOTHER?

AM I *YOU?*

She held her breath as she dialed, because it would not have surprised her to learn that the last occupant of this room was still present in the form of microbes and viruses and small insects that bored into the mucous membranes and ate your glands. She stood up and brushed at herself as if insects lay on her clothing and skin.

But it was too late for Stephen, she thought. He shouldn't be up. Barrett wouldn't let him.

"Fucking *whore!*" she said in the brown air of the room.

Which was what Barrett, she remembered, opening another beer, had said to her during one of their less splendid moments. She'd gone into Philadelphia, to a fabric show, and she had stopped at the studio of Edwin Slovitz, who lived on journeyman salaries from teaching design and drawing at Drexel and at Temple, and who'd been, for as long as she'd known him, the man she most admired and feared. He worked in a big loft over a plumbing company, and she had associated him, since the afternoon in question, with the high, tough Philadelphia-cockney voices of the men downstairs in the shop. It had been a little like being across a border on a map.

When she'd called, and he asked her why, she said, "I thought about you. Well. I think about you."

"How's the architect?"

"Great. He's terrific. We're terrific. I didn't want this to be a test or anything, Eddie."

"For who?"

"For me, dumbo."

"And me?"

"You were always good at tests."

She took a cab to the red brick building, and she walked up two long flights. He was broad but not fat, and the muscles of his neck and shoulders were bunchy-looking, thick. He wore what every painter and writer and composer — and no architect — of her acquaintance wore: a faded dark T-shirt. His arms were short and furry. His smile was like a child's, and he used it infrequently, as if preferring to hide inside his curly red beard.

"This is my place," he said, pouring hot water into unmatching cups for their instant coffee. "These are some of the pictures I'm doing right now." He gave her a cup. "This is my life." He sat on a large cube of wood painted gray. "What do you want from it?"

His face, for all its furtiveness, was as kind as she remembered.

She had been fascinated by his round bald head, and she wanted, even as he challenged her, to reach a hand to rub its smooth-looking top. "You were my friend in school."

"Sarah, I was your *lover* in school."

"You were a friendly lover. Didn't we have a lot of fun?"

He considered her question, and she remembered the earnestness with which he had both listened and answered when they'd been together. She used to call him The Judge, she remembered, for the sobriety and profundity of his attention. "That's why I went around — you remember this? I cried. You remember the crying? I said those things about love? I think you can recall them. We were up by the Schuylkill —"

"Eddie, I'm sorry. I was younger. I was screwed up. I'd met this handsome, smart man and I wasn't thinking. My values were still forming."

After a pause, and a sip of his coffee, he cocked his head and then moved, as if he'd made a decision. He went to the old-fashioned gas stove with its curlicued iron fittings, and from the drawer beneath the oven he took a roasting pan. Inside it was a plastic bag which he brought back to the cube. He began to roll a joint. When he was finished, he rolled another. "It's tough, forming your values," he said. His voice sounded a little like her father's, she remembered thinking. "Those old values kick hell out of a girl growing up. And if she's been in the sack for six months with a man who happens to have invested the majority of his emotions in her, well, the old value-forming process is going to take its toll on *him*, I'd say."

She watched him lick each joint to seal it. "I was hoping I could look at your work, Eddie."

"Charge the old cultural-value batteries, Sarah?" He stood and went to the stove, returned with a book of matches. She looked past him, down the long, broad loft at the large canvases stored or propped to be worked on. There was little furniture, a lot of equipment — saws, miter box, rolls of canvas, plastic bottles of paint — but very little mess. He had always been a clean man, and she remembered how when they lived together she had preferred to shower in the morning while he had showered at night, before bed. He said, "What we can do if you like, in that case, is toke together a little bit and then go back there." He gestured at a wall of bookcases behind which, apparently, he had a bed. She would have bet her carfare home that it was a mattress on the floor. The sheets would be clean. "We can fuck each other's brains out for old times' sake, and for the gargling-out of our presumably formed-by-now values, and then we —"

She knew it was her expression that had stopped him. His eyes had gone squinty and very cold — "Snake Eyes," she had called that face. But he had never been monstrous, only easily angered, and she knew that he'd seen her confusion. She heard children playing ball in the playground outside. She heard the foreign-sounding men downstairs, chattering while they worked. "I'm sorry," she said.

She labored at not crying, but he had seen enough to be thrown from the ease of his anger toward concern about her. And that brought him close, she figured, to feeling pain about her again — which was what had wakened his temper in the first place.

"I'm really sorry," she said. "And you're right. This is stupid. This is the middle-class housewife getting her rocks off. And I did *not* come up here to get laid by the fine arts, Eddie, I swear it. I just kept thinking about you."

She tried to read his face. When she'd mentioned sex, she'd understood that he wanted to go to bed with her for all kinds of reasons. And, she admitted, she would have happily gone. Now, if she was to have any honor, ever, in his memory, she'd have to keep her goddamned bourgeois thighs together and waddle away home.

"I'm too rough," he said. "I'm sorry. It was something out of some opera, though. Or I thought it was." He came closer, then, and put his hands on her shoulders. "I forgot that I loved you. I forgot to feel what you might be feeling."

"How did you mean that?"

"Do you want to stay?"

"Eddie, you shithead, I can't stay here if you love me. I *want* you to love me. I don't know. Never mind. Forgive me. Please, forgive me. Don't forget me, all right? I'm sorry."

"Sarah, *I'm* sorry. I — do you think I should call you, and we try to meet up?"

"I think we're stuck in our lives, Eddie."

He pondered that, even then, in his judicial way. He smiled his beautiful smile, but sadly. "Yes, we are."

"We are," she said.

She blew her nose on the harsh toilet paper of the Motel Dreadful, not knowing whether she wept for Edwin Slovitz and Sarah his girl, or Barrett and Sarah his wife, or Stephen and Sarah his mother — though she *ca-an't hear you.*

And even though she had barely been late that night, and Barrett had known that he was to get Stephen after nursery school, he had sensed — he had seemed to smell — a difference in her. After dinner, when Stephen was watching a National Geographic film about whales and they were clearing up the dishes, Barrett said, "What?"

"What what?"

"Really. What happened. What went wrong?"

"I told you. Good trip, the usual brilliant new designs that none of our clients will want except in tan or champagne like all their friends ordered, and the city was the city."

"Who'd you meet?"

"The usual suspects."

"Where'd you eat?"

"Barrett, what's this about?"

94

"Something happened. You — feel funny."

"No, I don't."

"I mean to me."

She hadn't meant to cock her head that way, as Eddie Slovitz did.

"What's that?" Barrett said. "That little whatever. It isn't you. You know it's not."

"You shouldn't tell me what's me, honey."

"Oh, no, *honey?* I don't care if I sound like some suspicious, impotent, fat little husband —"

"You aren't fat, you aren't little, and I can testify that you are far from impotent. For goodness' sakes. Listen. You remember Eddie Slovitz? That painter? Edwin Slovitz?"

He didn't set down the tureen he'd been drying. He dropped it onto the brick-pattern linoleum of the floor, and it broke. She started to cry. She knew she wasn't crying about the tureen. He said, "Whoops. An accident. Like how you're going to tell me you ran into your old boyfriend by accident. Could you not bother? Would that be all right? You fucking whore."

And she said — this was as embarrassing as any moment in Eddie's loft — "But we don't *do* things like this, Barrett."

"Oh," he said, his face filled with disgust, some of it for himself, she knew. "Oh, well. Then you just consider it undone, Sarah, all right?"

In the room of the Motel Dreadful, she looked at the oleaginous chicken she had not eaten. She looked at a streak, near the bathroom door, of what she was certain would be matter from somebody's nose if she examined it more closely. She saw her satchel of clothing, the keys to the car, her good leather wallet containing photographs of Stephen and Barrett and her parents. If Eddie Slovitz were here tonight, she thought, she'd make him pale, and then she'd make him blush.

*　　*　　*

He'd complained to Lizzie that he felt like a private eye in a television movie, catching calls at six in the morning and driving out to Christ-Knows-Where, New York, for coffee and intrigue. Stephen, practicing his beverage-pouring with Lizzie's saucer and sometimes her cup, remarked that the man who called might be a preacher if they were meeting in a town called Christ. Stephen raised him one: "It might be God."

Stephen turned, the glass coffee pot wobbling in his hand, and considered the possibility. Then he said, "No," and returned the pot to the stove.

"How do you know, sweetie?"

"Grandma, God wouldn't need to use the *telephone*."

And here he was at 7:15, in West Eaton, drinking more coffee than he wanted with Loren Macy, Attorney-at-Law. Macy's hair was huge with tight, dark curls, his beard was closely trimmed, and his suit looked expensive. His tie was a reproduction of a Van Gogh painting, and he wore it with a boldly striped shirt with a plain white collar. He was maybe a few inches over five feet, had thumped into the tiny diner on high-heeled cowboy boots. His handshake was very powerful, competitive in its pressure, and his grin exposed the tops of his gums. His voice was one of the deepest that Willis had heard.

"You're kind to meet me, Mr. Mastracola."

"It sounded important to you. How can I help?"

"Of course, this is about Loren Junior. You figured that out." Willis nodded, started to sip, smelled the sourness in the cup and put it down. "Food?"

Willis shook his head. "I'll eat some toast, margarine on the side," he told the waitress, who seemed about eleven.

Around them, men in feed caps ate eggs and sausage. One man smacked his lips as, a napkin spread over his tie and plaid sportcoat, he ate a bowl of oatmeal. Willis thought of cigarettes, and his gums ached as if he were teething.

"Now," Macy said, drinking his coffee. "Loren Junior is in trouble. It's a tricky business, because Lois and I wanted him to fit in, of course, but within individuated parameters. We didn't want him just *conforming*, understand, just to make it easy, but we *wanted* it easy. I'll admit that. But: your parents take the lonely road, I guess you end up on it too."

"Mr. Macy, you can take everything I know about being a parent and put it in your coffee cup with room left over for sugar and cream. And I did it — I've done it — for almost thirty years."

"It's a crapshoot, you're saying. Right. Right."

"And what a lot of crap it involves," Willis said, drinking the coffee as punishment for shooting off his mouth.

"I built the place myself, you know." Willis nodded. "I made a lot of mistakes, but we're learning to live with land, how to take care of a house in these winters. We're also learning limits to idealism. I'm trained at NYU. I'm a practical man, though my house might not look it. One of my precepts is becoming Learn the Limits. Well, Loren Junior took the cue from what Lois and I did — I mean, I've heard the talk. I know we're called 'the last hippies.' Which we aren't, believe me. But that's the exaggerated, simplified, Woodstock Nation version of our lives. So be it. Except, I think Loren Junior picked up on it in those terms too. Just because we lived there for the summer carting our water by hand before I got the plumbing done right doesn't mean we didn't bathe and care for our teeth. Same as now: we'll be putting in a windmill to generate power by the early summer, so we use kerosene lamps at night in the meantime. That doesn't mean I don't read case law and write my briefs. Understand?"

Willis knew that he needed to say nothing. Macy was delivering his summation to the jury, and he didn't need Willis's help.

"So Loren Junior, who is *not* a wonderful athlete — believe

97

me, I know. He wants to play ball without, well, playing ball, if you know what I mean. I mean, he wants to be on the teams and participate with the other boys. But he doesn't want to have to jump through hoops to do it. And he's heard enough from Lois and me about coercion, about knee-jerk patriotism, about individual liberty — he won't pledge the flag, he won't sing 'The Star-Spangled Banner.' He also believes in the separation of church and state, as we do, in a major way, though that hasn't come up yet. As you no doubt know, they want to throw him off the team."

"I don't imagine the principal will let that happen. You maybe ought to talk to her."

"I go to the top, Mr. Mastracola. You're one of the town fathers."

"Fatherhood again."

"There you have it. I'm curious about your take on Loren Junior."

"I think you should talk to the coach and the principal over at the school. That's the top you mentioned needing to get to."

"Well, she's your wife. You'd automatically tell me to check with hcr, wouldn't you? But —"

"The way I see it, Mr. Macy, this is still a free country. It's messy and sloppy and people track all kinds of shit all over the floor on account of its being free. You can do that here."

"I was going to suggest an interview for your paper."

"Was I supposed to be taking notes?"

"With Loren Junior."

"You want me to interview the boy."

"Sort of 'Rebel Up Close' kind of feature, yes. Don't you think it would garner some real readership?"

"I think maybe in the high school newspaper it would, yes."

"No, I meant in *your* paper."

"No."

"No?"

"Mr. Macy, the last child I interviewed was my grandson, on the subject of his participation in dodge ball games in gym. I don't plan to run that in my newspaper either. My back is sore, I got to stand up a while. You'll excuse me?"

Macy put on wire-rimmed glasses with small lenses and studied the bill. He looked at Willis over the top of his glasses as if surprised to find him still there. "I'll get this," he said.

Willis found himself driving the back roads on his way to the paper. He wanted to telephone Lizzie and talk about his sizzling temper and how he'd held it, but at the expense of third-degree burns. Thinking of Lizzie, and the phone, made him think that it had to have been Sarah last night when it rang four times, then stopped. Lizzie, in her deep sleep, had murmured, "What? Is it Sarah?" and had fallen asleep while he whispered goofy, untenable reassurances. In the morning, though, she'd known. Her face had looked so soft and sad, he'd thought of their early days, and learning her history, which he always thought of as tragic.

"It isn't," Lizzie always said. "It wasn't. That embarrasses me. I was a tough, independent kid and I made some choices and I lived my life." Thinking about tragedy, he didn't dwell on her affairs, the botched and bad ones, the ones that simply petered out. That, he thought, is what happens to a woman in the world. He liked to note, at such times, that he was not nearly as possessive and jealous as he thought he tended to be. The sciatic pain going down his leg or the hollow, nauseated feeling between his breastbone and his navel immediately indicated otherwise. But for him the worst was double: the child she had, the child she didn't.

She had told him her story in bed, early in their loving, and he'd heard the click of her mouth as she whispered at the ceiling in the dark. And he'd asked — because, he always remembered,

99

he was stupid and uneasy and filled with fear for her as much as lust and affection — "You mean you can't have a baby?"

And she hadn't answered. She'd nodded. He heard her hair move on the pillow beside him.

"So," he'd said, "then *we* can't have a baby. You want to do dogs, cats and parakeets, or should we adopt?"

"Flippant jerk," he announced to his recollections, driving from West Eaton toward Burroughs, rubbing at the underside of the leg that pulsed like the engine of the car. He sang along with someone on the radio whose voice he knew well. He couldn't remember the singer's name, and he was furious when he pulled into the alley beside the office. He thought: We should have gone for the parakeet. They always come with a cage.

•

HERE WAS her mother. Her *mother*, she thought, intoning the word inside so that she heard its syllables the way they used to hear records played too slowly on their cheap girlhood turntables, as if a monster drawled basso in a cave. *Ehm-uth-awr*, she told herself. But she couldn't feel what she'd feared and wished. She felt no snapping into place, no need to sigh the way you yawn your most relaxed, most yearned-for tiredness, no arrival. And therefore she felt no ease in her having surged from everyone, no justification and finally no confidence that she had gone anywhere but too far away from her child and from Elizabeth and Willis Mastracola, and from Barrett.

"Sarah," the small woman said. She breathed it out, she crooned it. "Sarah." The woman closed her eyes, then opened them wide. They were large and full and blue. "Do you think we could —" She held her arms out, and Sarah stepped forward automatically and was hugged, hard. She put her hands lightly on the woman's shoulders and felt her head against her own travel-soiled clothing — against, she thought, her bitch's hard heart. *I ca-an't hear you.*

"Hi," Sarah said, rolling her eyes at her own banality, stupidity. "Hello," she said, "good to be here."

"Call me Mother," the woman said.

Sarah stepped back and looked at her, at the harsh twill trousers and denim shirt bulging at the pocket from pens and a small spiral notebook. She wore those rubber half-boots you see on herb farmers on educational TV, Sarah thought. Her eyes were pretty, her features sharp, her forehead high, her hair a dark thicket. Sarah saw some Stephen in this woman's face, especially in its upper half and in her pallor. She looked older than Lizzie.

"No," the woman said, "that's fine. I understand. You know my name. Gloria Dodge. Will you call me Gloria, dear?"

Sarah found herself reaching to shake hands with the woman from whose womb she was born. She heard herself say, "How do you do." She watched herself follow the little woman in, past a low, broad airtight stove and over polished pine boards, past sofas and chairs that had piles of newspapers on them, and past a wall of shelves filled with textbooks and journals and collected objects — driftwood, pottery, stones. She sat at a round, dark table on a chair with a woven hemp seat, and she found that she was shaking.

"It's the worst time," Gloria said, "the early spring. It's always as cold as autumn up here. I'm going to make you a little fire, and then we can talk. I've been waiting since — my, since John F. Kennedy was killed, to warm you up and talk to you!"

Gloria, kneeling at the open woodstove, touched a match off and lit the pile of paper and kindling, then closed the door. She turned wheels on the door, listened to the air roar into the stove, adjusted the wheels again and returned to the little kitchen section of the open first floor.

"I can make you a pot of tea," Gloria said. "Or something stronger? Did you eat? Would you like some dinner?"

Sarah shook her head even as she thought how stolid, how ungracious she must seem. She wanted Gloria to like her, she thought. Or she thought that she ought to want to be liked by this woman who had denied them the chance, almost thirty years before, to riddle whether either wished to woo the other for long. "Tea, please," Sarah said. "I do feel a little chilly."

Dead of frostbite, she thought. Frozen hard as a stick of sausage in the back of the freezer because of an icy heart. *Feel* something, she commanded. It's your *ehm-uth-awr.*

"This is a nice house," she said as Gloria brewed tea.

"I had it built by an architect who was selling these kits. Plans he'd made for log houses. He gave a discount if you hired him and his two architect friends to build the house. I think they did a lovely job. They even came back to caulk out the drafts when I complained a little. Nice boys. I only had to stick pins into the little dolls a couple of times, and back they came."

Sarah snickered automatically. Gloria didn't. She looked sweetly earnest. "My husband's an architect," Sarah said. She thought she sounded like an idiot at a bingo game. My husband's the man who pumps your cesspool out. Oh, how thrilling, and mine's the man who changes your oil at the FastLube.

Gloria sat and poured a red-brown tea. "Sassafras," she said. "The Native Americans taught us how to use it."

Sarah leaned over to inhale a brackish steam. She said, "Mm."

"How long have you been married, dear?"

"Oh, God. Since — seven years," she said.

"To an architect named —"

"Barrett."

"Oh, he sounds lovely. Is he kind? Is he handsome? Are you rich?"

"Why would you ask me that?"

"Isn't it the way the fairy tales end? The queen's daughter runs away and marries the pauper who turns out to be a handsome prince who makes her happy and rich?"

"Is that how you see us?" Sarah asked. "You're the queen and I'm the daughter who ran away?"

"No," Gloria said, reddening. "No, you're right. Fate parted us. You had nothing to do with it. Well, you know."

"That last part I can buy." Sarah disliked the sullenness, the resentment she heard in her voice. She looked up to see, at the edge of her vision, Gloria returning with a plaid blanket that she draped over Sarah's shoulders. It was the plaid of old shirts. She had seen sad, filthy men with no homes who slept at 30th Street Station in Philadelphia wearing that plaid. It was good to feel the warmth, but she was uncomfortable when Gloria held her shoulders and ran her hands along her shoulder blades and neck. She sat stiffly until Gloria moved to her chair again.

"This isn't easy for us, is it?"

"No," Sarah said. "I guess not."

"I've been frightened since you answered my ad."

"Me too."

"What did your husband say?"

Sarah shook her head. She shook it slowly, as if commenting on her actions, not as if answering. "I didn't tell anybody," she said.

"Oh. Not your —"

"No."

"Will they be hurt?"

Sarah nodded. "Everyone will be hurt," she said.

Gloria poured more tea. They drank what tasted to Sarah like the smell of India ink, and then Gloria sighed and said, "I suppose there isn't any more cordial way of doing any of this. Except for us, of course. Our meeting, I mean. *That* can be lovely, can't it?"

Sarah heard her mouth tell the short, pretty woman, "You threw me away."

"Oh, no!" Gloria said.

"The baby in the goddamned Dumpster at Christmas. Moses in the bulrushes." Sarah felt a quivering that seemed to begin inside her organs and resonate. "I used to look at pictures of orphanages. You know how hard they are to find? I used to want to vomit when they ran a piece in the papers about so-and-so's *adopted* daughter. Never just daughter. *Adopted* daughter. I didn't throw you away, lady. You threw me. You tossed. I *got* tossed. You know?"

Gloria clasped her hands at the edge of the table, and Sarah saw what she might have been as a girl: tautly contained, often still, but with intense eyes that didn't seem to blink.

"I apologize," Sarah said. "I'm sorry. I apologize. That was infantile of me. Of course, there's all kinds of childhood stuff going on right now. But I should — this has got to be horrible for you. I'm sorry."

Gloria leaned forward, over her hands, and said, "Oh, no. This isn't horrible. It's terrifying, but it isn't horrible. It's wonderful, really. It's what I've wanted since I had to let you leave."

"No," Sarah said.

"No," Gloria agreed. "Since you were adopted away from me."

Sarah shook her head. She said, "No."

And Gloria said, "Since I knew I couldn't care for you and had to, to —"

"Give me away. Unless you got paid?"

Gloria stood up. Her chair rocked and Sarah thought it might go over, but it didn't. Gloria's eyes looked enormous and bleached, as if the blue itself had drained away when the blood had fallen from the flesh of her face. She clasped her hands in front of her stomach, as if it ached, and she said, showing even and very white teeth, "I was not paid. I wasn't a baby farm. A brood mare. I was a young girl. I was pregnant by a man I couldn't marry. Who wouldn't want to marry me. I was trapped. It wasn't my fault that I was trapped."

"By me," Sarah said, slowly standing, as if Gloria had threatened her.

"All right," Gloria said, "by you. By my stars. By my fate. By yours. It could have happened to you."

"What?"

"In those days? If he had a, if he carried protection, or if you had the courage to get fitted for a diaphragm, if you could find a Sanger clinic, if you were bold enough to make him wait while you squatted there and put it in, if you could ask him if he was wearing protection. *Then* you might not get pregnant, if the odds weren't against you. That's what it was like. We didn't go around wearing sponges and shooting foam up our crotch and pulling out flavored contraceptives with spermicide and little bumps and ridges on them. It was a time when you were *embarrassed* having sex. Being a woman. It could have been you. It could have happened to you. Oh, don't think I'm scolding you," Gloria said. "I don't mean to."

"You just did a fabulous imitation of it," Sarah told her, yawning, though she meant not to, sitting down because her legs felt weak. "You just did this terrific sociology thing about victims and how you blushed while you screwed, but you didn't remember to say what you *did* with what happened because you didn't want to ruin the mood. I know this sounds like some kind of egomaniac kind of thing to say to the person who hatched you and rolled your egg so unwillingly out of the nest, but I am not really sad for your trials, Gloria. You got me all the way up here, out of my life, away from my child and everyone else, so you could —"

Gloria's hand was in the air, a traffic policeman's signaling *Stop.* "You decided to come," she said.

"You advertised."

"You answered."

Sarah had come to the absolute end of the trip. She had to stop.

Gloria said, "You didn't answer *me*. Did you?"

Gloria's face was still pale. Most of the lights in the house were dim, and she stood away from the direct glare of the overhead kitchen lamp. Her white face was a stiff mask. Her bright eyes seemed not to blink. A steady chugging pulse in her neck counterpointed the hard, slapping beat of her own heart, which seemed to Sarah to rock her a little where she sat. She felt as though Gloria, who stared at her with Sarah's own eyes — with what she saw in the bathroom mirror, in the face of her own small child — was slowly examining her. Sarah yawned and shivered, and she felt Gloria inside her skin, slowly fingering the membranes, prodding the organs, pushing aside a rope of slimy gut to better see, to evaluate. Gloria's low, harsh voice said, "You answered your*self*. Isn't that a fact?"

She couldn't remember, the next morning, how she had answered, or what Gloria had said in reply. She remembered how Gloria had gestured and how her lips had moved, but she recalled no sounds. She saw them, as if from above, climb the stairs and walk to this room. She remembered how cold she had been as she closed the door and pulled blindly at the covers, as she tried to fold her clothing when she tore it away from herself. And she woke up cold, with a shoulder that ached from the way she had curled, had forced herself into a ball, almost, under the blankets that Gloria had left for her. They were made of heavy knitted squares of every color of wool Sarah had seen, all of them connected with black. It was like lying under something you could see in a microscope — what the skin of some animal *really* looked like. Beneath two of those covers she was trembling with cold.

She squinted up over the edge of the blanket to see what kind of room she was in. The walls looked like logs, a window next to her bed was bright with morning light. She heard birds, and they sounded frightened, or as if they were swarming. When she wrapped the blankets around her and sat up to look, she saw that they were calling from reeds and small trees near a pond.

Pretty, she thought to say. When she did, she felt unbalanced, because she was searching so hard for good thoughts about what was, after all, craziness from first to last — from whatever this woman, whoever she was, had done to her infant, to *her*, to Sarah's own attempt to make something out of nothing, a pleasure out of her criminality, a happy sight out of, after all, a hundred goddamned nothing but birds.

"Pretty," she whispered.

Her clothes were gone. She had left her plumber's bag in the front of the house, downstairs, she thought she remembered. But the clothing she had worn, everything but the T-shirt and panties she'd slept in, were gone from the rush-bottomed chair on which she'd thrown them as she fell — all but passed out, she thought — into sleep. "Call it coma," she said.

A photograph of Albert Einstein hung on the wall. Or maybe it was Albert Schweitzer. She could rarely tell the difference because both men were so dreamy-looking, so transported, and both had bushy white mustaches, and both were often confused, by seekers-after-heroes, with Christ or one of the more mistreated saints.

"Hello, I think I'm maybe your daughter?"

She shook her head and rewrapped the heavy covers around her. She had thought to enter with dignity, with mystique, even. She had thought to show this woman, whoever she was, what she had thrown away. How pathetic, thinking to show off for this stranger who had possibly found her inconvenient on the day of the birth that Sarah, for one, had not requested. Hello, I think I'm maybe your daughter. But maybe I'm the night nurse. Maybe I'm delivering pizza. Maybe I'm a maniac on the loose. No: the maniac on the loose maybe came and stole her clothes. All right. So she wasn't the maniac on the loose. So maybe she was the pathetic daughter of this weird woman who loved either Einstein or Schweitzer and stole the clothes of her long-abandoned kids.

"Hi, Stevie, kid," she whispered. "Hello."

On the wall across from the window there were pictures of birds that looked like serpents or insects — Currier and Ives, she thought, wondering again how her clients could request these ghastly and very expensive pictures of nature looking like a maniac on the loose. So she had birds out the window and birds on the wall, she had one of the bushy saints, and behind her, on a little shelf set on the wall, as if it were an icon, she had an antique porcelain doll. It was delicate and very white, tubercular-looking, and someone had dressed it in thick, delicious lace. The doll's blue eyes looked down at the bed, Sarah noted, clear and blue and insane, as doll's eyes always looked. Even Barbie, in the model that featured menstrual cramps and bulimia, looked less like a runway model than a — why, yes — maniac on the loose. This old doll looked like the kind of person who might steal your clothing while you slept.

The doll's mommy, and maybe Sarah's, knocked on the door and said, "Breakfast time." She *sang* it, three chiming syllables, the first two on the same note, the second descending, flat and sustained. Sarah found her sneakers and, in them and two heavy blankets, she went down to find, if nothing more, her clothes.

They were folded next to the only place that was set at the table. They had obviously been washed and dried. A thick pottery plate of toast and a vast glass of orange juice, hot coffee in a pottery mug that matched the plate, and her laundry — what more, she thought, besides reason and pleasure in her life could she ask for?

Good morning, Mommy.

She said what she could: "Hello."

The woman turned at the stove and beamed, her white and even teeth bared, her eyes as blue as Sarah remembered when she woke, the hair as almost-black, not nearly as shot with gray as you'd expect. She put down her red potholder and advanced on Sarah, her arms spread wide. She was short, chubby, very pretty inside the extra flesh, thick enough at the thigh for Sarah to hope that, if she was this woman's child, she could skip selected portions of her legacy. Gloria smelled of detergent and lavender talcum. She embraced Sarah lightly, but she kissed her on the cheek. "I know I'm your mother," she said. "I can feel it."

Sarah moved sideways to sit at the round, dark table, from which she could look out the window over the sink — birds, this time at a feeder in the window. She drank coffee and said, "Mmm."

"Chicory," the woman said. "I dry it and grind it to mix with French roast."

It tasted a little like coal tar, and Sarah again said, "Mmm."

"It grows in soil like this, full of clay. You can find it at the side of the road — they look a lot like dandelions, but they're coarser. Look for them in the morning because they close by afternoon."

"Okay," Sarah said, "I will. Thanks for washing my clothes. I didn't hear you come in."

The woman pushed her thanks aside with a flapping gesture. "What's your favorite food?" she asked. "What do you think of the most when you think about breakfast?"

Sarah obediently — she was being someone's possible child — closed her eyes for an instant, then found that she felt too vulnerable so she opened them. She said, "Frosted cornflakes."

"But *why?* My lord, they are so bad for you. All that sugar is just poison."

"That's why. My — I wasn't allowed to have them. I always wanted to. So that's what I thought of."

"I wanted you to want something I could make for you."

"This is great. This toast and all is terrific. Thank you. This is great."

"You were going to say 'my mother,' weren't you? Just before."

"That's who she is," Sarah told the pretty little woman who

stood at the table like a waitress. Sarah's throat closed up as she said, "Elizabeth Mastracola is my mother."

The woman sat down as if to eat. "I understand," she said.

Sarah said, "Excuse me, but *you* understand? I thought it was supposed to be *me*. I thought *I* was the one we were all going to worry about understanding everything."

"That's how children think," the woman said, her lips forming the words with such precision that Sarah grew angrier.

"Excuse me for not worrying about how tough this is for you," Sarah said. "I'm the one left her husband and baby and work and everything else and just took *off*. I mean," and Sarah's throat constricted again, and she thought about tearing it out for betraying her, "I mean, I did not put you out for adoption, lady."

"Gloria, I told you. Gloria. Or — I suppose you could call me Mother without betraying anyone. Tell me about your baby, your husband. Please. Don't be angry. We can get through this."

Sarah stalled by going to the stove for more coffee. "You want some?"

Gloria shook her head and smiled. There were tears in her eyes, and she wiped at them with great public care, using the hem of her apron. "I'm sorry," she said, "this is as difficult as I was afraid it would be."

"What I can't figure out," Sarah said, "is why I came."

"For your mother?"

"If that's who you are."

"Oh, it is."

"Was my father — was the man a little chunky?"

"He was what we called burly, yes. Oh, don't worry. You haven't got my figure. You did get my eyes. I'm glad of that. The eyes are the gateway to the soul, you know. I used to think, when I was a girl, that because my eyes were light blue, people could find my soul more easily. They would love me more, I thought. But they didn't."

"What happened? To the man?"

"Oh. Do you want his name?"

"No. All right."

"Arthur. Arthur Hughes. Art. He was a nice fellow — no husband, of course."

"He was, what? Wild? Irresponsible?"

"He was in love with death. He enlisted because he wanted to go into the Green Berets. He liked fighting. He used to get into fights in high school, fights in bars. He was big and strong, he had thick, very powerful legs. He never got arrested, for all his rambunctiousness. He could talk his way out of anything. He joined the army and he became a Green Beret and eventually he was sent to Vietnam. He died in the Annamese Mountains doing something terrible. I knew he would."

"So he didn't run out on you?"

"Well, things don't *happen* like that, that simply, do they?"

"Yeah," Sarah said, "they do. They could."

"At any rate, the man who sired you didn't know I was pregnant by him."

" 'Sired,' " Sarah said. "So that left you and me and the family death wish."

"Oh," Gloria said, smiling, opening her arms while she sat at the table, "I love *life*."

Sarah motioned at the window, at the calling of birds. "Well, you've sure got enough of it," she said. She stood, taking her clothing, shuffling in untied sneakers and the long blankets toward the stairs. She said, "I'll be back in a little while."

"Yes," Gloria said, "you will. It makes me so happy that you will. We can plan our day. I won't kiss you again right away, as much as I want to. It makes you uneasy, I think. I've always believed in letting people take their time in getting used to a new situation."

"Every twenty-nine years qualifies for a new situation, I'd say. That sounded pretty bitchy, didn't it?"

"Everything you do or say is a gift to me," Gloria said.

"Could I make a call?"

"There's a telephone in the bedroom down the hall from your room," Gloria said. "Please help yourself — and don't thank me. I thank *you* for being here."

Sarah only afterward realized that she had said "You're welcome" as she went upstairs. She was thinking about Stephen.

In the room that was smaller than the one she'd slept in, among stacks of magazines about nursing and public health and the study of nature, in the darkness of drawn blinds and a dim yellow glow from the lamp near the telephone, in the smell of lavender and some piny cleanser, *in my mother's room*, she kept thinking, Sarah dialed the area code. She thought of impulses leaping microscopically through the wires. She thought of the phone at the other end. She thought of a bony wrist with its smells of sunshine and soap and a boy's innocent sweat that she used to sniff when she bathed him or changed him or helped him pick out clothes for school. She used to bury her nose and forehead in his stomach as he lay, open to her, on the changing table. She used to blow air out onto his belly and make bubbling noises, and he used to shriek his delight. That time had been so long ago, she thought. She thought of the telephone ringing there, and of Stephen's hand about to pick the receiver up. Maybe he was in the kitchen on his way to answer it. Maybe he was in Willis and Elizabeth's bedroom, upstairs, having run along the hall as the ringing began. Then we could *both* be sitting in my mother's room, Sarah thought, trying to talk like any of this made sense.

She closed her eyes as the phone rang harshly, as if very close to where she was. Did she want to be so many miles away? She pushed her ear close to the receiver as if to prove how dearly she prized her son. Phrases filled her mouth like saliva, and she swallowed. They returned: Hey, Mom. And: It's me, yeah. I know. And: Stephen, baby, it's your mommy. And: Daddy, I'm sorry, Daddy. And: You could have *trusted* me. She swallowed again. Then she hung up, thinking, Well, of course. Everyone's at work and school. You're the only one sidestepping time around here. The rest of them have to keep living. She found it almost unbearable that their lives ticked on without her. We're a windup toy, she thought. And she answered herself: That's what all the runaway mommies say when the household they fled keeps living.

Then she thought of Barrett. And why don't you call home? she asked herself. The real home, where your husband and your child are supposed to be?

Because I've telephoned there so many times, and heard it ring along the windowpanes and copper pots and baskets from France and bottles of extra-virgin olive oil and the fresh rosemary and bolts of fabric and catalogues of furniture. I know what an empty house sounds like when you call it. And I know Barrett. And of course, of course, he's gone to weep on their shoulder. You sissy: I'll tell your mommy and daddy if you run away.

She heard her child's voice — the same sneering, panicky tones of her *I ca-an't hear you* — and she saw herself: a woman wrapped in blankets, sitting on the bed of the woman who had yielded her up forever, making telephone calls in her brain, speaking several conversations in her head. With her eyes closed. With a curl on her lip. With her eyes weeping while her mind conducted transactions remarkable for their self-pity and unreality and despair. And with your child someplace else, you fucking whore. What makes you any different from the nature lady downstairs, with her cooking spoon for magic wand?

She telephoned the house in Bucks County. She hunched — no, she cringed. But Barrett didn't answer. To prove to herself how brave she was, she dialed once more to try to reach her parents and, she'd have bet, her son. The nasty buzzer-like ringing of the upstate exchange was falling onto her mother's kitchen, her mother's bedroom and the flooring that ran along the hallway to the room she had used as make-believe seraglio through high school. There was a cough, and she thought she'd heard her father through the phone. Of course, it was Gloria. Just in case I wondered if she was waiting for me or anything.

She went to the room she had slept in, and she dressed. In an adjoining bathroom, with pictures of leaves or plants or Venusian invaders — she made an adolescent's face at them — she found a new toothbrush and she cleaned herself up. She noted again that her satchel was still missing. In these haunted-castle movies, she told herself, they always are.

Downstairs, infuriatingly, as if Gloria had timed her, two cups of coffee-of-sorts were freshly poured. Gloria pointed to a pile of dark, misshapen cookies on a plate. "Gingerbread," she said. "Do you know that song, 'If I Knew You Were Coming I'd Have Baked a Cake?' " She sang the title with the brio she'd used in calling Sarah to breakfast. "They're made with wild ginger. You'll find them milder than you're used to. I supplemented with dark molasses for flavor. I knew you were coming, you see."

Sarah, as if compelled to, ate the head of a gingerbread man. "Mmm," she said, as she had for the coffee. The taste was raw and unpleasant. "Why are some of them without faces?" she asked Gloria. And then, before Gloria could answer, Sarah said, "Did a lot of women answer your ad?"

"Ads," Gloria said, her eyes bright, her lashes fluttering, as if she'd been complimented, flattered, and sought modesty. "I must have run hundreds over the years. But I was never systematic, you see. When I found an interesting-looking newspaper, I ran a little ad. I thought: You never can tell. And I did get a number of replies. One of them almost fooled me. She turned out to be a crook. You've no idea how many dishonest people read the papers. She thought I might have money. But I don't. And she gave herself away. By that I mean that she tried to get more information from me than she gave. I knew she wanted to know what to say. I dropped her flat. But you: I knew you were the one."

"Born in the right place at the right time, huh?"

"From me."

"Too bad we didn't have a chance to get acquainted."

"I understand your anger," Gloria said, smiling.

Sarah thought that Gloria was forcing back the corners of her mouth. She thought that maybe Gloria wasn't smiling at all. She looked away, because it had been like looking at a clown. Clowns frightened her. You couldn't ever know what thoughts a clown was thinking, so with clowns you never were safe. She put the sour cookie down.

"You're resentful and you're hurt, Sarah," Gloria said. "Did I tell you the best part? I called you Sarah too. I did. I told the nurses: 'This one's a Sarah. S for Solemn. Your little face was so serious. You knew we had to be parted, I remember thinking. Oh, I wept. I wept!

"Tell me, Sarah. *Really* tell me. Was your childhood terrible because of — it?"

"Because of you? No. It was great. I had a great time."

"Were you resentful?"

"I just told you. It was a piece of cake."

"You weren't — I don't know: hurt? Wondering?"

"Defective? Busted? Thrown away? Me? Why should I be? They loved me. I had my own room. My father tried to punch a kid who insulted me and almost had a stroke or something, something terrible. Because of me. They were good to me."

"Sarah, *I* love you."

"Thanks."

"Will you be patient? You came here to me, so you'll give me a chance, won't you? Come out on my calls with me. Spend a day with me. Will your family understand?"

"Of course," Sarah said, biting into a cookie without thinking.

Gloria clapped her hands. "We'll have fun," she said, smiling. Sarah studied her tooth marks in the gingerbread.

The door to the hallways was pounded on or kicked. Karen rang the intercom buzzer. Someone knocked on the door from the General Office. The outside line began to ring.

Lizzie stood up, moved her chair against her desk and walked to the far right-hand corner of her office. There, on a wall rack, hung an old raincoat for emergencies and an umbrella. She leaned her head against the coat. She smelled chemical waterproofing and maybe autumn leaves. She rolled her forehead against the cool, hard fabric as the intercom buzzed again, as the telephone continued to ring, as the door to the General Office was rapped sharply with knuckles. She thought: So which of you's my daughter?

But the face she saw inside her eyelids, and the face she saw as she moved back to her desk and her day, was Stephen's. He'd wet his bed again, and had come to her bedroom from the upstairs bathroom smelling of soap and Willis's after-shave and holding himself, in his blue-and-white-striped bathrobe, too straight.

Lizzie, in her slip, and reminding herself of a scene from a film she barely recalled starring a ferocious Anna Magnani in *her* slip, went to sit before him on the blanket chest and squeeze him to her. Stephen said nothing. He dropped his head forward as she let go, and the top of his head rested above her breasts. She rubbed his shoulders and the back of his head, rubbed along his tensed spine, whispered, "It stops. Everything like this, after a while, just stops. You don't have to do anything. Except relax. Let it happen. Nobody cares. And then you let it go away. It isn't your *fault*, Stephen."

In her office, as her guidance counselor for the college-bound told her about eleventh graders exploding into tears, as they delineated ways to head off the panic and pain of their students, Lizzie thought of Sarah, and she thought of Sarah's child.

The counselor, a woman who had been pre-law in college and had grown to loathe her history classrooms, said, "What?"

"Nothing," Lizzie said. "I was thinking about kids."

"This place would be all right," the counselor said, "if it weren't for them."

He stayed in Espanola. He didn't know why. It was too far from Santa Fe, it wasn't much more than a location for hot roads and heavy traffic, fast-food joints and the usual New Mexican drive-through liquor stores: Bring me your tired, your Native American. He stayed in the Arrow Motel, with its red neon Indian bending a bow to shoot, if you followed the probable trajectory, Jake's Dirty Shorts Laundromat. It was hot in the room in spite of the air conditioner stuck through the side window. It was dark and airless and small, and all of it was the color of sand, except for the coverlet, which was made of something that felt chalky and was the same pink Barrett associated with the interiors of wounds.

He stayed in Espanola, and he did know why. Its lack of shade and silence, its emphatic service to the underclass, meant that he was different from Sarah. She would be in Santa Fe, able to make use of shade trees and restaurants that dentists and their wives could comment on after seeing photos of them in *Gourmet*. She could drink frozen margaritas with women from Texas and Oklahoma who were in Santa Fe to spend money, to stroll on legs longer than he was and to say "Fuck you" to anyone they wished. He was here with the long-distance truckers and the drunks and the people who weren't homeless, precisely, but who nevertheless hadn't homes.

He ate Mexican food and spent his pre-nap moments vomiting. He slept and he dreamed of the Martian landscape he had driven through — the pink hills that ran to pink plateaus and then the far distant mountains that seemed almost close in their blue-pink clarity. Everything he saw he seemed to see through magnifying lenses. He dreamed that Stephen wept. He dreamed that Sarah would not respond to him. She stared, but not at Stephen, with an immobile face, and his rage made his dreaming boil. He was going to slap her, and he knew that he would slap her *hard*. He knew in his sleep that the blow, delivered mostly with the heel of his hand, would slam her face back, but that she wouldn't fall to the ground of the airport they stood in as Stephen, standing alone near a saffron-robed Moonie with round eyeglasses and a loving smile, repeated to him how wrong he'd got it — that life was *delicious*. The music of the airport was giving him a headache, he shouted at Sarah, and she should have known that it would. She didn't respond, and he felt his arm swing slowly around, he saw his body uncoiling like a batter's bringing his bat around in slow motion. His entire body was launched at Sarah, and he woke in an explosion of pain, lying on his back on the dark, gummy carpeting of the Arrow Motel, blood on the floor and on his hands and his undershorts.

"Okay," he said, as if someone inquired after him or were alarmed. "It's fine. A dream. Just a dream. You always say that: Just a dream. *Ow!*" He sat, shoulders against the bed, his hand pressed hard to the cut on the back of his head. He had driven himself, somehow, into the far corner of the bedside table. He saw his blood on it, and wondered how much blood, now infected with precisely what, had been spilled on the surfaces of his room.

"I can walk all right," he said to no one's solicitous questioning. "I'm fine. I do this all the time." In the bathroom he washed his head and saw the bright, plentiful blood, remembering that scalp wounds were said to look worse than they actually were. It sounded like a *Reader's Digest* fantasy to him, because the bleeding simply wouldn't stop. He turned on the shower and was about to sit on the tiled floor until he thought of what might have been washed down that drain. He compromised by endangering his feet and standing, chin on his chest, under the cool water in his boxer shorts. Water doesn't stop bleeding, he thought. On the other hand, he had no idea what to do. How do you treat a self-inflicted blow to the back of the head when you're in the Arrow Motel by yourself?

Sarah often woke him as his more kinetic dreams approached a crisis. She said that he dreamed loudly, that he seemed to always have nightmares, that he ground his teeth and interrupted his buzz-saw snores with cries of anger and defiance. He muttered a lot of warnings, she told him, as if he ought to be controlling himself. "You're always getting people," she said. He had told her his most nonchalant "It's get or be got, Sarah," but had been puzzled. For he rarely remembered the experience of the dreams she swore, from outside them, he thrashed in. Several times he had hurled himself out of bed — "levitating," Sarah called it. He knew that she blamed him for the depth of his uncontrol. He refused to apologize for his nighttime mind, and his refusal, he knew, seemed to her a kind of extension of his secret angers, and she resented his failure to repent.

"I'm all right," he said in the shower. The water that sluiced off his stinging cut seemed only pink, or even clear. "I'm going to be fine." He would tell the fat, taciturn woman with a dirty cast on her wrist behind the motel desk that he had soiled a towel with a nosebleed, and he would offer to pay. He would find a drugstore and buy antiseptic and keep his wound clean. He would buy aspirin for the headache and because he had read that an aspirin a day can prevent heart attack and stroke. He didn't think that the pain running down his left shoulder to his elbow was his heart, but he would begin to treat himself as if his heart had grown weak.

Why not? Everything else seemed mildly disabled.

He had all of Sarah's souvenirs of their trip to Santa Fe, including the Chamber of Commerce map. Paseo de Peralta, he remembered from before his nap. You drive in on the Paseo de Peralta, and you look for the Palace of the Governors. You look for the Indians selling silver and pottery outside of the museum.

He thought of Sarah's electric wheel and the kiln they had bought after much careful research. He thought of the riverbank smell of the clay under wet, reddened rags. He had the bloody towel around his shoulders, and he thought of his head as something she had pulled up on the wheel and then shaped. He remembered her narrow back bent over the wheel, the intensity he could read in the line of her shoulders and upper arms, the sense of flexibility about her forearms and the remarkable tension of her neck. He often wanted to kiss her neck, and not out of passion: he had wanted, he understood, to interrupt that total absorption. He had wanted to force her to let him come *in*.

And instead, without discussing it, without preamble, she'd gone out to the little shed they had made a pottery room, and disconnected the wheel and kiln. She hadn't dramatized the decision by smashing the bisque and slip. She had merely ignored it all from that Saturday morning on, in the third year of their marriage. He hadn't known her to enter the shed again. After they had made love desperately one night, had been remote from one another in their lust but were satiated, he had asked her why she didn't make pots anymore.

"I took it as far as I could," she said.

"No," he said, "you were good."

"Good doesn't cut it" was her answer. He was pretty sure she'd pretended, after that, to be asleep.

So: the Paseo to, it looked like, Washington or Grant, and then down to West Palace. He would park at the Convention Center or sneak into a hotel lot and walk to the Palace.

The thing in his arm was tension. He was far too young for

something like that to be, you know, he simpered, drying himself with the remaining thin, narrow towel. Tension. Take an aspirin, plan your glide paths when you go to sleep, come in on the Paseo and walk around in your sunglasses and find your wife. Antibacterial ointment for the scalp, aspirin for the head and, you know, and then the drive to Santa Fe.

Call Stephen.

The front desk: tell her about the towel.

Call *Stephen*.

He would handle that when he came back. The front desk, the whitewashed adobe drive-in liquor store for something sour mash-y, the ointment and aspirin, the Paseo and sunglasses and the Governors' Palace and pots and then Stephen on the telephone. Sweetheart, it's Daddy, hello.

The temperature in Santa Fe was dropping, although the sun was brilliant, so he passed tourists in short-sleeved bright cotton and couples in matching dark leather jackets. Everyone wore sneakers except for the women in espadrilles. The infrastructure people, the Indians and Hispanics and the frequent mixtures, were only in transit — in cars or buses, and moving from one or the other to the side and back doors of restaurants and bars. He followed traffic in the circle around the inner city, not turning off to go uphill to the houses of artists and gallery dealers, the shaded elaborations and extenuations of primitive dwellings — Adobe Upscale — where the young professionals scored cocaine with which to impress each other. At last, he followed a car down East Palace to the Posada, which he thought he recognized from their visit. There was an office up front, in a wing of what he saw was a late-Victorian mining magnate's version of a hacienda. He drove past the office and saw that guests stayed in small adobe cabins. Each seemed to have two or three apartments in it. Hotel workers moved about the walks and lawns, carrying trays or bundles of piñon wood from the main house to the pink-orange bungalows. He parked beside a pool that hadn't been opened for the season yet and strode off as if he had a right to be there. He found himself on the map and walked due east toward the Palace.

He felt the sour mash, which he'd taken as a stay against the pain of his self-inflicted cut and as a kind of antidote to what the dream had been about. You are not responsible for your dreams, he firmly instructed himself. Nor, today, are you responsible for the sour mash, which is also self-inflicted. People in the street struck him as wealthy. They walked with the sort of arrogance tourists adopt in order to assert to other tourists that they are far from unfamiliar with the town — nearly locals themselves, you could say, having dined here once already and having endured their altitude-sickness headache. A lean man with close-cropped gray whiskers came loping by in body-hugging shorts with a big black Labrador retriever on a bright purple leash. Barrett believed that he had never seen anyone as happy as the dog seemed. He was jealous of the loping man's thigh muscles, of the dog's complete gladness.

A heavy, pretty Indian woman in a man's felt hat carried a closed tray of what he was certain was silver she'd not sold. Her face was sealed to him. She leaned against a wrought-iron fence at a bus stop. She suggested disappointment. He considered offering to buy something, a gift. Yes, and who would receive it from you with pleasure? What would this person think you were trading it for?

In the bright setting sun, men and women sat against the wall outside the museum of the Governors' Palace. They wore licenses on tags on their jackets or shirts. They were dressed in expensive leathers or bright traveler's cotton — variations of the tourists' costumes. The men mostly wore boots, though some wore sneakers. They sat on blankets or boxes, their silver and pottery arranged with care and tapped, from time to time, with feather dusters. Tourists broke the sunlight over the goods and the vendors, throwing shadows upon them. "This is all my work," the Indians said softly as shadows dropped on their turquoise bracelets, dark pottery, traditional fetish figures and solid-silver money clips. "This is all my work," they said. "Feel free to touch it." One young man, tall and fat, drinking hot coffee from a paper cup and squinting into the sun, pointed to his wares with a broken car antenna and named their prices. Then he tapped the antenna against the ground with increasing loudness. Barrett felt the man's anger, and he had to smile. The young man didn't smile back. He beat the rhythm of his rage.

When Barrett had very slowly, with great care, walked behind the tourists and in front of the Indians, had paused at the pots and especially the black ones, always her favorite, he was near the courthouse and Burro Alley and he hadn't seen Sarah. According to the map he could, if he were in his car, go right a short distance on Grant, left onto Johnson, drive several blocks to North Guadalupe and take it to 285, driving north toward Taos. And, just like that, he could slip out of Santa Fe and be very much elsewhere. That was what Sarah could have done, with her long legs and narrow back and the muscles of her neck and upper arms that he had watched as she worked at the pottery wheel.

She could so easily have driven away! Now he felt the despair he knew he should have felt earlier but that the energy of motion itself had kept at bay. He wanted to cry like a boy. He would do it with Stephen, he thought. Tonight he would call his son and sit in a bar among the hip and in-transit. Tomorrow he would waken early and eat a decent meal in someplace friendly, and he would divide the map into grids. Was he not a man who worked mathematically? Who else could divide, and understand the divisions of, a pattern of dwellings? He would use his fine-point mechanical pencil and the edge of a shirt cardboard and he would create a system whereby he would then conduct a search. Man, he told himself, marching toward the Posada past pottery stores and jewelry boutiques, is that animal capable of searching with more than his senses. Yes. But he would so much rather, to tell you the truth, have been that black dog running in his collar as if he were free.

"Venus's looking-glass," Gloria said. "It likes the gravel near the edge of the road. It's a purple kind of bluebell that a lot of people confuse with Indian tobacco. Now *that* has poisonous seeds. Of course, who'd be eating them? It's a bluebell too. Scarlet tanager! Did you see him? They *flit* across the road!" Gloria drove with a sawing motion so that the wheel was never still. Unless she pointed at a plant or a bird, or a red squirrel panicked on the buckled, pitted asphalt, she gripped the wheel with intensity and drove as the rhythmless dance.

And suddenly, on a dirt track that heaved the car right and left as its wheels more often straddled the road than occupied it, Gloria said, "I was a wild girl. No excuses. My father didn't rape me the way they all seem to do these days. My mother wasn't a drunkard or a dope fiend. I went bad. Actually, I believe I started *out* bad. I did mischievous things. I broke precious objects through carelessness. Food spoiled on account of my neglect. They didn't love me, of course, and, looking back, I don't blame them. We didn't have an affectionate household to begin with. I started bent and I got crooked. Shoplifting. Stealing money from teachers' purses, and boyfriends from my so-called girlfriends, and smoking in the girls' rooms and on the street corners, and into the bars at half past six with bad boys on motorcycles from the dog-food factory and the truckers on their way here and there. I don't know that I much enjoyed the sex, though I surely pursued it. I can tell you, I don't miss it now. I've — if you don't mind my raising the topic — I've stayed to

127

myself, if you understand me. Self-control and discipline have been my watchwords since I straightened my life out."

Sarah sat against the door as they bounced into the hardpan dooryard of a paintless, bleached-out clapboard farmhouse that didn't seem to have been planned but that had grown like a fungus — enclosed entryway, side mudroom, backroom addition, a further addition to the side of the back in a different gauge of clapboard. On the front porch, which was long and like the kind of gallery Sarah recalled from the Southwest, a child watched a cat that glared at the child. The cat was white with a tail that looked bobbed. The child was almost as white, with red-rimmed eyes and a filthy sweatshirt over a disposable diaper and shoes that looked too large.

"I'm not making excuses for myself," Gloria said. "I suppose I ought to apologize. I'm not sure I'm doing that either. I'm trying to tell you who I was."

"Did you, I don't know, get religion or something?"

"I'm too much of a scientist for religion," Gloria said, laughing, as if Sarah had been awfully naïve. "I'm discovering — I'm learning about what holds the universe together. I'm learning how it *works*. The orderliness of the cosmos is terrifyingly beautiful. You feel unworthy of it sometimes."

"You do?"

"Oh, yes. I do. You will too, once you learn its parts."

"Parts," Sarah said.

"I have to see this woman's father. He's dying. He's been dying for an awfully long time. It's some kind of cancer, and he won't go to the hospital and she won't make him go." Gloria pointed to the child, who now stared at them instead of the immobile white cat. "That's his son," Gloria said. "His son and hers."

"Her *father* —"

"Yes, ma'am. She's her brother's mother. Isn't family wonderful?"

Gloria left Sarah in the car as she hauled her black doctor's satchel to the house. Through the unscreened front door she spoke to a small figure who leaned in and out of the dimness of the house. Then Gloria was inside, and Sarah and the child regarded one another. Sarah tried a smile. The little boy cocked his head, as if he too were a cat.

Through the spongy-looking walls of the house and over the hard-baked mud of the yard and through the closed windows of the car came a wail, someone in terrible pain. The child looked up, then stared at the front door. Sarah watched the cat, which leaned forward along its forepaws and seemed to go to sleep. The child went back to studying the cat. And Sarah thought about the wonder of families. She closed her eyes and drifted in the shallows of sleep and was wakened by Gloria's entering the car and replacing her satchel in the back, buckling her seat belt and starting the engine.

"What was that yelling?" Sarah asked.

"The daughter. Her father's pain was bad, and she started to fall apart. Again."

"She really loves him."

"Call that love," Gloria said. "Why not?"

"Those poor people. That horrible life. What could you do for him?"

"I could kill him, I suppose. Smother him with a pillow. Let her collect whatever insurance there is and get on raising whatever it is she gave birth to."

"The cat, maybe," Sarah said, and had trouble with the tone of her giggle.

Gloria said, "But weren't they strangers to you, Sarah? Didn't you — I always thought this. I thought about you all the time, understand. Didn't you feel *outside* them? The ones who raised you?"

Sarah found herself thinking with her hands, remembering

how she had hurled the wet clay against the board to work the air bubbles out. She smelled the rich, dark cellar smell of the clay. She heard the low hum as the kiln began to heat. She thought she could remember when, with a stinging tautness in the back of her neck, she looked at the mound of clay and decided not to work it that day, or again. She thought of the figure at the door of the bleached-out farmhouse, the stillness of the child on the porch.

"You think you're entitled to this, Gloria? All right. Yes. Sometimes. When we fought. Sometimes when we didn't. Yes. So what? I might have been furious or crazy, but I always eventually knew or remembered: I could have been in an orphanage, or raped by those fathers and foster fathers and uncles you've been hearing so much about lately. You know what you hear on TV."

"I never watch it. I read."

"Fine. *I* see TV. I saw it. Kids hear things. School, for the children, is like a giant television set. I always knew what I'd gotten away from. Been taken away from. *Rescued* from. You know what, Gloria? This isn't fair to my — ask *them* what you need to know. Because they were there with me when I was feeling it."

Gloria strangled the steering wheel and slammed them over ruts. She looked up at a hawk hanging high over the hilltop they were on. Sarah thought the hawk was the luckiest creature on the face of the day. In a low, calm voice, Gloria asked, "Why ever did you come, then, Sarah?"

"I think it's about the kid I've terrified by taking off from him."

"My grandson? The boy you —"

"My child. Not your grandchild."

"Oh, what's yours is mine a little, Sarah. It's a biological fact. And if you don't know if you love your own child —"

"Don't say that."

"Isn't that what *you* said? Isn't that something about why you came?"

"Not *whether* I love him."

"Oh."

"About what it *means*," Sarah said. "Loving. Families. Just what it means. You're the one to talk about not loving kids."

"Oh, I loved you."

"Later on."

"Maybe."

"That's so terrible to say," Sarah whispered.

"You don't want to believe loving can stop, Sarah."

"For me it can't."

"Prayer? Or fact? I work with facts, Sarah. Loving is possibly a learned behavior. I'm not certain. I do know that some of me is continued in some of your son. In my —"

"No," Sarah said. "He isn't yours. He's not. Maybe I am. Maybe, strictly speaking, I am. Stephen isn't."

"Well, don't get excited, dear. Don't be alarmed. There's nothing to worry about. Oh! That little peek of orange and black: the Baltimore oriole. They're such shy birds. Tell me about your husband. Relax. Tell me all about your husband."

About the smell of phlegm on his breath because of his panic over losing a bid, over a bank's rejection of his plan for a suburban branch, over redesigning a former Railway Express depot for a maybe debt-ridden shoe company, over his annoyance with Stephen, over his sentimental worry about Stephen, over his rage at Stephen's nursery school teacher, over his jealousy because Sarah danced too close with the man he'd considered including in a partnership. About Barrett in bed, lean and athletic and strong and very exciting and — these were the words she had never permitted herself to even think — never quite enough. And so what did she want?

Not *what*.

Don't riddle me, you fucking whore.

Not *what*.

Who.

Oh, please. *Please*. You want your Jackson Pollock lookalike? You want that feisty, temperamental, selfish man who probably still gets into fights at parties? That shaggy red beard and those big hands on those funny short arms? Please. Eddie Slovitz? Oh, Sarah, please.

I do, maybe.

Your noble savage. Your metaphor. Your goddamned cliché.

Maybe so. Maybe so. Maybe, seven years later, so.

"Well," Gloria said.

"Excuse me?"

"Absolutely, dear. Are you hungry? I made us a lunch. I grilled kidneys and sliced them. With pickled onions on pita bread. How does that sound? I have to visit the little boy who fell off the haywagon. Did I tell you about him? He was standing on top of the bales, showing off for somebody sitting outside a house by the roadside. He didn't see the electric line that ran across the road. Oh, he wasn't electrocuted. But I'll bet you he was shocked! That wire plucked him off the wagon and knocked him to the road, and fast. He wasn't wearing a shirt. It must have been a girl he was trying to impress. There's a boy with road burns, I can tell you. He wouldn't let his mother — she was driving the tractor that pulled the wagon — he wouldn't let her take him to the emergency room. He got good and infected, believe me. I'm sorry about you and your husband."

"What?"

"Now, now," Gloria said. "A mother can tell these things."

And maybe no man at all, Sarah thought.

At the office, Stovall Stratton was setting type. He sat at the keyboard before the high metal rack and assembled the words. As he pushed and pulled, reached high and low, his legs and arms moving, he looked like an organist at the Yankees' farm-club games in Oneonta. Stovall knew that he was one of the last Linotypists and letterpressmen, and was as prized, therefore, as the last plasterers and caners. His round, hairless head — pale as his open shirt, pale as the white undershirt beneath it, pale as the flabby, strong arms with which he inked the slugs and the halftones cut for them in Oriskany Falls — sat quite still on his sloping shoulders. While his limbs moved, his head rode placidly, his weak eyes behind thick trifocals swiveled up and down, from close to medium to fairly far. He looked a little like a machine.

Willis walked toward the stairs to his office and stopped again to hear Stovall's music. He listened to a religious station that affirmed God's love for everyone, even blasphemers, with a heavy thumping beat: Move me to your rhythm, Jeeee-sus / I'm a wall-flower at the final heav'n'ly *dance!*

He sat before his Royal 440 manual typewriter and tried to make his thick fingers hit the right keys. A woman in the DeMott Infirmary in Norwich was one hundred years old, and Willis was telling the world. Except, he found, he was typing another letter to Sarah that he would tear up into confetti, since he suspected Stovall of inspecting his wastebasket — a born-again spy in the service of Jesus.

> *Sweetheart,*
> You have to remember how, when they put Stephen onto the pillow beside you, you loved him completely and right away. We didn't have a pillow. We used Mom's arms and chest to cushion you, with me afraid to touch you because I might break a part off or something. But we loved you at once, absolutely and immediately. No qualifications. No hesitation. Every cell inside each of us had been speeding toward you, we were both convinced, since the day of our birth. We remain convinced. We're talking about you as our fate and us as yours. I don't think you can shake that stuff off, Sarah, like sand you pick up at the beach. Beach? Sarah, I'm talking about a *beach?* I'm talking about our entire lives, all of ours, of course,

Barrett's and Stephen's and yours and ours. I have my suspicions about how all right it is with Barrett. But Stephen! And us, Sarah. Tell me your troubles, and I'll tell you mine. Or I won't. Whichever you want. Be all right and get back to Stephen. When we know that, we'll be all right too. I used to lie in bed on weekend mornings with you spread out on my chest when you were tiny. I used to hold you in place. You used to pull my chest hair to get yourself up so you could look down into my eyes and drool on me.

Willis had to stop. Listening to the cluster flies buzz against the window, he lit a cigarette and then pulled the page from the typewriter. He found he couldn't tear it. He put it into a brown kraft envelope and sealed it with tape, then he pushed it into the middle left-hand drawer of the desk, where he kept material for which he didn't have a category in his files. The clacking of the Linotype came up through the floor along with the amplified guitars and windshield-wiper bass of rockin' Jesus. Willis thought about Stephen, who now, after he washed and dressed for school, walked past them every day as they drank coffee, calling good morning from inside his daily defeat as he went into the pantry to do his morning's wash.

SHE FLED to her bedroom if not into sleep as early as she could. Gloria had cooked them gluey lamb shanks and an acid-tasting potherb that she said was sheep sorrel. "You can boil these leaves up good and make a kind of rennet. Do you know what that is? Sort of a pudding? Sort of — did they ever feed you Junket? It's like that." When Gloria brought a decanter out of the darkness of the rest of the first floor and into the bright light of the lamp that hung from a rafter over the dining table, Sarah knew it would be dandelion wine. But it wasn't. Gloria poured some into a small green glass on a short stem. "Dogberry," she said, and Sarah thought of large dogs lifting their legs on bushes in the woods near Gloria's house. Laughing at Sarah's expression, Gloria said, "It's also called mountain ash, sillyhead. Would I give you *dog* to drink?"

In her ancient-looking flowered housecoat, in bedroom slippers and a cardigan she wore over her shoulders — everything in a different shade of orange, Sarah noted — Gloria crossed her thick legs and leaned back against the ladderwork of her old cane chair and sighed. "It's so good to be sitting with you after a pleasant meal, Sarah. Did you like the lamb?"

Sarah nodded. "I'm awfully tired," she said.

"But we can try, can't we, to get to know each other?"

"I don't think we will," Sarah said. "I lived a lot of my life already. I've got a whole old set of problems. I don't know why I did this."

"Yes," Gloria said. "You wanted me as much as I wanted you. These connections aren't severed. They exist, and we either follow their demands, their requirements, or we don't. But they're part of our lives. You can know me as your mother, Sarah."

Sarah felt her shoulders curve, her head bend. She almost slapped the wine glass back onto the table. The weight, the pressure of this failure and the others, she thought, would crack her bones. She felt them splintering. She felt her organs, one by one, swell beneath the crush, then wetly explode. "I could have met you on the bus," Sarah said. The words grated against the back of her throat, and her tongue felt sore. "I mean, what's the big connection? You were a wild kid and you fucked some boys and you got knocked up and you got rid of it. Listen. I mean this. I'm glad you had some options in your life. I'm glad things worked out for you. But — listen, I'm sorry, Gloria. But you don't mean anything to me." She watched Gloria as the words reduced her, as the tone of her muscles receded with the color of her round, pretty face. "And if you don't mean — well, you don't. I'm sorry. But then who am I supposed to be to my baby? Who's he to me? What about my — shit, Gloria. What about my parents? Who could I possibly be to them or them to me or anyone to anyone to *anyone?*"

Gloria pushed herself forward. She nodded, once, as if in response to a request. She put her hands on her thick thighs as she sat sideways to the table and leaned in Sarah's direction. "This will not kill either of us," she said.

"It ain't Atlantic City in the summertime."

"From what I read," Gloria said, "and I see an awful lot of newspapers, neither is Atlantic City."

Sarah sat back as Gloria leaned forward. She required that

she not weep. Yet she felt the tears come at once from under her closed lids. Gloria cried too. They cried alike, Sarah saw, cheeks unmoving, tears sliding down as if on a business separate from that of the face. Thank you, Sherlock Holmes.

"May I tell you something, Sarah?"

"Not that the man who — not that he died of AIDS."

"He died of wounds, remember?"

"I'm sorry."

"I'd be dead by now. I don't believe there *was* AIDS then. There was plenty else. Syphilis and gonorrhea were what frightened us. And pregnancy, of course."

"At least you caught *some*thing," Sarah said. She even laughed. She raged at herself for cajoling, for trying to cajole, the misery out of this dessert. A perfect dessert, she thought, telling herself that if she called it *just*, there would be terrible consequences exacted by her on herself. "I'm sorry. About everything. I'm not what you wanted, and I can't be who you might need me to be."

"You're my daughter. You're smart and tough and a professional with taste. I admire that. I'm proud to know you."

"Stop it, Gloria. There isn't any *us* to us. You know that."

"And you're a mother," Gloria said, giving no indication of listening. "I'm a grandmother. What can I do but thank you? And ask that —"

"*No*," Sarah said. "Don't ask. You will not meet him. No. He's in another life, Gloria."

"I understand," Gloria said. "Shall I tell you something, though?"

Sarah shrugged. "As long as you understand what I'm telling you about Stephen."

"I hear every word you say. But listen to this, now. What so upsets you about your lack of feelings for me? Your discovery that everyone in the world is so separate that there isn't hope for — what: conjunction? communion?"

"Family."

"All right. Let me suggest this. Let me suggest you didn't learn that from me, here, in the worst of Pennsylvania at a bad time."

She watched the precise movement of Gloria's limber mouth. It was like watching your teacher in the heart of a lecture. You knew you had to pay attention, but you kept seeing the tongue inside the mouth, the lining of the lips, the way an *s* or *l* was shaped, and you lost the direction of the language you saw forming. "I'm sorry," Sarah said. "What?"

"You knew it, I said. Or you thought you knew it. Or you were frightened you thought it or knew it. You came down here so I could be proof to you that a family can't work. That a lover or marriage or being a parent — Sarah: being a *child* — can't ever work. What you say you've taken away from here, the lesson you think you've learned, is what you brought in."

"So I'm just —"

"Oh, it isn't anything simple. You've fallen into an old well. It's almost empty, but at the bottom there's enough despair to drown in. The sides are slimy and mossy, and the stone's too smooth to climb. That's where *you* are, Sarah."

"Who put me there, though?"

"And you say you aren't a child, Sarah? They're the ones who read the world as something that happens to them."

Sarah sat up, then stood up. She nodded. "And you say you aren't a mother?"

"No, you did."

"No," Sarah said. "I told you that you aren't mine."

As she walked from the table, taking care not to stalk angrily or in defeat, she squinted as if to penetrate the darkness. She wanted to remember the little house. Her mouth was filled with its tastes. Her stomach ached from the foods she'd been fed. She wanted her visual memory sated — with the bright, fairly inexpensive area rugs that were well chosen from good catalogues and middle-scale stores; with the litter of objects on tables and shelves, some of them interesting, most the stuff of touring: stones, dried-up starfish, shells and feathers, leaves affixed to matte board and sprayed into glossy permanence; some imitation Meissen platters, a long oval ironstone platter with interesting raised decorations, a couple of semi-fraudulent pots with traditional Acoma designs in brown and black and white painted on what felt to her like bisque imported from Taiwan, where it was mass-produced for the Indian industry; few books outside nursing manuals and guides to birds, flowers, weeds, mushrooms, trees, the common poisons, the basic diseases. As she walked, she tried to peer at them again. But Gloria had lighted the house for their meal in imitation, Sarah thought, of Gloria's mind: the bright light had pooled around them, and everything else had been sealed back into the dark.

I must be so goddamned predictable, even to a stranger like my mother, she thought. For there were her other underthings, washed and dried and folded, and there was her bag. In a doubled brown paper bag were a jar of, probably, dogberry wine, a plastic bag of gingerbread cookies, a plastic bag of what looked like nuts — doubtless the dried ovaries of dragonflies, Sarah thought. Something for early departure: the flag lowered in graceful defeat? Interesting woman, Gloria. Just not interesting enough to, you know, *know*.

Sarah lay under the covers and wiggled her toes against the cold cotton of the sheets. She turned onto her shoulder and, surprised by almost sleeping, was jolted to a wakefulness. She closed her eyes and tried to lull herself. She told herself that she was drifting. She told herself that she was lying on the air and drifting toward sleep. But she thought of herself as standing, and in someplace dark and mean. She thought of a stairway, of having been stolen away to it from a party upstairs. She watched Barrett hurry down the stairs from the loft. He rushed. The stairs sounded hollow, and she wondered if Eddie, upstairs, stoned and smirking, very pale, with sweat in little beads on his forehead and neck, could hear them going away from him.

Barrett didn't look up at her, she remembered, but she could feel the urgency of his need for her to hurry down and away before Eddie reclaimed her in person, or before — and she remembered how she waited to feel herself do this — before she was tugged back up into the smoke and stink and music and chatter by what you might as well call tethers. Wasn't her slow, languorous descent a proof to Barrett of how hooked to Eddie she was? Or wasn't that pace, that bitchy provocation, her attempt to stall herself before she left Eddie Slovitz as, since midway through her dance with Barrett, she had speculated she would?

Sarah remembered actually saying to herself these words: *I am falling.* She let herself clump stiff-legged, hippily, down the stairs toward Barrett. *I am falling into some kind of love,* she told herself as she went down each dark riser to Barrett, waiting below. *I'm allowed to be happy. You're* supposed *to be happy. I'm allowed to feel like a girl instead of a muse. Instead of the assistant muse. Handmaid to the painterly muse,* she said, but not aloud.

His back to her, his long pale hands propped on either side of the narrow door to the street, his head lower than his shoulders, Barrett — this new man whose back was turned to her, but whom she knew she could force to turn around — said, "Could you kind of hurry, Sarah?"

And she said, through a grin she wouldn't suppress, "How come?"

"I'm dying to kiss you," Barrett said. "Frankly." Then he did turn around to lean on the door, his hands at his sides.

"Frankly," she mocked.

He shrugged. "That's me," he said to her, six steps up.

She jumped off the stairs, forward and down, curious about what he would do.

He stepped forward and caught her, and they stumbled together.

"So that's you," she said. She said, "All right."

"Not all right," she said in the room in Gloria's house. She went barefoot from her room to the stairs. Other lights were on downstairs. The set was being struck. She ran on her toes to the room with the phone, and she tapped out the numbers in a hurry. It rang in the Bucks County house. She waited ten rings and hung up and called the number in New York. Stephen answered.

He said, "Hello? Mastracola residence?"

She whispered, "It's your mommy, Stephen. It's Mommy."

He said, "Huh? Excuse me? Mastracola residence."

She shrieked her whisper: "It's *Mommy*."

"Oh," he said in a long, soft, sighing syllable, "Mommy," he said. "Daddy said he'd get you back from Santa Fe. When are you coming home, Mommy? Start really soon. It's a hell of a hard drive, he said."

"Baby," she said, "Santa Fe?" The stairs made cracking sounds. In Gloria's room in the dark, her son on the line, her husband in Santa Fe maybe because he was as crazy as she was, Sarah heard Gloria on the stairs. She was filled with fright. "Mommy'll call back soon, baby. Oh. God. Tomorrow," she whispered. "I love you, Stephen, sweetheart. I'll call you soon. I love you." She pushed the receiver onto the cradle of the old, bulky telephone and she heard the extension downstairs give half a ring. She ran on her toes to her room. She turned off the light. She listened at the door. No one came up the stairs. No one walked in the hallway. No one talked on the phone to her son, who had made a sound that reminded her of what his body did at her breast: fasten on hard at the mouth, go limp in her arms so that nothing on the rest of his body was tense or clenched or in need. Her left nipple, the one that had troubled her during nursing, felt suddenly sore. The feeling went away at once. She heard again the long letting go of his voice when she returned to him as sound that pressed at his ear and inside his head.

She packed. She put on laundered jeans, socks, sneakers and a cotton sweater against the chill. She sat at her window and looked into the forest that surrounded Gloria's pond. Through the screen she heard what sounded like a goose, but hoarser. It stopped, and then she heard a *chug* sound, over and over. Insects made spirals of sound — they started low and soft, they rose as if on a piano scale and got louder and then, as she waited each time for the next loudest note, they stopped. Then they started again. The light went from a lit-up pearly blue to blackish blue, as if ink fell down the side of the sky and pooled, and then it was dark. It was never completely dark, for her eyes were used to it, and the light in her bedroom was off. Through the screen she saw the silhouettes of weeds or scrubby trees at the pond. Gloria, she knew, could name everything that stood or grew or hunted or was eaten. She would know what was dying from what deficiencies and what would grow to take its place. There was nothing at the pond or in the world, Sarah thought, that Gloria didn't know by first name and couldn't be said to have somehow digested. Except Stephen, she thought. Not him. Sarah would see to that. And maybe except for Eddie Slovitz: she didn't know anyone who kept too much of Eddie that he didn't want to give. To lend, she amended. She thought of a gavel, of a motion amended and the gavel dropping to make the amendment official.

At the foot of the bed, still looking through the screen, she pulled a cover about her and curled against the cold. She felt breezes on her face, and she smelled the sour, green odors of the pond. She stuck her hands between her legs against the cool wind and thought of closing the window, but she felt too cold to remove her hands or to leave the blanket's shelter. She closed her eyes and remembered when she had lain like this.

They were making love, she and Barrett. It was winter, the

bedroom was cool, they had seen to Stephen, asleep, and they had snuggled under the blankets, shivering. Their comfort in each other's temperature had turned to appetite. Barrett was in one of his angry, big-eyed, tight-lipped moods, and she was surprised that his lean body appealed to her. No, she wasn't, she remembered thinking even then: there was, in that harsh, at first unapproachable, but finally quite approachable sullenness and — that was it — cruelty, an appeal for her. At few other times, but often at times like these, he had to do with hungers. She thought of his body then as angular, with edges, like something metallic that might cut her. She moved her hands on him with care and greed at once, and she knew that the combination made his sexiness a kind of anger, he grew so huge and athletic. The more carefully but persistently she moved about his body, the more stirred he became. She licked, she nipped with lips, she bit just a little, she pushed her fingers into his mouth, his ears, his anus, she burrowed with the top of her head and prodded with her knees and thighs, and he held her, kissed her hugely, cupped her buttocks as she lay on him, pulled her on and in and suddenly, as she'd thought he would, he surged — seized her so that her back and arms hurt, and turned her over, bruising her thighs with his knees, hurting her breasts with his head, pushing her back against the headboard while she lay beneath him so that her neck was at a difficult angle and breathing wasn't easy. He grunted the same noises, over and over, as if he were conversing, but maybe with himself, and in a language no one else could speak: Uhm-*hm* uhm-*hm*.

Sarah remembered how, in the dark room and under her closed eyes and in the world inside her senses, she reached back and held the headboard with both hands and, at the same time, splayed her legs beneath him, so that she lay as if bound to the bed, as if his unwilling victim. She became hot and more liquid as she thought of herself that way. I'm all tied up on the bed, she thought. I'm helpless on the bed. He's pushing it into me, all the way up, oh Jesus, and I'm all tied up on the bed.

And like the wind from Gloria's pond, like something that had entered her body by surprise, she realized — arms cocked out, and legs, nothing but breasts and stomach and crotch beneath him — that she was. She was bound on the bed. She was helpless, she was as good as tied, she was hungry in her senses but not exactly for this, for all of this, for most — for any, goddamn it — of this. Not exactly, she thought in Gloria's house. Not quite. But as close as you can get to being right: not exactly, not for all, not for most, and close enough to not for any. She raged with want, and she didn't, and she was nearly tied to the bed.

"No," she said.

Barrett said, "That's right."

"I mean it," she said.

"You mean this," he said, forcing her thighs wider, forcing her buttocks closer to him, forcing his finger in next to his penis so that she was stretched and filled too full. "You mean this." He pumped into her and she held her own knees so that her vagina was open to him, she held herself wide for him because she wanted and didn't want this and she was filled with him and sick, simultaneously, with herself. "You mean this," he groaned, and collapsed on her, almost whimpering, lying still in her, his legs prone between hers as she continued to lie, her arms cocked and legs spread, as if she were tied to the bed.

He rolled over her thigh, apologizing when she winced as his leg pressed the side of her knee. When he lay beside her and said "Mmmm," she rolled to her right side and pressed her hands between her legs, drew her knees up toward her face and dropped her face down along the loosened sheet. She wept in the darkness in silence. He said "Mmmm" again, and stroked her back and buttocks. "Mmmm." She wondered whether women were born with a talent for weeping in silence so that after a rape or a semi-rape or a self-rape, a dual rape, a straight-out vicious fucking, they could cry and not have to talk with the owner of the penis about his sorrows over their failure to understand what everyone had meant in the dark.

So it became necessary in the home of the woman whose womb she had inhabited to think about Edwin Slovitz. They had lived together for some months, though not officially until the very end. Instead, each had kept an apartment and they'd commuted, usually late at night, by bus or foot or sometimes by cab, from the bed of one to the bed of the other. She'd been painting, then, with what Eddie had called a muddy palette. She asked and he told. That was the trouble with him. That was also, of course, the good news too. You asked him, and he told you.

"Am I good, Eddie?"

"Well," he said, standing in a towel, his little bit of belly, even then, showing over the towel, and his thick, peasant muscles — for lifting, she thought in Gloria's house, for carrying over very long distances — drew her eyes to his chest and shoulders. There was nothing that he couldn't open. There were few objects he wasn't able to lift. He painted, as a rule, with fairly large brushes because his muscles were made for thick, broad strokes, an almost impasto surface that defeated his efforts to be delicate. But he could always be careful, when he wished, and knew how to control his paint. He was a student, too, as she wasn't. He never talked about painters or painting: he lectured, often raising a finger to point straight up as one of his reddish brows might rise. And when she asked if she was good, he'd said, "Well," and she knew that he sought a way to say no without crushing her. She remembered her thought, as he searched. She'd thought: I could walk over to you and brush against you and take that towel off as slowly as I like, just looking into your beady little painterly eyes, and fuck you half to death shuddering. And you would

147

open your eyes afterward and, still panting, you would say to me, "Well, it depends on what you mean by *good*. What you want to do. What being good can get you to in your work. You know?" And she wouldn't. She knew it then, she knew it now. She wasn't good, she didn't know. She had taste. She was bright. She wasn't an artist. She was, he had told her during a fight, "something of a murky dauber." She had tried to tear off his ear. And they had made love on a mattress on a floor, Eddie pulling her clothing away and climbing on her, jabbing at her, both of them sweating and Eddie bright red with their remarkable lust, and he had stopped.

"What?" she'd asked, panting.

He lay on her, his jeans at his thighs, the zipper tearing at her leg, his hand in her underwear, her nipple wet from his saliva, and he rose, taking his hand from her, and propped himself above her.

"You look like you're doing pushups, Eddie. You're doing bedroom calisthenics."

"I'm trying to hurt you," he said. He shook his big head slowly.

"No," she said. "You're making love."

"I'm afraid I'm making fuckin' *war*, Sarah. I'm sorry."

"Oh, Eddie, it's all *right*. We're loving."

"I want that very clear," he said. "We're making love. We *love* each other."

"Of course," she said, understanding nothing. "Of course. Eddie!"

"What?" His eyes were closed, and she felt his elbows shudder a little as he held himself away from her. He looked so sorrowful. He looked as if he had been given the very worst of news.

"Get on top of me," she answered. "Get inside me."

And he had smiled, giving in to it at last to grin like a balding boy. "You still trust me?"

"When you're in, will you let me know?"

"Jesus, what a bitch," he said, smiling.

"How will I know when you're in?"

And he'd descended slowly, his weight on his arms, so that his penis brushed her, then rubbed against her, then prodded very gently, then lay unmoving on her as she moved her groin up against him and then seized him in her hand, finally, and drew him in. She kept her hand on him and they lay together against it an instant, and then she moved her fingers away and thrust her belly up.

"Oh," he said. Then: "Am I there yet?"

"There," she said. "There."

"You're sure?" he said, moving on her in a wonderful rhythm, as if they danced to a Latin song that would prove too quick to keep up with. But they kept up. He said, "You're sure."

"Sure, you big bully. You bastard. *Okay*. Okay. God. Yes. Sure." And then, because he'd taken control, she said, "Well. Wait a minute. Let me — ah: is *that* you?"

And he had doubled the rhythm for an instant or two, and she had, she remembered on Gloria's bed, howled. Eddie bellowed. They collapsed and he rolled to the side at once.

"What, Eddie. God. That was — what?"

"I didn't want to be too heavy on top of you."

"You think I didn't hold you up before?"

"Well," he said, "now that you mention it."

"So get back on," she'd said.

On Gloria's bed she fell asleep as if she'd just assisted her husband to rape her. Or as if she had made a sweaty, teasing love with Eddie Slovitz. She dreamed about neither man, but about her son. They were downstairs in a hotel, and she was tying his necktie for the nursery school open house. His neck looked very thin and frail inside the white collar that she buttoned for him. When she knotted the tie she smelled his breath, which reminded her of milk. His eyes stared past her, at something they ought to be worried about. But he wouldn't look at her to tell her what he saw. She couldn't move from her kneeling posture to look, because her neck didn't function and her shoulders ached. She waited for Stephen to say. Stephen stared behind her, and she forced herself to stand, wincing, and to turn, and Stephen screamed. The lobby wall, vast and directly in front of her now, was a giant window. Figures loped purposefully, confidently. They were coming to the hotel for her and Stephen, and she had to protect her son. She reached behind her, didn't feel him, didn't dare to look, and even as she despaired of seeing him, she took a step toward the window to confront the silhouetted figures who filled her with fear. She cried a warlike cry at them and forced herself to raise her hand.

It was the hoarse, desperate cry that woke her. She was screwed up tight on the bed, and the moon was high and bright above the big pond. She still heard the sound of her terror as she folded the blanket, stripped the bed, piled the bedclothes and her towel at the foot of the bed and closed her satchel. She looked at the bag of provisions from Gloria, and she opened her case to put them in with her clothing.

At the little desk, perhaps a child's, she used a pen from a jar of pens and pencils to write a note on a piece of floral stationery she took from a box in the drawer. The flowers looked like tongues and tentacles, she thought. She closed her eyes, and in the dim light of the small lamp she'd turned on at the desk, she wrote, with no salutation:

> I'm sorry to run off. That's what I'm doing. I don't know what to say to you that will be useful or comforting. You do need some kind of comforting, don't you? Who doesn't! But we're strangers. That makes a kind of sense. You gave me up, I guess you had to give me up, before we could know each other. So what's left to us is biology. I'm afraid biology is mostly responsible for a lot of the shit in my life and everyone

else's, so what I'm saying is I guess there's pretty much nothing for us to use to have a relationship with. We started out as strangers, and we're left with what we had. I hope that can be enough for you. Thanks for wanting to know me. This is a pretty big disappointment, isn't it. But thank you.

Sarah

She went quietly, but not like a sneak, down the steps. Turning past the kitchen area, walking through the stubby living room, she paused at the shelves of books and curiosities. In the granular, lightening darkness of early dawn — the birds began their lush, loud calling — she looked at the fake Acoma pot. She took it with her when she went outside to the Blazer and turned the engine over and left.

The tall, broad-shouldered one from Oklahoma or Texas, he forgot which — the one with the big men's shirt of rayon or silk that was open to below her breasts with the tails knotted just below the open buttons — came back sideways. That is, she had to take a major sidestep to regain her balance as she returned from the room that had the bar. All of these people kept their hotel rooms open and assumed that the corridor was theirs, that in fact the Eldorado Hotel was theirs. She had jet black hair in a short hairdo, almost that of a man with a grown-in crew cut. She wore tight black jeans, black boots and a silver-chased black snakeskin belt, and her white shirt and pale skin seemed to gleam.

She had begun to insist at Coyote Café that he drink tequila on ice. "Forget the salt lick," she'd said. "Our *stock* lick salt. That's tonguing a drink. The people I know like to use their whole mouths on alcohol." So he was drinking tequila, shuddering when it went down, becoming *muy borracho*, which he assumed was the idea and which he thought not a bad one. But

151

he kept moving his head, as if Sarah were going to wander into the party that a local architect and his lover, a tough man who ran an adobe construction business, had taken him to at Coyote. They'd fallen away, the bar at Coyote had closed at around ten, and the tall men and women they'd been drinking with at the bar decided to move the party back to the hotel by way of three Mercedes with seats that Barrett thought might have been made of human skin.

The women smelled of Poison and cigarettes. The men smelled like a combination of the car seats and almond soap. Smoke hung low in the room they'd been drinking in for a while, and Barrett, though he moved his head, had little hope.

"I have little hope," he said to Marylinn Conover.

"For what, little man? You tell me your hope, and I'll give you the odds."

"Seeing her."

"Oh. Well, her. The one wandered off on you and your boy."

"Sarah," he said.

She looked at him with her alarmingly green eyes. She studied him and he stared back, intimidated. She had little lines in the corners of her eyes that he found as compelling as anything about her — as if she had stared so long at phenomena he hadn't yet discovered. "You think they're too much too?"

"Who?"

"My eyes. You been looking into my eyes like I'm what's his name, Svengali, or Caribou the Magnificent, one of those conjuror hypnotist types. They too much of emerald, do you think?"

He could only shake his head.

"On account of I bought them this way against my own better judgment. I hate when I do that. Listen to yourself, I always tell myself, but then I think, How can I trust a gal who keeps talking to herself in boutiques?" She turned away and bent forward, stuck her hand with her drink in it toward him. He took the drink, and she worked at her face. When she leaned back, and turned to him again, blinking her eyes, they were gray. She held the lenses on her palm and then, sticking her long fingers into the pocket of his sweated-wet shirt, let the lenses slide in. "Do I look too washed out this way?"

He again only shook his head.

" 'Cause that's what you're stuck with, son. Now you got it all natural, untouched by cosmetologist, surgeon or psychiatrist — the real me, original tits, ass, eyeballs and noo-rosis." She took her glass back and drank. "You ever design a building that was real, you know, *real* beautiful? A work of art for the ages and all?"

"No," he said. "I did a car showroom one time that was pretty remarkable, given the budget and the climate. I still like to look at it. Why?"

"I never knew an architect that did much more than buy his dope by the eighth of a kilo, invest in vineyards or minor league sports teams, try and diddle the interior designers, and go around having penis envy for painters and video artists who mostly starved to death all their lives, that's why. I mean, where *is* the Leaning Tower of Pisa for our time? You know?"

He leaned in close and whispered, "Somebody ought to spank your ass for talking like that to a bona fide servant of the middle class. Somebody ought to — "

"I know," she said, nodding, "punish me. I turn you on when I, in a manner of speaking, lift my leg on you. Come on over here to this table with me, son." She pulled him by his shirt toward the kitchenette of the suite and pushed aside bottles and a bowl of lemons and limes. She sat and indicated for him to sit. She rolled up her left sleeve and bunched a muscle at him. "My pecs are even better, and no saucy talk back, it's just a fact."

"You work out hard," Barrett said, thinking of Sarah in her

iridescent body suit, panting in front of an exercise program on
TV.

"I do everything hard," Marylinn said. "Now you show me
yours."

One of the tall men from Oklahoma or Texas gave a little
whistle and went to stand behind her. He had white hair combed
over in a prep school cut, and he looked to Barrett like an evil
older child. Several men and women joined him as Barrett, embarrassed to stop, rolled up both of his sleeves and tried to make
his arms go taut.

Marylinn took hold of his bicep, worked her fingers around
to the tricep and said, as if she were judging a melon, "Not bad.
But you're going soft, son. Now, let's do this this one time
without burning cigarettes under us or any other kind of sadist
torment. Let's just wrestle to see which of us has, you know, the
biggest dick."

"Bigger," the evil child said.

"Whatever," Marylinn said, finishing her drink and holding it
up behind her for another woman in a shirt and jeans to fetch
for a refill. "Big, biggest, bigger, or Vienna cocktail frank, am I
right?"

She set her right elbow on the table and he set his beside it.
She used her left hand to pull his forearm snug against hers, and
he felt as though they were in bed in front of a crowd. I used
to call that kind of thing a nightmare, he thought, feeling a sort
of pleasure and shame at once.

"Let her rip," Marylinn said. "Who's got a cigarette for the
champ?" A short man in a black suit over a black shirt that was
accented by a silver and black string tie put a cigarette between
her lips. He brushed her upper lip with his finger and she turned
to look at him. "You want to take liberties, old fella," she said,
"take something gonna do either of us some good. Best thing *you*
can do is come up with a match." Blushing, the man in black lit
her cigarette and smiled a dying smile at the others.

And with her lit cigarette wobbling in her mouth, with smoke issuing from her nostrils, Marylinn made Barrett's hand tremble as he tried to hold it erect, never mind push her hand back and down.

"Strong lady," he said, sounding weak to himself.

"And you know what it sounds like to me, Mister Barrett with a double *t?* Way things are happening, it looks like you left your kid as much as the little woman did. In case you ever wondered how I saw your situation. Though who really gives too much of a shit, am I right?"

"Hey," Barrett said. "Marylinn?" His tone made the man in black lean closer. The evil child shook his head, as if Barrett were going to make a dangerous and entertaining mistake. The woman came back with Marylinn's drink. Barrett looked at Marylinn, at her thick lower lip and her almost aquiline nose, at the lines around her eyes and the speculative wrinkle of her forehead, the close-cropped glossy black hair. He put her arm down hard and held it there. When she tried to yield and withdraw it, he continued to press the back of her hand and arm against the sticky, littered small table.

"Now he's done it," the man in black brayed.

Marylinn looked up at him and said, "*Won't* you go find yourself a Mexican boy and lay silent for the night? It's an embarrassment, it really is."

Marylinn leaned back to Barrett, and someone in their audience said, "Whoo-ee, boy."

She took the cigarette from her mouth and brushed a kiss against his lips. She leaned further and whispered in his ear, "So you went and beat a girl, Mister Barrett."

He replied into her ear, "What would you have said if you'd beat me?"

"That you'd have to end up doing *me*," she whispered.

"Whoo-*ee*," the commentator called.

"And now?" Barrett found himself able to say.

He leaned back to look at her face. Most of the others had gone off. The little one in black had lingered, though, and Barrett said to him, "Nice meeting you. Good night, I guess. Is that right?"

"Night, now," he answered and backed away, calling, "Night, Marylinn, honey."

Lighting another cigarette from the pack on the table, Marylinn asked, "You're not going to ask me to do you a hum job, are you?"

He said, "Marylinn, I don't even know what those are."

"Good boy," she said. "I hate doing it. It's just so much *entertainment*, if you know what I mean. Which apparently you don't. That's good. But I tell you what. I'll show you all the rest. If you promise not to be mad on account of I know it and you don't." She stood, then picked up the pack and the lighter and held them in the hand that wasn't grasping his. "Anyway, Mister Barrett, you could maybe just know a little more than you believe you do. And I am no sore loser. Now, you recall that fellow with the big shoulders and the white hair? His name is Pempler, Georgie Pempler, and his older boy — he's about thirty now? another one of you architects I was talking about — he's got nose medicine, and I believe that Georgie brought a little for purposes of acquiring energy on the long drive home. You take this, and you wait a minute or two if you would, and I'll join you presently with the party favors."

She put a room key in his hand. He knew he was in the hallway of their floor. He knew he was close to fourteen feet tall and considerably closer to invincible than he'd earlier believed. He had turned a woman's eyes from green to gray, and had bested the champion of the Philistines, although he couldn't remember if she was named David, Goliath, Samson or Delilah. He accepted that his erection was so enormous just then that he would soon have to shuffle if he didn't find her room. He should have known: it was the one in the vicinity of the party that wasn't open.

Inside, in its surprising neatness and in the absence of double-headed dildos set in readiness on Marylinn's armoire, he cupped his loins in appetite and pride. The door slammed shut behind him and the small man in black clothing stood before him. Barrett hadn't noticed that he wore a very thin mustache. Barrett decided to take Marylinn's tone. "Well," he said.

"Unwell," the little man said. He came closer and Barrett lost his tumescence and his sense of exceptional health.

"Look, mister."

"Mister? Thank you? I kind of thought there you were gonna call me boy or something in the realm of derogatory. Thank you."

"Isn't this Marylinn's room?" Barrett asked. He didn't *think* he had actually whined.

"It sure is, son. Mine and Marylinn's. We're what you would call a set. You know, horse and saddle, brush and comb, man and wife?"

"Wife? You're her husband?"

"Dick Tracy, you've come home at last." The little man smacked Barrett's face with a funny, sharp, chopping blow. Barrett sat down.

"Whoa," Barrett said.

"You almost missed the floor there," the man said. "I'll help you. No. I really insist." His little toe whipped into Barrett's neck and he was lying on the floor. He wondered when the pain came. The man seized his ear between two fingers and the pain came. It went down his jawbone and into his neck. His arm began to throb with the pain he'd felt in his motel room. The cut on his scalp felt raw. His collarbone ached. So did his chin and temple, because the man had whipped his hands on Barrett's face again, and he was going down to the floor.

"Shit," Marylinn said from the doorway. "Goddamn *shit*. You promised me and you promised me again and now you do the same damned goddamned *thing*, Gordon. You're gonna get arrested, I am never gonna get myself laid the way I like to, and we're both going down in the annals of exiled Oklahomans as nothing more than boo-jois trash. Is *that* what you want? What in *hell* did poor Barrett ever really *do* to you, Gordon?"

Gordon rebuttoned his silky jacket and rubbed his hands together briskly. His face was red and sweaty, but he was the happiest-looking man Barrett had seen in a week. "I believe I am not going to comment," Gordon said. "I believe I am going to let actions speak louder than words."

"Me too," Barrett said from his hands and knees on the floor. "No," he told Marylinn, "I can do this one." He pulled himself up on a coffee table made of bright tiles inside a wrought-iron frame, and he finally stood. He didn't know what part of his body to clutch at, except that his loins no longer figured in his list of possibilities. "I believe," Barrett said.

"Oh, no," Marylinn said, holding up a little plastic envelope. "I went and got the goods and everything."

"Why don't you and Gordon here do some together. It'd bring you closer," Barrett said. "Gordon and *I* have got as close as we can get, I believe. And I am not sufficient thereunto for anyone else, Marylinn. I loved meeting you. I'll remember you the rest of my life. You're a better man than I. Good night."

He felt a repeated gentle pressure on his arm. When he looked, he saw that Gordon was behind him, cordially patting him *au revoir*.

He limped along the corridor, even though he'd taken no blows on the legs. He rubbed at the arm that Gordon had stroked, but not because of the stroking. He nodded at the Hispanic bellman in the lobby of the adobe fortress. The bellman didn't nod back.

Why should he? Barrett thought, turning onto West Palace

and clutching himself, all but carrying himself back toward the Posada and his car. Why should he bother acknowledging a drunk who would leave behind a child six years old? Who had driven two thousand miles to find his wife down the front of the shirt of a woman from Oklahoma? As he passed before the Palace, he reached into his pocket and pulled out, one at a time, then shook in his hand like dice, her extra set of eyes.

Because no one in a small town goes to a restaurant without visiting with the entire dining room, Lizzie and Will drove a dozen miles of back road, and a dozen more of highway, to what Will liked to call a roadhouse — a long, low building with several dark rooms in which you ate steak or roast beef, or the requisite deep-sea and therefore low-cholesterol fish, and where no matter the cost of the Burgundy to follow, you started out with a glass of whiskey on ice or, as Will and Lizzie did, dry martinis. She wore a dark olive-bronze dress with long sleeves, and she looked like a smart, tired woman in repose.

"Take it from an older man," Will said, "you look — what?"

"Nothing." She accepted her martini and, when the waiter left, she drank and looked into the dimness of the room.

"For chrissakes, Lizzie, you can't *see* anything in here. That's why we came here. You're not looking at anything, you're look-ing *off* the way you do when you're not fighting when you're fighting."

"I don't know whether it was right to leave Stephen with Karen that way. It's an imposition on her, and Stephen probably figures he's going to spend the rest of his life there. He's probably peeing his pants and staring at nothing the way he does."

"The way you do, too. That isn't what you're worried about. We were a little desperate for a night alone, weren't we? So we could sit here and bullshit each other about not having a fight?"

"Will," she said, "you and I are very nearly the same age. You talk more and more about being old and sick, and I don't feel old or want to feel old. We were going to be *young*, remember?"

"I didn't mean to screw up our plans by having all those birthdays, Lizzie."

"It isn't birthdays."

"You're not, surely, going to say something about a frame of mind."

"Not now," she said.

They sat in their silence until the waiter took their orders and left. The room chimed glassware and furniture, people talked loudly, and Lizzie raised her glass at the waiter, who nodded that he would bring them another round.

"Good gin they're serving tonight," Will said. "Don't you think?"

Lizzie shrugged.

"I didn't expect to break any news," Will said. "I was just trying to show you a different way of groveling."

"Idiot," Lizzie said. "I'm not laughing. I'm not smiling. And I'm not forgiving you. Will," she said, leaning over the table, "we haven't got *time* to be old. Understand? We can't fuss around. We have to get what we can right now. *Now.*"

"I'm game," he said, leaning toward her. "Want to leave and go home?"

"And pick Stephen up later anyway?"

"And —"

"And," she said.

He said, "And." He wrote a check and left it on the table, and they walked to the door, waving like embarrassed school-children at their waiter. In the car Will said, "A good country-woman will slide over and sit next to her man."

"In a stick-shift car, Will, she's going to get the knob of the gearshift caught between her legs."

"I love that."

"Drive, and don't be juvenile."

"I thought the *idea* was to be juvenile."

"Just young," she said. "Young enough."

At the bottom of a long, swooping hill on Route 20, near the turnoff for Eaton, the River Road cuts through less populated countryside, and it dips at points toward deep bends in the river. Willis followed the River Road until they were near a narrow iron-and-wood bridge that went over the river into pasturage. He turned his lights off, and very slowly he drove them toward and then over the bridge. On the other side he turned right, and they bumped and wobbled behind old willows and aspen that grew above the riverbank like a hedge. He shut the engine off.

"I don't believe this," Lizzie said.

"Are you wearing stockings?"

"Well, of course I'm wearing stockings. Pantyhose. How can you be dressed up unless you're uncomfortable?"

"Then we're going to get you comfortable," Will said. He reached for the hem of her dress. She slid lower on her back. "I take it," he said, "you're not fighting the idea."

"I'm spreading my legs, Will. Can you remember back to what that means?"

They made love in their clothing in the front seat of their car. There was the rising and falling drone of insects, and an owl called. And then, carried on the wind as pollen is, came the almost inaudible sound of people calling to one another in a field or the dooryard of a farm. Lizzie and Will were public, they were in the actual world undiscovered, they were thrashing in the front seat of a car like teenagers.

"I keep waiting for you to make me stop," Will whispered.

"So do I. This is crazy. This is crazy."

"I'll stop. You want me to stop?"

"It's my impression," she whispered, "you'd have to be shot to stop."

"Let's wait, Lizzie."

"Wait?"

"I mean, let me . . . Let's slow down a little."

"Oh," she said. "And me with my dress halfway over my head and my ankle banging into the gearshift and all."

"Shut up a minute. Let me —"

"With your pants halfway down over your ass like that. It's a cute little ass, Will."

He said, "This isn't slowing down a little."

"No," she said, "it doesn't feel like it."

"All right," he said, "then don't wait." Lizzie giggled, and Will plunged ahead.

And then he was slumped over her, wrapped around the wheel, the gearshift and the console box. He made a sound of satiation. Then they lay in silence a while.

Lizzie said, "I am so hungry."

"Didn't I take you out for a meal?"

"There's nothing here I especially want to eat," she said. "Though . . ."

"Though," he prompted.

"Well, you never know."

"Will you tell me when you *do* know?"

"Will," she said, "where do you think Sarah went?"

"Shit, Lizzie. Didn't we come out here and go crazy so we wouldn't have to talk about it?"

"Like when your father died. And we all but raped each other half the night. I know what you mean. But no, I think."

"No, you think what?"

"I think we did this because we got horny for each other because we love each other. I've been with you longer than I was alive before we met up, I think. Let it just be what's good about us, all right? If we happen to be a little desperate, it's like salt. No, an herb. It's like rosemary."

"This is like rosemary?"

"All right," she said, "marjoram."

"Getting laid in the front of a car is like marjoram."

"That's right," Lizzie said.

"No wonder," Will said. "No wonder Sarah did something crazy. She's your daughter."

"I really hope so," Lizzie said.

Will half kneeled on the seat to reach her. He kissed her forehead and her temple, her cheek and ear and neck, and he began to trail his lips over her throat. "If this *were* a restaurant, I know exactly what I'd recommend for a second course," he said.

"Thank you," Lizzie said, "but I know just where to find that when I want it. What I can't find is Sarah. Do *you* think she went to Albuquerque?"

"Santa Fe," he said.

"That's what I meant. Santa Fe."

"No. I don't know. I think what matters is she went. Stephen's stuck here, we're stuck here, and Barrett's running around like crazy because she bugged out, Lizzie. She left. That's what matters. *Where* really doesn't. I think the man is minus a wife."

"And the little boy a mother."

In the darkness, he nodded. Then he said, in a warning voice, "I'm getting ready to zip this zipper up, Lizzie."

"Oh," she said. "What you need to do, then, is pull that little metal tab there at the bottom."

"Yes," Stephen told his class and Ms. Thorndyke, "it's true. My mother and father are spies. Now, if your parents are spies, you get to have a lot of fun. It is also very scary and very lonely because you have to be alone a lot or stay at your grandmother's house or a hotel in a foreign country. The fun things, you get to play with your father's and mother's gun. They always take the bullets out and put on the safety thing, switch, so the gun can't shoot by mistake. My mother never wears disguises. Disguises are, you look like somebody else with whiskers. You could not have a lady who is a spy with whiskers. Unless she was spying on enemy people who were hiding out in a circus or something. That never happened to my mom. But it did to my father. He has to wear disguises a lot. He wears different kinds of hats and things. He smokes cigars and pipes and things so the enemy people don't know it's him in the airport or the hotel or places like that. My father carries a Uzi machine gun in his suitcase. My mom carries a little gun that you hide under your belt buckle. They have passports and things but they don't use their real name.

"The thing about spies is, danger. There's a lot of danger. If somebody from the enemy side sees your mom and dad and tells somebody else, well, that's it. You can imagine. The enemy people use poison gas in a, whaddya call those? *Umbrella!* It sprays out. So when it's rainy and you're a spy, you have to be really careful. They also use guns, of course. And knives. My mother hates to carry knives because they cut holes in her stockings and dresses and underwear. So she mainly uses her gun when she can. My dad knows that karate stuff with his hands and feet.

"He goes disguised as an architect a lot. They make up buildings like stores and banks and houses. My father once made up the plans for a moo-zee-youm that had a lot of famous pictures in it, but the moo-zee-youm people liked this other lady's plans better so it didn't get built the way my father planned it. He was home from being a spy. That's what he does when he isn't on a mission.

"My mom goes disguised as an interior designer. They tell you what color rugs and paint to use and what kind of tables and chairs and sofas you need. She says it's a little boring. But she *loves* being a spy. I think that's probably so she doesn't have to, you know, be bored so much.

164

"When she's home from spying, she picks me up at school. She drives a car that's really low, like a Corvette, kind of, except it's a lot faster. It makes that *vroom* noise, and knives come out of the side of the wheels to cut up your tires if you're chasing us. If the coast is clear and it's safe, my mom comes and gets me and I get into the car and she always asks me what I want for my snack. She says, " 'What'll it be, kiddo?' "

He looked at the class and stood with his arms at his sides. He looked at Ms. Thorndyke, who leaned in the far corner of the classroom and looked at him with her eyebrows raised. Stephen shrugged his shoulders at her. Ms. Thorndyke shrugged her shoulders back and smiled a sad smile.

She said, "Thank you, Stephen. Are you finished?"

"He's crying," a girl in the front row called to Ms. Thorndyke. Stephen shook his head.

Ms. Thorndyke took a step toward the front of the room. Noel Kelly, in the middle of the row near the windows, got out of his seat and walked with long steps to where Stephen stood. He took Stephen's hand and pulled him back to Stephen's seat, two behind his. Stephen let himself be towed. Then Noel returned to his seat, and the class looked at Ms. Thorndyke. Noel folded his hands on his desk and breathed as though he'd been running.

"Yes," Ms. Thorndyke said, "thank you."

It was Saturday morning near the end of April, and though you could get away with a light sweater where the sun shone, it was cold in the woods and especially in the shadows of spruce and maple, quaking aspen. Lizzie sat on the rock with her legs drawn up and her arms crossed for warmth. She wore what Will called his barn coat. They had no barn, only a disorderly garage and a wooden outbuilding for storage. But Will had insisted, when they bought the house, on buying from Agway a flannel-lined blue denim jacket with a corduroy collar that was cut to fit livestock, perhaps, or farm hands bigger than men ought to be. And every Saturday, whether he raked a leaf or two before he grew bored, or sorted the bottles from the cans for the recycling center, Will wore his barn coat. Today he was meeting with Mariah Kasselbaum and the others on the burning issue of whether an arrogant boy could decline to salute his country's flag before the commencement of an athletic event of about as little importance to the nation as the identity of the Speaker of the House of Representatives. And Lizzie was in Will's barn coat, listening to Stephen as he swung by a river on a rope.

Stephen was singing, and Lizzie was grateful. It was almost familiar, what he wordlessly sang, perhaps a movie theme, but slower than she remembered. She imagined him — for she stayed out of sight; *cowered*, she might have said — drifting back and forth on the hawser line with his eyes floating on the big trees and the blue-silver water that frothed between rocks and poured surfacelessly toward the turning, where willows thicketed the bank. His small voice rode the morning on a higher, frailer level than the sounds of limitless motion that the river made. As long as she heard his voice, she thought, she would not interrupt him.

The surface of the soil, under leaves and pebbles and fragments of branch, was so cold that her fingers grew numb. But her nails were short and strong, her fingers powerful, and she found the butts that Will had buried. She counted half a dozen, smiling at first for the contact — the communion: you were here, and here I am, and here we are — and then frowning because of his bubbly cough and his pallor, his inability to walk a flight of stairs without panting. They had sat here, sometimes together, often taking turns, and listened to Sarah as she scolded dolls or sang songs about loss and sexual ravening with no sense, Lizzie had prayed, of what they meant.

Once, she had followed as Sarah, maybe four, bundled against October winds and carrying her small, pink metal suitcase filled with small, pink rubberoid dolls — Lizzie forgot the name of the set; it was something nauseous, she thought — played at the huge, protruding roots of the tree beside the river.

"I'm taking care of you," Sarah told the dolls. "That's what mommies do. I am your mommy and you will listen. Do you hear me?"

Then her voice piped higher and became indecipherable as, presumably, the disobedient dolls, each in a tiny costume with an aspect of pink to it, talked back — a specialty, even then, that Sarah was mastering. "Don't you *ever* say that to me, young lady. Is that clear?"

Lizzie remembered hanging her head and being torn between laughter and a good, hefty cry over the echoes of her untalented parenting.

The dolls replied, and the Sarah-mother changed her tone. "Well, of course, darling. That's perfectly fine. And I can show you how." Lizzie heard herself being competent, fastening a leader to a line or fixing the butterfly nuts on a miniature wheelbarrow. But Sarah knew that Lizzie never gave up on a point, and she returned, in her scolding, to the essential theme: "Don't you *ever* go to the river all by yourself. Don't *ever* go alone."

They should have whacked her ass, Lizzie thought, and made damned well certain that she didn't go. The dolls were having their say again. She and Will were proof that you are not born to be a mother or father, that it doesn't happen because you love a creature or fear for it or, as Will did, crouch over the crib a dozen times a day to listen to its breathing because it was no feat of imagination for him — it was real and proximate, like rain on dark mornings — to see his new daughter suffocating alone as she slept. We should have tied her to the bed once she learned how to walk, Lizzie thought.

"Don't you *ever* go without your mommy and daddy. Do you want the witch to eat you up? Because she will, sweetie, she will."

Lizzie remembered crying, in her stormy brain, What witch?

What was the menace that her child identified and her mother didn't? She remembered thinking, Let me *in*, goddamn it.

"Don't you *ever*," Sarah said.

Lizzie supposed that it made sense, then, to remember their trip to Utica, and a department store closed now for years, the Boston Store. She bought towels there, and cookware, and sometimes she found fancy socks for Will. It was on a Saturday morning, and she and Sarah, maybe the same age as Stephen, though Lizzie thought she'd been younger, were strolling among television sets and radios. A nature film was on, and there were close-ups in slow motion of a cormorant diving for fish off the coast of Maine. Sarah had asked if the fish was Big Bird, and the saleswoman had stared instead of applauding, she remembered, and Lizzie had grown angry. The air had the thick, exhausted quality peculiar to department stores, and colors seemed distorted under the fluorescent lighting. Lizzie found herself staring at hundreds of rugs that weren't as cheap in price as they were in quality, and when she reached for Sarah to move her along to someplace where breathing wasn't such a chore, she saw that she was alone, her daughter gone.

She called out to her and got no response except on the faces of preoccupied clerks and the question, from a little boy to his mother, about why that lady was making so much noise. She walked back through the television sets and toward the kitchenware department, calling for Sarah, asking clerks if a little girl had been found. She finally asked a clerk to call a supervisor, and a bald man who seemed about thirteen, in a dark brown suit that might have been his father's, accompanied her and gave his assistance by hectoring any number of saleswomen who might have been twice his age.

After another trip through the flickering damned television sets and the hi-fi components that were playing "Mambo Italiano," she turned left instead of right and, with the supervisor gently breathing through his mouth, and thereby achieving a sound not unlike that of a dog who has raced through a field, she came to the very small book department and there she found her child.

Sarah sat in a corner — she had created a corner — between a low bookshelf and an absent shop assistant's stool. Books had been dragged from their shelves and laid on their sides three and four deep in a line from the shelves to the stool. Behind the wall of books that separated her from the business of the store, leaning her back against the emptied shelves, her knees drawn partway up, her heels dug into the carpeting, holding a book — Lizzie forgot what it was: photographs of athletes, maybe — was Sarah, pretending to read. Lizzie knew she was pretending because her eyes were closed. She posed as a little girl who was reading a book. She had hidden herself, or secured a redoubt, and was making believe. Lizzie watched the tears run down her face from those closed eyes. She remembered sinking to her knees and reaching out to touch her daughter on the arm.

Sarah didn't turn. She kept her face toward the book. She sniffed and opened her eyes, blinking them.

"Good book?" Lizzie remembered asking. You matter-of-fact bitch. You could have *hugged* her. She was *lost!* But I did hug her, she recalled. Right after that, I dove for her. That's fine. But first you had to be casual, right?

Sarah, looking at the book, said, "Boring."

She couldn't be after her mother, at last, Lizzie told herself. It couldn't be one of those desperate searches for where you came from, she thought. Sarah's too old for that. She's too much in her life for that. Lizzie's mouth filled with saliva and her head ached under her ears, as if she had eaten something sour. So *few* adopted children make that search, she heard herself lecturing Will, as if the idea were his. Not Sarah, she thought.

Then Lizzie heard an object go into the water. The river suddenly roared louder, and the birds above the shadows over her, working in the sun, stopped calling, then began again. Lizzie shrieked, "Stephen! *Stephen!*"

She rose and ran in the same motion, leaning toward the bank and closing her eyes against the whipping branches she plunged through. There he was, a small, slender boy in a warmup jacket that said *Eagles*, his feet together at the knot in the rope, his arms casually crossed to hold the rope against his chest, slowly spinning as the rope danced in lazy, narrowing motions. In the water, a long evergreen branch snagged among stones was quivering as the water pulled it. Stephen watched her, not the branch she was certain he had somehow hauled to the rope with him and carried out above the river as he swung, then dropped to flush her from her blind.

She wondered, as she fought her breathing to a normal rate, whether she was willing what she saw, or whether Stephen's smile was also, and precisely, Sarah's. It said, *Got you.*

On her day off, Gloria washed her daughter's bedding and towels. She remade the bed with clean linen and vacuumed the room. Downstairs, she adjusted the pottery on its shelf, pleased to have been plundered. As if to a listener, she said, "The other pot? Oh, that one's in my daughter's house. Her husband's an architect. They're doing quite well, I think." She sat in the kitchen to drink a cup of sassafras tea. She used the bark as well as the roots, and the tea was brick red and thick. "Ah," she said, reaching for the telephone and calling the business office. "Oh, hello. Would you tell me what to do about a break-in? No, no, it's over, dear, thank you. I mean, someone came in here and didn't take all that much, to tell you the truth. A little food, a few items from the shelves — I think it was some hippie, to tell you the truth. You know, wandering in the woods? I live pretty much in the woods. Someone just got into mischief. But what I was wondering: what if they used my telephone? Could we, do you have a record of the long-distance calls from this number? If you could run a few by me, I could know whether I called them. Yes, dear, thank you."

Gloria poured more tea. She had read that sassafras tea might be a narcotic. She had heard, even, that Indians used to drink it to help them with trances for their rituals. She closed her eyes partway and nodded listlessly, as someone who had never taken drugs might think to imitate someone who had. "Ten little Indians," she said, as if through stiffened lips with thickened tongue. "Li'l."

Then: "Yes, dear. Uh-huh. Yes, I did call that one. And yes again. *Ah.* I knew it. Never called that. Wouldn't know — where? Burroughs? Where *is* that, dear? Oh, of course. Yes. I've never been to that part of New York. Yes. What was the — two eight at the end? And no others. Well, somebody probably called home, don't you think? Can't blame a child for calling their mother, can you? Yes, I'll note it on the bill when it comes, and you — yes. Yes. Thank you, you've been wonderful, dear. Bye-bye."

Gloria cleared away her teapot and cup, saying, as if to the same listener, "An architect, yes. Uh-huh. Well, I was impressed *too.*"

She went outside and slowly walked down the wooden steps of the deck toward the pond. The boat, a little aluminum pod, drifted on its line at the dock as the wind blew over the water in short gusts. She stepped in and untied it, let it move as it would, then rowed until she was near the center of the pond. A bass leaped and splashed. "Welcome back," she said. The pond was ringed by rushes, duckweed and tall, spiky duck potato with its broad leaves. If she were to stand in the boat and look north, she could see down into a couple of valleys, shaped like folds on a dark, dirty cloth, in which pockets of settlement had been stubbed into the stony ground. On the clearest of days she could look at individual houses and, pointing, name genital herpes here, impure-water diarrhea in the infants there, incontinence there, carpal tunnel syndrome in that one, in the farm wife, over there. (Vitamins and exercise would be *her* prescription, over-the-counter B$_6$, but of course she was only a nurse.)

Gloria didn't teeter in her boat, though. She sat slumped, as if exhausted, and let the sound of shrieking red-winged black-birds roll over her, and the hum of insects, the splash of fish after punkies, the gentle slap of water on the pod. She had grown so tired, she wanted to lean back and sleep. The sun broke through, and she felt the weight of spring sunlight on her forehead and neck.

Gloria's neck was as sore and tired as when she had gone to see Dr. Armandine at the hospital. She hitchhiked there from school because she couldn't ask her parents for the ride and because the bus driver on the rural route was her mother's cousin Larry Angel. She got there almost too late: the man who picked her up — he worked at the tile factory — had been pretty sure that Gloria, with her tight sweater and her pouty mouth, was desperate for his services. But she'd cried so hard, with as much mucus running down as tears, that he'd surrendered to the possibility that she needed something different from his dick. It was almost dark, and she'd got out on the wrong side of the hospital. By the time she arrived at the emergency room, Dr. Armandine was ready to leave.

"That's what happens," he said, leading her from the examination room off the ER to a little room with tables and magazines and the smell of hundreds of cigarettes. The light, she remembered, was a kind of ragweed color. "You are going to have to learn punctuality and *care*," he said, his small mouth pursing, his tired eyes looking cranky. He had no hair on his face, and she was afraid that if she felt the red top of his small head, it would feel damp, like a rotting plum.

She said, "Yes, sir. Doctor."

"Yes. How far along?"

"I'm a month late."

"Pregnancy confirmed?"

She nodded.

"Parents?"

"What? I have them. I have two parents. I didn't tell them, though. I can't."

"Of course. Money?"

"Money?"

"Surgical procedures cost *money*, Miss — I'm going to call you Miss, let's see, Monroe. Isn't that a nice name?"

Gloria started to cry again.

"You can afford this procedure?"

"I have money for college. I saved some. My grandmother left me a little so I could go to junior college."

"Oh, this'll educate you, I daresay, Miss, ah, Monroe." He sat straighter, leaned his head back as if his neck were sore, and Gloria's neck suddenly felt tender, filled with crushed blood vessels, incapable of motion without great pain. She winced. He said, "Yes, I know. You've always been a good girl. Well, we'll make you a good girl again. You'll be as good as new. Call my office in two days and do as the nurse instructs you, Miss Monroe."

She sat back, he leaned forward, and he patted her on the thigh. Her leg jumped, her neck responded to the motion, and she straightened herself slowly, biting her lip.

"No," Dr. Armandine said, "you can relax now." He smiled, rubbed the top of his head as if an insect were biting it, and left.

In her boat with her eyes closed, drifting, Gloria remembered saying to her daughter, "I was kind of wild." She thought: I was really only kind of simple, in the end. Because I never called Dr. Armandine, and I did tell my parents, and I let myself be treated like a whore, and they gave you away on me. They went with me, they showed you to me after you were born. *This here's your punishment*, my mother's eyes told me. They brought you in, they took you away, and some lucky lady harvested me. I was simple, and so was everything after. That's flesh for you: mysterious, then simple.

And I still do love the night we made you.

Gloria let the oars dip into the water and, as if her wrists were lamed by the carpal tunnel syndrome she was sure she knew how to cure, she rowed halfheartedly toward her graying wood dock, tied up the pod and walked inside.

She looked at her scratch pad and, still standing, dialed the number. Taking a deep breath, she listened for the ring. The first wasn't finished when a child's voice said, "Hello?"

"Hi, sweetheart?"

"Mommy?"

"Oh, dear. No, I'm afraid I'm not your mommy. But she did ask me to call you. Is your name —"

"Stephen," he said.

"That's right. Stephen. But I have to make sure it's the right Stephen. Your mommy said you were the only one who would be able to tell me the name of your town, darling."

"She did?"

"Hurry and tell me, darling."

"Burroughs?"

"Burroughs, New York, right? And you're seven years old."

"No, I'm six," Stephen said. "I won't be seven until next — is Mommy with you?"

"And you go to the, let me guess, Burroughs Central School?"

"Yeah, but where's Mommy?"

"Goodbye, dear," Gloria said, hanging up gently. Her face

felt twisted. She rubbed it and rubbed it. She looked at Sarah's note, affixed by magnets to the refrigerator door. She said, "See you soon."

In the Arrow Motel in Espanola, he woke to wash aspirin down with whiskey. He smelled himself in the room, and the sourness, instead of dismaying him, felt like a fact he could count on. The pain on the surface of his head was a fact, the sensation of slow, juicy tearing inside his head was a fact, and so were the bruises on his face and throat and belly, and so was the soreness from the arm wrestle. He lay in bed again, but he pictured himself upright, squinting into the awful white glare of the skies here, leaning at 20 degrees against the facts of his life: his wife had gone from him, and he had fled the aftermath of that departure. His child was marooned in the world his parents had left, and Sarah had gone to someplace else, and he had guessed wrong. That was the fact he leaned upon with all his weight. This new planet was huge, too big to navigate, and its gravity made you weigh ten times your weight on earth. He had known, in bone and balls, that Sarah was in Santa Fe. He had come to Santa Fe, risking time, income, Stephen, the chance to find her anyplace else, because he knew his wife so well. The fact that he couldn't find her in a fairly small place suggested just how well he knew her. He was rubbing his left bicep, he noticed, although he had wrestled with his right. Another fact for the bag of facts. When is a bag of facts a bag of rattlesnakes? Answer: when I am holding the bag.

"But not to worry," he said, rolling over and off, standing and walking upright, like a human male, into the shower. The stream of hot water made his sore scalp sorer, but that was a fact and he was therefore alive. Good news. "I bring Good *News!*" he cried in the shower stall, smiling into the hot, tin-tasting water like a television evangelist. "I am risen, children of Israel and

Espanola! Dial One–Eight Hundred–Credit Card to specify in what direction I shall aim my prayers on your behalf. I am arose!"

Forty-five minutes later, Barrett sat in his motel room drinking takeout coffee without sour mash and eating a fajita. He'd opened his door and propped it so that heat came in, but also some air, in its pungent Espanola blend of diesel fuel and distances, and with it the enormous sky. With his fine-point mechanical pencil he was working on the Chamber of Commerce map. The work got a little detailed, he realized, as he bent so close to the shiny paper he saw his shapeless reflection on its surface. Although he used computer programs now, he had trained by drawing his own framing plans. And he saw that his proposed search looked more like a rendering for the framing of a house than it did like a sane man's pursuit of his wife.

He cackled a little. Call it laughter, he thought, what the hell. And he added, in the waste ground between South Guadalupe and Pranzo Portare, a little code: *All joists 2" × 8"–16". To bear live load of 40 lb./sq. ft.* He filled in some of the grids and erased and redrew until he had, superimposed on Santa Fe, what he labeled, where Galisteo crossed the Paseo de Peralta, *First Tier Framing Plan.* He drew in headers and trimmers. He debated tripling for headers near the chimney — it rose from West Manhattan, through Read and Garfield — but settled for doubling. You don't want the client to think you're padding for a share of the contractor's skim in the name of safety.

He folded the map and put it in the pocket of his last clean khakis. He counted his money and forswore wondering what would become of his business. He considered showering again, because his chest, back and armpits were wet once more, and he felt as though the fuel-laden air had settled on him like a heavy, damp powder. But it was already early afternoon, and there was a wife to be found.

He parked at the Posada, smiled at the man who worked at a hydrant near the swimming pool, and he flapped his map, overlaid with a drawing for an impossibly framed, unworkable house, as he held the city in his hand. He knew that his smile was aggressive. He knew that his steps were too long. He was on a mission, and he looked it. He wondered if someone would point him out to the police. He forced himself to shorten his strides. Just look pleasant, he instructed himself. Look reliable. He wondered, following a sign that directed him along the Old Santa Fe Trail, whether Sarah had left because he was unreliable.

He knew that he'd been *too* reliable: reliably himself. And Sarah was tired of the self he was. Marriages, you know, some of them just end up kind of *ending*.

You're a fucking drag, Barrett, you know? That's why. Your neckties and your suits, your town board meetings and your zoning seminars and your conference table and your plans and plans and plans, more goddamned rolled-up paper than an asswipe factory. Laying it out, drawing it up, sampling programs, stocking up on the specialized software, offering caution and counseling the house-proud on their BT-fucking-U heat-loss correlations. The woman is looking for a little *adventure*. The artist guy in his, probably in his white painter's overalls and bare chest. Sandals? They wear sandals anymore? In his costume, is the point. Doing his dabbing to rock 'n' roll on the radio like the rest of the jerks he'd been to school with. Talking about "color weight," except saying it with a lot of "like" thrown in, "like *tight*, you know, color weight," saying "gestural" and, please, "surface." And of course fucking his wife.

There would have to be a lot of forgiveness, he thought, looking at the other tourists on East De Vargas Street. There would have to be a lot of forgiving each other. He was outside a narrow adobe church called San Miguel. Its original walls and altar, the sign said, went back to 1610. Nobody had forgiven anybody since 1610, he thought; what am I going to do with a woman I can't even *catch*? Find, he corrected himself, find. Fathers carried babies on their backs in little carriers, and mothers carried infants

177

in slings against their breasts. He was not about to enter a church, sit on an old wooden bench, stare up at the Tlaxcaltecs' version of Jesus rising from southwestern clay and cry out loud in front of strangers that his wife no longer loved him. Face it, he would not cry before these people, She doesn't want me anymore. Nor would he discuss the implications in this new, fanged, rattling fact for Stephen, the orphan of parents still alive. About face, son. About face.

He turned west and walked with his longest paces, bearing a smile so broad his face ached to rival his head, toward the Palace and the rows of Indians selling their sterling silver collar pins and turquoise earrings. He went in the direction of the Coyote, vowing to pass up the margarita he wanted so much, and he paused only at the end of the gallery, where a chubby Indian girl of fifteen or so was waiting for an Anglo woman in her sixties to make her purchase. The sun was in the girl's eyes, and it cast a long shadow of the Anglo woman's arm as it passed back and forth over the jewelry laid out on black velvet. The girl squinted against the sun and her eyes moved, following the shadow of the arm.

Fathers holding children's hands passed by, and Barrett went in their direction. He saw a boy and girl and mom and dad in pastel clothing, and he wanted to make jokes for the children, to suggest to the parents where to eat a late lunch. But he could only stay to himself. You leave that, he thought, and you get flailed by small, mustachioed, snarling men. He was supposed to only walk and sweat, to look for his wife, whom he was frightened to find, he admitted. But that was all right, he thought. You don't have to be frightened. Because you won't find her.

He went into small, carpeted galleries and big stores bright with pawn jewelry. Mass-produced pots stood on shelves beside the dark, burnished pots of the Montez family. A small, incised black bowl was the work, a hand-lettered sign said, of Evening Snow Comes. The bowl had the San Ildefonso signs for good harvest and good luck. The woman who sold him the pot was tall and thick and made up like an actress or a dancer. She had applied her makeup, he thought, because she thought she ought to be stared at. The makeup, her bearing, the flatness of her gaze, made it clear that no matter how hard you stared, she was not going to be concerned. She packed the bowl in a box filled with S-shaped pieces of plastic. "Your purchase is safe," the saleswoman said, tossing the box up and catching it. "So relax and have a good day."

Relax and have a good day, he instructed himself, sticking his credit card in his pocket. You lose that, Pyramid Builder, and you can *walk* home, because you're almost out of gas money and the account has less than mouse droppings in it. You relax and have a good day. He was carrying the gift, the offering, for Sarah, whom he knew he would not find.

Isn't that called prayer? He asked it in the voice of the TV evangelist he'd been in the shower at the Arrow Motel. "Isn't that *prayer?*" he couldn't prevent himself from saying as he turned east off Ortiz onto Water Street. And, lo, like a something in the desert. Like a — like a something in the desert. There was the Coyote, and it was obviously the outskirts of the cocktail hour. He stood near the entrance to the Hotel St. Francis, meeting the stare of the handsome, annoyed bellman whose flaring nostrils suggested to Barrett that he wore the aura of Espanola. He cradled the white box in its white plastic bag, thought of the shiny pot, its shape that she'd relish cupping her palms around. It would bring him luck because it was a prayer and an offering, and he would learn to be a man his wife might continue to love. It wasn't only her loss, the loss of the woman to the man in his no doubt fucking *beret*. The loss. It was, it was that she had come to despise him, Barrett thought. It was that she must turn her face from him so totally. And this talisman and offering, whether anybody loved anybody ever again, might anyway save him from her scorn.

Softly, conversationally, pushing his legs in place against the sunlight that rose around him like rising water, looking across at the Coyote, where the margaritas and the tall women perched, he wondered, "Wouldn't you call this praying?"

Lizzie sat on the edge of the bed and tried to find a tale in *The Juniper Tree* she could read to Stephen, whom she had tucked beneath his mother's girlhood blankets and who lay with his arms limp outside the covers, his eyes unfocused, as if he were ill. Karen had assured her that these stories were some of Noel's favorites. Lizzie was having some difficulty. She started the title story, about the rich man and his good and beautiful wife who loved each other so very much but had no children, despite the wife's prayers.

"That's a little boring, don't you think, sweetie? Let's try and find another one. I don't even know what a juniper tree looks like. Ah! Here's one we know. Let's try it." Stephen didn't reply. She started the wintry beginning of the Snow White story, but faltered as blood from the queen's fingers fell onto the snow and she thought, " 'If only I had a child as white as snow, as red as blood, and as black as the wood in the window frame!'

"Yuck," Lizzie said, hearing her voice grow tight and phony, "too much *blood* for me. I say we give this book one more chance. Okay? Let's turn to — here: a nice, short one about goblins. You know what they are, Stephen? Little creatures, little sort of —"

"Gremlins," he said listlessly. "Like the movie."

"Well, I don't know. Why not? Goblins, all right?" She began desperately, and realized too late what she was reading. She felt like one of those absurd, Technicolor talking creatures in the cartoons Stephen liked on Saturday mornings. She had run off a cliff and was charging through the air, unaware of the necessity that she fall. " 'Once there was a mother,' she read, 'and the goblins had stolen her child out of the cradle. In its place they laid a changeling with thick head and staring eyes —' Stephen," Lizzie said, "do you want to *hear* this?"

He looked at her for the first time since she'd supervised his getting into bed that night. His eyes were miserable. She looked from them back to the book and skimmed, looking up as if to make sure he was there, then back down to the book.

"Stephen," she said, "it ends happily. The goblins bring the baby *back*. Shall I read it to you?"

He said, "No, thank you, Grandma."

"Do you feel all right, sweetie?"

"Yup."

"Not sick?"

"Nope."

"But you're miserable, right? You feel horrible inside?"

His eyes welled, but he turned his face so that he looked at the ceiling. Lying flat and still, his arms at his sides, he looked to her like a sarcophagus in a church in Europe with its carving of a crusader. The pillow rustled as he nodded.

Lizzie stood, set the book on the schoolgirl desk she had bought for her daughter, and put a knee on the bed. Looking down at him, she lay down gently and put her arm across his waist. Her own face was in the pillow, turned a little toward his ear.

"After school," she whispered, "I'll come in the car and I'll pick you up. We'll drive someplace together. We'll — maybe we'll go to the mall in Binghamton and go to the movies. We'll get Grandpa, we'll make him leave work early, and we'll go see a movie."

"I don't know what's playing," Stephen said.

"Something, I think, with guns and cars, and a lot of guys get shot," she said.

"What's it called?"

"I forget. We'll look it up in the newspapers. If you don't like that, we'll find another one. There's lots of movies, Stephen."

"Yes," he said. "Okay."

"Good. So look for me in the car, and come a-running."

"What'll it be, kiddo?" Stephen said.

"What's that mean, sweetie?"

"It's just a thing some people say."

She stopped, finally, after running in the straightest line she could manage — Pennsylvania Turnpike at Bedford through to the Mechanicsburg exit, where she got off and followed back roads too quickly, turning into one featureless strip of plastic-covered stores and gas stations, driving out the other end, driving a dozen miles of badly maintained country road to find another cluster of shops selling nothing she wanted and people with faces she wouldn't choose to see. In Landisburg she let the car idle near a self-service car wash, and then, in the back of the car-wash parking lot, near a coin-operated vacuum cleaner on which a *Broke* sign had been hung, she turned her engine off and looked past the tall, thick tube of the vacuum cleaner to face high, bright green privet that formed the back wall of the lot.

Barrett was in Santa Fe. She couldn't imagine why. Stephen was at her mother's house when he should have been home, in Doylestown, with Barrett. Her mother was at a log house in the middle of Noplace, Pa., putting spells on birds and feeding turtle-vomit teas to disfigured people in the hills. Her mother wasn't her mother, and her adoptive mother *was* her mother, so Elizabeth Bean Mastracola was not her adoptive mother. You get adopted, she thought, and you end up working it out like an accountant. If they hadn't adopted me, I'd be dropping calf in rural barns on the Pennsylvania border, 1.97 billion trillion light-years from where I live. I'd be fucking with mutants and bearing their cloven-hoofed offspring. I'd be — what'd she call it? I'd be a little wild. That's right. And, anyway, even *without* her I was a little bit wild. Searching for something to belong to, her mother called it, who was her mother, as opposed to the woman who delivered her and left her off. No stork: a brown United Parcel Service truck brings the babies, she ought to tell Stephen.

I ca-an't hear you. Except I can. If I don't belong to you, Stephen, where do I belong?

Sarah looked at her odometer, trying to gauge how many miles she'd fled, how quickly, and where the fleeing had begun. In Bucks County? In her birth mother's house? And why had she been so frightened?

"Why not?" Sarah said, putting the car in gear and driving to the shed that housed the car wash. She put dollars in the change machine and used the quarters to wash her car. She paid for the hot rinse, the extra soapy wash, a second hot rinse, a spray-on hot wax and a hot-air buffing. She scrubbed from her windshield the caked blood of bugs and moths, the pasted fragments of their wings and antennae, the mud and dung of Gloria's road. The red Blazer shone. She had even washed the tires. She was soaked from the thighs down, and suddenly as tired as she'd been throughout the trip.

Trip, she thought. How about stumble? How about fall?

She changed more bills into quarters, and she drove north on State 15, crossing Route 81 and the Susquehanna River, until near Straustown she found a small general-goods store with gas pumps and a telephone in an old-fashioned booth with a door. She dialed her house and heard the emptiness at once. She decided to decide that she did not smell urine in the hot booth. She dialed her parents' house and licked her bottom lip, rehearsing, as the ringing began. And, like a headache that you're suddenly aware of, she understood why Barrett had gone to Santa Fe to find her. Because he thought she loved it for the pottery, or for the time they got so drunk that their lovemaking — the first such occasion since their wedding, which had frightened them both — was not only uninhibited but fun. She had realized that all she needed to do was drink too much for their loving to go wild. Presumably, she thought, as the phone rang and as the ringing did make her head ache, Barrett didn't know that she didn't need it to be him under and over and on whom she toiled. She hadn't slept around, but she hadn't needed Barrett anymore, she thought. Was that possible? Had Santa Fe shown her how unnecessary he was to her? That early in their marriage? She pictured Barrett's earnest, narrow, handsome face, his forehead wrinkled in bewilderment, his mouth turned down in a sexy, sullen pout. He'd be lost there.

He'd be lost, Sarah thought.

She hung up and dialed the high school, was connected after four rings, went through someone else and then, automatically, she said, "Mommy? It's me."

N EAR COUDERSPORT on the Allegheny River, Gloria made two admissions: that she was exhausted, and that she was lost. Being lost was her own fault, she told herself as she lifted her nylon suitcase that converted into a square knapsack, and locked her car. She let herself into her room at the White Horse Inn, a stucco motel with a small chipped plaster horse in front of its flagpole. She smelled at the fake peonies on the bureau and put them into the top drawer. It had been her theory — it had been her *belief* — that, once on the move toward Sarah, having lived for two days and two nights with her, she could not be separated by distance or disdain from her daughter. She had aimed herself toward New York State in almost a panic, driving as if in pursuit of Sarah. And she'd known better. Or, anyway, she knew she knew better now. But she'd been on the trail, certain she would find her way. She'd been wrong, and she admitted it. "Always admit your mistakes," Gloria told the rest of the room as she stood with her back to the uncomfortably wide, high mirror.

She would buy a map in the morning if the person at the checkout desk couldn't help, and she would drive unswervingly and reach her destination. *Destiny*, she thought, is inside *destination*. And, for the whole of this late afternoon and night, she would rest. She would prepare her mind. She thought her soul was pretty well prepared. It had been harrowed by experience, the bulk of it lonely. She had paid what she thought of as her penalty. She was not in the debt of humankind or family. She held that word and weighed it as you hold a river stone, black and dripping, cold, rounded by millions of gallons pouring over it: family. She said it *fam'ly* to herself, considering how she had forsworn material possessions and the comforts of marriage. She had known, she thought, she had known all her life that her ultimate attentions were reserved to her eventual family.

We'll be a happy family again, she thought, remembering how her infant had been brought to her and taken away, the beginning of her punishment. She had held her child and she had wept, and they had taken her away. Then Sarah had returned, a little pinched, a little crabby, a little frightened, Gloria thought, wondering why. But she was a *handsome* woman, slender and strong and straight-backed, muscled almost like a man, she thought, and with angry blue eyes like her own. Though I'm not an angry person, she reasoned as she took the plastic bottle of disinfectant from her kit and scrubbed the basin, then rinsed it, then replaced the cap on the bottle and the bottle in her kit, then washed her face and hands and throat, using the soap from the plastic dish in her kit.

These things take time. She nodded at the mirror. Time. She nodded again, seeing her eyes as Sarah's. The fatigue was doubtless emotional. This is a very emotional time, you know, she told herself in her most understanding nurse's voice. Even though you're hardly very old at all, and though you keep yourself fit and eat, lord knows, the right foods, you're going to become spiritually drained at a time like this.

From the open knapsack-suitcase she took a clean cotton nightgown and heavy socks that doubled as bedroom slippers. She contemplated her early supper and long sleep. She opened the brown paper bag she'd carried in and removed two thick sandwiches on the yellow bread she made from her own blend of cattail pollen and good wheat flour. From her traveling flask she poured the dark birch beer she made. The cocktail hour, she heard herself say to a child in her house. Music played, the sunlight brightened the pine floor, the child sat smiling with a book by someone important to read to be well read. It's the cocktail hour, she heard herself say to the child.

She hadn't lifted her creamed herring sandwich, nor had she tasted her beer. She rewrapped the sandwich, poured back the beer and sealed the flask. Straightening her clothes, taking her key and her purse, she made her third admission, that she was lonely enough to weep and not stop, and she went outside. She walked the length of her wing of the motel and came to the front wing, at right angles to hers. There, the sun shone hotly on the white stone or plaster horse, on the wagon wheel in the hub of which were planted red geraniums, on the soda machine near the office and on the elevated concrete swimming pool. In her heavy denim skirt and wrinkled khaki blouse, she entered the indoor pool and sat in the aluminum chair she almost tripped on.

A family at the far end — Gloria had to squint and peer through the hot lights — was squabbling. The little boy wanted to cannonball in and was told that he might not. "Practice your diving, Bobby. We paid for you to learn how to *dive*," his mother said. She was a short, scrawny woman in a small one-piece bathing suit that showed, Gloria thought, a wisp of pubic hair. She felt her lips purse. It's natural, after all, she thought. But still her lips tugged down. The father lay back in a chaise and read a newspaper, reclining on the fatigue he no doubt felt he had earned by driving rudely and too fast, Gloria thought. A smaller boy dutifully chugged back and forth at their end, the shallow part, holding on to a buoyant board.

"Let him jump if he wants to, Syl," the hubby-daddy said.

"Fine," his wife said, peering at the child in the water as if the pool were writhing with lamprey eels. "Fine. You'll remember not to remind me, Mister Free-and-Easy, how much the diving lessons cost you?"

Gloria squinted along her legs at the child who didn't wish to dive. She looked and she looked, and she said, with no words, Over here.

The boy, perhaps eight or nine, looked around, then sat sulkily at the edge of the pool.

No, Gloria told him, *here*. She thought of treats, of sweet satisfaction, of tricks and the neat secrets of the scrumptiously puzzling world. Over here.

Bobby, his head hanging, began to amble along the pool. He looked at moss, she thought, or fungus growing on the tiles. You can watch small *worlds* grow up in tiling cracks, Gloria thought. You can see half the rural wilderness in broken streets. The Egyptians and Sumerians domesticated cows and used their milk for cheese five thousand years ago. You can boil up burdock leaves for greens with dinner, but *never* try to eat the leaves of rhubarb, which are poisonous. Stand this pencil straight up, and we'll use it as a sundial to tell whether it's dinnertime. We can make our fire for cooking dinner in the woods with milkweed down for tinder. "Hello, Bobby," she said, smiling. "I'm Gloria."

He stood before her, and she lay back so as not to frighten him. His face was soft and pampered. His expression was inward, unkind. He stood before her and waited.

"Are you bored?" Gloria asked.

Bobby shrugged.

"Did you ever hear the expression 'An intelligent person is never bored'? Grownups always tell that to children. Isn't it dumb? It's so easy to get bored. All you have is your computer game and your portable radio and your brother in the back of the car driving you crazy. And just when you think you can, I don't know, *let go* and not have to sit quietly while your father drives, they make you dive instead of jump in. Right? Parents are *always* like that. You know who's not? Grandparents. I'm a grandparent, and I can tell you: I am not like that."

I can focus a beam of light with my magnifying glass and set a little clump of goldenrod on fire. Apricots and pretzels make you fart as much as beans. I pressure-cook my beans for half an hour so they'd never give you gas. Rub red alder tea directly on to heal your hives. I can show you how to collect tadpoles in a jar and watch them grow to frogs.

"My name is Gloria, and yours is Bobby. Yes, I know. Grandmothers know almost everything, Bobby."

The scrawny woman with, there it was, the flagrant pubic hair interrupted the light between Gloria and Bobby, who was just about to relax with her, and she said, "*His* grandmother knows more than the other grandmothers, even. Just ask her. I'm sorry he's been disturbing you."

"Oh," Gloria said, sitting forward a little, "hello. He's a lovely boy," she said of the pouting, fat, ungenerous lout. "He hasn't been disturbing me at all. I was just about to see if he wanted to take a walk around the grounds. There are all *sorts* of interesting weeds and, oh, insect galls on this vegetation."

"Vegetation?" the mother said.

"Incidentally," Gloria said, "a little hydrocortisone on that rash on his leg —"

"Is that what that is?"

"A mild dermatitis. He's probably allergic to some of that vegetation I was talking about."

"Dermatitis," Bobby's mother said.

"Nurse talk."

"Oh, you're a *nurse*. Wonderful. Great. Robert back there, Bobby's dad, is a hospital administrator in Sayre."

"Love those administrators," Gloria said.

"I'll bet you do. He tells me how much his nurses love him, and I say, 'Watch it, big fella.' You know?"

"You know those nurses," Gloria said.

"Oh. No, I didn't —"

"Of course not," Gloria said. "Shall I fetch the hydrocortisone?"

"Please don't bother," Bobby's mother said, reaching for her son's shoulder and all but towing him by the loose flesh of his upper arm. "I couldn't let you bother. Nice to meet you. Bobby, say bye." Bobby said nothing and so did Gloria. The family, when it was clustered at the shallow end, and when the mother had chattered in a whisper at the father, coalesced under the protective arm of hubby-daddy, and they collected towels, board and newspaper, and left. As they approached on their way to the stairs, Gloria closed her eyes.

She heard them pass. She smelled their tanning oil and the chlorine of the pool. Bobby's flip-flops scuffed past, and she opened her eyes, then closed them again. When she was alone at the pool, Gloria sat forward and held her face in her hands. This is traveler's exhaustion, she told herself, nothing more. This is the fatigue of pursuing wholeness. She straddled the chaise longue as she stood and she thought a sexual thought. She thought of someone standing over her that way. Then she stepped, retrieved her purse, heavy with pocketknife, plastic bags, medicated wipes, compass and magnifying lens, and hauled it away toward her room.

She changed into her cotton nightgown and put on her slipper socks. She sat on the side of her bed and ate her sandwich and drank her birch beer. The herring felt thick and slimy, the bread just a little bit sandy, and she didn't unwrap the second sandwich. "That's fatigue for you," she said. That's what you risk when you get yourself out in the world. But she had made a start. She had covered distance, she had settled herself a little, and she was on her way. She sipped the birch beer and enjoyed its astringency. She was, as the travelers say, en route.

"You know what got us over," Marylinn told him, "was that motel you picked out. Once I saw the Arrow, I knew you had to be selling drugs on the pueblos or guns to the drive-by shooters in Albuquerque. Or worse. And it was worse, wasn't it, Mister B?"

She had sought him at the better places, thinking the Arrow he had mentioned was the name of a suite or bungalow or wing. Then she had looked up Arrows in the telephone directory and then had simply asked a policeman who was napping in the parking lot of a bank near where Catron ran into North Guadalupe. She had driven over in the Mercedes, parked outside his room and looked in through the propped door. He'd looked up — stripped to the waist, sweating onto his new grid overlay for the neighborhood east of the Canyon Road galleries. Sarah had been in none of those. He had looked into each one that was open, searching for his wife among paintings of cowboys on horses that reared from rattlesnakes, and of Indians enmeshed in ritual visions, and among contemporary Anglo versions of pots that Indians had thrown and painted for a thousand years. He had tiptoed on thick green carpeting and shining parquet floors, on long, bright boards of ponderosa pine and on antique Armenian rugs laid down for the feet of buyers of antique Indian blankets. And, working on the houses of artists and gallery owners, the big new vacation lodges and old haciendas, the final neighborhood in which he could envision her, using a shirt cardboard and his fine pencil, he made a search grid that looked more and more like a designer's rendering of a jail cell, bar by bar by bar. He was drinking sour mash on ice and not telephoning his son. He was a husband and he was a father, and he couldn't find his wife who had fled him, and he hadn't a word of assurance or comfort or even a sense of the pleasure he might take in lying to offer false comfort to his son. Marylinn had looked through the door, wrinkling her nose at, he had no doubt as he looked up, the airlessness, the smell of his sweat, the dishevelment and surrender of the room.

She had walked in, shaking her head and smiling, as if he had offered her a large gift in total surprise. She had stood before him and had dropped her bag, had raised her short brown leather skirt and taken down a pair of small emerald-colored panties. He'd thought of her contact lenses. He had put them in a tissue in his suitcase. Then she opened her cream-colored collarless shirt and removed it. Stepping out of her shoes, she had said to him, "You want this, Barrett, you're gonna have to do a little work anyhow. See can't you find the fastener back here."

Ms. Thorndyke drew the shades, and Stephen shuddered. He had to pee, he had needed to pee since he got back from lunchroom, and it was much worse now. Sometimes, when he could hum to himself so he didn't hear himself saying that he had to pee, he could go for a long time more, holding it. But now he wouldn't be able to hum because Ms. Thorndyke had drawn the brown-yellow shades against the bright sun of the early afternoon, and she was turning off the lights. She was going to tell them a story.

She liked the way she told stories. She liked the way her voice got low and the little girls' eyes got wider and their mouths got tight when the scary parts came. Stephen knew how much she liked that, and he was angry even while he shook the way he did when he was cold. He swung his legs wide and hard and they banged together and flew apart. He wanted to hum so *I ca-an't hear you* the feeling about needing to pee couldn't come in.

194

He knew this was what his mother meant about the emergency feeling. Even if she was coming home now, the way Grandma said, he knew she had the feeling because he had it right now. And maybe Grandma *was* a liar like him. He still loved her, but that made it tough for him to figure out what was really happening and what wasn't. He was a dirty liar too, and he was pretty sure Ms. Thorndyke didn't believe him about his parents being spies. It was stupid to say that. But he had loved telling them. That was how he knew that Ms. Thorndyke loved the way the children's eyes followed, and their lips pressed hard against each other. They didn't want to believe him. They were pretty sure they didn't believe him. But they kept listening, and he liked the way that felt. He figured Ms. Thorndyke did too.

He moved from side to side in his seat and clasped his hands on his desk. Noel Kelly looked at him, and Stephen thought he might tell Noel, if he could ever live long enough to get to the end of school, what this was all about. Noel just watched him with his quiet eyes and his almost-smile. Noel looked like a judge or the person on TV who took care of the orphans.

Ms. Thorndyke sat on the front worktable with her legs together, swinging a little, and her hands on the edge of the table on either side of her legs. She leaned forward and wrinkled her nose. Stephen thought that was disgusting. But her eyes were always nice, except when she wore her glasses. Then they got big and she looked like a giant bug. She said, "Boys and girls, girls and boys, I have a story to tell you."

Everybody leaned back when she said that. Stephen, though, leaned forward and put his face down and bit on his arm while his legs swung in and out, in and out.

"Once upon a time, in the queendom of Minerva, there lived a family of vitamin makers. Everybody in the queendom had to take their vitamins every day, of course. There was no question of that. They *all* wanted to be healthy."

Stephen remembered when his father brought home vitamins shaped like TV creatures. He couldn't remember their name. But the vitamins tasted good, and Stephen ate most of the bottle of them while his father was watching the football game and his mother was in Center City looking at furniture for the business. It was called mission something, or maybe that was the vitamins' name. After a while they tasted too sweet, then worse, and he threw up. Also the Eagles lost, and his father was not happy about any of it. He should have told them that, instead of the spy lie.

"But the father of the vitamin makers' family got very sick. It surely wasn't from a lack of — what?"

"Vitamins!" the class screamed back.

"That's right. It was a strange disease, and it affected only males. The father got sick, and then his two sons. Soon, they were too sick to make vitamins, and the royal family and all the dukes and dukelings and courtiers and clerks and generals and soldiers and parking-lot attendants grew too weak to do their work.

"Now, the mother of the vitamin makers had been lost at sea many years before. But there was a daughter in that family, and she was strong and healthy and very, very smart. She was in the, let me see, yes: fourth grade. She was nine years old, and very tall for her age —

"Janine! Are you interrupting the story? Do you have to —"

No! Stephen called inside his head. Don't say it! He knew all you had to do was ask for the pass and you could walk down the green hallway to the first stairs on the right and go down the steps and turn right when you got through the door and there, on your left, in the big white-tiled wall, were the doors to the bathrooms. But he wasn't ever sure of the turns when he was walking there. And he hated to have to walk up in front of the whole class when they knew he was going to the bathroom. He seized each hand with the other and rocked and swung his legs.

"What color was her *hair*, Ms. Thorndyke?"

"Dirty blond, Janine. Just like yours. Now. This daughter, whose name was Sasha, had watched her father and her older brothers make vitamins for years — ever since she was an infant, in fact, and lay in her cradle, singing softly to herself as her father and brothers used retorts and precipitates and Bunsen burners and test tubes and all the other apparatus that vitamin makers have to know about. She went to Minerva's court, but was not allowed to see the queen because the courtiers were afraid to bother her and because they could not imagine why a mere child, and a *girl* child at that, must disturb Her Majesty — who was already quite upset about her vitamin-deficient queendom.

"So home went Sasha. She was undaunted. This is a wonderful word, boys and girls. It means you may be afraid, and you may not be allowed, but you know you're right, and you know you're not going to hurt anyone, so you go ahead and do what you think you must. Undaunted, Sasha set about making vitamins, just as she had learned by keeping her mouth closed and her eyes open and her mind always working hard."

Stephen shuddered, and the sweat on his forehead made him think he had the same disease as the vitamin maker and his sons. He knew he was going to lose this one. He was going to lose and he was going to be ashamed. They would smell him in the hall. They would laugh on the staircase. The office would call his grandmother and grandfather and everyone would want to *talk* about it.

"She stayed up late far longer than she should have, and she labored far too hard for a child of her age. But she did what she had to do, and by dawn of the third day, when she had hardly slept or eaten, Sasha had manufactured enough vitamins, all in the shape of the Sacred Swans that drew Queen Minerva's Royal Boat, and she set about the queendom — fortunately it was a compact little queendom — leaving a small bundle of vitamins in silver paper tied to every doorknob she came to. The family dog, whose name was Hugo the Huge, for he was an enormous Newfoundland, carried the vitamins in his special dog knapsack.

"By dinnertime that day, Sasha had delivered all the vitamins, including a big batch for the court. She limped home on feet that were sore from walking the queendom. She fed Hugo and gave him the thigh bone of a moose for his reward. She gave her father and brothers their vitamins and some soup she made by following the directions her mother had written in her cookery book before she was lost at sea, and then Sasha fell into bed, exhausted."

Stephen put his head down on the desktop. He covered his head with his hands. He swung and swung, but he knew what was happening, and he felt sorry for his mother with the emergency feeling, all alone in Santa Fe.

"When the sun came up, people were surprised and delighted to find their vitamins, and everybody took the correct dosage. Sure enough, they started to feel well at once. Queen Minerva demanded of her courtiers why she had not been told about this new vitamin maker. When they told the story of the nine-year-old girl, she punished them all for not paying attention to those who deserved it. And she announced that she was going to reward Sasha with anything she wished.

"The Royal Boat took the Royal Canal to Sasha's house and brought her before the queen, who was strong and broad-shouldered and also, of course, attractive in a very competent way. 'What is your fondest wish?' asked the generous queen.

" 'For my family to be well and for the courtiers to be spanked and covered with molasses for the flies to annoy, ma'am,' said Sasha.

" 'But those are two wishes. You must choose one.'

" 'The health of those I love, Your Majesty,' said Sasha.

"And *poof!* When Sasha came home, her father and brothers were stirring with new health. 'Where have you been, Sasha?' her father asked. 'And what mischief have you gotten into, dear child?'

" 'Oh,' Sasha said." And Stephen lay his head flat on the desk and closed his eyes and pressed his thighs together and sighed. He felt warm and, for a moment, as if he were sleeping. He kept hoping he was asleep and only wetting his bed. " 'You'll find out,' she said.

"And Sasha's father looked deep into her eyes —"

Behind him, Stephen heard the clattering as children's feet touched the floor. They were moving away from the puddle. He heard the sound he'd been waiting for, the quick breath before the calling out.

Eddie used to take her around. Where are you going tonight? What are you doing this afternoon? Oh, Eddie's taking me around the Ninth Avenue markets — "Avenoo" was how she used to say it, her version of Philly talk. Eddie's taking me around to the Phillies game. Eddie's taking me around to the museum. She had always been aware, the summer and part of autumn that they were lovers, that she was burgeoning. She could imagine elders discussing her, telling each other that Sarah's coming into her own. What a woman she'll be, she could imagine them saying to one another. What a woman she's becoming! But, in spite of burgeon and bloom, she had been thoroughly taken that summer — taken to bed, taken around, taken care of. She knew they would never stay together, just as she had known that she and Barrett wouldn't stay together. While knowing this with Eddie, she had known, too, or she had feared, that no subsequent lover, no marriage, no condition or event she could imagine, would make her feel so *wedded* to something outside herself, while still so much in the process of becoming Sarah Mastracola, as she felt in the summer and fall at the end of her youth in Philadelphia with Eddie Slovitz.

It was one of the tropical Philadelphia summers, when the only air that moved some nights was down off Delaware Avenue near the docks or at the other end of the city, near the Schuylkill. Eddie preferred the docks because they were more dangerous. He swaggered a little more when he walked — no, swayed, rocking from side to side to show them he was dangerous too. A tug was tied up one night, and they sat at the end of the pier near where its hawsers were looped because Eddie insisted that it was their city too. In the darkness of the unlighted dock, as Sarah waited for flesh-eating men and drug-addict rapists who would sidle from the warehouses and dark parked trucks to tear her clothing and then her limbs off, Eddie told her, "Listen." She heard the voices of the crew as one of them cooked something mixed with onions, as another apparently read out loud with a lot of pauses and indecision. The water that smelled like gasoline and swamp was slapping a little, and the tugboat moved against the pier. After a while, with her eyes closed, she felt as though the pier, too, rocked on the Delaware River just across from Camden. Loose plates on the Walt Whitman Bridge, above them, clanged as cars went over. She kept her eyes closed, imagining the light cast by the crossing cars. Her sweat cooled, her hair stopped feeling sticky at her forehead, and she turned to Eddie, thinking that she would kiss his shoulder, which was hard but not bony, and instead she fell asleep.

When she woke, it was beginning to lighten, there was an early lie about coolness in the air, and traffic was starting on the bridge. The men on the tug were silent, and Eddie, on whom she leaned and up at whose face she had looked on first awakening, was asleep. His eyelids were jumping and his brows were raised, and she watched him as he dreamed. He looked like a surprised child, in spite of his beard and his baldness. She moved a little closer, causing him to stir slightly, and she tried to see what his dream inside him was.

She woke him when she mushed her wet eyes and runny nose against his shoulder.

"What?" he said.

She shook her head. "Go back to sleep," she told him, over the black water and under the yellow-gray sky, listening to the bridge rung by early traffic, preferring not to say that she had reached the furthest she could get in him (or, therefore, anyone else) and that she thought it as terrible as knowing the fullest, foulest details of your own death to learn what she believed had just been disclosed to her by Eddie's locked, secret dreaming.

On the other hand, she thought — she was squinting now into the afternoon light of late April, moving with dense suburban traffic that she would lose in twenty miles when Binghamton was well behind her and she would risk a state trooper on Route 12 and run like hell for home — on the other hand, there was Stephen. He had always told her his dreams. He came into their bedroom late at night and, often, stayed beside her, under the covers, not between her and Barrett, as she had expected, but on the side away from his father, where it was only mother and child.

Once, she remembered, he had dreamed the same terror-dream for weeks, it seemed, without halt. He gibbered and wept after the first time. Thereafter, he presented himself by her side as she slept, poking her with a single finger, standing, when she turned her lamp on, with his eyes closed and his long, slender neck exposed at the open V of his pajama tops. "Same one?" she would mumble. He would reach his hand and raise his knee at the same time, and she would lift the covers on her side of the bed and let him sidle under them. He lay along her, pressing close to her side. The first night, she had held him, and he'd moved against her breasts and belly and she hadn't minded but had known that she should. After that night, she'd moved the covers for him, then had lain on her front and reached for the light switch, and Stephen had lain alongside her, touching, and had whispered — his breath smelled to her like cloves — about the flying men who had come to lift him above the floor of his room and immerse him, with the same movements night after night, in the same series of bathtubs.

Barrett learned to sleep through their ritual, and Sarah didn't blame him. She didn't mind having Stephen to herself that way. And it took several years for Barrett to begin having his nightmares, his somnambulistic fights, his terrible sleeping rages that resulted in broken light bulbs and not a few blows to Sarah's arms and head. When she woke him, she rescued herself as well as him from assaults and obligations. "I was saving us," he would tell her, blinking, before he fell back asleep and she sat up, panting a little and, sometimes, bruised. "They were coming and I had to save us."

She remembered that she had thanked him whenever he saved them from his dreams by slugging her. "We always dreamed crazy," Sarah said in the Blazer outside Kattelville, on 12, "and we always stayed in what you might call touch."

She wondered what she might have done if Stephen and Barrett were having their nightmares concurrently. She thought: I'd have stuck them in bed together and I'd have slept on the sofa downstairs. No, she thought, because then Barrett would be thrashing around and pounding on the son he was presumably protecting from invasion. You could slam your wife in the name of salvation, she thought, but it was really too much if you decked your kid while he was sheltering from his own interior storms. Maybe that's why they invented king-size beds, she thought: to keep families from wiping themselves out.

She remembered her mother and her first king-size bed. Her

parents had gone to New York City, where her mother had to attend a conference on running high schools. Her father was going to the exhibition of Colonial broadsides and newspapers at the main library on 42nd Street while her mother went to meetings. She was going to skip the alleged banquet and evening session, and they were going to see an Arthur Miller revival at Circle in the Square, downtown, after dinner together someplace on 14th Street. When they came home and unwound Sarah from the telephone cord and liberated her stayover sitter, and when Sarah affected boredom and asked, "So how was it?" her mother, she remembered, had smiled a broad smile and said, "I slept on my first king-size bed, Sarah. It was *enormous*."

Sarah was fifteen, and she'd known enough to ask, "What was, Ma?"

Her father's large eyes had grown huge, and he'd reddened. All he could say to her was "What? What the hell? *What?*"

But her mother had said, "Biggest damned bed I ever slept in my entire life, Sarah. There was enough room to keep the suit-cases there with us, if we'd wanted to. We could have stuck you and the telephone under the covers, too."

Sarah remembered losing the tempting, terrible image of her rampant father and her lust-crazed mother performing unspecific atrocities upon each other. She had thought, she remembered, of her mother in pajamas, asleep, stretching and kicking with her big-nailed toes. "Gag me, *please*," she'd said.

Her father had said, "What?"

"Gag me with a spoon," her mother had said, in a decent parody of Sarah impaled by disgust.

In the Blazer, she grinned about the hotel, about the bed, about her mother's unsophisticated aplomb and about her father's confusion. Of course, he had known for years, she knew, that he was required, from time to time, to assume confusion — a camouflage suit, she thought, a mask from a German opera about disguises, or greasepaint and a false mustache — and he did it quite professionally and well. It gave him pleasure, she believed, to be outsmarted by the women in his family.

He probably did belong to her, she thought, as much as any person ever had.

You're always thinking about *possessing* people, she told herself.

Yes, and the opposite too, she thought, remembering Eddie as he sat on a wooden milk crate opposite a canvas he'd leaned against the wall, and smoked the unfiltered cigarettes her father had until recently smoked. He sat and looked at his picture, his left leg crossed over the right, holding his ankle, waggling his foot, leaning back by pulling against his ankle, and sending up blue-gray streams of smoke she liked listening to him sigh away into the air as she read in bed and affected independence while staring at his powerful back. She remembered a night for two reasons: because she had wanted to be stroking him and wouldn't say so, and because she envied him the ease, the terrible separateness, that enabled him, without apparent reluctance, to position the canvas and carton so that he could sit before his picture with his back squared toward her, yards away in the bed, and read his own mind.

Barrett saw Sarah and Eddie Slovitz on the verge of parting when, just after meeting her, he began to imitate a man who had fallen, with life-threatening velocity, in love. He felt as though his crash-dive plummet toward Sarah were crumpling his face, distorting his voice as the G-forces mounted. They were across a circle of eight or ten artists and the herring gulls of art — part-time gallery salesfolk, curators in training, a professor of art who wrote mostly about people who wrote about configuring video images, and a couple who specialized in getting laid by the same artist on the same night. Then there was the bald guy with the big shoulders who wore a sportcoat over a twenty-five-year-old seersucker shirt, striped, with big collars, and the woman beside him whose height and tense slenderness, whose frizzy dark hair and vast blue eyes and pallor made Barrett leave the ghetto of architects drinking Laphroig and slowly, still studying her, walk across the room.

The circle of artists and scavengers was convened, of course, for the passing of joints. Several went around at once, as if they would smoke dope the way a chorus sings rounds. The one with the shoulders and big neck and shirt open on a hairy chest was rolling a joint from the communal plastic bag — supplied, no doubt, Barrett thought, by one of the architects or gallery people — while he stuttered a cough and slowly, reluctantly, released what he'd pulled in. The progression was clockwise from him, and Sarah, the woman with the eyes and hair and the sad mouth, was at the end of it all, receiving the smoked-down roaches and — he saw that the others never noticed, for they were happily screwed up and, therefore, sealed over in themselves — holding them an instant, looking about, then leaning to stub them out in a big ceramic ashtray on the plant stand behind her. Sometimes she got them into the ashtray and sometimes she jammed them into the earth of the blooming Wandering Jew on the planter. Each time, Barrett saw, she looked with a kind of despair at the man in the old-fashioned shirt. He had the manic look of a man afraid to see the face of the desperate woman beside him.

The sculptor who was their host on Vestry Street in New York, a man named Harry with sweet eyes and, Barrett thought, from what he knew, the biggest gift in the long loft, put on one of the ultimate camp records: Sophie Tucker, virtually on her deathbed, singing Johnny Mathis hits. It was like listening to a truck imitating a bird. But there were lush strings, and she looked so innocent, so bewildered, as she ruined the smoking by absently stubbing the joints out and looking at the big, frightened man with a regret Barrett thought he would trade happiness to have directed at him.

As one of the artist-vampers called out, "Hey, who's got the joints?" Barrett came through the circle and crossed the naked floor to reach the bearded man and the sad woman.

"Would you care to dance?" Barrett asked her. She looked startled, as if the idea of dancing didn't occur among her island people. "Oh," Barrett said, bowing — *bowing* — and turning to the man she was with. They were the same height, Barrett was surprised to see. It was this fellow's width, his big chest and belly and shoulders, that made him look shorter. Barrett had the sense that this man was so packed, so dense with energy and muscle, that he could explode. Barrett was very reluctant to be the explodee. "Listen," Barrett said, "I'm sorry if this is a drag for you, but do you think anybody would mind if I danced with your wife?"

"This is not my wife," the big man said, rolling a joint while he looked at Barrett. The man's chin was lifted as if he were about to make a provocative point, or detect the rat that Barrett might have brought along.

"I am not his wife," the blue-eyed woman said. "Are you — I didn't hear the beginning of it. Are you asking me if you can dance with him, or him if you can dance with me?"

Barrett said, "I was trying to be polite to everybody, but I had this, you might call it an *impulse* to come over here. I was back over there, with the businessmen and criminals and architects? I ought to admit to you now, I'm in architecture? I saw you, and I really wanted to dance with you." He turned back to the man and said, "Is that all right?"

She said, calling it loudly over the party din, "Why do you keep on asking Eddie?"

Barrett offered his hand. "Eddie," he said. "Barrett."

Eddie held up the joint and the bag of dope to indicate that he would be unable to shake hands. Barrett noted that Sarah closed her eyes at that point.

"Am I making trouble?" Barrett asked.

"I don't know," Eddie said, lifting his chin again, "are you?"

Barrett smiled at Sarah and slowly nodded his head. She looked at him while the dirty-song queen sang the Johnny Mathis arrangement of the theme from *Picnic*. And Barrett remembered at the end of that night, and even now, in Santa Fe or hell or wherever he was, the look on Sarah's face as she raised her left hand to the height of Barrett's shoulder and, staring at Eddie, stepped up to Barrett, turned toward him and began to dance against him. She understood that something was impossible. She was moving like a train down a track, farther and farther from whatever it was that she and Eddie knew, the instant she looked back, that they couldn't have either then or ever.

Barrett could fancy, as he told himself this story, that he had stolen Sarah from Eddie Slovitz. But he knew better as they danced in Harry's loft in New York when they were students, her cold small fist inside his hand, her body against his as if his feeling her body and her feeling his didn't matter to her. And he knew it now. Sarah and Eddie had tried for something together and failed, and they knew it, and Barrett did too. He thought, in Santa Fe, that he had probably never forgiven her the enormousness of what she had tried for with Eddie, or the breadth of her sorrow for its loss.

Marylinn had made him lie naked on the harsh polyester sheets of the Arrow Motel while she, wearing no clothing but her cowboy boots, had slowly nibbled her way up the length of each leg, stopping to brush her face and hair over his groin, but not otherwise touching him. Every time he moved, she'd barked, "No!"

She'd pushed his legs farther apart and had crouched between them, her lips just above his penis, and she had spoken into it, still not touching him, as if it were a microphone, and Marylinn was on the air. "Obedience and discipline," she whispered, her warm breath making him jerk and bob as if his penis were a sapling, she a storm. "If we're going to establish an orderly life, we have to have obedience and discipline." He leaned up, as if working on his stomach muscles, to watch her spread her lips wide and *hush* her breath onto him. "Self-reliance is part of this exercise," Marylinn said, raising herself onto her knees and lifting her buttocks into the air. He saw her support herself on one bent arm as the other moved between her legs. She closed her eyes and moved her hand, then opened them and said, "Lay *still*, Barrett." She hummed to herself and breathed hot breath on him, slowly moving her hand and beginning to dance her buttocks side to side, back and forth. "Oh, Barrett," she said, "this one's gonna be so good." She said, "So good" again, then, "So good." She said, "This is taking no time at *all*, little guy, and —" She moved her body, moved her hand, she breathed heat down onto him and then touched him with her tongue, then lowered her head as he raised himself all the way from Pennsylvania through New Mexico into her mouth.

That had been the early exercise before the day's excursion. Barrett hadn't drawn a grid, or bought a souvenir for Stephen, or gone into Santa Fe. He knew by then that though he was frightened of finding Sarah, finding her or not had not that much to do with his fears. He was a husband, he was a father, and he was riding in a Mercedes on a seat he knew was made of human skin, and the woman who drove them over the Rio Grande on New Mexico 5 was a thousand years old and incapable of fear.

She hadn't spoken since they left the motel except to say she was broadening his education, since it was clearly what he'd come there for.

He had said, "I came here looking for my wife," keeping his voice low and even, hoping that his casual understatement would persuade — if not himself — Marylinn.

She had leaned over, sliding her hand up and down his thigh in what he thought of as her collegial grasp, and she'd said, not looking at the road but into his face, and for long enough to frighten him, "Now, Barrett. Now, I *told* you already, so let's keep the cows with the cows and the bulls with the shit, all right? I believe I did make it clear that you came here for two reasons only — to meet up with me, and firstly to run just as fast as you could away from everything you packed too tight into your life. That's why I'm taking you here. Not another word after you kiss me hello again."

As if the traffic coming their way at 65 or 70 were incidental, Marylinn leaned over with her hand companionably on his leg and she extracted a long, tonguey kiss that she finished, as he leaned back, by ducking forward and licking his lips.

They drove through more of the usual pink-orange sandy land-scape of what Barrett was certain was another planet, until they turned off the main road and went over a long livestock grate that marked the beginning of the Santa Clara pueblo. The dusty road went between cliffs, and then over what Barrett thought of as desert. There were hills, gray and blue and blurry far off in all directions, but near them he saw nothing but sand and scraggly piñon, gnarled cactus. It seemed like a good place to be driven by this woman in this car. The air conditioning was low, and while he looked through tinted windows at Mars, he smelled the cheap motel soap and, beneath it, Marylinn's skin. The perfume she used, he thought, only filtered but never suppressed the odor of her flesh.

Vegetation increased, and there was even a little grass, and then the road narrowed and climbed, and cliffs rose to their left. They were yellower than the pink-orange of the desert and foot-hills, and the sky above them seemed brighter, a lighter blue, less pearly. Marylinn stopped at a little cabin and paid an Indian man in uniform and signed a book. She got them parked on a scrubby lot past the cabin and motioned him out of the car.

"There," she said, pointing at a path. He saw that it went to a series of wide wooden stairs and then a winding, sandy track, then very narrow wooden steps, more bends and turns of track, and then cliffs, high and distant, with a ledge halfway up, and wooden ladders that went from the ledge to the top. Although two more cars were in the lot, Barrett saw nobody else on the trail or on the cliffs. "The Puye cliffs," she said. "We're about seven thousand feet up, and the air gets thin. You're gonna pant like we're in bed before you get there. This here we're on is called a mesa, by the way. You heard of them in cowboy movies more than likely. Welcome to your mesa experience. Now you're not a virgin anymore, almost."

As usual, Marylinn led and he followed. He was breathing hard before they were up the first broad flight of steps, and by the time they had got to the narrow, winding track, he saw black spots and was reaching harshly for breath. He never quite caught it. He speculated that this was not the moment for telling Marylinn that he was uneasy about heights of more than two feet, and that on multistory jobs he walked, whenever possible, with a hand in manly friendship on the shoulder of whichever contractor he dealt with so as to keep himself from plunging eight or ten feet to his death. Marylinn's hips and legs before him did not remind him of bed and of her extraordinary hunger and invention. They looked to him, now, as wonderful stanchions, handholds against the increasing steepness of the angle at which they climbed.

When they reached the ledge, and he insisted on looking forward with terrific interest because he was afraid to even consider looking down and back, he saw, heaving for breath, that the shadows he had noted at the foot of the caves — and all they had climbed to was the foot — were really entrances. Caves had been carved in the sandstone four and five hundred years ago, according to the leaflet Marylinn had handed him. He thought of small, wiry dark-skinned people, crouching here, cooking, carving — and that was when he forgot himself a little. For the rock had been carved, ten and twelve feet above the ledge they stood on, and he traced with his eyes the shape of a lizard, the radiant ball of the sun. Barrett rubbed his fingertips against the tan, coarse stone of the cliff above an entranceway.

"This is the most I ever believed about religion," Marylinn said, pointing to the glyphs on the stone. "I mean, up here and all, with all this, you can get tempted into believing something, couldn't you?"

She looked wounded in the cruel light and thin air, and Barrett, wishing for breath more than sustaining it, put his arm behind her hard back and pulled her into a kiss. There was no tonguing or chewing, there was nothing erotic for him as he kissed her. It was sorrow and inability and gratitude and loss and brotherhood, he thought. And only you would end up kissing her like this.

She pushed him away, but left her hands on his chest. Her hands rose and fell as Barrett tried to catch his breath. Marylinn looked at him and her mouth fell into a sort of sneer. He smiled as if he understood her expression, and she reached to gently slap his cheek. Then she looked away and, gesturing, turned and marched them on, toward a ladder that narrowed at the top. "You go ahead this time," Marylinn said, "so's I can catch you — well, I couldn't do that, could I? Maybe I could?"

"You could break my fall," he said, straining to fill his lungs and failing.

"Sugar, I have *done* that already now, haven't I?"

And Barrett, nodding somberly, then looking away, had started to climb. He heard Marylinn below him, and he sensed the country spinning out beneath and around him. He shut his eyes and thought that he could lift off and give himself to the air and fly, the way it was possible to let go of the side of a dock and lie on the dark, frightening surface of the ocean and, giving yourself up, be held afloat by the sea. He felt the ladder narrow, so he knew he was approaching the top. With his eyes still closed, moving slowly and breathlessly, he pretended that when he reached the top and rolled over clumsily he would find Stephen and Lizzie and Will waiting. They would greet him with glad cries and gesture behind them. He would look up in exhaustion to see Sarah, wearing, say, her baggy white shorts and a crisp, clean white T-shirt and sandals. He couldn't think of one word that she might say. He reached up and felt nothing and knew he had come to the top.

Barrett opened his eyes and saw the barren, sandy surface of the clifftop. Now he would have to step up and to the side, with nothing above him to hang on to. Now was when he would fall, he thought. He stayed where he was, breathing as if he had run for miles. He didn't know how to move on.

Marylinn, below him, rapped on the heel of his shoe. "Hey," she said.

He said, "Hey."

"You stuck?"

"I believe I am," he said, closing his eyes again.

"You could jump off backwards," she called up to him. "You could do one of those two and a half harpoon willie gainer backward tuck things they do on the Olympics. You know? Or just let go and do a bellywhopper but backwards. What's that? A spinewhopper?"

He didn't answer, though beneath his eyelids he was seeing himself fall and fall and fall and strike the ledge, then bounce off, go limp and roll the rest of the hundreds of feet down, bouncing from time to time off jutting boulders, his tattered body growing bloodier through the tan dust as he fell off the Puye cliffs and out of New Mexico and his marriage and his life and the world.

Marylinn rapped on the back of his shoe again, and he started. She said, "Easy, son. Climb back to me. I think we've got as far as we'll get. You back on down to me and I'll keep you from pitching off."

He leaned his forehead against the final rung. He knew that if he looked up he would see condors and vultures circling. He had seen them in the desert on the way, and had noted them in Santa Clara when they'd arrived. But he hadn't felt at the time like something's meal. He kept his eyes closed, and he stayed where he was.

"Were you thinking of that, Barrett?"

"What?"

"You know, what I was joking about?"

"Were you joking, Marylinn?"

"Some," she said in a flat, harsh voice he didn't remember.

They stayed that way on the narrowing ladder, and then, coming toward them from the back of the clifftop, Barrett heard the voices of children and then the voice of a man and then a woman. The steady wind was warm and peppery with sand. The sweat on his back and neck began to cool and he felt a shiver coming up his spine the way a sneeze begins. He opened his mouth to sneeze, but nothing more happened: he felt colder than he'd felt, and he hung on, starting, suddenly, to sweat again, to bow his head beneath the sun. He shifted a leg and began to let his foot drop toward the rung below.

"Or maybe we'd have found out we can fly," Marylinn said, lightly touching his foot, guiding it to a lower rung.

We could make a terrarium in an old pickle jar I have. I could show you how to mix charcoal with sand and lay that into the jar set sideways on the table. We'd put topsoil over that, and the mosses, the black medick or some other kind of clover, lichens on rocks, knotweed. Water everything, and close the jar. You'd have the natural world under glass.

Like everything else, it was a matter of timing, of assuming a certain deftness, of not admitting even inside the car as she sat staring — in, admit it, some panic — at the school buses, at the parents and probably grandparents in their cars at the end of the crescent-shaped drive where the children came out the door and down the hill. You asked at the Superette and they told you where the school was. You looked at your watch, you drove around for a little while, you drank coffee and ate a sandwich in the car, and then it was dismissal time. We'll wear rubber gloves and paint with bleach on colored paper. We'll heat a little jar of mothballs in a pan of water to make crystal shapes. Come here. Come here.

Someone might be there for him, probably *would* be there, but you have to act. She thought, I've always acted when I had to. Darling: here. She tried to imagine what the grandparents would look like. Sarah had, with great reluctance, shown her the pictures in her wallet: of a tall, wiry, nervous-looking handsome man with worry furrows above his nose, and of the boy, her grandson, *her* grandson, with his parents' height and with Sarah's and her large eyes. The boy looked like her, Gloria thought. And why shouldn't he?

Sodas were in the cooler on the back seat, and medication beside them just in case. Refrigeration made the phenobarbital taste better, pediatricians said. They prescribed it as an anti-convulsant for high fevers in kids. She herself was in favor of using brewed willow bark as a tea to relieve fever, but the phe-nobarb made you so sleepy, and of course the point here might be sleep, not fever. If necessary, her grandson could sleep all the way home.

Gloria wasn't sure, she had to admit, what she would do once they *were* home, though heaven knows there were enough projects, from building an aluminum-can birdfeeder to making a planetarium with punched-out constellation shapes in a cereal box. But she knew that grandparents had rights, and women had rights, and she was a grand*mother*, and everything, now, was going to be right. Things get wrong, but they also get right. It happens in your life, no matter how difficult the years have been. It happens, and if you make your plans and buy a bag of ice at the Superette to chill the various flavors of soda and the phenobarbital, red as lollipops, and then you sip your coffee and pick the pieces of chicken heart and liver and gizzard out of the homemade mayonnaise in the sandwich and you wait, the better days finally start.

As the children straggle down, listening to something inside their minds or hearing their digestive tracts gurgle — what do they do as they walk so undeliberately, so inattentively? — all you really need to do is open the box of chocolate-covered doughnuts so the rich chemical-vanilla smell rises in the car, then wind the passenger-side window down and lean your chinny-chin-chin on the window ledge and watch them approach.

The child who walked with his legs awkwardly apart, as if chafed or injured. No: look at the dark stain at the crotch of his jeans. The child bearing the large note that would doubtless be about the stain. The child with the green book bag. He is looking so far inside himself, he doesn't see the cars at the curb. Life's so dangerous for little boys who don't look up, she thought. I see so *much* in my practice, she thought, as if replying to someone's remark that Gloria hadn't raised boys, never mind girls, and never mind *girl*, the one girl.

Come here.

We can string dried beans and peas and woven bits of grass into a necklace for your mommy. We can make shapes with sand on glue. Sand is worn-down bits of igneous, sedimentary or metamorphic rock. If we find sandstone, that's a sedimentary rock, then we'll have reds and browns and yellows. I can show you places on the hills and near my house where wind, rivers, rain and even people walking on paths made erosion happen. Erosion means things wearing away, and you can make a shape on paper with what's left from wearing away.

Come here.

Sarah's wide eyes and mine, she thought, looking from the drive to the rearview mirror, watching herself watching, then diving across the seat to crouch at the window and say, in a whisper, "Stephen! Here!" He couldn't hear her, she thought. But Stephen looked up. To call to him but not in the hearing of anyone else — only a mother, a grandmother, could urge the thought across the air like that. "Stephen?"

She beckoned: Come here, darling. And Stephen, wide-legged, pale, looking ill now that he was close, looking febrile, the nurse thought, came a little closer to the car, then stopped.

"That's right, darling. You're wise to be cautious. But look at my eyes, Stephen. No, really, darling: look at them. They're the same as your mommy's, aren't they? Aren't they your mommy's eyes? Stephen, I'm your other *grandma*. Stephen. Look."

He said, "*My* mommy?"

"Can't you see her in my eyes? But we have to hurry, darling."

"Where? To Mommy?"

"That's my Stephen. Hurry, darling. Remember, I am not a stranger. This is *not* talking to strangers, because I'm Mommy's mommy. And *that's* not being a stranger, is it?"

A car honked behind her, and Gloria wanted to turn to see. But she knew that in moments like this, the non-sensory element, the telepathic element, was particularly important: the unspoken speech between parent and child, grandparent and grandchild, the language of cells, the secret, silent communication of the DNA.

She levered the door open and swung it gently out. She smiled her grandest, gentlest nurse's matter-of-fact smile. She pushed the seat belt into place across him, resisting her own powerful need to embrace him, to feel his vertebrae all in a row, to see his healthy teeth and gums, to feel his bony arms. She was careful not to breathe in his face: children hate the stale breath of grown-ups, she knew, and they could hate you for a sour stomach. She started the car, she looked back, and she saw, three cars behind her, standing beside the open driver's side door of some low gray sports car, the elegant, long-nosed, wide-mouthed woman in expensive business clothes whose white, horrified face and gesturing arms, whose long legs moving her from the sports car toward Gloria's, simply had to belong to the poor stupid bitch who had thought to own her child.

Gloria pulled out and drove sedately. She wouldn't drive back past the school, she knew. She would drive straight away from the woman who still ran toward her. She would find her way out of Burroughs, and she would get them, driving at the legal speed, back home.

"What's your favorite cookie?" Gloria asked the child, who stared at her with Sarah's eyes. "Grandma loves to bake," she said.

JESSIE NEWBOLD was at the desk downstairs, taking ads and engagement notices, accepting small items about high school dropouts who had completed training at quasi-respectable schools that trained people to load baggage onto airplanes and deliver coffee to firms that rented their coin-operated machines — *Join the Airline Industry! Earn Top Dollar!* or *Food Service Means Fast Growth!* She was part-time and more or less kept her own hours. Will knew she was working when Stovall Stratton's Lite Crucifixion station was switched to an all-talk station that lonely people called to state their opinions about changes in the order that were upsetting them. Through the floor, over the clang of the Model 5 Linotype, from which Stovall, on Jessie's days in, seemed able to crank more noise as the matrices dropped through the assembling rig, Will heard admonitions of ecological disaster and protests that it wasn't really a matter of their being Hispanic that was offending the caller — it was their *hygiene*, it was the smell of their peculiar *cooking*, it was their *noise*. He always saw Stovall on those days as the mad-organist Phantom beneath the Opera, slamming the brass down, pounding the lines into shape, cackling as hot lead squirted over the words.

Jessie liked to call out her ideas as the people on the radio called in theirs. She was communicating, and often she did so while customers were discussing advertising rates or essential impending events. So, today, Will was standing at his desk, palms down on either side of his typewriter, leaning over it, eyes closed, hearing Jessie say, "I think we *oughta* have the draft. They drafted my husband. They drafted my youngest boy. No reason these kids with their green hair and naked half the time can't serve. Maybe those Arabs would listen a little better if we had a draft. Anyway, that's just my opinion."

This was Jessie's answer to a question about a display ad. Will wanted to shake his head, or laugh, or call out to Jessie that she was fired, or maybe hurl a little invective around. What he was doing, at the end of a long, gagging, bubbly cough, was drooling blood and sputum onto the typewriter and the page he'd been working on, about the toxic emissions of the local pharmaceuticals company. He hung his head in some pain, but mostly in fear. That was why his eyes were closed. And of course the bright little red blots on his copy were not encouraging. He thought it best, overall, to keep his eyes closed and stand there a while. If he did that, furthermore, he would not have to contemplate cleaning up his copy — he did acknowledge this double-entendre with a flecked, small smile. He wondered: Did you carry the whole machine into the bathroom and run water over the platen? Did you sponge it down with the tail of your shirt?

He decided, at last, to tear the page out of the machine, keeping his eyes closed, and toss it in the direction of the wastebasket. Then he stuck his fingers into the space between the roller and the support behind it and wiped back and forth. He rubbed his hand on his dark slacks, reached behind him to find the arm of his oak swivel chair and sat. His legs were out before him, partway under the desk. His hands, he found, were clasped and on his solar plexus, as if he were praying. He had not chosen to pray, and anyway, he thought, Lite Jesus wasn't on the radio today — Jessie and the citizenry of the airwaves were conversing now on the matter of sonic booms near the Hancock Airport outside of Syracuse — so he lay each arm on an arm of the chair and directed himself toward rationality.

He found that he had a cigarette between the fingers of his right hand, a book of matches, open, in his left. He saw that he was going to smoke a cigarette. In a way, his actions made sense to him: he thought best while smoking, and surely this was a matter deserving of thought. On the other hand, there was the gag, the bubbly sound in his chest, the pain, the long rasping cough, the bloody little spatter.

Jessie called to the radio, topics having kept the pace of the world's fast-breaking news events, "Well, of course he kept it a secret. It's his White House, ain't it? He's the President, ain't he? Who's supposed to know better?"

Will thought of dogs eating poisoned woodchuck day after day in the fields, of fat people buying candy bars at the Superette, of rummies grabbing their daily liter of Four Roses, of men and women in business — say, at the pharmaceuticals plant — who pumped out what gave their townsfolk, and maybe them, cancers of the reproductive system. He sighed the smoke out and waited for a pain in his chest, or another cough, but, except for a sense of impaction and a little heaviness under the breastbone, he felt fine. He felt serene, in fact.

He was crying, suddenly, and he couldn't explain it. He wiped his nose with the hand that held the cigarette, using the back of his hand like a kid, and as he cried he thought of his daughter and he thought of her son. With his other hand he wiped his mouth, and he decided that he would not look just now to see if his hand had got bloodied.

Each time he thought of Lizzie, Will directed himself to study the issues of the day as reported on the air and through the floor joists. But the discussions now filled him with scorn, with rage.

His fury extended to Jessie, a victim to whose noise he was. He continued to want to lift the phone and call Lizzie, who would just about now be leaving to pick Stephen up at school. He knew he mustn't. He knew that if there was a secret he must keep from her, it squatted inside his body today. It was a terrible secret to live with, he thought, inhaling the smoke and waiting for it to bite. It didn't. It seemed to crouch wetly inside him, filling his chest. It was the worst secret, he thought. And the only person he needed to say it to, the only shelter he sought from its meaning, was the former Lizzie Bean.

But he did pull himself on the chair's casters toward his desk, and he did punch her number on the phone. Karen answered, to say that she had left early to fetch Stephen, that she herself was leaving now to get Noel and then go home. Was it urgent?

"Oh, no, Karen. No. I'll see her soon enough in person, won't I?"

He sounded so tranquil, he thought she would imagine him talking to her from the outskirts of a nap. He sounded like a healthy man, he thought. Perhaps he was. Perhaps he had a bronchitis. Perhaps a polyp the size of his fist adhered to the wall of his throat. You can get those, smoking.

"Of course," he told himself, hanging up and shaking his head in disgust. He jammed the cigarette into the ashtray and felt the heat of the coals on his fingers. "You spit a little blood and smoke two, two and a half packs a day, the first thing you think of is it's the *smoking* makes you sick. You think of — " He would not say the name of the disease. "You think something like that, you're a hypochondriac. You've got a cough." He coughed. "If you gotta cough," he said in Groucho Marx's voice. He couldn't say another word. He leaned back in the old swivel chair and it creaked. He crossed his fingers on his belly, and he listened, through the floor, to admonitions and rejoinders.

*   *   *

224

Sarah was at the edge of town, touring her childhood house. She put down the white canvas plumber's bag and unfastened both latches. As if this *were* her home, as if she really lived here still, she carried the clothing that Gloria had washed to the pantry and she checked the washer: Stephen's underpants and undershirt, pajamas, some of his socks, some bedclothes — colored wash with white, she scolded in her thoughts. Now she knew where she had learned to violate that particular taboo and why she always mixed the dark and white because it saved the time she thought of as wasted in sorting. "Let's all sing it, ladies: Fuck what's orderly," she said. She moved the sheets and Stephen's clothing to the dryer and, noting that she had failed to check the lint filter for overloading, she turned the dryer on, tossed her own mixed darks and whites in with maybe too much soap, and switched on the washer. "Hey," she said very quietly, under the chirr and gurgle of machines, "I'm home."

She carried the bag of food to the garbage and dumped it. "Lizzie, meet Gloria, my mother. Gloria, meet my, well, mother, you know?" Then she removed the fake Acoma pot and carried it in her left hand as she strolled through the house. Some of the furniture was probably good, she thought, rubbing her hand on the old harvest table at which they dined during holidays and on state occasions. The Hepplewhite sofa table, the low Stickley bench, the maybe Shaker sewing table — she'd live with them. The sofas themselves were a little shabby, but that's what happens when you get comfortable. She knew the North Carolina manufacturer, and the frames were good. At a window in the far corner of the living room, looking over the dead end of what was more of a shady lot than a street, she sat at the oak library table where she used to do her homework, when forced to do homework. Here was where she had written thank-you notes at gunpoint after Christmas or a birthday. She reached under the lip of the chunky table and felt where she had scratched an execration on parents and their maleficent rules.

She carried the pot upstairs. The master bedroom was in disarray, as it always had been, even when she'd been enjoined by its occupants to straighten up her own room. There was the mail-order catalogue her mother had been reading while she used the blow dryer on her hair this morning. She read so as not to be bored by a chore she not only resented, but by her devotion to which she was embarrassed. On her father's bureau, clean underwear, and shirts from the dry cleaners, were stacked in two teetering piles that propped each other up. His disorder was always neat, she noted: he piled the smaller undershorts on the larger shirts and the socks on top of them all. He was a symmetrical man, she told herself, and that ought to tell her something about him. She didn't know what, though.

The town's alarm went off, deep and frighteningly loud, insistent. Almost at once, she heard the sound of volunteers' cars and pickups accelerating to the firehouse for the location of the emergency. She walked past the larger bathroom down the hall to what had been her room. During her second year of college, they had called it the guest room once or twice, and she had responded, over the phone from school, with low-grade hysterics. She stopped and let breath wince slowly out of her — Stephen was sleeping here, she saw. She picked up some of his shirts, tossed on the floor at the end of the bed. She put her nose to them and inhaled. "Aren't you still a baby," she said.

His papers were on her desk. She felt, suddenly, that she mustn't read what he had written in school, and not because she was violating his privacy. She was afraid of what he had said about his mother, who had left to go crazy in hers, or go to southwestern Pennsylvania, or go to her birth mother, or — wasn't it pretty much this simple? — *go away*. It seemed to her to be a lot wiser and easier and less of a hemorrhage to set the

Acoma pot on the desk, on his desk and hers, and to leave the room as much to him as now she could.

The siren kept sounding as she walked to the little bathroom where, on the white towel crookedly hung from its ancient dime-store aluminum rack, there were three lovely smears of boy mud — one for each of Stephen's hands and one for his face. It was like looking at a relic, preserved in a bog in some northern country in Europe. It was like the Shroud of Whereverthatwas, in which you saw Christ's face.

Downstairs, the back door slammed and feet moved heavily, hurriedly, across the kitchen floor. A man's voice made what Sarah would call soothing noises. Her mother's voice responded, higher than she remembered it, the syllables coming in gulps, in bites. The air in the house seized up with emergency, and Sarah moved to Stephen's door, to hers, to theirs, and then she ran, calling, shrill, she feared, as a schoolgirl: "What? Mommy, *what?*"

The village cop, big, earnest whatsit, Pierson, stood behind her mother, who stood at the telephone and said, "No, it's not about the elementary school, sir. It took place there. It's about my grandson being kidnaped *from* the elementary school. Would you people consider that as something of an unusual occurrence? Would you kindly get a little *excited?* Could you break a *sweat?*"

"Stephen!" Sarah said.

"No," the policeman said, "Ben. Ben Pierson. Hey, Sarah, how are you?"

"Yes," she said, "excuse me. Did she — did my mother say, did she mean kidnap when she just said it?"

"Well," he said, as if to adjust matters to their actual proportions, "it does seem that somebody in one of those old tan Eagles — you know those humpy cars so high off the ground, with the round back and the four-wheel drive? Back when AMC wasn't part of Chrysler?"

"Jesus!" Sarah said.

"Great cars," Mr. Pierson agreed. "They were ahead of their time, of course. Like the old Studebaker, that was before your day. The back and the front looked so —"

But Sarah screamed, so he stopped. She did it again, and Mr. Pierson stepped back. Her mother hung up and, while sirens went on, came forward to seize Sarah, to shake her shoulders, to step back again and hurl her fist around, slamming it into Sarah's shoulder and knocking her a pace sideways with its velocity. Sarah nodded and wept louder. Her mother stepped in and, shaking her head, embraced her, kept pulling her in, and Sarah went limp against her. "Mommy," she said. "Stephen."

"Some wild woman with hair sticking up all over, frizzy and electric-looking, she got him to come over while he was walking out of school to where I was supposed to meet him. I came late, just a *little* late, you know those afternoons when I have to sprint to get away from the office, and he just went over and looked in the window and listened and she talked, he got in, they drove away. Like that. I'm so sorry, darling. Five minutes, or one minute —"

Sarah, this time, stepped back and put her hands on her mother's shoulders. She shook her head as she spoke, and then told her, "I know where he is. I think so. That's Gloria."

"Who's Gloria?"

"My — oh, shit, Mommy." She leaned on her mother and whispered to the side of her face, "The woman who had me. The hatcher. Birth mother. The one who gave birth to me?"

Her mother went so white and so quickly, Sarah thought she would faint or throw up or simply stop breathing, then, forever. Her mother said only, "Oh."

"Yes, there was this ad."

"You took it out?"

Sarah smiled and shook her head. She wanted that gesture to

say *Never*, but she had no idea what her mother thought. So she shrugged. So her mother did. "You didn't tell me about this when you called. From wherever."

"No."

"But that matters, darling. Doesn't it?"

"I sure wanted it to, I'll tell you that. But you maybe can't believe how little it did. Does. Amazing, isn't it."

"That you ran off, searching for her, without telling Barrett or Stephen or us or anyone *why?*"

"This is what you said we wouldn't say, Mommy."

Then they both stood very still, looking at each other, their eyes simply leaking onto stiffened faces because they had got beyond tears, though their bodies didn't know it yet.

Behind Sarah, Mr. Pierson said, "The ambulance and fire-truck boys'll be waiting at the school for instructions."

She thought of the earnest men, their radios crackling on their belts, the loud voice of the county dispatcher buzzing from the speakers on the two yellow fire trucks and the yellow and white ambulance truck, all the lights and panting engines and coiled hose and the gawkers about them as the men walked to and fro, waiting for something reasonable, like a fire or collision or heart exploding out of someone's chest. She laughed, one desperate whoop that she caught.

Her mother raised her eyebrows over wet eyes as if to ask, Well?

Sarah said to her, very low, "I know where she took him. I'm pretty sure. I was there. I'll find it again."

Her mother said, "Let's go." Then she said, "Wait." On a small yellow tablet she scrawled a note. "Would you see that Will gets hold of this, Ben? So he doesn't go nuts when we all turn up missing?"

He took the note and, frowning, read aloud: "*Sarah back. Stephen gone. We're fetching him. Call from road.*"

Her mother said, "That's, that means we'll call him from our being on the road, Ben."

"He doesn't need to call you, you're saying."

Sarah let another whoop out and couldn't stop it as it descended and then began to rise again.

Her mother looked at her, hard, and said, "You're right. Everyone in this house is crazy. Except you, Ben. Can we take your car, Sarah? Ben drove me back in his."

"Why?"

"What?"

"Why'd you come back here? Did you come to get me?"

Her mother, checking in her purse for money, shook her head. "No," she said in a level, sensible tone, "girlish hysterics."

Sarah whooped again and her mother nodded.

"Ass over teakettle nuts," her mother said, tugging her arm and leading her out.

"Nice to see you again, Sarah," Mr. Pierson said, holding the note for her father. "What ought I to be doing here, do you think? And can you suggest where you're off to?"

This time her mother laughed, a bark about nothing funny.

"Hopeless," Sarah agreed as they went, breathing hard, to the Blazer.

"Us or him?" her mother asked.

He slept naked and a little drunk, and when he woke it was to remember how he'd fought for sleep in the merciless room, its air conditioner cranking and pulsing and seeming to heat the walls and floor. He'd finally sipped on sour mash until he'd gotten stupid and had lain flat on the scouring sheets and passed out. And now the chugging of the air conditioner made him feel that he had wakened in the moist, dirty cabin of a wretched cargo vessel toiling up a green, corrosive river toward an inland catastrophe. But he woke, he knew, in the Arrow Motel in Espanola, New Mexico, and it was Marylinn at the door, her hand dropping from the light switch to hang by her side. It was a large, strong hand, he knew, and he kept his eyes on it as he climbed through fatigue, the whiskey and the immensities of self-pity under which, as if inside layers of dense wool, he'd been sweating. The hand lay so helplessly, he thought. This was going to be sad.

Marylinn was wearing something like silk or rayon pajamas, he observed, and tall high heels of the same black suede as the thin belt that drooped around the waist of the sheer, shimmering gold-colored jacket or pajama top. Her hair was all over her face, which was pasty and damp. Her lipstick was gone, her neck was mottled, and she was breathing fast. He watched her body inside the gold suit, and then he looked hard at what he had thought was shadow on the jacket and one leg and the other calf of her clothing.

"You're all stained up, Marylinn," he said, wondering whether he was supposed to cover himself, cover Marylinn or make conversation.

"Stained's a good word for it, Barrett. You want me to close this door? Even if it's kind of stinky in here?"

"If you wouldn't mind," he said, pulling the sheet casually across his lap.

"I've seen so much of it, darlin', I've got it memorized by now. But you do as you please." She closed the door and walked to the closet, which was a cheap folding louvered door over a small depression the height of a tall child. Pushing it open, she felt for something, still watching him, and pulled his suitcase out. "You want to pack, or you want me to do it for you?"

"I'm leaving?"

"You're leaving, son." But she stopped and lit a cigarette she took from the small suede purse on a gold chain that she wore across her chest. "Oh," she said, exhaling, "what a fuckin' *night*.

But that's what you go looking for, I believe. A little proof. A little evidence of life on other planets, including this one, am I right? Look, *you* do the packing. I just have to sit and smoke a while."

She went to the room's chair and sprawled in it. Like a prurient boy, Barrett looked up her legs, from her strong ankles to her crotch. "Why do I have to leave *you?*" he said with what he could have sworn were suggestive tones.

Marylinn smoked with her head back, and she said, almost to the ceiling, "You're not leaving me, darlin'. You left Stephen, remember? So what you're doing, you're going *back* to him is what you're doing. And your wife. She's probably home by now. Or gone to the high grass, and forget her."

"And you?"

"We are too grown up for this kind of talk."

"Right," he said.

"And don't you sulk. Listen: Gordon is really *riding* tonight, you understand?"

"Your husband?"

"The guy with the fast hands?"

"You mean — you're saying this guy is after me? Still?"

"Still? Forever," she said. "It's part of it."

"What?"

"*It*. What happens. What we — do. Look," she said, gesturing at the marks on her clothing, "I was with this guy tonight."

"I tried calling your room."

"I just told you: I was out."

"On a date."

"All right," she said. "We were doing what you do on dates."

Barrett thought of slippery sex in a sacred, forbidden kiva on a pueblo at midnight. And he found himself in a fever of jealousy. The cut on his head throbbed, the hangover he kept blinking his eyes against throbbed, and he stood, wrapped the sheet around his body like a cape, knotted it loosely against his chest and took the suitcase to the bureau.

He said, trying to decide whether to roll or fold his dirty socks, "Old Gordon burst in the door."

"No," she said, "he bought the duplicate key off of the woman at the desk."

Barrett imagined the door opening in, as if he were Gordon, and seeing the clothing on the floor, Marylinn on her hands and knees in some tall, tough westerner's bed.

All he could say, like a sad child, was "I tried calling you."

She sat forward, her knees together, and stubbed the cigarette out. "Don't make me remember you as such an innocent creature," she said. "Please? As some, I don't know, *boy* I got busted up?"

He settled on picking up handfuls of clothing and reaching to stuff them into the bag while he stood at an angle to the bureau so he could see Marylinn. He felt lovesick, as he hadn't since his childhood or, anyway, since he'd learned from Sarah how much Eddie Slovitz had mattered, even after they'd crashed and burned and died together and had come to the party, where Barrett met her, as a kind of sentimental courtesy to Harry, the host, who had taught them both and who loved them as a couple. He felt nauseated, suffocated, weak of limb, as he had when he was fourteen and dying of love.

Marylinn stood up and, her legs a little apart, her hands clasped before her, smiled an ordinary smile that seemed to imply nothing more than her pleasure in seeing him.

"You're so beautiful," he said, surprised not to hear his voice cracking like an adolescent's. "Thank you."

"Thank *you*," she said. "I always wanted to get to know one of you northeastern intellectual architect or artist guys."

"And?"

"And didn't we do some kind of knowing," she said. She strode to him, extended her long arm and broad hand and he shook it.

Then she leaned in and kissed him. He closed his eyes and inhaled, wanting to keep some of her inside him. She pulled her hand away and stepped back. "Good kisser," she said. "Bye."

"Is it blood, Marylinn?"

"This, you mean?"

He nodded. So did she. "Whose?" he asked.

She said, "It isn't mine, darlin'. I'm whole and entire. I'm off. Bye-bye, Barrett. Good luck with your family. Hurry home. Go home." She waved, as if he were some considerable distance away, and then she walked to the door and went out.

He actually felt a surging at the bridge of his nose, a pressure on his eyes. He hadn't wept for Sarah, and here he was in Espanola at the Arrow Motel, having traded vast quantities of body fluids with a woman who had twice refused the condoms he had urged they use and would probably die of AIDS or her husband's abuse, and he was close to tears at her leaving. He told himself how lost she was, and he nodded as he dressed. That was part of it, he thought, part of the energy of her attraction. She was a lost person. She was homeless and drifting and as much of a waif — for all her seeming sense of direction, the placid surface of her wild needfulness, the money that generated the confidence she and her husband radiated — as any hairy madwoman of seventy-five wearing three raincoats and two hats near a big-city soup kitchen.

And aren't you the good fellow who can rescue her, he sneered inside his sore head.

No, he answered. Nor Sarah. Nor Stephen either.

Nor me, he thought as the door, which apparently gave the illusion of locking, much as the air conditioner generated only the sounds of the making of coolness, opened in. "Welcome to the Arrow Motel," he told Gordon, "the hostelry where it's all made up."

Gordon closed the door and stood. He was wearing black

clothing again, and his high-heeled cowboy boots had silver edging at the toes. He nodded, smiled a quick smile. Barrett stared to see whether he wore his mustache.

"I'm packing," Barrett said, rising from the edge of the bed where he'd been lacing his sneakers. They were black and high-topped, and he'd always wondered, wearing them, just what it was he pretended to be in them. "Actually, I'm packed. What I meant was, I'm leaving. Now."

Gordon nodded again. He wasn't all *that* little, Barrett thought. He was narrow, he was short. But he was also compact, and there was a hard look to his chest and neat neck. His arms, as Barrett knew, were powerful enough, and his small hands were very fast. The skin of Gordon's face was shiny, and his dark eyes were flat. He looked like someone else wearing a Gordon mask. The narrow forehead under his shiny black hair was unfurrowed. Except for the crow's-feet at his eyes, Barrett thought, you wouldn't know that he moved the muscles of his face. He wondered if you could sneeze or yawn with your face that tight.

"Did you commit sodomy with my wife?" Gordon asked. The word sounded like "wahf."

"Sodomy," Barrett said. "I don't remember what actually qualifies as sodomy, but, no, no, I'm sure I didn't. We. I'm pretty sure we didn't."

"She suck you off?"

"How do you mean?" Barrett asked, because he could think of nothing else to say.

Gordon said, "Sure. And did you fuck her in the ass?"

"Your wife?" Barrett said.

"Did she hum on you?"

"Guaranteed no," Barrett said, sidling along the bed because there was no place to back toward. "Guaranteed," he said, shaking his head and crossing his arms. "Never."

"Then you're a lucky fella," Gordon said.

"Thank Christ," Barrett said.

Gordon said, "I don't see any need for you to die of your wounds."

Barrett sat down on the bed because he couldn't stand.

"Of course, that's right now," Gordon said, walking toward him.

So Barrett thought of himself as lucky when, not twenty-five minutes later, he picked up Route 25 to get himself to 40 and the East. He was alive. His lip was split in two places. The bruise under his eye, which Gordon had given him the first time, was puffy from the blows it had received tonight. His eye was beating as if something behind it were trying to push it out of the socket. The cut on his head was bleeding again, he thought, but that would be difficult to determine, since Gordon had crushed his face into the lamp shaped like cowgirls on green pottery horses, and the ceramic base as well as the bulb had broken all over him, slicing a little of his scalp and some of his cheek. He leaned to the right to make his sore ribs more comfortable, and he failed. His groin ached. It had ached for two days from Marylinn, but that had been the dull interior thud of the exhausted prostate, whereas this pain came from being kicked directly in the nuts with a metal-shod cowboy boot as the boot's wearer, whirling in the air of a small, sweaty motel room, cried martial-arts fright noises without changing his facial expression.

He remembered movies in which men faking upper-class British accents told about having been vanquished by superior odds, but not before they'd given a good accounting of themselves. If he could move his jaw without very bad pain all over his face, but especially under the left ear and along the jawbone, he would imitate the actors imitating Englishmen, and he would dismiss himself as not, in fact, having given a good accounting of himself.

He was driving quickly now, not looking at the speedometer but staying with the sparse traffic as it moved toward Tijeras in little lighted clusters. The sky was pressing down purple into the blackness, and the purple would soon get granular, he saw, the way it does just before dawn. And he would drive through a piece of Texas and then Oklahoma and start, then, to head up north, maybe catch I-80 in Iowa and begin to get home. He knew he would drive to Will and Lizzie's house in New York State. He knew he would go to fetch Stephen. He knew that he would tell them how profoundly he had failed to bring Sarah home.

But, beyond a lot of empty talk, he hadn't any plans. He would end up in Pennsylvania, trying to make a living. And he would probably design, one way or another, some unexpected day, a wonderful house that he would see constructed for next to no profit. And he would want to write to Marylinn, he would want to think of her opening the mail in some black-tiled foyer that matched her husband's slay-the-lovers outfit, and he would want to see her face as she read how he had all but given a wonderful building away for the sake of — call it his art. Or his shame. Or her scorn. Or her voice behind him near the top of the Puye cliffs as they imagined how you could lean out onto the pearl-bright air and possibly fly.

"You virgin," he said to himself, leaning south for his ribs but heading east, "you boy." Making the words caused such pain in his gums and jaw and the sinuses behind his nose that he started, finally, to cry. Crying hurt too. And, thinking that, he thought for real about Sarah, whom he had wept over before in his life and for whom — he realized now it was the finality of losing her — he wept again tonight. He wished that he could tell Marylinn that he was gripped by what she'd accused him of fleeing. He wished he could say how his head and face and balls and belly and chest and arm were throbbing like one wound.

He saw the sign for the Santa Rosa pueblo. He winced for his ribs as he changed his posture at the wheel. Free for a while of grouped traffic, alone on the dark highway under the terrible wide sky growing lighter and somehow huger, he thought about how intimately and thoroughly he must know his wife to understand that he needed to abandon his child and drive to Santa Fe because, of every place on their continent and the other continents it was possible to reach, she would, he'd known at once, come here to the little city in which, given several days, he could not help but find her.

They'd run along the Chenango River and parts, according to the signs, of the Erie Canal. Gloria thought that would explain why, in the minutes before dusk turned into evening, as they passed above Towanda, having just dipped into Pennsylvania, she kept singing the same tune silently inside: *I've got a mule and her name is Sal / Fifteen miles on the Erie Canal.* Every time she reached *Canal,* her inner voice pounced on the word and broke it with enthusiasm into pieces: *Canal.* She must have learned it in grade school, though she couldn't remember. When Stephen woke, she would ask him to sing it with her. He'd want to know, she thought, that they had driven along the famous canal of story and song.

Of course, he'd been living near parts of the canal. There were signs up and down Route 12. So perhaps he wouldn't be that interested. And he might be groggy from the phenobarbital. He'd cried, taking it, because of the taste and, she assumed, because here she was, her hair unkempt, her clothing rumpled from long riding, and there was the anxiety. You learn about anxiety when you care for people. You learn how a mother may weep when you hold her feverish child. You learn how an old man can attack you with his cane from a sitting position when you try to give him his insulin shot. Even *suggest* a blood profile to some of the farmers in the raggedy tattered houses in the hills and they stare at you with those empty light eyes under chewed-looking eyebrows and spit tobacco juice on your feet.

And here was a little boy, she thought, who must have felt frightened at once — strange woman, strange car. Yet he'd come to her, she thought, tucking the blanket over him where he slept face down, curled, where he'd plunged willingly into sleep to escape the confusion of their wheel-squealing flight, pursued by that long-legged harridan who ran as if she might actually catch the car and lay hold of some piece of it and pull. That was his grandma, Stephen had told her. "But I'm your grandma too," she'd said, perhaps too sternly. He'd grown frightened, and all at once. She'd half expected his bowels to contract with the fear.

Grandma Mastracola.

She snorted as she passed a pickup truck that pulled a horse box. Mastracola. It sounded like an Italian soft drink, she thought, and then she giggled. Of course, she was not a bigot, she declared and promptly agreed. She'd been caretaker to enough minority groups in her time, including the families at The Bend. Probably they'd once been slaves, descendants of slaves. Probably they'd all settled at The Bend, which was now nothing more than a hollow off a track that went to long meadows from where the one-lane country road dipped at a sharp angle in the two-lane. If you followed the track, if you had four-wheel drive, you came to what they called The Hollow and the four shacks made of small trailers to which clapboard, building paper, scrap, tin roof, stolen unfinished lumber and, she thought, probably candy bar wrappers had been added over the years. One of them, an uncle who didn't have a wife or children, was dark-looking, black-looking. The others had bleached white skin and broad noses and red hair and even freckles. She'd midwifed children there and seen two of the old people off. She kept a baby in one of the families alive through a bad winter when no one in the county had money, it seemed, for food or milk, much less medicine. So don't call *her* a bigot, thank you.

Mastracola. She probably fizzed when you poured her out with pizza, Gloria thought, snickering to herself. With those long legs and arms, she looked like she could do you some damage. And she looked young to be a grandmother. So did Gloria, of course, Gloria thought. But not quite that young.

But Stephen had looked into her eyes, she remembered. He had stared in and stared in, and she had looked out at him the way you do to call to somebody you love and say, *Come in, dear.* And he'd been reassured. She saw that. He had known Gloria's eyes as his mother's eyes. She wondered if he could tell that they were also his. He had stared in and then he'd taken the single step, and then she'd had him inside.

The rest, she intoned, was history. Whatever that meant. The rest was soda and cookies and his being overwhelmed by fear, and then the phenobarbital. When she'd stopped on the road outside of Oxford, New York, in front of a dark, cluttered antiques store with a big sign that said *Old Buttons*, and had reached back for goodies to offer him, he'd looked at her with his pale face and wide eyes and he had said, "What'll it be, kiddo?"

"Kiddo?"

"Just a thing you say after school around my school. My new school. I'm not changing *schools* again, am I?" That was when his eyes filled and his pallor made him look shocky and she went for the phenobarb.

So Gloria was driving southwest, down through Pennsylvania, with long hours ahead, with her grandson asleep on the seat beside her. The lights of houses and cars began to glare powerfully, and the air around them had gone black. She had seen herself, when she set out, in her car in darkness, driving with a child. But even after recalling Sarah's pictures of him, she couldn't summon his face in her visions of bringing him home. She looked down as she thought that, but saw only the blanket, the boy shape curled beneath it, the whiteness of his fists and back of his neck. The fists seemed so tight. "You know there's nothing to worry about," she cooed to his sleep. "Grandma's taking care of you."

There were laws, she knew. Grandparents had rights, grandparental rights, and in the event of the parents' divorce or of disagreements or death — her lip lifted as she catalogued the joys of marriage — the courts had made it clear that grandparents, too, had rights. She'd never heard of any judge denying a grandmother visitation rights. And wasn't this a kind of visitation? She imagined herself saying that to a state policeman who had stopped her and, gumball light swinging, his headlights flashing, stood outside the driver's side window in her imagining and lectured her on the severity of what she'd done. But don't you know the *law?* she heard herself saying. Don't you know about the rights of grandparents? We have rights, too. But our records show you gave the mother up, she heard and saw the stern policeman tell her. And she heard herself reply, with great confidence, that there were extenuating circumstances, that, anyway, it wound up with the baby being *taken*, not given away. And didn't you law enforcement people know the difference? The policeman asked her if she wasn't taking this particular child and did she think two wrongs et cetera. Behind the wheel, with Stephen asleep on the seat beside her, in her life and not her daydream, she shook her head as if to disperse the scenes inside it. "I don't hear a word," she said.

She did regret her daughter's inability to give of herself more. That behavior struck her as inconsiderate. Gloria had spent most of her life in bringing the benefits of science and scientific knowledge to the people who needed what she knew and what she could do. "A lifetime of service," she said as she drove. "A lifetime." And hadn't she spent so many of her hours and days in searching for her child? Hadn't she sought to undo the mistake of a sad, confused, even tormented adolescent girl? What if they had stayed together and married and brought her up? This sort of behavior made it clear that, even then, given that her father lived and her mother had forced the issue with him, *still*, she thought, Sarah would have found a way to put herself ahead of the family. "A lifetime," Gloria said.

Dear Sarah, she wrote — and she could see the page as it trembled in her daughter's fingers — I posed the question in towns and cities from rural Pennsylvania to Kingman, Arizona: AM I YOUR MOTHER? You answered because you knew I was. You knew long-distance and with no other knowledge but your heart's assent that I was your mother. That I *am* your mother. Yet, in my home and in my daily routine and even in my arms, you denied me. After a lifetime of service and searching and remorse on my part, you knew me, you recognized me, yet you'd not acknowledge me. I will have to content myself with believing that you showed a child's natural resentment toward her natural mother, given what we've been through and given what I believe to be a lingering immaturity on your part. Also, it may well have been the surprise. I assure you that I mean no harm to your child and my grandchild. Of course, you could never think your mother would harm this baby! This is the secret of eternal life, Sarah. This is our gene pool. This is our happily ever after.

She stopped writing the letter and squinted at oncoming cars. She was very tired now. They would have to find a motel or sleep on the road. Management would now become a problem. And anyway she found, with a painful urgency, that she wanted to not have to try anymore to say to Sarah what she really didn't know how to make clear.

It was the pain of smelling your skin, Sarah, and not having bathed it.

The frizzy, silly hairdo you wear, and I never, ever, brushed your hair and talked girl talk with you about how the stars wore *their* hair.

Your high forehead, the same as mine. When you were ill as a child, I didn't put my cool palm on it that you would remember feeling later, and I never reassured you as I've reassured the closest I can get to you, your baby, that you'd be all right.

The dreams in your brain that you never told me.

The changes in your body that I never explained.

How if you were sick and we were alone I would have slept beside you as your mother and nurse. Awake at night in illness or pain or under thunderstorms, to keep you safe.

How I didn't explain as I raised you that your father was dead in the war. It would have been a safe lie. I would have taught you the spelling of *widow* for your grade school compositions. *My mommy was a widow very young.*

I was, though, wasn't I? Women can be widows alone.

In nursing school I always carried myself stiffly, with dignity. I tried to stay by myself. The others understood promptly enough. They might go drinking with college boys and medical students. They might give themselves away, cheaply and coarsely. They did. I had done it younger. I knew about wanting to throw myself away. I knew about giving myself away. I knew about trading. But I was a student nurse then, and I had risen above a difficult life of poverty and neglect. I won't claim abuse. I won't lie. Every other girl I meet these days who's rubbed herself raw and thinks she's going to die of it decides she's been abused. I've seen the eyes of the girls who get raped by their fathers, by their mothers' boyfriends. I know the difference. I won't claim it. But there were difficulties. I was not an easy child. You weren't either, Sarah. I can tell. It would have been difficult between us.

I comported myself as a professional. And I still do. I am a nurse, my work is taking care. I've always known my work. I'm taking care of Stephen now, she thought, yawning on the highway from New York State, driving her grandson through Pennsylvania, down toward the hill roads, some nearly corrugated by frost heaves, that ran past oily green ponds, through densest tamarack and spruce, in the tremble and gleam of aspen and then, at last, to Grandma's house.

In the litter of Noel's play, among miniature metal racing cars and a brace of pirates' pistols, to the synthetic death-ray noises of Noel's alliance with the forces of good on a video game, while Karen poured a dark ale slowly down the side of a pilsner glass, Will Mastracola whined. He heard his voice and hated it. He hated that he'd had to run for help, that he wasn't home at the telephone — "I better get back to the phone," he said.

"I wondered about that," Karen said. In khaki twill pants rolled at the ankle and a baggy dark blue mock turtleneck, she looked comfortable and, studying the head on the ale, competent. He thought how much he would rather stay with this woman and let her tell him what he needn't be frightened of than sit at home and overload his lungs. But she wasn't about to offer comfort, only beer. "Here," she said, sounding a little annoyed as she handed the glass over. "I brought it back from the Chesapeake. They brew it there. It's real."

He drank and tasted nothing, smiled as if overwhelmed, and reached to the breast pocket of his shirt. She lifted a finger and shook her head, and he shrugged his apology.

"Karen, this is great, but I should go back."

"*I* think so. I mean, you're welcome to stay, Will. Night and day, just bang on the door, you know that. But *I'd* be near a phone."

"I'll finish this another time."

"I'll save it in a plastic bag," she said. "Turn it *down*, please, Noel."

"He's been great for Stephen."

244

"But we know what Stephen needs. Or who."

Will nodded.

"And the father's not coming back?"

"Jesus, Karen, who can tell? He's not the stablest guy — is that a word? Stablest? You know. He isn't on all four wheels all the time to begin with. Of course, Sarah's not what you'd call pacific either."

"But she's his mother. Lizzie's not."

"Did you ever watch the rocket launches? The moon shot — no, you're too young. The space shuttle? Any of the rockets going up?" Karen, looking back at Noel and then at Will, nodded. She stood, as he did, in the nervous pause in their motion toward the door, and he stepped again toward the front of the house. "There's a point, when they're on their way home, and, you know, it's time to worry about whether things are working right, whether the heat shields are holding so they don't burn up when they hit the atmosphere — the ground loses radio contact. They're on the other side of the moon, and the radios don't work. I always think of it as the dark side of the moon. That's where Lizzie and Sarah are."

And for all the alertness of her eyes, the movement of her lips and cheek muscles, the prompt nod of her head, Karen wasn't listening to him, Willis thought. He moved so he was ready to seize the knob on the front door.

Karen put her hand on his arm and left it there. He put his hand over hers, then raised her hand and kissed the cool long fingers, the large rounded knuckles. She said, "Why, Will. Lizzie always said you had that southern gallantry."

"I had southern ancestors. *My* gallantry is out of Red Bank, New Jersey." She patted his cheek, and he thought, walking across her wooden porch and down two steps to the short walk flanked by privet going green, there wasn't a woman in his life, except for maybe Jessie Newbold — and *she* got money from him for working the hours she liked while dictating what he heard through his floorboards — who didn't, one way or another, run him.

He walked the short way, past the three identical stone colonial houses in a neat row, each separated from its neighbor by eleven feet of yard, the owners of which refused to speak to one another. Burroughs was dark and closed. Only the Superette, the pizzeria, the Kwik-Fill and the Legion bar were open. He walked past the *News* building and looked to see whether a Ku Klux Klan arsonist was on the job. As usual, none was, which meant that his pieces on Aryan Nation, Christian Identity and the freelance bigot bikers from the Vermont–New York border were having no effect except to diminish his ad revenues. He had always calculated that he'd know he was in the running for a Pulitzer when the lads with the gas cans got in touch.

Goddamned peace in the high Chenango, he thought. Back to writing about hundredth birthdays and the weddings of the unlettered rural poor. And the women in his family on the road. He smoked a cigarette while he sat on his porch, listening for the telephone. He thought about Sarah in the pictures Lizzie took. She shot most of them, and he spent his time dodging the camera because he didn't like the way it seized you up, being photographed. You forgot to be yourself. On the other hand, he had always been grateful when Lizzie took pictures of Sarah. Bad or good, he didn't care. He felt a kind of relief, as if he knew, then, when the camera flashed and its drive mechanism whined, that they had some of her to keep.

Yet he never looked at the pictures. They saddened him too much. Instead of signaling what he'd thought they might save, the photographs instructed him in what they had lost. When he looked at the photographs of her in braces before a dance, too sore and too socially devastated to smile, in a gown that proved how glamorous she was, or so her father had insisted, he wanted to weep. They had a photograph of Sarah and the boy who was sacrificed to her first date. He was holding the door of their car as Sarah slid in. And there, he remembered, a little out of focus, stiff as a cabbie being mugged, was Willis Mastracola, driving the miserable couple to the movies in Norwich. The only film he would approve for them had been showing at the drive-in, and Will remembered the stiffness in his neck and shoulders, as he drove them home, from having sat motionless for the one hundred minutes of a full-length cartoon about a deer. He tried to remember the name of her date. The only one who was memorable, besides Barrett, and besides the kid in college he had almost beaten for mistreating her, was the painter she had said she was dating, while they knew she was living with him. Stavitz, Starz, Slovitz, he thought, lighting a cigarette. Bobbie Slovitz. *Eddie* Slovitz. One tough man, Will thought. The telephone rang, and Will began to gag on the smoke in his chest as he stood to run for the door.

Lizzie walked with long strides down the path from the little building that housed the public restrooms on Route 81, south of Great Bend. Sarah studied Lizzie's waist, her thighs outlined by her dress, the big shoulders and long arms. I could almost be her daughter, Sarah thought. Allowing for everything being different, she thought, you could, if you looked at us quickly, see a couple of tall chicks with long arms and legs and think, Oh, a mother-and-daughter team of poetry-writing nuclear-particle brain surgeons who are probably great in bed.

Lizzie, looking miserable, said, "The phone smelled like everybody with bad breath driving a truck between Binghamton and Harrisburg. Does this go to Harrisburg?" Sarah shrugged and Lizzie did too. She said, "He thinks we're crazy. He's furious that we left without him. Five minutes, he kept saying. Five minutes and he could have been there. He said we *wanted* to go without him."

"That's ridiculous," Sarah said.

247

"Of course it is," Lizzie said.

"It's not a pleasure cruise, I hope you pointed out," Sarah said, drinking from the can of soda she'd bought at the machine outside the bathrooms. "It's not as if we're on a mother-and-daughter mall crawl."

"I pointed out," Lizzie said. "I pointed. He pointed too. I did that thing you do on public phones when you want to shout but you're being discreet?"

Sarah laughed in a kind of hiccup. "You hissed, right? You pronounced every syllable ve-ry care-fully and you hissed it?" Lizzie nodded. "But what, Mom?"

"He sounded awful. He was breathing so wetly. He said it was from running to the phone, but I don't know."

"He has to stop smoking."

"We have to start driving," Lizzie said, getting in. So Sarah went around to the driver's side, got in and headed them back down to the highway while Lizzie talked about Willis's health and his conviction that he was old.

"Smoking makes you old," Sarah said.

"He knows that. I know that. I *tell* him that. Last time we really fought about it, really had an argument. I said he's growing senile lungs in a middle-aged body."

"Was that received well?"

"He looked past me at the table, you know, as if he were tasting something? And then he looked over at me and said, 'That's really good, Lizzie. That's a smart one.' "

"Bastard," Sarah said. "We have to make him stop."

"Don't we."

"Well, I'll help, Mommy."

"Sweetie," Lizzie said, "I think you've a few other problems right now. Which we are scrupulously not talking about."

Sarah looked ahead into the traffic bound for Scranton and Wilkes-Barre, and she became fastidious about checking her wing and rearview mirrors, about noting her speed and inspecting her oil pressure gauge. She passed a truck that was going too fast for her to comfortably pass, and then she speeded to stay ahead of it and then forgot, and he passed her close, ducked in ahead of her with a vengeance and a backdraft that made the Blazer rock. "I'm driving wonderfully," Sarah said. Then she said, "Oh, you mean like why did I not tell Stephen where I was going? Or Barrett? Or you?"

"You don't have to tell me," Lizzie said, rubbing her temple, looking out her window at nothing but soiled grass and featureless road. "You're a grown woman."

"And a daughter," Sarah said. "And I know whose."

She saw Lizzie turn toward her and wait, face very tight and teeth together.

Sarah had to say, "And you *do* think I should have told Stephen. Well, I did. I left him a note."

"Sweetie," Lizzie said, "he peed his bed every night. He peed in his pants in school at least every other day. He got into every kind of trouble except murder and arson and trying to assassinate the governor. He told these immense tall tales, these *lies* about you and Barrett. I think Noel Kelly saved his life, that's my — Karen Kelly's little boy."

Sarah blinked her eyes a lot, which she found preferable to driving the car across Route 81 into oncoming traffic. She assured herself that tears would not run down her face. After a while she said, "Yeah, but you should see his act if I don't leave a note."

Lizzie reached across and cupped her chin, held it in her hand. Sarah dropped her head's weight onto Lizzie's palm and they rode that way for long seconds. Sarah breathed in the way you do when you've been crying. Lizzie patted her cheek twice, then removed her hand. "He never let us see it," she said.

"We're good at secrets, he and I."

Lizzie said, "And Barrett?"

"He brings home the bacon. He's a bear in bed. He ends up hating me half of the time we're together. The rest of the time he worships the oriental carpet I stand on. I'm pretty sure we're finished."

"Finished?"

"Well, I think we've done what we can do."

"And — you just end it?"

"When you get to the end," Sarah said, "then you're there. I mean, where do you *go* after that?"

"And Stephen?"

"Barrett won't contest custody."

"You've been reading about divorces, it sounds like."

But Sarah shook her head and smiled a small smile. She said, "No. The people I hang around with, designers, furniture makers, antiques people, it's in the air. Half of my profession dies of AIDS and the other half thinks it's going to die and doesn't of divorce."

"That's so old-sounding," Lizzie said, in either admiration or distress.

"And you sound so inexperienced," Sarah said gently.

They slid into a silence that lasted for miles and was broken at last by Lizzie, rubbing her temple again, saying, "So you felt that you needed to see her, this person who advertised, and you went."

"And I didn't discuss it with you."

"I told you," Lizzie said, "you don't have to. It's your life."

"And I didn't discuss it with you," Sarah said.

Lizzie shrugged.

"I think it didn't have anything to do with you, sweetie." When Sarah called her that, Lizzie's head swiveled. "It wasn't a comment on your being my mother. You were scared of that all the time I was growing up. Whenever *that* allegedly happened. I knew it. You talked about it all the time, like a smell in the room that you figured, well, what the hell, mention it, since it's stinking everything up. Bad wording. Nothing about it stank. But you kept *talking* about it, and it just wasn't a big deal with me. I thought. *I* was always pissed about having to compete with you for guys. Well, that's what I thought. That's what I was thinking. And Daddy, he would turn mauve every time you said something and I was just this kid who was high on her hormones, I was only thinking about how to justify getting laid in terms of high romance."

"I loved being your mother," Lizzie whispered. "When I wasn't figuring out how to kill you while you slept, I really loved being your mother."

They went silent again. Then Sarah said, "And then I went crazy."

"When you saw the ad?"

"Or before it. Stephen kept on needing me, and Barrett kept on needing me to be different about needing *him* and — I don't know. I was going crazy. I went back to see Eddie."

"The painter? After all these years?"

"Yeah. Painter, years, him, the whole thing."

"You mean — you mean *he* —"

"No," Sarah said. "I don't think so. I don't know. I just needed to see him. So I saw him."

"Was it — nice?"

"Nice, Mommy?"

Lizzie compressed her lips and goggled her eyes, and when Sarah turned toward her silence and saw the face Lizzie made, she gave a long, climbing call of what sounded, even to her, like delight.

Sarah studied the road very hard for a while, and when she turned again, saw that Lizzie was rubbing her temple again. She reached down beneath her seat, missed it, looked back at the road, then reached once more beneath the seat. She came up with the emergency kit and offered it to Lizzie. "Unwrap the duct tape," she said. "It's Barrett's crisis-intervention kit, containing everything you need for comfort and survival when your car or child or wife breaks down. He omitted the Valium and the gun, but there are aspirin in there, and you can wash them down with some of this soda. Can't you see him putting it together? Can't you see him deciding what an emergency is? No razor blades, no Thorazine, no block of wood to bite down on when they amputate without the anesthetic or when you can't breathe the same air you've been breathing for the past seven years. Well, six. No: seven, I guess. And no thongs for tying yourself to the crucifix until you can borrow the hammer and nails he also omitted that you need to fasten yourself on with. But he did supply *Goodnight, Moon,* so in case his wife took it on the lam she would have to run nose-first into *that* and thus pump her remorse up high enough to stop her breathing for a while. And a little thing of aspirins."

Swigging the soda, refastening the silver tape around the kit, Lizzie said, as if in response to something Sarah had said, "He's a nice boy, though."

"Oh," Sarah said, "that."

"Mm. Is he?"

"Sometimes. He's doing a lot of booze. Not that *that* makes him a war criminal. He's got some secret people inside his skin too, though."

"Like the rest of us," Lizzie said.

"I guess."

"Sweetie," Lizzie said, "why did she take him?"

"Nutsy Gloria? Mother Nature? Only because she's deranged and evil and driven. She's even sad. She just has this power of making you forget she's an actual person when you're with her because she is so busy organizing the entire goddamned universe around *her.* She can prove it while making a soup out of snakes. Poor Gloria, I guess."

"Her."

"So you never met her."

"Lawyers," Lizzie said. "There were lawyers who used to specialize in these adoptions, and our attorney had heard of one, and, no: I couldn't have met her. I couldn't have."

"No, I don't guess you could. I'm going to kill her if she's touched him."

"Why would she touch him? Hurt him, you mean. Not —"

"Well, who *knows?* She has to own everything. Everything. She can't leave anything be, me or him because he comes from me, or I don't know. Anything. A lot of need in that lady."

"As soon as we get there, we go to the police. Agreed?"

"As soon as we get there, we go to Gloria's and beat the living shit out of her and fall all over Stephen is what we do as soon as we get there. We can call the police whenever you want, whenever we stop, but we *go* for my son. Why'd you adopt me?"

Lizzie sat back. She said, "Oh."

"You know, instead of having me?"

"I couldn't have any more children, Sarah."

"Any *more?*"

"Any more."

Sarah didn't say anything. She tipped the soda can, but it was empty. She turned the radio on, and the stations she'd been tuned to were fuzzy or lost. She punched the button until she pulled in a station from Allentown that had just finished something by Queensryche and was now going to play something that caused Megadeth, or was sung by them. She turned it up a little and settled in behind the noise.

Lizzie turned it off. "I got around pretty much," she said. "I was a normally sexually active young woman, considering how neurotic and screwed-up and feeling screwed-over I was. I had affairs. You call them relationships now. As if getting into bed with someone defines relationship. Hello, let's fuck."

Sarah raised her eyebrows at her mother's language, realizing as she did that the eyebrows were her mother's response, often enough, to her own language.

"I seemed to be one of those very fertile women as *well* as crazy, a little. I got involved with men. I got involved with a particular man. I got knocked up. Hello, jig-jig, rockabye baby, and I *knew* he'd be a lousy father, and I'd be crying all over the baby instead of feeding it, and we really got to where we couldn't stand each other a few days after we'd been to bed in a torrent of appetite, you know, lust, call it whatever you like. All of that swept-away-by-desire stuff. And then we had nothing to say. *Nothing.* And I made the decision on my own, without telling him. Undemocratically. Unfairly, I'm sure he'd have said if he'd ever learned about it, which I think he didn't. And I was right.

"So I aborted. I mean, I went to a doctor. It wasn't a clinic, but it wasn't one of those so-called back-street butcheries, either. Just a lousy doctor at a small hospital in the country who botched the job. Well, he killed the kid all right. He just happened to mess me up too. He didn't intend to, of course. He was young and stupid, just like me. I just happened to be the one with the fallopian tubes and ovaries and womb, and he just happened to be the one with the chain saw and monkey wrench and crowbar."

She laughed hoarsely, her face by now covered with her tears, no longer pretending to be unmoved by her own story. Sarah had been crying through most of it. They drove while they wept and made sniffing noises and then nose-blowing honks.

Sarah said, "Too bad Barrett didn't stick a bottle of wine in his emergency kit."

"Sweetie, wine wouldn't touch this. Well, in a way. In a way, you know, and this is *not* a motherly pep talk, it's a happy story. It's a good story. I couldn't conceive anymore because of the story, so I got you," she said. "Sarah. Sweetie. God. How could I ask for better news than you?" Lizzie blew her nose again, passed a paper tissue over to Sarah, and then said, "Wine wouldn't touch it."

When they were past Wilkes-Barre and heading for Scranton, Sarah said, "I'm going to kick in Gloria's *ass*."

THE DESERT looked blue in the morning light for just an instant, and then the pink began to seep down. He saw scrub, piñon and the barrel shapes of cactuses, and the cactuses that looked like people on the verge of falling into the sand. Traffic ran very quickly, and as much as Barrett looked at oncoming cars or into the passenger-side windows of cars that passed him doing 90, he saw no faces. He was on the highway of blistered concrete and boiled tar and he was surrounded by desert, accompanied by faceless drivers in unidentifiable small trucks and long cars. He was used to the pain of his ribs and his arm and his breastbone, he was used to the stink of his sweat and his breath, and he was on the way to try again to be father and husband, though he suspected that he would never get home. His suspicion, stronger than his fears about Sarah and her Slovitz, stronger than his doubts about the comfort he had wished to supply to his son, was that he would be murdered on the highway by brigands, by hallucinating motorcycle gangs, by drug smugglers in souped-up black Trans Ams. He was sipping sour mash judiciously, and he knew that he should stop for coffee and the vitamins in orange juice, the carbohydrates in toast. But he was taking only nips, watchful because he had to be watchful, he had suspicions about his fate.

Each time he shifted to accommodate the pain in his ribs, he felt a slow, nauseous tug below his belly, and he knew that either Marylinn had damaged his prostate or her husband's dancing feet had so insulted the health of his testicles that he was in need of repair. The more he thought of that growing pain, the more it grew, and soon it was overwhelming the soreness of his ribs and of what he thought might be cartilage between the ribs that had torn from the bone. In half an hour, with the sun low but bright and directly in his eyes, so that he slouched with the visor down and peeked from beneath it at the road whose surface soon would seem to boil, the pressure between his scrotum and his belly was insistent and intense.

The sign said *San Caliente Mission* and a number of miles that he missed. His foot began to pump the brake and he checked his mirrors, because he was doing, he thought, at least 85, and he would need a lot of runway. Another sign came up, and the schematic showed a right-hand turn, and he dove into it, fish-tailing on the grit that lay on the clay of the tributary road. He was driving southeast now, and there was nothing around him except low escarpments of sedimentary rock in which minerals broke the light into rainbow glints as he passed. In a mile, a sign indicated the mission, and in another couple of miles there was another sign. The road had straightened out, the rock formations had fallen away, and there were the parallel converging lines of the narrow rutted track, and the desert, and then in the extreme distance, more to the south than the east, the low blue ranks of foothills to some mountains he would never see.

A wooden signpost with a wooden sign, a finger post, the lettering of which had been bleached away, pointed at the mission. It had been small and, of course, adobe. The right-hand side of the front wall remained, and, wonderfully enough, the entire doorway, and some of the squat tower. Everything was scorched from fire, and the semicircular arch of the entrance was missing the inverted-triangle keystone at the very top and many of the smaller stones of the intrados that should have lined the interior of the archway. The doors had been burned away or stolen. The piers and springers were covered with unreadable graffiti, as if an inner-city gang had come out here on a class trip from, say, Amarillo or Albuquerque to practice with their spray cans. There wasn't any back to the mission, and the low tower was crumbling away. He saw, walking in under the damaged arch, that the steps that would have gone into the tower had been removed, and that the tower was held up by two and a half shattered walls. Paper and the remains of picnics littered the inside, although, he noted, there really *was* no inside. In was the same as out, here, and up was no different from down. He looked for condoms, and when he saw two, and then three, and then many, he nodded, as if satisfied by the level of degradation. He nevertheless wanted to shout or weep, and he was disappointed when he couldn't.

The bird droppings on the walls and sand floor led him to expect giant humpbacked vultures staring coldly down, and when he looked up, almost cringing, he saw nothing but smaller, unidentifiable birds that darted above the soft garbage, the greasy white paper sacks in which, he thought, many small snakes in a slowly writhing knot could wait.

In the farthest corner of the defunct courtyard — it was only a shattered, smoke-blackened corner, the walls were gone — he found what he supposed was piñon burned black. It had been a campfire, he thought, a cooking fire. He saw what he assumed were chicken bones or rabbit bones that had been thrown into the fire to burn. Like a frontier scout, he put his hand to the fire. He felt nothing but charred wood. He squatted on his heels and sucked a small sip from the bottle of mash while he considered announcing to San Caliente that two, maybe three white men had passed this way ten, maybe eleven hours ago and had overcooked their lime and turmeric chicken. Maybe it wasn't chicken. Maybe it was man. Maybe these were some of the numerous small bones of the hand. Barbecued honey-and-mustard-glazed adolescent hand. Slow-roasted, foil-wrapped grown-up architect's hand. I see your fine hand in this, he thought, not snickering as he expected to. Not only wasn't he funny, he was frightened, he realized. Because people *had* been here and wasn't it — this ruin, this limitless desert country over which you could see drug enforcement people in their boxy government cars and half-wrecked Jeeps come swerving over the sand far enough away for you to make your escape in your sleek, tightly sprung, stepped-up sedan — a perfect place to be killed in?

Who was going to murder him? he wondered. He wiped at the sweat that lay beaded in solid, heavy, oily drops on his forehead. He wiped with his hand beneath his chin. He opened his shirt further and wiped at his chest. He wanted to take his clothing off and bathe, and the sweat now bubbled from him. And suddenly the pain, perhaps from the angle at which he squatted, became intolerable. He stood and delicately — as if he were helping Stephen in a public restroom, he realized — aimed himself at the sand. He saw the blood in his urine. I'll take the body-temperature rosé, he told the waiter who was stooped and heavy-lidded, like a vulture. He watched the blood as it pooled on the pink sand, going dark, almost brown, then turning rosy and soaking in, leaving only a dark stain on the surface of the desert. He watched that evaporate. As soon as he was done, he felt the need to do it again, but nothing emerged from him, and he tucked himself away as if his flesh, bruised on the outside and broken within, were a soft, frightened child.

Barrett looked up at the sun. He supposed that he wanted to wail for mercy. When he saw the tower more closely, squinting at it, treading in the sea of his sympathies for himself in the middle of the desert, he saw the rose window. The glass was gone, of course. He thought that maybe he had never laid it in, the architect, the builder of San Caliente, but it was, without question, a crude, small circular window. Its mullions, shaped like teardrops with the trefoil decoration at the rim, converged toward the tiny round center. It was a Catherine window, and some person building in the desert in America, who had seen the medieval wheel windows of Europe, had built this window to boast to the Indians he labored to convert, in this sculptural language of such elegance, about the prowess, the richness, of his god.

Barrett raised the stubby square bottle of sour mash to the window and took a somewhat unjudicious drink. But it was a celebration. And anyway, there was the matter of the blood he had pissed and would doubtless piss again very soon. Squaring his shoulders, delicately working his fly, he performed as promised, moaning a little when he saw how red his urine was when it arced to the ground and disappeared. He cradled himself when he was done, and he zipped.

"Drink this," he said, regarding the rose window. "This is my whiskey. *This*," he said, pointing with his Chuck Taylor sneaker at the ground, "is my blood."

He hadn't heard the Land Cruiser roll up, and yet he was certain he'd been listening, with at least one ear — he turned his head to aim an ear at the high, battered green truck — for the people who would kill him before he could drive home to reclaim his child and organize the search for his wife. He made certain that the bottle was cradled in his arms against his chest, so that he would not appear to be a man who staggered with a bottle in the courtyard of an ancient mission that had been so nobly decorated. The air was utterly clear, the sky cloudless, limitless, the desert everywhere, the sun very heavy on his head. He squinted at the truck and set his legs.

When the driver's side door opened, he said, "Here it comes."

He looked about for the vultures. He checked the white hamburger sacks for signs of serpents on the move. "Here it comes." He closed his eyes and waited. Then he opened them and saw a tall, thin, hairless man who stood with his arms about a small, equally thin woman who was wearing a powder blue short-sleeved sun suit and a little girl with very red hair in white shorts and a T-shirt that advertised the Hard Rock Café. He wondered if, beneath her light blue scarf, the woman was as bald as her husband.

Barrett looked at them, and they stared back. They were not the death squad he'd expected, and he thought the fact of his salvation merited a toast. He removed the bottle from where it lay against his breast and held it before him. The touring family stepped back.

"Quite," Barrett said. "I understand. I've been a father in my time. There's nothing to fear." He made a half-bow, then held the bottle against his left leg as if to hide it from their pained eyes. He walked in a crab motion, scuttling, keeping himself between the bottle and them, until he had passed beneath the arch and was near his car. "Nothing to fear," he said, almost singing it. With the car between the family and him now, he turned, opened the door, looked past them to the Catherine window and nodded at its builder. He sat inside the car and started it up, leaning into the air that came from the panel. He locked the doors, belted himself in, settled his crotch, angled his ribs and barely tasted some mash before he capped the bottle and set it on the seat. "Nothing to fear," he said, as he drove back into the desert, certain that he would find his way to Route 40 and then east to where his child, at least, awaited him. Perhaps he was not supposed to be killed now. "There is nothing to fear," he said. It was what he told his son about his inescapable dreams, or the lightning-flare thunderstorms that made his bedroom windows shake, when the boy came panicked to his parents' room and, wide-eyed and pale in the darkness, handed himself over to Sarah for rescue. He assured himself, probing across the desert for the way east, "There is nothing to fear."

He remembered Sarah sailing down a flight of steps somewhere, to land against him in a flurry of their arms and legs. He had tried hard to catch as much of her against him as he could. He remembered the cheap-candy taste of her lipstick and the coolness of her tears. He insisted now, tasting sour mash and what he swore was his blood, that there were tears.

That was when we were so nice, Barrett thought. We were such nice kids together, he thought.

"Frankly, we had a dandy future, I'd have said," he said.

We just ran out of it a little bit, he thought. But we were nice. We thought there was nothing to fear.

Gloria spoke to herself about fear. On the road with Stephen, exhausted, still for a while at the side of the road, she tried to cope with her fears by reminding herself: they had looked into one another's eyes, the family's eyes, really Sarah's eyes when you consider. What it was was Sarah looking at Sarah. Maybe call it Gloria looking into Gloria's eyes. If A = C and if B = C, then A = B, Gloria thought. It was the eyes, which are the windows of the soul, looking into each other, repeating each other. So that meant it was the soul of one and all that looked inside the soul of one and all. That's what family means, Gloria thought. She was trying to sleep in her car after she parked it alongside the stained picnic bench she would as soon let her grandson dine from as invite him to eat from the fingers of unwashed men on the streets of some septic city. But she was too full of cold coffee and too jolted by unexpected bursts of energy that made her pulse race and her neck and cheeks feel sweaty. So she lay in the darkness, watching the reflections of headlights on the chrome of her rearview mirror, watching the car fill up with light and empty out into a gray flatness when each car or truck had passed.

Soon, when she couldn't close her eyes anymore, when the light poured in and rose from the metal of the door handles up to the door frames under the windows and then along the windows up to the chrome that framed the mirror and then the windshield and then to the metal molding at the window, and when she still could not force her jumping eyelids to be still, she sat forward and held the wheel with both hands and rested her forehead on her knuckles.

The skin of my hands is still soft, she thought.

He's breathing too deep. He's breathing too hoarsely, from too deep in his throat, she thought. In the lights thrown by passing vehicles he looked too sallow, and Gloria knew why. She had given him too much. It was natural to make a mistake with phenobarbital when you're dosing a child this large. And she knew that she had panicked. A nurse never panics. Her supervisor had told her once, over a Manhattan, "A nurse finds out why she panicked. She only panics once. She examines *herself* when that happens, not the patient. And it never happens again. Or she isn't a nurse."

Of course, her supervisor was also a lesbian cannibal, Gloria thought.

But it was true. She had in fact responded unprofessionally. It was Stephen's fault, in a way. Well, that isn't fair, she reproved herself. He's a baby, not much more. Of *course* he's going to be confused, grandma or no grandma. Especially if the grandma is new to him. And he'd grown very frightened, and he was thirsty and hungry and scared, and instead of comforting him, she had spoken harshly. She would have to make that up to him. It happened all the time in the practice, but you have to make it up.

He had looked like a little bird, Gloria thought, leaning forward in the motionless car, listening to Stephen's stertorous breath. *Stertorous*, we like to say in the trade, she thought. She had simply ignored his flailing arms and she'd cupped his jaw in strong fingers and introduced the thick eyedropper over his wriggling lips and in between his teeth as he parted them to cry out. She had squirted the phenobarb, and she made sure that he swallowed it before he realized that it was the same bitter liquid he'd protested against earlier. As he weakened, as they fought, she had held him again and filled the dropper and emptied it into his mouth again. And then, as he drowsed in spite of himself, she had done it twice again. "Sahnt-ameters," she said to herself, using the European inflection of a doctor for whom she had worked.

She leaned back again and tried to sleep. It felt as though she saw in spite of something having hollowed out her eye sockets. She didn't know if she could move her legs. She was too exhausted to lean again and seize the wheel and steer the car. They would have to rest together, and she knew that her galvanizing pulses came from fear. She knew that she was afraid to sleep because she didn't know for guaranteed sure that when she woke her grandson would be breathing right.

Just *breathing*, she admitted.

Simply not true, she answered herself. Unverifiable, unscientific, untrue.

Gloria composed herself. She looked at Stephen's slack and almost jaundiced face. She hoped he dreamed. She hoped, closing her eyes and insisting they stay that way, that Stephen dreamed something merry. She hoped that maybe he dreamed about their studying in her side yard with the hose and a little incline of dirt that she'd rake clean of vegetation. They would watch the hillside erode, then talk about how erosion affects us and how to build erosion blocks. Would a boy dream a dream like that? Keeping her eyes closed, Gloria sadly shook her head on the backrest of her seat. She would have to learn about being a better grandmother, she thought. She would have to learn how to play.

Gloria made her mouth smile. She gave a little waggle to her head, as if she were a child playing. And, she instructed herself, you remember that you looked in one another's eyes, into the family's eyes. He understood. He saw your soul, so he knew. She thought, I think that's a fact.

But wouldn't it be good to have a pet for him to play with? Children like animals. Children *are* animals, she thought, and she imagined herself waggling her head like something at play. She thought she might actually be sleeping now, but she wasn't sure, and she was so tired, she was reluctant to check in case she woke herself up. Momma needs her rest, she announced inside herself. She corrected herself at once: Grandma. Grandma needs her rest.

But wouldn't it be lovely to show him a puppy with drooling wet jaws? That she would have to wipe with a towel? And then at once wash the towel lest the child forget it had been in an animal's mouth and touch it to his own? Dogs were so messy, evacuating everywhere, and constantly, and eating what made them sick.

Dogs and lovers, Gloria thought, are the creatures that return to what makes them sicken and sometimes die. Though of course you can't die of love, can you?

Oh, yes, she said, waking or in sleep or floating just under the surface of her sleep, in the locked tan car at the side of the road. She had seen it glistening in the headlights when she pulled in on the verge for her rest. Dogs leave their bowel movements everywhere, and in damp places especially the evening and morning dew seems to collect on their waste, in a kind of silvery network. It glistens in the light. It looks almost metallic. It looks like the silver strands you hang on Christmas trees, one careful piece at a time.

Then a cat, she thought or dreamed she thought. Once she had owned a cat, a big ginger-colored cat she had named Birthwort, the family name for wild ginger. She had felt *free*, at first, with animals, she heard herself protest. She had bought a sixteen-gallon tropical fish tank and filled it with miniature golden carp. It had been restful, watching the bubbles of the aerator come up, watching the slow, emotionless feeding of the fish. And one afternoon she had returned from her rounds to find Birthwort on top of the tank, holding himself on the iron rims with three paws and fishing with the other. How she had shrieked! She had swung her kit at the cat, had missed, had stumbled into the tank and had pitched it over. Fish flopped on her clean softwood floor, slimy water lay on everything. The cat had sat on her bookcase, licking its paws and observing her.

She swept the fish into a dustpan and threw them into the woods for the porcupines. She swept up the glass and threw the frame of the tank and its aerating machinery into the back seat of her car, on a canvas tarpaulin, to take to the dump. She had poisoned the cat.

It was lonelier, she heard her voice say, a little sorrowfully, but it was clean and neat. When you live alone, you must be orderly.

She hoped her grandson wouldn't vomit from the phenobarbital. She gagged, or thought she heard herself gag. Which was silly. You know that nurses don't gag about vomit. They clean it up. They rid the room of its cause if they can. Not that she had to relish a soiled environment. Not that she wouldn't labor to remove the source. She heard the boy wheeze, and she wondered whether he suffered allergies. She had lots of antihistamines, of course, but they did slow the metabolism and make you sleep. She hoped she wouldn't have to use them. Or she dreamed she hoped. In her sleep, or in her dream about sleeping, Gloria hoped her pale, restless grandson deep in sleep was well and delighting in a long, lovely dream.

Stephen could feel his mouth stretch, and he felt like he was smiling. He was running with Noel and some of the girls from

his old class, in Doylestown. They were screaming words he
didn't understand. Noel and he were laughing. No, they weren't.
They were not laughing. They were crying. The girls were
saying something about being covered with poop and Noel was
crying. It made Stephen so sad that he began to cry. They were
running away from the girls. The girls were running after them.
The girls got bigger because they got closer. They were two
teachers, Ms. Ng from Doylestown and Ms. Thorndyke from
Burroughs. They chased them and got bigger. Noel was crying
because they were covered with poop. Everything was stinky.
There were big animals chasing after the teachers. Everybody
got closer to the big window at the edge of the field. The window
went as far as the field. On the other side, Stephen saw his mother
and his grandma and grandpa. They were crying too. They knew
the glass was going to break. Stephen thought he would get yelled
at if the glass broke. But the teachers were closer. The animals
were coming too. But they weren't animals. They were men.
They were mean men, very big and sweaty and covered with
mosquito bites and sores they itched at while they ran. They
were going to hurt everybody. Stephen saw their yellow teeth.
His mother came to the window. He saw her mouth move. She
was calling him. He looked at her mouth. He loved to watch his
mother's mouth when she shouted. Sometimes when she scolded
him her lips began to move funny and she started to laugh.
Sometimes she kept laughing and sometimes she got angry because she was laughing so she stopped and hollered worse. He
watched his mother's mouth and she was saying *Daddy*. Noel let
go of his hand and went to the window. Stephen turned around.
The big man near the teachers was his father. He had the Walnut
Face. He was angry. He was running toward them with long
slow steps. He just kept coming toward them. Stephen turned
to see his mother. His grandma was there. She was running the
shower but there was no curtain and no tile floor underneath.
She was just turning the faucet. Stephen looked for his mother.

He turned around and his mother and father were washing the car. They were shouting at each other. He heard the glass begin to break. He was on the other side, crying. He knew the glass was going to cut him when it broke. He called Noel. He couldn't see anything because the water was in his eyes. He heard the men roaring like lions. He heard the glass break.

Sarah's head did not begin to ache at that moment, nor did she feel a twinge at the back of her neck or a soreness under her breast or the sudden racing of her pulse or sick sweat. She felt nothing, as far as she could later estimate, as far as she can puzzle it now, on damp days, on bad afternoons, when there's too much rain or snow turning purple at dusk, after too much wine with nothing to laugh about. She thought, days afterward, and now, still, she thinks: I should have felt *something*. Aren't there obligations on us? Shouldn't I at least have done *that?* Surely, she thinks, I should have felt it when he —

They did not require that she fly there. She couldn't have traveled again right away. Her father went. Handsome and white, even down to the hair on his chest and his arms, he drove himself to the Hancock Airport and flew by himself to make the identification. He said they were cordial and a little bored.

It was to be a good deal later before he would tell her the rest. His eyes watered and his nostrils flared when he did. His voice tightened down and he had to force himself to speak. But she pleaded with him, and he did.

Curved like a baby in the womb, her father said. Curved and black, the arms pulled up against the mortuary sheets. Sooty, her father said. Mouth agape with the tongue burned away. She wept in her father's arms. She kneeled on the living room floor and lay her head in his lap and he surrounded her with his arms. She should have *felt* it when it was happening, she said. He told her No, no. But oughtn't she? It is one of her questions now, afterward. Shouldn't she?

But she couldn't help it, Gloria insisted to herself. Fatigue is finally undeniable, she thought. In the dirty light at the side of the stained road, Gloria wakened and smelled the foulness of her breath. She heard trucks gearing up outside as they passed. She heard the usual sparrows and finches in the brush and trees at the edge of the pullover. She heard Stephen snuffling, still asleep, and she knew he was in trouble. She smelled the urine and knew it had soaked into the seat of her car. She would wake him, somehow, and clean him at a roadside restaurant. If she had to, if he couldn't be roused, she would use medicated wipes from her kit and throw away the offending clothes and wrap him in the blanket from the back of the car. She had clothes for him at home. She opened her window and started the car, eager to be moving, and eager for the greasy winds to fill the car and blow away the stink of the child, her own foul smell. Nostrils pinched with disgust, Gloria drove. She was doing what was right.

Lizzie and Sarah had passed the tan car hours before, Lizzie driving now and Sarah falling into and waking from small units of sleep to gasp or stare, then see her mother's hands on the wheel and then her mother's face, then falling slowly, chin on her shoulder or chest, head on her window, into one more unrestful doze. She forced herself up and out, like someone pulling herself out onto the edge of the swimming pool after a lot of laps. She gasped as if out of breath. Lizzie studied her face and saw the indications, under Sarah's eyes and on her forehead, of how many years Sarah had been waking. She smiled at the thought of her daughter waking up. She used to watch her sleep. Of course, all mothers did that, goofily, dreamily, watching the miracle of breath and of oxygen pouring up into a brain, of the twitch of mouth and shake of eyelid hinting at what teemed inside, out of sight. She used to be afraid that Sarah wouldn't waken.

Sarah, looking up and over, saw her mother frown. "What?" she said.

Lizzie said, "Small memories. Nothing, really."

"Do you forgive me for, what could you really call it? Visiting Gloria? Siccing Barrett and Stephen and all the worry about us on you and Daddy?"

Lizzie nodded. She thought of Barrett's face the night he brought Stephen. Barrett had looked like a cheap, crooked Halloween mask, like a skull. Stephen, she thought, had worked so hard not to shout, to scream and thrash. He had so obviously wanted to. His eyes had moved toward everything that moved. They never focused on one point. He had the look of people in hospitals awaiting a visit from their surgeon, or a pain pill from the nurse, or any hint about the disposition of their next ten minutes, or any reassurance that they *had* ten minutes. "Yes. I do. And I forgive you everything else in advance, sweetie," Lizzie said. "Do you forgive me?"

"For what?"

"For what I did when I didn't know I was doing it? For what I won't know I'm doing?"

Sarah nodded. She thought she ought to make it official because her mother looked so grim, so sad, so much, at once, unlike a sister or cousin or friend, and very much only her parent. "Yes. Thank you. Yes."

"We'll get him back," Lizzie said, hearing something familiar not in the words so much as in the rhythm of her reassurance. Then she remembered. She heard Stephen comforting his grandmother and thus himself with the certainty that Daddy would get her back. That his daddy would have a *hell* of a drive. But his daddy would get her back. Lizzie thought he probably would not be getting her back. She sighed, and Sarah looked for the source of the sound. Lizzie thought, as Sarah watched her fingers loosen and rewrap themselves around the steering wheel, that Barrett was probably having a hell of a drive.

He had slept a few times after the visit to the mission. Each time, he had known from a waning of his vision to pull over and close his eyes, and, each time, he had turned off the ignition and slumped onto the passenger seat, tucking up his ankles, sleeping like a sick child. He had wakened each time to drink and gag and shake his head as if observing the commission of a wrong. He had purchased food and whiskey and fuel, and he had voided blood. Now, in the solid dark, having stopped by the side of the road three times in the last hour, sheltered from the oncoming cars by the open doors between which he stood, he had urgently urinated thin blood. The last time had so hurt his back and loins, he had shut the front door, crawled onto the back seat and locked himself in. He'd put his head on the seat, his nose near the junction of the seatback and its bench, and he had closed his eyes and fallen again into sleep. He thought he was at the eastern rim of Texas or in Oklahoma now. He didn't think it mattered because he didn't think they would let him get home. *They* were not Central American death squads, or architectural critics, or clients, bankers, contractors or rubbish haulers. *They* were the forces arrayed against him. *They* were his luck, which was septic, like a wound. *They* might prove to be smugglers running money to be laundered, or drugs, or Iranian counterfeit hundred-dollar bills, or genetically altered bull semen. *They* might be serial killers searching for a chest to open and place a potted plant in. *They* might be witchy women handicapped by innocence or friendly needs and sand-shark husbands. *They* might be him. He didn't think their plans included Barrett's going home.

When he woke, hot and stuffy-headed, gummy of eye and tight of jaw from clenching, from grinding, at his unremembered dreams, he felt the pressure of the blood and pus inside his crushed plumbing. His kidney jumped as if a little animal were trapped inside. He thought he would have to throw up. He crawled backward, kicking at the door, until he stood on the sandy side of the road and looked at barren yellow-green land uninterrupted by buildings or hills or anything larger than small trees in the blueness before dawn. The trees were silhouetted, and he thought he stood at the edge of a randomly planted orchard that a fungus disease had destroyed. He imagined the trees as soft, like mushrooms. The windy wakes of brightly lighted double rigs battered the car, and he felt it rock as he leaned against the frame, staring at the shadowy, low, sick trees, depositing blood on the lunar soil. Looking over the roof of the car, he saw the same uneasy landscape.

He reached into the front seat and made his breakfast: half of a Baby Ruth and a quantity of sour mash. He coughed when he drank, but he drank. He walked around the car and sat behind the wheel, propping the bottle beside his right thigh. You might better leave the cap off of it, son, he said to himself in Marylinn's deep voice. Because how else can you get at the contents, you know? I should be thinking of Sarah, he thought. I should be looking for a shop that sells cowboy souvenirs.

Little boy, he thought.

He might also, he thought, be looking for another liquor store. He wondered how early they opened in whatever state he was in.

"What state are you in?" he said, pulling out behind a tractor without a trailer.

"Disreputable," he answered. "No," he said. "What state are you in, and the guy says: shitty. No. The guy says: fucked. What state are you in? Fucked." He took a sip and was surprised, on returning the bottle to its niche beside his thigh, that he found the lights of what appeared to be a big white Lincoln in his rearview mirror, close. He leaned his foot on the accelerator until the Lincoln dropped back. "What state are you in, and the guy thinks a minute, he says, and then he says, forlorn." Barrett stuck his tongue out and made a merry face. He checked it in the mirror and then he looked for the Lincoln's lights but they were passing him, the driver was pounding his horn in little stuttering burps, and then the Lincoln was in front of him, close enough to make him work on the brake. "Forlorn," he said. "Angry men and a state of forlorn. Distant women and Catherine wheels." He felt the tingle and then jab, then a kind of thrill of pain in his left elbow and forearm, a dazzlement of deep ache, and he suspected the receipt of a harbinger. He added a slow, controlled drink to the menu of the moment. "San Caliente," he said.

The lights of the Lincoln pulsed and he knew he should stand on the brake. But he suspected the driver was toying with his sense of caution and his affliction by melancholy. He had lost his wife and frightened his child and betrayed his ethics with dangerous women. And now this plowboy, this cowboy, this bully from the state of forlorn, was endangering his safe return.

They, Barrett thought. Here they are. The lights pulsed, the Lincoln grew larger before him, and Barrett thought: racing shift. He reached for the stick to gear down, but noticed he had seized the bottle of mash. This is no time for tippling, he thought, but he was worried lest he spill the whiskey, so he held the neck of the bottle and worked with the brake, two pitty-pats, then a loop to the left, being careful not to fishtail, then a stern pass, and you drop in ahead of him, of them. *They*. He was a husband, he thought. He was a searcher in the grid, he was a tourist in the state of forlorn and a husband, he was a father, Barrett thought. He steered with his left and held the whiskey with his right and he pulled out into the tractor that he seemed to have passed before the Lincoln came up. The tractor rose upon his car, and Barrett thought of rearing horses, of animals that mounted one another, snarling, in the wild.

He was sleeping in the blanket, naked as a baby, naked as a grandchild, Gloria thought. He looked almost golden, and Gloria wondered whether he had jaundice. There was no jaundice in their family that she knew of, though he might have hepatitis or liver malfunctions. The disorder of their life! She wondered just how careful Sarah had been with him, whether she knew how microorganisms from the bowels of dogs could infect a child walking barefoot in the grass. You *never* go barefoot, she would tell him. There are bacteria everywhere, and slivers of glass indoors, or pins, and then you need tetanus injections, and wounds on the sole of the foot are terribly painful, she'd explain. She held her breath and heard him breathing and she nodded to the road she no longer saw. She avoided vehicles, she tried to keep her control of the wheel, but she was going very quickly now, and frankly, she thought, she was noticing nothing. Some tourist, she thought, waggling her head as if she delighted in chivvying herself.

She instructed herself, or tried to. She attempted to tell herself the story of what was happening. And then the woman, the pseudo-grandmother, would tell Sarah, she thought. Sarah would call the police. The police would come to talk to her. This could take *hours*, she thought, just to register a complaint. And what was there to complain about? The grandmother has rights. Go complain about them and I'll sue you. Her jaw ached because she was clenching it as she thought of facing her daughter, her inconsiderate daughter, and reminding her: I gave you life. You have this child because of me. It isn't proper that he never know me. Go complain about *that*.

They would go home. They would bathe properly and eat a decent meal. She would cook chicken breasts or frozen fish for protein and minimal cholesterol. She would steam potatoes or cook noodles. She would make them a large, fresh salad. He would take to greens, she was certain. She would flavor the greens with vinegar. She regretted that it was a little early for dandelion greens, but she could make a potherb of chickweed and open a packet of dehydrated skim milk and mix him a pitcher. And *candles*, she thought. Light candles and — why not? — they could sing. They could pretend they were living in a log cabin on the frontier and it was somebody's birthday or they were sitting around the campfire, singing old-fashioned camping songs. What could a boy love more? Oh, she thought, and of course the wild gingerbread cookies, some with their faces and some with none.

"Are you all right, Stephen?" she whispered across the car to the boy whose face glowed in a bundle of blanket. "Are you following all these plans?"

He was sweating. His lips looked chapped, and his face shone. He moved beneath the blankets and was still again. They passed mileage signs that gleamed in her lights and disappeared, and she knew that the roads would shift, soon, from two-lane macadam to the chipped and battered country roads that led to the chalet and the pond. And the boat, she thought, smiling in the car and humming her satisfaction aloud. She sounded to herself like bees. They could row in the boat. They could look over the side. She would hold his ankles, if he liked — she would make him an observation box from a refrigerator container, and she would hold his ankles and let him lean over the side and peer into the dark pond at its very deepest point, above the bubbling cold spring that fed it. They would use her aquatic net and collection vials and she would show him the bass feeding on the blasturus nymphs they'd collect. "Don't worry," she said, as if to a boy in a boat on a pond who is held above the darkest, coldest point by the ankles while his head pokes into the water, "Grandma has you. Never fear."

Stephen heard voices and felt hot. He knew he was sick and home in bed. He knew his mother was taking care of him. He would be all right. He would tell her about wetting his bed and she would show him how to make it stop. "Never fear," his mother told him, and he leaned against the sound of her voice.

It was a little funny, he thought. Her voice was a little funny. But his mother was telling him not to be afraid and he would be all right. He was worried about his father. It was a hell of a drive, Daddy said. You can get her back, Stephen told him. But she *was* back. So where was his father? His father probably got her back and then went downstairs to wash the dinner dishes because that was his job. It was a hell of a drive, and his mother was home and his father was downstairs washing the dishes. He shouldn't be scared, and he would feel better soon. He was afraid he was going to upchuck, though, something bitter was in his throat and he was afraid he was going to upchuck. He told his mother, but she didn't say anything, and he knew he wasn't supposed to be afraid now, but he didn't know if that meant being afraid of upchucking too. He wanted to ask her, but his throat felt closed. He opened his mouth wider to get the air into his throat.

"Don't you dare sick up all over yourself," he heard somebody say. She wasn't exactly his mother, he thought. He thought maybe he was on the drive with his father and he forgot, but it was a hell of a drive and you could get sick on it. It wasn't exactly his father, though. This wasn't exactly right. He opened his mouth for more air.

Sarah shone the barely glimmering flashlight at the woods beside the country lane. They stood outside the car and leaned into the darkness as if, Lizzie thought, they were in a blizzard and leaning at the wind to see the way. Sarah thought she wouldn't mind if they were lost together just going someplace, because her mother was a kick-ass traveler. She'd forgotten that. But this wasn't *going*, she thought. This was screaming on the roads with so little rest you can't think except about the steering wheel. And now they were close enough to Gloria's house to walk there, almost, and she had gotten them lost.

It isn't fair, Lizzie thought. Sarah shouldn't have to be responsible for knowing where the goddamned bitch lives. Except she set this thing in motion, didn't she? Or was it the bitch who started the engine of the whole thing turning over? My daughter, Lizzie thought. It was my daughter who got us into this. The bitch got her into the world. I got her into plenty of trouble too, I'm sure. And she got us into this. All right. We know who to blame for what, and if you say a *word*, I will tear your tongue from your head, she told herself.

Sarah thought her mother looked crazy. Her eyes were zinging around like pinballs and she had a nutsy smile on her face, and yet she looked sad. Sarah said, "What?"

Lizzie, thinking that she wanted to hug this roving disaster area and kiss her a few times, said, "I'm just hanging around like the rest of us. That's all."

Sarah forced a whooping laugh, but didn't believe it and, she saw, her mother didn't either. Her answering smile was as faked as the laugh. "I can find it," Sarah said.

"I figured you could."

"I'll do it now. Starting right now, I'll find it."

"Let's," Lizzie said. "She doesn't — she's not a voodoo person or into Dianetics or something?"

"She does nature," Sarah said. "She cooks revolting food. Soft inner organs and the glands of lesser species, and she gathers slimy weeds to steam. She has this thing about everything being neat. She's a nurse, right? They take *care* of people, right?"

Lizzie thought of the nurses in veterans' hospitals and old-age homes who pulled the plug on brain-damaged accident victims, who injected lethal substances into the carotid arteries of sad geriatric cases. They did it for God, gods, higher callings, inner voices, instructions from alder trees or linoleum, Lizzie thought. Who knows? They were nurses too, she thought. "Yes, they do," Lizzie said.

"We'll walk in and we won't talk, all right? We kick her ass and grab Stephen and go."

"Right," Lizzie said, fastening her seat belt as Sarah switched the motor on.

"Or maybe just, I don't — something like, 'You whore monster kidnaping bitch weed worshiper, keep your goddamned hands off my baby.' You think?"

"We should have called the police," Lizzie said.

"How am I going to tell them why this happened in the first place?" Sarah asked. It seemed to Lizzie she was driving through the bushes instead of beside them. Insects smashed against the window, moths fluttered low on the road, and branches whipped the Blazer's antenna and roof. " 'How did this happen, Miss?' 'Well, officer, I left my husband and kid and took off after this woman who put an ad in the paper and who seemed like she might have been my birth mother, so of course I *had* to go, didn't I? I mean, the search is everything, officer, isn't it?' How would I do that?"

"That's not important," Lizzie said. She was thinking that they might just do one of their sullen, simmering, rage-flavored fights now, with Lizzie standing on the hood of the car and screaming, and Sarah smirking at Lizzie's uncontrol — the Mother of Cool in the halls of her high school, the Doyenne of Tantrums at home with her kid. "It's all a matter of *Stephen* now, darling. Isn't it?"

Sarah was almost crouched at the wheel. She thought they had come to the edge of the commonwealth-owned fir plantation where the road forked and you stuck to the left. The right, right? The left. She said, "You're right. No argument from me. Stephen all the way," she said. "But I don't want to call the cops."

"Oh," Lizzie said, instructing herself — threatening herself with teeth touching at the very edges, with hands screwed into fists — you will *not* state the obvious. You will live with it because you cannot die of it and just, will you just shut up. "Because she's your mother?" Lizzie heard herself nonetheless say, in a voice disguised as careless, but which jumped with voltage enough to char a joint of meat. Sarah knew the answer and decided that she wouldn't say it. She had always been better at silence than her parents, better than Barrett, too, she thought. Only Eddie had been able to outlast her, sitting with his back to the bed, smoking carefully, depositing the ash in his cupped hand, resting his hand on his crossed ankle and studying a point, he would answer if later asked, where two fields of color almost touched. It's the edges, Eddie said. What you have to focus on is where they meet or don't meet. Look at the edge.

"Jesus," Lizzie said, "Sarah, can we stop talking and get there? It's your *boy*."

And Sarah, happy inside for that instant, and in spite of her best wishes, because she had stepped away from or maybe stepped *on* Lizzie's need and instruction, kept still.

And all of them in cars, sealed in cars, belted into cars, naked in cars — Eagle and Blazer and Lincoln and Ford — and Barrett sailing off the road, and now, tonight, in the dark forest, the mothers who were locked in their cars were flaring the nearby forest with their headlights in tandem, not seeing each other, the brightness of their lights filtered by rising mist and a drizzle that simply, suddenly, appeared on windshields and branches and petals and the ocher lichenous stones that shone an instant like gold in the headlights which faltered, finally, and showed them less than they required. They chased each other, and no one knew who really led or followed. Everyone was undiscovered until Stephen, waking in the blanket on the seat of Gloria's car, choked, then moaned for air, then caught it and swallowed it hungrily down. He blinked and blinked, as if his eyelids were forcing the air in, and then he coughed up a thick, gray, slimy chunk of mucus and cried, "I'm coming! I'll be right there!"

Gloria said, "That's disgusting." She stopped her Eagle and in the midst of the chase, in mire and in darkness, she found a tissue and, knowing that her face looked angry and revolted, a little disappointed with herself for giving vent to her knowledge of bacteria and plain decent good manners — which, it was totally clear, this grandchild of hers had not been exposed to — she cleaned his mess, wiped his mouth and nose, placed the tissue in the brown sack she used for refuse while traveling, wiped her fingers with an alcohol swab from her kit, restored order to the interior of her car, turned off the overhead light and smiled what she thought was a fetching smile at Stephen. She said, liltingly, she'd have sworn, "There. *Now* we can go home."

Stephen remembered her, and knew that he had sat in the wrong car. He remembered her eyes, and he made an effort not to look at them now. Her eyes had been his mistake, he thought, unsure of what he meant. She opened her window a little and smelled the air.

"I love a rainy night, don't you, Stephen? Cold air is blowing down from Ontario, which is very rare this time of year. Usually the jet stream carries warmer air in from *below* the Great Lakes. Have you studied the jet stream in school? Do you know about the Great Lakes? Or where Ontario is? Oh! Listen, Stephen!" She pointed at the window, and then she opened it some more and smiled when rain fell onto her pretty face. "It's a jet plane," she said. "The passenger planes that fly from Philadelphia to the Midwest often fly over these hills. On clear days you can see them, silver and majestic. They look very low. Now, this is interesting. They fly faster than sound! Did they teach you the speed of sound in school? That plane is ahead of what we hear, Stephen!"

Stephen, knowing nothing except the surge of his anger, a kind of anger he didn't know about, said, "I'm cold. What happened to my clothes? Why did you take away my clothes?"

"Because," she said, turning the window handle very hard, cautioning herself to be careful, be gentle, and refusing to listen, "because you managed to vomit and shit yourself and be disgusting and vile." Stephen watched her close her eyes, and he wondered if she was going to hit him. He thought maybe he should say he was sorry. He started to cry. "Because you had an accident, darling," she said in a different voice, proud of herself for exerting the patience this child just barely deserved, and probably didn't. "You had a little accident, darling."

Stephen wondered if he had wet himself again also. He knew he couldn't stop crying. It was like not being able to stop peeing. He was being very bad, he thought. He wished his mother could get away from the emergency feeling like his grandma promised she was doing. He was pretty sure it was about time she came home. Except he wasn't home now, he knew. He drew his hand across his nose and sniffed.

"Don't *do* that," she said without moving her lips. Her face looked like a pretty mask that didn't move, and Stephen felt very frightened.

"What's going to happen to me, please?" he asked her. Gloria wondered at the fragility of Sarah's child. This was someone who'd been allowed to grow, but who had not been trained or guided, she thought. He said, "How come you're my grand-mother too?"

And Gloria said, "On the way home, I can tell you that story, Stephen. Shall I tell you a story?"

Hoping she wouldn't get angry again, and wishing she would smile so he would know it was all right to ask for his clothing, Stephen said, "Excuse me, are we going to my regular grandma's house? You know — "

He stopped because her face got stiff again. He thought she looked a little bit like his father when his mother called him Walnut Face. There was always someone hiding behind it, and he couldn't help getting scared. Stalk him, Gloria thought, think-ing of nets, of killing jars, of notebooks, of hot afternoons and mosquitoes and of getting down, as specimen and as notes, the precise nature of what she observed. Gloria thought of really getting to know her environment.

"I'm a regular grandma too, Stephen," Gloria said. "I am Mommy's mommy."

Stephen blinked and blinked. He worked, inside his naked body and his stunned brain, and, realizing what he would do as he did it, he urinated up and onto and through the blanket in the darkness of the car, knowing that she would smell it or feel it and her face would get stiff again, waiting, even as he answered her by saying, "How do you do."

They had gone past the turnoff twice, but the third time Sarah saw the corner of Gloria's outbuilding, a tool shed, and stopped, backed, turned onto the long mucky track that served as a drive up to the house that sat on the berm of the pond. The forest came to the sides of the track and the rim of the pond, and once they had driven to the house, they were sealed away from the road, Lizzie thought. Sarah said, "I didn't see any car tracks. I think we got here first."

"Maybe she's — from the way you describe her, maybe she'd get out with a broom or pine branches or whatever they use in the westerns and cover her tracks."

"Daddy gave me Zane Grey's *Riders of the Purple Sage* in my sophomore year in high school, remember?"

"I believe you commented on the appropriateness of the gift, yes." Lizzie felt a wave of stupid gratitude for the recollection, the familiarity — our history, she thought — as they sat in the dooryard of the mother whom Sarah had sought.

"Well, they use branches in dry ground. They can't do it without showing it when there's mud."

"Really?"

Sarah leaned over, happy for the excuse to touch her, and she banged her forehead on Lizzie's hard shoulder. "No. I just wanted you to be right. I wanted you to feel all right. I have no idea. But I didn't see any tracks."

"I'm going to look," Lizzie said, moving out of the car so that Sarah wouldn't see her cry. She pretended to squint at the ground, then wiped her face as if because of the rain. At the open door she said, "No tracks. Let's break in and set an ambush."

"I love ambushes," Sarah said, wondering why she felt almost giddy as they stumbled brainlessly in pursuit of a madwoman who had stolen her son. "First you hide the car, though. Every James Cagney movie I ever saw, they always hide the car."

"I'll stand watch," Lizzie said. "I saw those movies too. They have people standing watch."

"I wish we had a gun," Sarah said earnestly, suddenly overwhelmed by sorrow and dread. "If I had a gun, I think I would kill her, Mommy."

Call me that again, Lizzie thought. "We'll use our bare hands," she said. Sarah nodded and reached for the gear lever, and Lizzie slammed the door and stood back. The car whined up to the left of the house and seemed to Lizzie to barely fit between the house and the outbuilding. Its lights bounced and flared as Sarah used the brakes, and then it was out of sight. Lizzie heard a jet overhead. She clasped her arms across her chest against the mist and chill, the cold rain, and considered how she really ought to be wearing something besides low heels and mud-spattered white tights if she was going to chase a crazy kidnaper day and night partway across New York and most of the way across Pennsylvania and end up in some kind of gang fight in some forest that was noplace she'd ever heard of. She thought of Will because she wanted to say this to him, to tell him about Sarah, to comment on pain, to share it, really — to give it away. She thought of Will tucking Stephen into bed, Will showing Stephen how to wash his shameful sheets, Will in the woods near home with Stephen, sneaking cigarettes and telling him stories. She thought of the bloody tissues and blood on Will's pillowcase and how she was waiting for him to tell her. You wait all your life to wait like this, she thought.

Sarah came through the mud and whistled. Her mother looked tall and tough and beautiful, she thought, mud to her knees, her dress clinging to her body, her hair lying hard against her head. Her mother was one of those middle-aged pieces of ass young women resent. The older women sometimes have the grace to not know it, she thought, but that only gets them resented so much more. Her mother turned and smiled a sad smile and whistled back, as if they had made an arrangement, as if they used a signal they both knew. Sarah walked to the side of the house and Lizzie followed her.

"What movie are you using?" Lizzie whispered.

Sarah stooped, picked up a rock, slammed it at the window before which they stood, and reached carefully through the jagged glass and smashed mullion to trip the latch. "*Tough Broad*," Sarah said, not whispering.

"I never saw it."

"Stars Elizabeth Bean Mastracola."

"And her kid," Lizzie said, shooting herself in the head and heart simultaneously for having said it.

Standing on Lizzie's thigh and halfway in the opened window, Sarah paused, stepped back down, stood before Lizzie in the mud and rain and thickening mist, and she leaned her face close to Lizzie's. She paused because she was wondering how to say it. Lizzie reached up to touch either side of her face. Sarah finally said, "I forgot to ask: May I step on you? It'll be business as usual."

"As usual," Lizzie said. Sarah climbed, and Lizzie watched her daughter's buttocks in their dungarees at the window ledge. She reached up and gently patted them. Sarah wiggled once, then launched herself over and into the house.

Lizzie ran around to the front, and Sarah let her in, relocking the door behind her, leading her by the hand — I'm the last of the Mohicans, Sarah thought, remembering *that* gift from her father, which she'd also detested and soon set down — but enjoying her mother's big-fingered grip, and enjoying that she knew, more or less, how to get her around in the dark, and liking her mother's willingness to be led.

Lizzie smelled herbs, delicious herbs and a good pungency of roots. Maybe an interesting woman, she thought of this birth mother. She snorted. Of *course* she's interesting: she steals children and serves fried throats.

"What?" Sarah asked.

"Nothing more than losing my mind," Lizzie answered.

"Here," Sarah said. "This is the kitchen. No lights, right? We wait here, so we can get between her and knives and things. I don't think she'd have guns. There's an ax someplace, I'm sure. I'm hoping it's out in that shed, whatever that is out there. We have to jump on her and — Christ, Mommy. Jesus. God."

"Sweetie, what?"

"We don't know what we're *doing*. She found your house, she kidnaped Stephen, she might have *eaten* him by now. What are we doing here? I should have called the police. God, were you right. I should have asked Mr. Whatsit to call the police."

"Ben Pierson?"

"Or Daddy. Or waited for him, for Christ's sake. What was I thinking about? Was I thinking at all? My Christ. She took my *baby*." When she tried to imagine, even as she spoke, what Gloria might have done to him, or what he might — what terrible bewilderment and loneliness and danger — he might feel, she heard her little-girl's voice from the days on the road: *I ca-an't hear you*. Yeah, she thought. Well, maybe you should have, bitch.

That's right, Lizzie thought, reading her daughter's expression.

In the silence, in the alien odors of a stranger's life, Lizzie, feeling just then less like a rescuer than a crook, whispered, "Can I ask you something?"

"No."

"You sound like a teenager."

"I feel a hundred."

"Now you sound like Willis. But I have to ask something."

Sarah, forgetting to whisper, barked, "Please."

Lizzie made hushing sounds. Sarah did too, trying to show that she agreed with the need for silence. Lizzie whispered, then, "But I do."

Sarah tried to answer with silence.

In the darkness, Lizzie closed her eyes. "Why didn't you tell us?" she asked Sarah.

"That I'd seen her ad?"

"That you felt something powerful when you saw it. That you felt a need to go off and meet her. That you — that you weren't satisfied with us."

Sarah couldn't stifle her anger. She knew it rode on her voice. "It isn't that clear. It isn't that simple." She was horrified to find her voice as harsh as Gloria's.

"That you had to leave your husband and child without telling *them*."

"I barely told myself," Sarah whispered.

"I believe it. I do. You — what? You just burst into motion? The way people in musicals burst into song?"

"All of a sudden," Sarah said, not whispering, "all of a sudden, I was writing this incoherent note to Stephen and sneaking cash and clothes into the car and just *going*. I just went. That's right. Like bursting into song. Some song."

"Were you angry?" After a while, Lizzie said, "Was that clothing noise the sound of you shrugging?"

"I think I'm always angry a little," Sarah said. "I didn't know that about myself. I always thought I was a little sad. I even like that, the sadness, a little. Maybe I thought it made me attractive. I didn't know about the angry part."

Don't, Lizzie told herself. She did. "This is so selfish, but I have to ask you. At us? Was it — at your father and me?"

Sarah shook her head and seized her hair. She pulled very hard, but she said, calmly, "That wouldn't be fair."

Lizzie, remembering again to whisper, said, "Whatever happens in your stomach or your ovaries or your soul doesn't *have* to be fair. *Isn't*, usually. It's what happens, and then you deal with it."

"Not exactly angry," Sarah whispered. "Not the way people get *mad* at each other. Not like that. It hurts your throat, whispering this much."

"Yes, but she could hear, she could take him away someplace you *don't* know how to find." Lizzie listened to insects droning, to the noises of the house — a startling crack of contracting wood, the barely audible padding of an animal, maybe a cat, Lizzie hoped. She said, "Sarah. I have to admit something. I'm angry. I'm really angry." She commanded her voice not to quaver, her eyes to stay dry.

"At me?"

"Yes."

"Am I grounded?"

Lizzie fought the giggle. She suppressed it by compressing her lips so the laughter had to lie against her cheeks and palate. But the sound escaped with a farting noise, and Sarah began to laugh.

"I mean it," Lizzie said, laughing, endangering her grandchild. "I'm really furious."

"I know," Sarah said, laughing. "You probably should be."

"You ungrateful goddamned bitch, hurting us all like that."

"I know," Sarah said. Then she wasn't laughing anymore. She said, "I know." Shut up, she commanded. As usual, she didn't listen. "But are you grounding me?" she asked.

Lizzie wept in the darkness, pretending to laugh. Sarah listened and knew what she did. She instructed her hand to move to touch Lizzie, and as she waited to see whether it did, the lights of a car filled the narrow front windows and spilled along woodstove and furniture and rose along the post beneath the carrier beam and lighted them, one for the other, and then, shutting off, left them blinded in Gloria's house.

That's right, Gloria thought, watching her grandson chew on the edge of his blanket and close his eyes and cry. She turned off her headlights and pulled on the emergency brake. She turned her engine off and, thinking, Yes, that's right, you shake in your boots, you little animal, thinking too that he wore no boots, so she would have to carry him across the mud, soiled and vile and soiling her as he was carried. Gloria said, "Sit very still, now. I'm going to come around to your side of the car. Sit still."

She carried him, her face averted from the odor, from his flesh no longer jaundiced with fever and distress, but white and quaking because of the cold. At her door, her key ready, she admitted them promptly and said, at the threshold of her damp, chilly house, "I'm going to build us a fire in the woodstove and towel you off once you're warm. You will *not* permit yourself the luxury of wetting yourself again. Is that clear? I had a cat once who you remind me of. He wouldn't observe the proprieties either. I'll fetch you another blanket, and then I'll warm you up. We'll understand each other, Stephen, and then I'll teach you about the world."

She closed the door, reached for the rheostat on the wall and, as she found it and turned, smelled more than the smell of her house or the offending odor of the child. She smelled a perfume. Gloria didn't wear perfume because it attracted insects. A perfumed person was in her private house, she thought with an anger impossible to bear. She heard herself make a sound like a moan, like someone aching. No one answered, and she set the boy down — "Stand there," she said — and inspected her room, realizing that she had closed her eyes like, well, like the child. She saw only her house, no more. It looked inviolate. Perhaps, she thought, the smell was on the urinous skin of the boy. Perhaps he used his father's cologne, perhaps the alternative grandmother had embraced him, rubbing some of her chemical scent onto Stephen.

She regretted the noise she had made. Gloria walked to the airtight stove and opened the door. She had laid the fire already, because in a house heated by electricity, the stove is for emergencies. An emergency stove is pointless if you don't have it in a state of readiness. She would tell this to Stephen later tonight, she thought, when they pretended to be camping like the settlers who had slept under Pennsylvania skies, moving west. She lit the newspaper with the matches kept always at hand, and watched the paper burn, watched the pine kindling catch, watched the hardwood start to smoke. She closed the stove door and damped down the aperture until a very little air went through. This is efficient heating, she would say to Stephen. The stove reuses its own smoke. No one knows stoves like Grandma, she would say, smiling, and Stephen would smile in return.

Over the low crackle of kindling and small roar of fire, Gloria heard a sound like a whisper. She said, "What, Stephen?"

She turned and saw Sarah, who ran across the room with her knees and elbows pumping, as if she had to come a great distance to reach her. Gloria thought, for only an instant, that her daughter was running to embrace her, that her daughter had repented her flight. Lizzie watched Gloria's expression and, seeing the pleasure repose there, then leave, had a sense of Gloria's mistake even as she reached for Stephen and held him and felt his very cold fingers and arms so hard around her neck that she had to force her head back enough to watch the reunion between Sarah and — between Sarah, godammit, and the woman from whom she was born.

Sarah was surprised to find that she had not knocked Gloria down, was not battering her with her fists as she had thought to. Gloria reached behind her for the kindling hatchet and held it before her. Sarah stood, breathing hard, looking into Gloria's eyes and trying to find herself in them. Lizzie rocked Stephen, whispering, "Here we are. Here we are, baby. Here we are." Gloria stepped back to the woodstove and took hold of the handle of the door. She groaned as her fingers burned, but she pulled the latch down and opened the door. Sarah thought that somehow she'd intended to hurl herself into the flames. Lizzie moved two steps forward, as if to keep the woman from pitching Sarah, impossibly, through the eight- or ten-inch opening. Stephen remembered how Hansel was supposed to be cooked. The fire pulsed. The wheels of the tractor chewed on Barrett's car and his car locked onto the tractor. The engines screamed and they spun. Barrett heard the shattering of glass, he heard glass breaking without an end to breaking, and the scream that metal makes when it grinds and folds and erupts on itself. He closed his eyes and held on to the wheel and the whiskey bottle as the locked tractor and his car spun off the road and over each other, rolling into scrubby soil and punky trees to become the fireball from first the gas tank on the side of the truck and then the tank in the car as the cooking noises rose and the shards and powder of glass and plastic rained down onto the fire.

The fire jumped in her stove and Gloria threw the hatchet in. She sat on the bare pine floor before the hearthstone of the stove and cradled her hand as if it were a small creature, and she wept. Her head bowed over the hand she held, and she made little sighing, sneezing noises. Sarah looked around the room, stepped back toward the kitchen, took two steps toward the front door, then went across the room to Lizzie. She held her arms out and Lizzie lifted Stephen away and to his mother. Lizzie knew what Sarah had sought. She wanted to stay with them, to huddle with them, to finally wail as loud and as long as she needed to, but she went, instead, closer to Gloria and said, as if hesitant to interrupt, "Your medical things?"

Still holding the outraged hand, Gloria pointed by moving both of her hands toward the door. Sarah watched her mother as she moved quickly, as if she still were a high school girl studying dance. Sarah said, "Stevie, darling. Stevie, darling."

"No more emergencies," Stephen said.

Sarah knew that she couldn't lie. So she said nothing, only squeezed him to her, wrapping the damp blanket harder around his thin body. Then she said, in spite of herself, "No more emergency feelings. I guarantee."

"Guarantee," Stephen said. He felt cold and sore and wet and sick to his stomach. He felt absolutely all right.

Lizzie came back in with the doctor's bag and rummaged. Gloria said, "The yellow tube, please. And a little gauze, perhaps. Just lay it on lightly. Ah. Ah. No, that's all right. Ah." Lizzie found that she didn't mind touching the pretty little woman's flesh, and that she felt sad about the terrible red shape — the handle itself — that the stove had seared on her skin.

Gloria looked at the woman who crouched athletically, like a soldier, treating her hand. The woman studied her, and Lizzie, not knowing what else to do, nodded. Stephen closed his eyes while his mother held him. Sarah thought her mother's face, lit by the stove and edged with shadow at the temple and cheekbone, looked like a painting about sorrow. Lizzie called, "Are we all right?"

Gloria wondered if the question was meant for her. Sarah thought Lizzie asked about Stephen. Stephen heard his grandmother say something, but it wasn't to him. Lizzie held herself still. She knew how to wait.